Advance Praise for American Ending

"Did Mary Kay Zuravleff time travel to write this book? It's as if she truly lived in the past—all the details so vivid, and real—to bring us a novel of the moment. **It is the old and forever new story of immigration.**"—Jane Hamilton, author of *A Map of the World*

"How I loved spending time with Yelena in her vivid, terrible, and—most astonishingly—joyous time and place. Mary Kay Zuravleff's novel manages to capture all the struggle and the grief endured by this particular, unsung set of immigrants without ever veering into caricature or melodrama. **Wholly fresh and achingly believable.**" —Alice McDermott, author of *The Ninth Hour* and *Charming Billy*

"*American Ending* is an exhilarating new take on the great American immigration story. Mary Kay Zuravleff has given us **a vivid, unforgettable portrait of an immigrant community** and the wry, richly colored, and darkly enchanting stories it tells itself to survive." —Margaret Talbot, staff writer for *The New Yorker*

"In the dark of Pennsylvania's coal mines, **Yelena's voice is both the light and the canary**. Her struggles, and those of her Russian American immigrant community, are deeply felt and beautifully written. Immersive and compelling."—Helen Simonson, author of *Major Pettigrew's Last Stand*

"**I fell in love with Yelena!** So many stories of immigration focus on the men, but it's the women who kept the family together, had the courage to leave their villages, who stuck it out in a strange land." —Ana Menéndez, author of *The Apartment* and *Loving Che*

AMERICAN ENDING

American Ending

by

MARY KAY ZURAVLEFF

—BLAIR—

Printed in the United States of America
Cover design by Laura Williams
Interior design by April Leidig

Blair is an imprint of Carolina Wren Press.

The mission of Blair/Carolina Wren Press is to seek out, nurture, and promote literary work by new and underrepresented writers.

We gratefully acknowledge the ongoing support of general operations by the Durham Arts Council's United Arts Fund and the North Carolina Arts Council.

This novel is a work of fiction. As in all fiction, the literary perceptions and insights are based on experience; however, all names, characters, places, and incidents are either products of the author's imagination or are used fictitiously. No reference to any real person is intended or should be inferred.

Library of Congress Cataloging-in-Publication Data
Names: Zuravleff, Mary Kay, author.
Title: American ending / by Mary Kay Zuravleff.
Description: [Durham] : Blair, [2022]
Identifiers: LCCN 2022053428 (print) | LCCN 2022053429 (ebook) |
ISBN 9781949467994 (hardcover) | ISBN 9781958888001 (ebook)
Classification: LCC PS3576.U54 A64 2022 (print) |
LCC PS3576.U54 (ebook) | DDC 813/.54—dc23
LC record available at https://lccn.loc.gov/2022053428
LC ebook record available at https://lccn.loc.gov/2022053429

For my mother, my grandmothers, and yours

PART I

1908

1

I HOPED THE SISTERS I'd never met would never join us, and when they did arrive, I wanted to send them back—that's how American I am. As far as I was concerned, my parents had left the two of them behind and come here to give birth to me. "What do you want, a medal?" my little brother used to ask. He was born here, but I was born first.

Where I was born isn't how I was raised. Though I hailed from Marianna, Pennsylvania, I was brought up hearing that wolves talk and Old Believers rise from the dead. That a good woman can make soup from a stone, and a good man's snot is black with coal dust. I'm American, so I figured I didn't have to take what comes, the way Ma and Pa did. Our kind of Russian Orthodox is called Old Believers because they don't believe in making changes—or choices—but I aimed to choose some things for myself. That included a life away from the mines, where most of the men who aren't crushed or gassed end up dead from drink.

For years, I was at Ma's apron strings, pickling beets and cucumbers alongside her, boiling diapers, rendering lard for soap. "Yelena, Yelena, Yelena," she'd say, "What kind of mother leaves her daughters behind?"—a riddle where the answer was my kind of mother.

She didn't leave the family icon behind, or prayer books her father had copied by hand, or spools of brocade to turn any shirt into a shirt fit for church. She even brought over a tin of ashes scooped from their tumbledown hearth, given that every family has a domovoi who lives in the stove, and better the devil you know.

A few plump raisins set out overnight and the domovoi would at most hide our slippers or let the fruit flies in. Ma warned us that a nibble of pride or envy would make a monster of him, as if I didn't have enough to fret about. Surely, the domovoi would scorch what little food we had—or burn up our house with me in it—on account of my pride at being American and my envy of my older sisters, so treasured by Ma.

The Pittsburg-Buffalo Company supplied Pa with a single ticket to come to Marianna in 1898, and selling all they could, floorboards to doorknobs, only raised enough for one more ticket. If Pa came alone, he wouldn't get a house; if Ma came with him, they'd have to leave the girls behind. So Baba made up a room in their house for her precious granddaughters, and Ma and Pa promised to send for them within a year. But instead of getting their two girls back, they got me, their first American, on January 31, 1899.

I envied my sisters being pampered by the baba I'd never met, brushing the long wavy hair I admired in their picture, and our jeda, a tailor, sewing the matching coats that Baba described in her letters. I couldn't bear Ma's stories from when they were a family in Suwalki, roasting an entire pig over the coals for Easter dinner, decorating their fancy eggs, and eating Ma's famous skansi and blintzes oozing sweet cheese. I didn't want to hear about the three-day village wedding feasts when I went to bed hungry, cabbage and beans bloating me with gas, or potatoes and lard weighing me down like my baby sister's leg, resting on my gut.

Each night, Ma uncoiled her braided bun and dropped hairpins in her lacquered box painted with Emilion and his magic pike. She shook out her golden plaits, never cut because that was a sin, and carried them like the train of a dress into our room, letting go so she could hoist our stack of covers. She tucked the heavy wool blanket beneath our chinnny chin chins and perched on our bed, careful not to sit on her hair. Rubbing her swelling belly, she asked, "Russian ending or American ending?"

Bedtime was the only time I felt sympathy for my big sisters, knowing that Ma and Pa had slipped away one day without them. It was hard to sleep stewing over that, and I worried that my parents might want to begin again, again. Every scrape I heard was the trunk being dragged from under their bed, every squeak the wagon carting them away from us.

That was a Russian ending, and Ma's fairy tales were worse. For every wish come true, there was a catch, and you could easily end up worse off than where you started. She told us about the wolf who promised the bride a ride to her wedding if she climbed on his back, and instead, he ate her. "Eyelash to toenail," Ma growled, tickling us three.

Kostia, flailing to escape, smacked baby Pearl, who sprayed tears like a watering can.

"Russian ending, everyone suffer," Ma said and soothed our baby sister. "I'll give you American ending for my tender American children." She said "tender" the way the wolf might.

American ending meant the groom slicing open the wolf's belly and the bride jumping out unharmed. Her baba skinned the wolf and used the pelt to line their firstborn's cradle. "I heard it from the bride herself," Ma said. "I danced at the wedding and I ate their soup." She was proud of the cheery ending she'd tacked on.

Ma and Pa had come here to seek their fortune, and instead of Ma getting her girls back, she got me. Then Kostia, then Pearl, and now another one coming. She hadn't seen her older daughters in ten years. I didn't think we were suffering, but we weren't tender either. Most days we kept Lent—Wednesdays, Fridays, saints' days, and six weeks before Easter and Christmas—which meant no meat, milk, or eggs. Since we didn't always have them otherwise, I figured some rules were made to turn hunger into holiness. Why else, and why so many rules? I'd dared to ask one night at supper.

"You want we should be New Old Believers?" Ma asked, then laughed at the impossibility of such a thing.

"Katya, what nonsense!" Pa scolded. He told me and Kostia to wipe the smiles off our faces. "Americanskiy," he hissed.

Got that right, I'd thought, biting the inside of my cheeks to stop myself from grinning. Americans with their carnivals and crusted fruit pies, their mail-order catalogues and money-back guarantees. Americans not expecting the worst, so I wasn't expecting it when he knocked me on the forehead with his spoon.

Russian ending or American ending? The wolf ate the bride either way. In Ma's telling, the bride was cut free from the dead wolf's belly and lived to tell the tale. Another night, I imagined, the bride might be spared, only to have a wolf eat her baby in the spring.

Ma touched her lips to my forehead, finally cool after a long bout of scarlet fever. "You'll live," she said and crossed herself. She took her leave, and each footfall across the creaking floorboards rattled the crooked window frames. At the top of our hill, winds got smacked around and whined through chinks in the bricks—or maybe it was someone's ma. Our flimsy house shivered as if spooked. Lying like a body on top of me, the thick wool blanket weighted down my chest and scratched my bony ankles. If I didn't fan my feet out, the blanket squashed my toes, though I'd be a shivering, miserable mess without it. I was grateful Ma and Pa had carted the blanket all the way from Suwalki, and fretted about what was coming. Sleep whistled its lullaby through Kostia's crooked nose, and Pearl's pudgy thigh, thrown across my belly, pinned me down snug against her. Even so, I slept guardedly, as if two forsaken sisters might ride a wolf into the house and up the stairs, knocking the three of us to the floor to claim our bed.

2

AND SO IT WAS and wasn't a surprise when Baba's letter arrived. I was raring to start fourth grade, and hearing Ma and Pa's voices through the floor grate, I figured they were raring too. I pushed Kostia and baby Pearl apart from where they'd rolled into my hollow, climbing out of our bed and into the hand-me-downs Ma had remade for me. She'd finagled two dresses from one of my godmother's, saying I was "a scarecrow like your Pa." I had thatched hair and skinny arms, legs, torso—the stick figure of a child's drawing. What was round on me were my big saucer eyes, which didn't look Russian, and my red cheeks, which did. My clodhopper feet fit into my godmother's boots with just an extra pair of socks, and I hoped to wear those boots clear through sixth grade. Of course, I couldn't know then that my feet would never walk into sixth grade.

I tidied my stack of clippings before heading downstairs. People brought me scraps and sometimes a whole section of the newspaper; mostly, they gave me comics because I was a kid.

Ma didn't take to the mischief and lip of the comics, but me and Kostia loved funnies like *The Dream of the Rarebit Fiend*, which made sense even as they didn't. A man eats whatever a rarebit is and dreams he's been shot, the doctor telling him, "The bullet hit the splazetum in its descent through the calabash of his brulapsuski."

Foolish Questions was my favorite. I'd help Kostia sound one out, and we'd guffaw at people giving each other guff, the words so rude and ridiculous.

"Picking flowers?"

"No, I'm filling the coal scuttle with applesauce."

"Is there a body in that coffin?"

"No, they're shipping a box of sandwiches to Egypt."

Ma and Pa's squabbling downstairs drew me to the landing, where I looked out over Ma's pincushion bun and the apron she noosed around her neck.

Pa said, "That svoloch docks my pay for the boots on my feet, the pick in my hand."

"He acts like he owns us," Ma said. Above her sharp cheekbones, dark lashes fringed her wide, suspicious eyes. "We have less each year because of him."

Pa held her gaze and sucked air through his teeth. "That doesn't keep you from stirring the pot."

Ma pointed the spatula at her heavy belly. "You stirred this pot. I had to stir the pot for my girls, because ships don't take scrip." As she slid the spatula under a sweet potato biscuit, her shadow pranced along the wall, across the soot outlines of pans hung there by the family before us. All these years later, their rat poison still sat on the windowsill.

The girl in the family before us had died of her scarlet fever, and I wondered if she'd made it to fourth grade. I wondered if she'd learned to read her book of Russian fairy tales, leather-bound and written in English, now my prized possession.

"Gregor, Gregor, Gregor," Ma chanted, "All our years here and we have less than we started. The more you work, the more we owe."

"If I worked less, your girls wouldn't be coming." That's when he held up an envelope, ragged with Russian stamps, and shook it at Ma. "You packed our bags to come here, and now your wish comes true. Watch what you ask for." He turned his head and his spit sizzled on the side of the stove, *thu thu thu,* to ward against evil.

"I had almost lost my heart," Ma said.

"Nadja got her boys back just to ship them off to Pittsburgh." He was talking loud enough for Nadja and Max to hear next door, and I expected them to thump on the shared wall.

"I don't blame Nadja," Ma said. "She didn't bring her boys here to die underground. She says steel men live to meet their grandchildren."

"Her boy was nowhere near dying," Pa said. "Max cut into that vein, and while he could take what comes, the black damp knocked out the bird and then the boy—Daniil weighs little more than a canary. Nadja's sore because she didn't sense it."

Nadja claimed she could predict a mine disaster by the laundry on the line. Where Ma would snap Pa's shirt to shake off the grime, Nadja would rub a corner of fabric between her fingers, reading the soot like tea leaves. She coached Ma: "Greasy patches come before a cave-in—twice I saved Max's life from up here." She tilted her head toward our side of the joined houses. "She paid me no heed, and after that cave-in made a widow of her, she lost her girl to the fever." Nadja's face softened when she looked to Ma. "That's how I got you."

"I pay heed," Ma said.

"Heed this, Katya. You give too much away." Nadja tucked the clothes pegs between her lips, giving her a different kind of grin.

"I get more than I give," Ma told her. Ma's gift was being generous before there was a need, so people felt richer than they were. It meant they had something to offer.

"You won't get your girls back giving everything away." Nadja leaned over and let the pegs drop into her apron pocket. "You sell hren to the butcher, so take a nickel for a loaf of bread. Have them give you what your sewing's worth, or let them thread their own needles."

Nadja and Max had left Suwalki and made their way first to West Virginia and then, lo and behold, to Marianna. "The world is cramped!" they greeted Ma and Pa, who'd traveled five thousand miles—wagon to boat, across the ocean, then train to wagon and up Russian Hill—to live in a house mashed against their Old Country neighbors. Nadja welcomed them with bread and salt, Max with vodka.

"Hold back your horses," Ma told Max. She hung her icon of the Blessed Virgin on the nail where the last family had hung their family icon. Then she opened her stove to empty the ashes carried all the way from Suwalki. Max laughed at her superstition, but he spit on the stove—*thu, thu, thu*—and uncorked the vodka. The women stopped after the second round of Nasdrovyas, and after the fifth, Ma asked Pa, "How will you mine tomorrow?"

He said he'd come halfway round the world and deserved a drink.

"New country, same old Gregor," Max said, which led to Pa bloodying Max's nose. And their only friends in this country went home mad to their house on the other side of the wall. On their first day in their new life in a new country, Ma wept. "What was new?" she asked.

But what was new was my showing up nine months later, steaming like a fresh-baked skansa. Nine months after another knockdown, drag-out night, Kostia arrived as a big round paska. And the same for Pearl, though she was a tiny tea cake.

I watched Ma hack at the hambone to get meat for Pa's biscuits, and she pointed her cleaver at my two sisters in the photograph that had pride of place next to her Chinese pitcher. "Another baby just means I miss them more. It's like we turned our back on our girls to make a new family."

Ma always said my life wouldn't be worth a plug nickel if I broke her Chinese pitcher. As for my sisters' picture, I could close my eyes and see the tiara on Sonya's head and the ribbons threaded through Lethia's ruffles. In the photograph, they were both younger than me, yet they already had ringlets down to their waists. Straight as I was up and down, they already had waists.

Though the baby thickened Ma, she was still her curvy self, and Pa scooted up against her backside. He waved the envelope above her head like a teasing schoolboy. "Your girls have been living like kittens, being petted and playing with yarn."

"They won't here," Ma said. She bumped Pa backwards, and he plopped his rump into a seat as she lifted the kettle from the stove to pour an entire pot of tea in the deep bottom tray of his dinner bucket. She spooned boiled potatoes in the middle tray alongside the sweet potato biscuits stuffed with ham, onion, and horseradish, and two sour cherry pirozhki in the top tray. She fitted one tray inside the other and locked down the bucket's lid. Filled, the bucket weighed more than Ma's Dutch oven. They said a boy was ready for the mines when he could carry his heavy, sloshing pail.

I wished Lethia and Sonya would stay in Suwalki, though I envied them getting petted like kittens and sleeping in their own beds. After lurking on the landing, I tromped down the stairs in my new boots. "What did Baba write?" I asked, though I knew full well.

"You're in our business now?" Pa said.

No, I'm salting slugs in the garden, I sassed him inside my head. His blue eyes were like marbles in his pale pale face, which never saw the light of day.

Pa palmed the baby under Ma's apron, and my jealousy flared. Then his curls bounced with the racket of Max banging at our door.

Max yelled, "Get your big nose out here, already!" It was the start of school for me, but it was any other day for them, heading for the chilly damp mines underground.

I'd seen the huge map on the foreman's wall the day Ma dragged us there. Miss Kelly, our schoolteacher, had gone over Pa's contract with Ma, showing her where it said Pa could get paid in cash instead of scrip. I was terrified of Mr. Henderson and of his skunk-haired wife who ran the company store. He was the one who'd issued Pa his pick, miner's cap, candle, explosives, matches, and dented coal bucket on Pa's first day. He'd pointed to the number on Pa's bucket. Pa had held up his fingers to show he understood—two, four, four—then he'd used Mr. Henderson's pen to make an X at the bottom of a piece of paper.

"So many gifts," Pa had said to Max, and Max had told him, "You'll pay for them all." Max had tucked Pa's bag of black powder in his supper pail until Pa knew what to do with it. He told Pa to make sure they tallied his number on the slate each time he emptied the bucket into the coal car. He told him to stay on the foreman's good side.

When Ma took us to Mr. Henderson, I'd looked for the hulking Irishman's good side, then stared beyond him at the gridded map. Marianna was shaped like a bird flying west, our house up at the head and the mine down at its twiggy feet. However old I was, I still fancied that Pa, digging his way through the mountain, might pop up like a worm in our garden. But the foreman's map showed an entire underground city, shafts like taproots and tunnels branching off for miles. Numbered square by square was a grid of streets men had hewn out of rock, with train tracks and water running through one coal-lined town stacked on top of another.

In a honeyed voice we never got, Ma said, "If you please, sir." She set the contract like a doily on his desk as he looked her up and down, picking at his teeth with a knife.

Henderson tried sandbagging her, telling her the contract didn't say what she thought, that the words on the page meant something else, but he changed his tune when she recited what she'd read. "I'm afraid this is your husband's business, ma'am. Gregor Federoff needs to be the one to notify us."

"I have his notifying," Ma said in her sticky sweet voice and handed over a paper with her writing and an X at the bottom. I knew scrip wasn't money, and people carped plenty that the company store wasn't square. But the morning I heard Ma and Pa squabble about stirring the pot, I realized that she didn't care about getting more for her money at the company store. What Ma wanted wasn't offered there. "Ships don't take scrip," she'd said to Pa, eager for Sonya and Lethia to get on a boat to join us.

My memory of Ma standing up to the foreman was really about Ma standing up for her girls—she needed money for their passage—and I felt duped. I knew the future would be different once my sisters came, but it was as if they were changing the past as well.

"Get along now," Max said to Pa, and he saluted me with his shriveled hand. "Morning, Yelena. I came to make this nogoodnik put in his time."

Pa tucked his curls into his miner's hat and picked up his pick and pail. Max had all that Pa had, plus hanging on the end of his pick was a canary in its square cage. On Pa's first day, he saw miners carrying birds in little wire boxes—for music, for lunch, he had no idea. Ma kissed him on the lips. "Go lose us money, or they'll can you." And the men roared out the door.

Ma had saved me a slice of bacon, maybe because it was the first day of school. I lived for bacon, fatback, salt pork. Then she slid the letter from the envelope and laid it by my plate, as if it was a blintz that I should roll full of sour cream and gobble up. Pa couldn't read, and I couldn't read Russian. I thought of Pa on his first day, making an X because he didn't know what his name looked like or what he'd signed. Did he have the same dread as me?

Baba's writing was chicken scratch to me. So were the *Staroobryadtsy*, or Old Believer, prayer books Jeda sent, pages he'd copied in church Slavonic after his long day as a tailor. Ma told us how he'd call her over when he started a new Bible chapter, to watch him ink the outline of a big fancy letter and fill it in, adding a drop or two of gold. I wanted my grandparents to get on a boat and for Jeda to ask me to watch him ink in the leaves vining around the huge scarlet letter.

Ma and Pa had traveled wagon to boat to train to wagon to live in a house attached to people from where they left. It was a loop like in a Russian fairy tale, and there were other loops I returned to, raveling and unraveling the knotted yarns. They had to come here so I could come here, so I could be American. Together with Kostia and Pearl, our family was more American than Russian, but now more Russians were coming, wagon to boat to train to wagon.

In the precious photograph, my sisters were done up like little tsarinas, Lethia's white dress frothy as meringue and Sonya's with a fancy lace yoke. What did I have that was delicate? That was white? "Why don't I have a dress like Sonya's?" I asked my mother.

"She doesn't have it anymore," Ma said. The sisters I'd never met looked more like Ma than I did. They had the same wide, heavily lidded eyes as Ma, who swiped hers with her hanky and tucked the letter inside her apron against her heart, but she also slid a sweet potato biscuit on a plate just for me. She said, "Yelena, Yelena, Yelena, my girls are coming."

"Me and Pearl are your girls," I reminded her.

And she reminded me, "My Russian girls are coming."

3

WE HAD BLUE SKY and grass up on Russian Hill, but we also had the longest walk to the schoolhouse. We had to get past the Poles, Slavs, Irish, and Italians to where Maple split in half, west of the Oklahoma Patch where the Colored lived. I made Kostia walk out in front, else he'd stop in his tracks for a dead bird or a gimpy toad to stuff in his bulging pockets. Me and my two best friends, Maria and Olga, were right behind. Maria had on the Easter dress I'd outgrown as soon as Ma had finished sewing it. The skirt was so long on Maria that the dress looked to be wearing her instead of the other way around. She was sinewy, lithe as a cat, and sweet, but she could also fight like a cat if cornered. Olga in a new sailor suit was her stodgy self, her uncut hair braided down her back like a bellpull. I gave her braid a tug, just to hear her squeal.

Farthest from the mine, we had sweeter air and greener space than most, though our houses were stuck together and stingier in size. German, English, and Welsh lived in the ashy-aired valley, closest to the tipple and the tracks. They stewed in the afterdamp and dead-horse smell of the coke ovens. The rest of us were striped up the hill like veins of coal, and we each looked down on anyone outside our stripe. Because Russians were the last to get here, Russians were at the top.

I said, "I hope the schoolhouse doesn't smell like us." We'd smeared it good with olive oil, beeswax, and incense the day before. To me, having services in the schoolhouse made it more ours than anyone else's, though I still didn't want it to smell like us. "What's it going to take for the company to build us our own church?" Old Believers groused, but they also groused about Father Dmitri teaching us Sunday school in English.

Yesterday, as we'd made our way from Russian Hill past Pole Town, Chins Radchenko and his goons turned out to shoot off their slingshots and their mouths. Chins shook his head as he yelled, setting all his chins wobbling. The girls pinched their noses and said we smelled of cabbage or horseradish, which we probably did. They stuck their fingers up like goat horns. "Bah! Bah! Bah" they bleated, mocking Old Believer's scraggly beards, "Rushie, Rushie, go to church." How could I argue that I was American, wearing a headscarf and my long black monyik, carrying a sack of church podruchniks on my back?

After Sunday school, Olga directed us as we pushed desks and chairs to the back. When our fathers arrived carrying the family icons, her brother Sergei tilted them against the blackboard. He swung out the vigil lamps on their tiny hinges, filled them with olive oil, and lit each floating wick. Women burned beeswax tapers down to puddles, and Father Dmitri walked the center aisle—men standing on one side and women on the other—swinging his stinky censer into every corner up to heaven. With his sunken eyes, long fingers, and robe, along with his awful beard, he looked like the saints on the icons. We crossed ourselves three times and bowed down again and again, chanting the Lord-have-mercy prayer forty times—*Gospodi pomiloy, gospodi pomiloy, gospodi pomiloy.*

Father Dmitri taught us that "Lord have mercy on me, a sinner," was the only prayer we needed and that we should strive to say it with every breath. Traipsing to school that first day, I had a chant of my own. *My sisters are coming, my sisters are coming, my sisters are coming.*

Maria stretched up to right the strap of my sagging schoolbag. "Do you have a rock in there?" What I had was a rock in my heart.

"Teacher's pet," Olga chided. "Always raising your hand and now you brung a present."

I used to think that's what school was for, raising your hand, but Olga said school wasn't just for me. As for the jam in my schoolbag, "Ma sent it," I defended myself. I wiped my sleeve across my eyes.

"She's jealous of your smarts," sweet Maria said. "Don't be sore, Yelenie."

I wasn't crying about being called teacher's pet, which I hoped was true, or about Ma piling gifts at Miss Kelly's feet, which had been going on since before I was born.

We passed the plain English church and the Catholic Saints Mary and Anne, which had a bell tower and windows of colored glass. I'd never seen the windows from the inside because it was a sin to step into another church. If the company ever built us our own church, the icons lined up along the chalk tray would hang on the walls. Pa said the Suwalki church had icons four rows high and that boys like Sergei climbed ladders to light the top row and then snuffed each lamp out at the service's end.

Miss Kelly stood in front of the yellow brick schoolhouse, the same yellow brick as the churches and our house, the same as the whole company town. She was buttoned up to her chin, a ruffle circling her neck, and her linen skirt had been ironed flat, like a paper doll. A belt the size of an embroidery hoop cinched her waist. Her freckles were always a surprise, as was her shiny brown hair piled on her head like a giant loaf of paska. She took my rhubarb jam in both her hands and said, "Your ma is a gem. Hasn't she come a long way with her English?" That threw me, as if Ma took leisurely strolls with the English families at the bottom of the hill.

Ma said I was the one kicked her down the road to the schoolhouse while I was still in her belly. It was my godmother, Daria, who presented Ma to the teacher, who in turn admired the white lace collar Ma had plaited for her, all the while refusing it. Daria told Ma that she said, "I've done nothing to deserve this," and Ma told Daria to tell her, "That is what makes it a gift, like God's grace." That collar got Ma the alphabet with pictures of apple, bird, cat. Dinner got her a lesson in what to call dinner: *kapusta* was cabbage; *kielbasa,* sausage; *pirozhki,* a bun stuffed with onions and a smidgen of beef, or with sour cherries.

Seeing Miss Kelly lifted my spirits, as did the smell of chalk and linseed oil. Had she been pushing out our smells all night?

"Fourth graders," she pointed us to the back rows. Along with my Olga, there were three more Olgas, and I was glad to be born in January, or I'd probably be named for the first saint too. We were seated by age and alphabet, so Italians, Colored, Welsh, Polish—you name it—sat cheek to jowl. Chins Radchenko was right behind me, breathing down my dress. This was his third try at sixth grade, and though I'd never wished this on anyone else, I wished he'd go into the mines already.

Miss Kelly called roll. On the board was her chalk drawing that started each year, the parts of the apple. There was something for every grade in that apple. In his front-row seat, Kostia bobbed his curly head as he took in the bright chalk colors and the apple cut open to the core, arrows shooting off to label peel to pips. Being with Miss Kelly, even if it was crusts and gristle for dinner, even if it was Lent, there was school and I was fed.

She snuck in the rules as she went along, how to be excused for the outhouse, when we were allowed to crank the pencil grinder. But when she announced, "Here, there are no foolish questions," Kostia's hand shot up, and he grunted eagerly until she called on him.

My heart sank to my boots. "Beg pardon, miss," he said. "There are *Foolish Questions.* They's Yelenie's favorite. She has a big stack what she can show you."

The laughter started with Chins Radchenko right behind me, rolling me flat as it traveled up the rows.

"Filling the coal scuttle?"

"No, I'm throwing tin cans to my goat."

"Are you playing the flute?"

And while one said, "No, I'm biting my initials in an apple dumpling," another kid said, "No, I have a big stack what I can show you."

"That's enough, now," Miss Kelly said, fanning her freckled face. She tugged at the top of her high-necked blouse, undoing oyster-shell buttons the size of her button nose. I planned to pinch my brother silly at recess. "Aren't you a tonic?" she said to Kostia, then "Don't answer that," which set everyone off again.

She got us back to the apple, and the fact she aimed at us fourth graders was that each seed had the makings of an entire tree—a single shiny pip could give you a hundred years of apples. Our fourth-grade words were *pulp, pericarp, pip, calyx, pedicel.* Copying them over and over brought me back to our tussle with the foreman.

The day we climbed the hill home from Mr. Henderson's, Ma scooted me to the table and gave me a little onion to suck on, then she sharpened two pencils with a paring knife and worked a page free from her practice pad. She printed my name great big between the lines—Yelena Federoff—bearing down so hard that the letters had a gray-black shadow. She blew the dust away and handed me the pencil. Although it was a stub, I knew it wasn't a plaything. She said, "This is coal, too. You must use this to get away from the mines."

Rolling the onion along the roof of my mouth filled my nose with the smell of supper. Ma lifted her shoulders, neck, and head away from her ample bosom, growing tall in front of my eyes, and she stretched rows and rows of O's across the page.

She said, "To get coal to feed us, Pa crawls on his knees and breathes stink and dust. We patch our patches, we make broth from a bone, while the company adds up our debts." Ma rubbed her jaw, which sounded like rocks grinding together. "Pa is bent over pick, I'm bent over washboard, and you, my first American"—she tapped the top of my head with her pencil—"you will be writing invitations, asking ladies to tea."

Her loopy story turned my pencil into a magic wand filled with the very coal Pa mined. Even better, I had the power to change our donkey work into a tea party. Unsteady as I was with the pencil stub, I made my crooked marks as if I were writing with money or with food.

When Miss Kelly said, "Eyes front, if you please," I'd finished my words, filling two pages with apple parts. Though it wasn't even lunch yet, Miss Kelly tugged butcher paper off the other blackboard to reveal a red brick building topped by onion-domed towers, like the pictures I'd seen of Old Believer churches in Russia. She'd also outlined and shaded in rows and rows of red bricks atop a star-shaped foundation on the blackboard that yesterday had been lined with our icons. "Ellis Island," she said, "near the Statue of Liberty."

Miss Kelly held up a whole *Washington Observer*, the paper from Washington City a dozen miles away that I only got in dribs and drabs. The front page showed the same scene she'd drawn, except the building and grounds in the photo were teeming with people who looked to be carrying or wearing all they owned. She asked a third grader to read the headline: "Record numbers come to America." I thought of how Pa always said, "America came to me."

Miss Kelly read the number beneath the headline, "Eleven thousand seven hundred forty-seven immigrants," then handed her chalk to Nikki Popoff in the back row. He knew to go to the board and translate it for us all: 11,747. Last year, we'd learned that a mile was a little more than five thousand feet, and a foot was about the size of a grown-up's foot. So 11,747 people lined up, toe to heel, would stretch for more than two miles, which I tried to imagine. Miss Kelly said 11,747 was a record, the most immigrants to arrive at New York City's Ellis Island on a single day.

Nikki Popoff, who came here from Suwalki, sent up a cheer, which some joined, but there was plenty of razzing as well, led by Paddy Hanrahan. I was caught between the two. I wished my godmother or Nadja's boys were still in school, so I could follow their lead. Nikki Popoff was one of ours, even if he'd come by boat. Paddy was Irish and Chins Radchenko was a Pole, though they were born here—Chins spat on my neck with his razzing. I was American, too, but I lived on Russian Hill and was Russian Orthodox. It was Maria elbowing me that got me to clap for Nikki, for Ma and Pa coming into Baltimore, and for Miss Kelly, who Ma called an Irish wisp. I didn't clap for my sisters, who were coming whether I welcomed them or not.

"Open your primers," Miss Kelly told the first graders, and she emptied a scoop of dried beans in the well of each open book. "Count as high as you're able," she encouraged them.

She told Nikki to stay at the board, then she said, "Yelena, if you please." It was an odd pleasure to hear my name said once rather than the usual three times. "Angelo Giordano, won't you join her?" There was an "Ohhhh," from the Italians at the two of us up there together, because they'd seen me coming and going from his house some Saturdays.

Our mas liked to practice their "pronounce," us kids winding the Victrola as they belted out songs. After, the boys passed around plates of prosciutto and provolone sliced so thin the painted patterns on the plates showed beneath. Mr. Giordano had carted Ma and Pa from the train station on their first day, and on their second, Ma brought skansi to Mr. G and a fly bonnet she'd sewn for his horse, Pezzato, setting off a tug-of-war of thanks that was going to this day. It was Mr. G who gave me the Russian fairy-tale book left behind by the widow who'd lived in our house. Her girl had lived—and died—in our house, which was spooky but also gripping. Though that was back before I could read, I'd stroked the embossed cover, Prince Ivan and the firebird who I knew from Ma's stories.

Standing up at the board between Nikki and Angelo, I showed all my work the way Miss Kelly had taught us. I snuck a peek to the right and saw that Nikki and me had the same numbers. Angelo had to erase and redo his three times until his totals matched ours.

One day of immigrants:	1 x 11,747	=	11,747
One week of immigrants:	7 x 11,747	=	82,229
One month of immigrants:	30 x 11,747	=	352,410
One year of immigrants:	365 x 11,747	=	4,287,655

When Miss Kelly asked the first graders what they'd counted, Kostia had finished his whole scoop, a hill of beans that only amounted to 120. What would 11,747 look like? 4,287,655? If four million more foreigners showed up, would I count for more or less? And in our own house, what would two more beans matter?

The boys ran wild at recess, turning every race into a contest. We girls jumped rope until there was a ruckus around the side of the schoolhouse, then, like idiots, we ran toward trouble. I saw my little brother pinging pebbles at Chins Radchenko, who was tormenting a rat in a crude maze built of twigs and mud. Kostia liked animals more than most people, and this rat was in a bind. It darted toward every escape route opened and blocked by the boys, who cheered the fix they'd put him in. I thought the rat might outlast them or win them over, but its spunk and determination egged them on.

Olga's brother Sergei objected when Paddy Hanrahan pelted the rat with coal chips. "Knock it off!"

Chins lifted the hairless tail and dropped it in the rain barrel, where the plucky rat came up swimming. "We have enough of your kind here," Chins said, knocking the rat's grip free from the edge. "Go back where you come from." Olga and Sergei had come from Suwalki.

Angelo ran a stick around the rain barrel's lip to keep the rat from holding on, while Kostia tugged on his sleeve in vain. "It's me, Angelo," as if Angelo would stop because we'd sat together on the Giordanos' divan. Kostia's chest was heaving like an accordion, and his long fringed eyelashes held on to his tears. Though I'd planned to pinch him for embarrassing me in front of the school, I cupped his shoulder and aimed him outside the circle, toward a gaggle of boys shooting marbles. It occurred to me that my big sisters might prove useful someday.

Then I called Chins a blockhead, which I'd pay for, and Maria told Angelo he had noodles for brains. "Oh, yeah?" Angelo said, "You people cross yourself wrong."

Olga, the defender of the faith, reached back for her own braid and gave him a couple lashings with the tasseled end. "No, you do."

When Old Believers crossed ourselves, we started on God's good side—sheep and Jesus on the right, sinners and goats on the left. Catholics did it backwards and barely bowed, where we went all the way to the floor, each person touching their head to a square podruchnik Ma had quilted. Ma said that Catholics, may they rot for all eternity, had broken away from us and changed the calendar. Our icons were flat, but they prayed to statues.

My old Easter dress tied with a sash that Maria tugged loose to give Angelo another few lashings, chanting, "You worship idols, so shut your trap." She and her ma ran a boarding house of young, unmarried miners, and she'd learned how to fend for herself. She was sweet, but you didn't go against her.

Chins Radchenko sang, "Shut your trap, nya-nya-nya." He splashed water from the rain barrel at Sergei. "Hey Ivan, tell your girlfriend to mind her own business."

"That's not my name," Sergei said. Ivan is what they called all the boys who walked to Sunday school in their rubashka shirts, brocade along the collar and down the front.

"Go kiss the floor, Ivan," Angelo said.

If Sergei got in a fight, Miss Kelly would send him home, where he'd get another beating from his and Olga's father, Horse Belsky. Olga told me that Sergei had lost his side tooth getting between their ma and pa. He said, "I'll kiss the floor after I kiss your sister," and he smiled his gap-toothed grin.

That shut Angelo up—his older sister Teresa was a famed beauty—but it didn't stop Chins, who pushed the rat's sleek head under water until finally it drowned. My chin quivered with rage.

"Any foolish questions, smarty pants?" Chins lifted the rat out by its tail again, this time bringing it close to my face. Since it was dead, I wasn't scared or sick, only sorry for the rat. I thought of the first word I'd read, R-A-T-S, and the two x's for eyes on the Rough on

Rats box of poison that sat on the windowsill. Soon as I sounded that out, I ran around sounding out everything in the house, and that night, I slid my fairy tales from their hiding place. Stroking the letters sunk in the cover was magical, because now I could read them—so this is what *Russian* and *fairy tales* feel like. I paged to Prince Ivan riding on the back of a gray wolf and found the words with the sounds in the story. This is what *wolf* looks like, and *Ivan*, and *firebird*.

The boys must have thought I was frozen in fear, because I didn't squeal at the dead rat in front of my face. Sergei stepped between me and Chins, and he said, "There's your lunch, Chins. I hear your people love ratwurst."

We all hooted that Sergei had made two digs in one. Chins was Polish, so he ate kielbasa. He would never eat German bratwurst, let alone rat. He swung the dead rat high and then let loose of the tail, aiming straight for Sergei's head. But Sergei, who'd had plenty of practice at home, was fast enough to duck.

4

PA TROMPED HOME AT twilight, so cindered over his clothes looked to be made of blasting powder and coal. "That's about two bits' worth," he said.

"Too bad you're wearing it," Ma fumed, either at him or at the effort to hoist the pot of steaming water to clean him. Pa let his overalls down to his waist and knelt next to the zinc tub in the corner, then Ma unfolded the kitchen screen around them so she could go at him with hot, soapy rags. Behind the screen, they boiled over in Russian, as if they'd been simmering since breakfast. I caught a few words I knew—*glupyy, byess, hvatit*—which was stupid, devil, enough.

Pa came from behind the screen wrapped in a towel, his furry chest steaming. "Kostia will be a miner."

"That may be," Ma agreed, "but America needs bridge builders, too."

"Who asked you?" Pa said.

"I listen. Nadja said so many people are just off the boat, and Mrs. Henderson told her if only there were bridges for them to jump off of." She leaned over to stoke the oven.

"You think you're bettering yourself, giving my jam away to the teacher." Pa lifted the zinc tub as if it were a teacup and emptied his bathwater out back where I toted his dinner pail.

It was my chore to wash out Pa's dinner bucket, the battered trays reeking after a day in the mines. Ma said she was glad I had come along for the job. Tobacco chaws stuck to the sides, and the bottom was slimed with mine slurry and mule mess. Inside, the trays were smeared in a vile paste of honey, horseradish, pork fat, and smashed potatoes, along with cherry goo and coal ash. I held my breath and scoured the pail with lye soap and water.

The way Ma and Pa carped at each other, I thought Pa had maybe changed his mind about bringing Sonya and Lethia here. Ma ladled out our supper, and I raised my right hand to show Pa how I held my ring and pinky finger to thumb, middle finger hunched against pointer. I didn't want him smacking my noggin with his spoon.

"Horosho," he approved. "Our martyrs get buried alive, least we can do is make Christ on a cross the right way."

Ma said, "They would not budge." Not budging was most of our religion.

We crossed ourselves three times—*Gospodi, Isuse Hristos, Syne Bozhi, Pomiloy*—and fell to dinner, spoons knocking against bowls and slurping. We picked the chicken necks out of our stew to eat them corncob style. Once Pa was fed, he relaxed some, and after supper, I swept the kitchen floor beneath the table, each plank as familiar as him going on and on about his day. Stuffed into coal carts, they rolled down, down, down the tunnel to the city they'd dug out of dirt. The rooms were wide as our house but half as high, so even the Italians had to stoop, and they all ended up ankle-deep in chilly cave water.

Little Pearl reached out to Pa, who put down his mug of tea to take hold of her. The thumbprint he left on the mug was a black whorl, despite all Ma's scrubbing. He told how the mule boy walked Topsy from the barn, Topsy's ears brushing the top of the tunnel the whole way. "Then Max picks into a seam, augers the hole, stuffs it with powder." Pa fanned out his long skinny fingers. "He pulls that metal needle out, and I'm the one slides in a squib. That's how Max's hand got burnt, when a short fuse blew, so I'm the one lights the squib, too."

"Ka-blam!" Kostia hollered but also covered his ears.

"You feel the blast here." Pa thumped his chest next to where

Pearl rested. "I'm grabbing for the chunks shot out, we fill and dump our buckets fast as we can. When the whistle blows, it's coal that gets a ride. We walk to the scales on the tracks, wading through Topsy's mess."

Kostia's crooked nose twitched. "Where's the mule barn? I never seen it."

I got that if Topsy wasn't toting tons of coal to the weighing station, she was alone in the clammy dark, and I dreaded Kostia knowing, after the day he'd had. When Pa said, "Once them mules are down there, they never see the light of day," my brother drew his head in like a turtle, trembling between his rounded shoulders. Pa leaned in and said, "Don't be a sap. They don't know no different, down there in the dark. Their eyes cloud over and they go blind."

When we were settled under the covers that night, Ma started in on Emilion's story, which we could as easily have told her. Stupid Emilion was the laziest boy in his village. Rather than doing his chores, he goes fishing through a hole in the ice and manages to haul up the magic pike, who grants him wishes in exchange for being thrown back. What Emilion likes best is napping on the warm stove, so he wishes for a towering woodpile—"I ask it pike, do it"—and his horseless sleigh dashes to the forest, plowing through a crowd of villagers and running down a little girl, who dies before her mother can kiss her goodbye.

"Why not a little boy?" I asked, and Kostia pinched me.

You'd think Stupid Emilion would get what was coming to him, but Ma told how he ends up with red boots of buttery leather, a felted beret soft as a lamb's ear, and the tsar's daughter.

The next morning we made ready to do it all over again. Ma hadn't asked about my first day of school or told Kostia and Pearl the news. Maybe my sisters would take over the laundry or help with Pearl and the new baby when it came. I wondered if growing up in Suwalki, the two of them had learned all that Ma knew. Unlike Pa, Ma could read and write Russian, Polish, Lithuanian, and church Slavonic, more than all the men except Father Dmitri.

"Am I meant to take them to school with me?" I asked Ma in private, and she guffawed.

"My silly docha. What they don't know, they won't learn in school. They'll be home with me."

I remembered when I was home with her. Ma made all our clothes from other clothes, and I helped piece the scraps into the quilted podruchniks she made for church. I used to climb on a stepstool, and while Ma brewed brine to put up cucumbers, radishes, beets, or beans, I scrubbed them clean and tugged off the tips.

"Stand tall." She'd pull my shoulders apart like a wishbone. "No one showed me any better, and I'm too old to change now."

"You're too old to stand tall," I'd echo her. She was higher than I could count then, twenty-four or so.

Time and flour enough, we'd make black bread for the Finns who built us a porch swing, or for Maria's ma, her hands full with her boarders. Ma's hands around mine squeezed coffee grounds through a cheesecloth, dregs dripping into the dough. "What Polish use twice, Russians use three times," she'd say. "Black bread is dark as coal but not as hard. You work it with your hands—what is it to work?"

"Knead?" I guessed.

"Knead. My American gets stirred up."

"Mixed up," I'd set her straight, then I'd take Kostia with me to bury the grounds in the garden. That would be three times we'd used them: for coffee, bread, and the worms.

I had surprises to look forward to in school, like fractions being division in disguise or Miss Kelly showing us stereoscope cards of Ellis Island and the Statue of Liberty, but Ma's days were set, working to put food into our mouths and keep the coal dust out of them.

PEARL WAS AT MA'S breast when we came in from school, and lickety-split, Ma wiped Pearl's mouth, slipped the apron off over her head, and picked up a loaf pan of dough. We followed Ma next door. "Can I bake this with your stove?" she asked Nadja.

"Can I eat it with my mouth?" Nadja answered, which tickled them both.

She was taking us to Mrs. G's, though Kostia asked to stay put. He and Nadja's girl wanted to see if the fairy houses Kostia built in the meadow from twigs and cattails had gotten any visitors.

"Have you started supper?" Nadja asked Ma. "I can add cabbage and broth to ours."

Ma kissed her on the cheek, and we ran next door to fetch whatever would stretch it. Ma spit-polished my face, then scooped a fingerful of lard onto my tufted bangs. "So they know you have a mother." She ducked back into Nadja's kitchen, saying, "Turnips and a soupbone."

Kostia was so tickled he slapped his knee. "Soup doesn't have bones. Meat has bones."

Though I'd just walked all the way uphill from school, I was happy to walk down hand in hand with Ma. Pearl could walk—she could run—but not far. Ma strapped her high on her chest because of the baby in her belly, and when we came to Little Italy, Pearl waved her arms overhead, stirring up the garlic and stewed tomato air. Trumpet vines and morning glories filled Mr. G's trellises, and rosemary and sage bushes grew waist-high in his garden, along with shiny eggplants, spiky greens, and peppers galore. He had a grape arbor and an olive tree; fig trees he buried flat each winter and planted upright in the spring. Pa said the Italians paid more attention to their gardens than their children.

Mrs. G was at her clothesline, gathering ribbons of spaghetti she hung like laundry. "Katya!" She poured out her heart between kisses. *Smooch!* "Teresa and him, they come back married, can you believe?" *Smooch!* "A daughter's wedding without her mother, but thanks God a priest was there. Ludovico says he's a thug."

She pronounced it *thog*, which I thought was Italian. In one motion, she lifted a handful of noodles from the clothesline and twirled them into the basket under her arm, making a row of little nests. "He trails her like dog, his tongue out, eyes bulging. Vico swears to slit his neck if he sees them together, so they run off."

"Tell Mr. G to be happy she found herself a Catholic," Ma said.

I puzzled through Mrs. G's banter: Vico was our beloved Mr. G, the same as Ludovico—the same as the Vico who would slit the boy's throat for sparking Teresa. "Lenotchka," Ma tapped me on the head to get my attention, and she set Pearl on the ground for me to chase after. I pinched off a grape from their clusters, splitting its leathery skin in half to give Pearl the pulp, so she'd stay put. Ma asked Mrs. G, "Teresa loves him?"

"She beg Vico, 'Slit my neck, too!' and off they go." Mrs. G rolled her eyes back into her head. "Is talk. My Vico, he's good as bread. This week, he took his son-in-law to the mines for work."

"So it's jolly ending," Ma said. "Would you rather she married a nice Polish boy? Or a big boiled Paddy to give you grandbabies?"

Mrs. G pushed her body against Ma's. She said, "Maybe a Yewish son-in-law."

"Or a healthy mule," Ma said ruefully.

"Katya, oh Katya!" Mrs. G snorted. When they stepped apart, she pointed at the letter Ma had taken from inside her housedress. "Whose news is that?"

"Ma's," Ma said and unfolded to read, "'I hope Gregor is smarter than his father, the cobbler who can't heel a boot but charges you anyway,' 'I'll cry a mother's tears when I send the girls I raised as my own.'"

"Katya, your girls are coming!" Mrs. G threw a noodle nest into the air, like confetti, and pasta fell on my head and my shoulders. I thought of Maria saying Angelo had noodles for brains. But then Mrs. G said, "'*Send* the girls'? I thought you buy tickets for them to come, too."

Baba and Jeda were coming! That meant Baba could take a turn pampering me, and Jeda could write my name in gold. I couldn't speak until spoken to, but I did a little dance of excitement with Pearl in my arms, until Ma rested her heavy hand on my shoulder.

"We buy tickets for them," she agreed with Mrs. G. "But 'Maybe next time,' my ma says. How to tell Gregor? He's been so cross about paying their way and living with Ma and Pa under our roof. I thought my wish come true," she said, her voice cracking. "My girls wouldn't be alone and I could care for Pa."

Pearl ran back to hug Ma. I wanted to know why she had to care for her pa—was Jeda sick? Really, no one told me anything.

Mrs. G said, "So they don't come. You lose that money but keep your bed."

"That is not her way, to waste anything." Ma read again from the letter. "'The Raskoff girl, just married, is happy for the chance you give them. They will have a longer life in America than me and your pa.'"

"Dio mio!" Mrs. G said.

Ma slid the envelope back against her heart. "I have to tell Gregor she turned tables on us. Nadja says he'll get over it, what choice does he have?"

"That is why they're so angry, because they have no choice," Mrs. G said. She handed me the basket of noodles and scooped Pearl into her arms. "Come inside, my Katya. We'll toast. We'll tear our hair out."

I was ready to tear my hair out, too. I followed them into Mrs. G's kitchen, where cheese hung in nets from the ceiling. Salami, too, and sausage ropes looped from one corner to the other. Everything hanging. Ma sat in one of the heavy kitchen chairs at the giant table, and Mrs. G took two tiny glasses from her glass-fronted hutch, its overhead arch carved with oversized fruits. They must have brought their furniture from Italy, which I hadn't known was allowed. Mrs. G lifted the lid off an urn on the floor, and I tasted the fumes in the back of my throat. With a tiny silver ladle, she scooped up cherries and dropped them in thimble-sized glasses, *plop plop*. Ma and Mrs. G clinked the glasses, sipped the syrupy stuff, and gave a *whoop*. Ma wasn't a drinker, but the doll-sized glasses weren't for drinkers.

As Mrs. G arranged a plate of skinny white breadsticks and salami slices—sheer as the tissue paper over my Russian fairy-tale pictures—Angelo appeared, nice as could be. He helped himself to food and not only put a record on the Victrola but also let me crank it, as if the rat attack had never happened. The needle scratched its way around a couple times—*chew-wool, chew-wool*—before it turned the platter's ridges from sludgy strings into a sweet tune. "Beautiful Dreamer, wake unto me," our mothers sang, Ma's dress rippling like a cat in a bag. First verse, second, and by the time they got to "beam on my heart," they were crying over each other, Baby Pearl, and all the babies to come, including my sisters.

I pointed to the pink sky out the window and said, "Ma." Miners were passing on the street, and however mad Pa was going to be would be worse if he came home to a dark house.

"Don't go empty-handed," Mrs. G said, stuffing two salamis and a handful of biscotti into a sack. Ma carried that and strapped Pearl to me, because we had to climb uphill in a hurry and she had her belly to carry. If I ever got out of this town, I vowed to go someplace flatter. Though we slapped one foot down after the other, Pa's boots were already on the front porch when we arrived. Stinky and grimed in soot, he was an angry shadow with eyes and teeth.

"You weren't here!" he bellowed. Cap off, his forehead shone like his miner's lamp.

"Gregor, Gregor, Gregor," Ma pleaded.

"Now you know me! I need bath and supper, you don't know me."

Nadja waltzed in behind us with a stockpot and my little brother, champing at the bit.

"Papa," Kostia hopped on one foot with excitement. "Chipmunks are in our fairy house, they nibbled the roof away—"

"Who asked you?" Pa flicked him with his finger.

"Gregor," Nadja said and set the pot on our stove. "Save your breath to cool your soup. Katya left your dinner with me to keep warm." The bread we'd baked in her oven was sliced and steaming on the counter. She knew our kitchen as well as her own, and she lit the burner under the kettle and pulled out a chair. "Katya, rest up while his water boils."

She wisely scooted out the door to her house as Kostia hid behind Ma. Pearl squirmed against my chest, so I fetched her a biscotti and handed a deck of salami to Pa. I said, "Mrs. G sent this for you."

He took two slices of salami, rolling them up, cigar style, and shoved them in his mouth. "You," he growled. "You think you're so smart."

You weren't supposed to think you were smart. All I'd done was give Pearl and Pa something to gnaw on. He reached for the plotka he kept hooked on the back of the door, and my skin turned to gooseflesh. "I'll show you to keep your Ma out past supper, blabbing to dagoes."

Kostia darted upstairs. The last time he'd gotten whupped was for hiding Pa's plotka—Pa just nailed another broomstick with strips of new leather, which must have hurt more. I'd been whipped for not bringing in the wash and for cracking the reflector on Pa's miner's cap, but if I got the plotka for being at Mrs. G's, what would Ma get when he learned the rest?

"Water's hot," Ma said. "Let's scrub the day off you afore supper." He surprised me by handing over the plotka to her as she wrapped the screen around him, but he yelled, "You're in the danger zone."

Danger Zone was painted all over signs near the molten-hot coke ovens, billboards tall as me in six languages Pa couldn't read. It was a wonder he wasn't burned to a crisp or killed a dozen other ways in the mine, and that prickled my skin, too. Behind the screen, he was hollering at me. "Docha, get my pail clean as a whistle and then to bed without supper. You and your monkey business."

All the while I scoured his pail, I sassed it like it was Pa. *Is that mule kaka or did you make on your own bucket? I bet you've never seen a monkey or its business.* Upstairs, I threw myself on my bed and cried, though I hadn't gotten hit, and I blamed my sisters for already taking food from my mouth. The truth was I'd eaten more at Mrs. G's than what the rest of them had for supper.

I dug through my clippings looking for bad news and settled on the Darr Mine Disaster, which had toppled our chimney thirty miles away. "A muffled detonation, an ominous shake of the earth, sent a thrill through the hearts of the villagers today as miners met a painless death." I skipped over cleaved skulls, severed arms, and how many coffins. My godmother, Daria, would have found such details ripe. "Soon, our men will refuse to enter the mines. Already, two-thirds are negro or foreigners. Many foreign-born are unable to obey simple safety rules, as they neither speak nor write English." The talk of painless death and *our men* got my dander up on Pa's behalf, which wasn't what I wanted.

I slid my book of fairy tales from its spot. Thinking of the girl who'd owned it satisfied my need to wallow. I imagined her lifting the tissue paper to see Maria Marina, headdress big as antlers, then closing her eyes in feverish pain. Her ma pressed a cool cloth to her forehead and offered her bone broth, but her jaw tightened until she couldn't sip from the soup spoon at her lips. Maybe. Hers was a true story wrapped in fairy tales. Or the other way around, because I was making her story up, which was so thrilling it was probably a sin.

Hours later, I woke to Pa slamming the front door, moaning a sad song. I climbed out of my crater to see Ma between the stove and the window, balling yarn by the light of the moon. Her wheat-colored hair glowed.

"You weren't here," she gently spoke his words back to him.

"And how do you like that?" His pointy nose and long fingers cast a creepy shadow.

"I don't like our money going to vodka," she said.

"It's bad enough you give my jam, my bread, my skansa to the entire town. I have to learn from Max that I've been swindled." He seemed more hurt than angry. "I don't need your ma picking at me, but instead of sending us two children, she sends four. That Raskoff girl is Lethia's age."

"Fourteen," Ma said. "Same age as when I married you." She gave him a thin smile. "You're sad my mother isn't coming?"

"Zakroy rot," he snapped. "You tell everyone our business before you tell your husband."

If I told Kostia to shut his mouth, Ma would wash mine out with soap. But the worst happened after Ma said, "I only tell Nadja and Mrs. G. She knew what I wanted."

Pa swung the back of his hand across Ma's face, a terrible clap. She hunched over the table, a golden curtain of hair closing around her head. I'd never seen him hit her, and my heart went to my socks.

Wobbly as he was, he wobbled over and pinched the precious dreaded letter from the table. With his long fingers, he tore the paper so slowly that the ripping made no sound. Then he did it again and again—quarters, sixteenths, I'd just learned from Miss Kelly—before throwing the strips in the air, the same as Mrs. G had done with her noodles. Paper fluttered to Ma's hair, shoulders, and the floor.

"You always get what you want," he bellowed. "Are you happy now?"

Ma gathered her hair, jutted out her chin. "Nyet. I don't want fat lip. I don't want my pa to die without me."

"Your pa," he moaned, and he sounded contrite.

Ma moved past him to sweep up the scraps, emptying the dust-pan inside the stove. "Let the domovoi have it." Facing him, she held the broom like a pitchfork and the dustpan like a shield in front of her belly, her face swelling as much with tenderness as with pain. She said to Pa, "What is it I want? My children with me, safe and fed, my house warm, my husband—"

"Katya, Katya, Katya," Pa hushed her with her own name. Kneeling, he reached his long arms around her wide lap. "You want too much."

5

THE PRESIDENT WAS COMING to visit. Max said, "He's a lame duck, so joke's on us," but the way I saw it, he was the president of America, and I was American. Why wouldn't he want to see how we made do? Turns out, the joke was on me because the train bringing him here was the very train that my sisters and the two strangers would be riding into town. I couldn't make sense of it if I tried, that those foreigners would meet the president before I did.

In Sunday school, I tried to make sense of the church, asking, "Why is it a sin to whistle at the table, eat a crawdad, play cards for matchsticks?" Father Dmitri said the church doesn't answer to us, we answer to the church. Then he said, "We cut in a straight line the word of truth." Together, we sounded like *Foolish Questions*.

The grown-ups showing up for service were more interested in the president than God, and I listened to the men go on.

"Other mines, the boss comes in swinging. But Roosevelt wants what's fair."

"Ask me, I'd worked the extra hour, send the money home."

"That's another hour when the roof could fall in on you," Pa said.

"He upped the breaker's age to nine. Taft may well raise our boys to twelve."

"Here's what you do," Nikki Popoff's pa said. "Pay a visit to Doc and the postmaster, and they'll stamp a birth certificate says he's twelve."

Max said, "Or you could let him finish sixth grade."

"He had enough schooling," Nikki's pa said. "Your boys are too good for the mines—they have to work steel—and now I heard your Daniil went and married a Polish girl."

"I heard the same," Max said about his own son. "And Nadja thought the mines were dangerous." He fiddled with the sash of his rubashka, tricky with his damaged hand. "Yelenie," he said my name, "tell us what you know about Teddy."

I was so surprised to be asked, I stood up to answer. "He's why the mine whistle blows at six instead of seven. His wife, Alice, died on the same day as his ma. His youngest son Quentin is eleven, and he's got five others." At home, I would have been stopped by now. "He became president in 1901 when Leon Czolgosz shot President McKinley—"

"A Polack," Pa cuffed Max.

Chanting started inside, *Gospodi pomiloy, gospodi pomiloy, gospodi pomiloy,* and we hustled to get in before the last pomiloy. I tugged my favorite podruchnik from where I'd snuck it in the stack, a square of blue velvet and satin triangles cut from Ma's old coat. Everyone touched their heads to prayer squares she made; "from the hem of our garments," she said at home.

Church Slavonic still sounded like fancy gibberish to me, and I followed what Ma did, crossing myself and bowing to the ground three times and three times three. When we weren't doing that, we were supposed to stand still as a statue. I was fidgeting too much for Olga's ma, who flicked me on the head the way she'd flick a fly off a loaf of bread. She could somehow sense when I shifted my weight to one leg, though my skirt reached the ground. Then she glared at me with her black eye, a fresh shiner courtesy of her husband, Horse.

I found our family icon of the Madonna and child along the wall. Pa said smiling people were simple or up to something, but the only part of church that made sense to me was baby Jesus's smile. Soon Ma would have a new baby, and toting up all of us and the two strangers coming, there'd be ten in our house. Sonya and Lethia would take our bed, and Ma had scared up a mattress for Pearl, Kostia, and me to sleep on, crosswise like hillbillies.

Father Dmitri swung the smoldering frankincense toward every corner. The chunks he fed the censer looked like raw sugar, but the funk of the billowing smoke was moldy as Methuselah. While I wasn't ashamed to be Orthodox, I didn't want the president getting a whiff of us. Miss Kelly had drawn his portrait on the chalkboard, and his big bushy eyebrows and wide cheeks stuck out around the icons.

After Sergei snuffed the wicks one by one, we kids fell over ourselves to get outside. Pearl jumped on the swing, stumpy legs dangling from the flat board. The way she talked, "Push Pearl!" sounded like "Push pull!"

Nadja and Ma joined the men on the stoop. Lately, some of the biddies had taken against Ma for boycotting the company store. They called her a troublemaker, though it was no skin off their noses, and we were the ones had to walk all the way to Deemston to shop.

Pearl yelled, "You want down! Yaney, down!"

"Who wants down?" I teased. She ran to Pa, who lifted her in the air. Nadja and Max's littlest one, Rita, was younger than Pearl and had taken a shine to me. She climbed into my lap, and I listened to the men rant some more.

"Henderson will give him the royal tour, and nothing will happen."

"I'll give Teddy a tour," Max said. "I'll take him deep down in the Rachel shaft, in and out if you know what I mean." He yelped when Ma stuck her elbow into his side. "Hey, you're not even my woman!"

Pa laughed. "She showed you."

Olga and Maria called for me, and Ma pried Rita's fingers loose. "You don't want to be a rotting egg, Lenotchka."

Olga had bunched her monyik between her legs so she could jump the rope Maria was turning with my godmother, Daria. I jumped in behind Olga, but the slight Maria kept lagging behind, making the rope go catawampus. We collapsed in laughter, out of breath.

"What kind of name is Roosevelt?" I asked Daria, who made it her business to know things, especially anything grisly. She's the one who told us that Father Dmitri came here because his wife and two kids were killed in a trolley accident.

She said, "Roosevelt is Dutch."

"Our cleansing powder is Dutch," I said. I wasn't sure what country Dutch people lived in. Windmills were Dutch. "What religion is Dutch?"

"Not ours," Olga said. "Pa says he'll make us give up the church."

"For what?" I asked, and Daria said, "For Lent," which upset Olga.

"You should confess you said that," she said.

Daria said, "You don't like it, go gargle with soap. I'm almost a married woman."

Getting married meant having babies and feeding them from her breast and soaping down Jimmy Kasmiersky, who kept the coal carts in good repair but didn't actually mine. She'd have to sleep with him instead of sideways across the bed with her sisters, which might be a step up.

Daria was going on about working for Doc, who let her order his supplies and keep his patient files. Then she lowered her voice. "Chins Radchenko's ma had a boil in her armpit, and Doc took a splinter out of Pyotr Sokolov's piska." Doc's office was a good fit for Daria, who was drawn to blood and pus. It was Father Dmitri's gory Bible stories that kept her coming to Sunday school. She flounced off to find Jimmy, and Olga and Maria headed home hand in hand, leaving me to eavesdrop on the biddies behind the schoolhouse.

I heard Nikki Popoff's ma say, "Who leaves their docheri to be raised by Jid?"

Jid was their word for Jew. I'd never met one and didn't know that any lived in Suwalki. Father Dmitri said that Jews were God's chosen people until they killed his son. Then we were.

"Didn't that Jid make your monyik? You bragged that she finishes each buttonhole with a little strip of cloth, and you have a coat she made, too."

Ma finished her buttonholes with a strip of cloth and was trying to teach me how.

"Coats have buttonholes. Also, she makes a generous collar, considering."

"I'd like to know how she gets the milkman all the way up the hill."

"Maybe she promised to swap a daughter for a jug of milk."

"So she's a go-getter." That was Vera Sokolov, mother of the splintered Pyotr. While the other women were wide-hipped and buxom, Vera was thin as a skeleton, and her cheeks were sunken. "When I had female trouble, she brought me kapusta soup and brown bread."

"That may be, but some say Katya brings you a loaf of bread and leaves with your shirt."

Until they spoke Ma's name aloud, I thought they were just running their mouths. But they were dragging Ma through the mud! I pushed off from my hidey-hole and took off up the hill in my monyik, which was like running inside a sack. Ma was worth more than the lot of them, always helping them out and trying to better herself, yet the only one defended her was Vera Sokolov. Ma said Vera had been through the wringer.

My sleeves were wet with snot and I was out of breath when I hung up my church clothes. "What is it?" Ma asked. I didn't even know all that was eating at me. I wanted to push her away and also mash myself against her and the baby rolling around inside her. I was carrying on like a Holy Roller.

Ma pulled me down on my bed with her. Tomorrow, it wouldn't be my bed anymore. Pearl climbed in and petted my hair. She was usually a terror, running into trouble so I had to follow her, but that day she claimed me. She'd taken her clothes off down to her raggedy underwear, and her copying me made me feel hateful and abandoned, selfish and neglected.

"Why didn't you leave things alone?" I cried, struggling in Ma's grip.

"We'll be a whole family," Ma said. "I never forgot my girls."

I imagined Sonya and Lethia stepping out of their photograph in their billowy white dresses and ringlets to see my little sister, whose frayed undershirt was made from a dress made from a flour sack. Pearl's front tooth had been knocked out by an ice ball, and you could see a piece of coal that had stayed under her skin when she'd scraped her elbow running down the road to meet Pa. I closed my eyes and said to Ma, "They called you a Jew." It was probably true, since no one told me anything.

"Baba was raised that way," Ma said, and my eyes flipped open like a doll baby.

"Jeda copies the Bible for church," I objected. If Ma didn't defend herself, I would. Jews nailed Jesus to the cross, which seemed worse than what we said about other religions.

Ma wiped my face with her hanky. "He used to say, 'Suwalki was out of Orthodox women, so I found myself an Orthodox Jew.' His parents never spoke to him again."

"In the same town?"

"Same town, same church, same celebrations," Ma said. "His ma and me, we had the same birthday. I left flowers at her door, and nothing from her, not a smile. One birthday, I see her walk out to my bundle of roses, and she crushed them with her boot."

Now I felt sorry for Ma and for me both. I blubbered, "If you brought me flowers, I wouldn't step on them."

She laid her head on my pillow facing me, Pearl at our heads. "My baba lived in my village and wouldn't look at me. Your baba took your sisters in when I made Gregor come here."

"Made him?" Here was the past changing again. As many times as I'd heard about the fliers posted in the town square—TICKET PAID TO AMERICA—this was the first it occurred to me that Pa couldn't read a word of them. What kind of mother leaves her children behind? She knew what kind.

Ma said, "Twice, our priest filled the belea with water to baptize Ma Orthodox, and she changed her mind on the church steps, said 'Maybe later,' and went home."

"Maybe later" was what she'd written in her letter about coming to America. She'd given her and Jeda's tickets to strangers rather than come meet me.

Pearl twisted around Ma and me like pretzel dough. I whispered to Ma what I couldn't say out loud. "Are you a Jid? Am I?"

"I am my mother's daughter," she said, stretching her head on her swanlike neck.

She didn't deny it, and I said, "I am my mother's daughter," with as much loyalty as shame. Holding my cheeks in her hands, she touched her nose to mine, but I couldn't look her in the eye.

6

AT TEN EACH MORNING, the Cokeburg train pulled in beneath our coal tipple, where chutes poured their loads into freight cars, then it delivered passengers to the station a half mile beyond Marianna. For the president's visit, the company built a parade stand by the tipple and a staircase up from the tracks. It was the dirtiest spot in town, silted by years of soft coal sliding out the chutes and surrounded by slag heaps.

Before we headed to the parade stand on Monday, Miss Kelly had us wax our chairs and desks, in case the president came round, though I figured it was mostly so we'd blow off steam. The president's bushy mustache, scrunched eyes, and horse mouth watched us work over our desks. We teased Paddy Hanrahan, whose hair was slicked down and parted in the middle. His da was one of the miners chosen to escort the president down the mine shaft. I was glad they'd closed the mine for the day, so Nikki Popoff was with us and could recite his "Ode to a Miner" at the ceremony. We knew the chorus by heart:

> For a plate at the table, you need meat and potatoes,
> but when the plate's missing, you'll need plenty to drink.
> Raise a glass if you're able, raise a toast to the miner,
> digs your coal for a living 'til he digs his own grave.

Miss Kelly had us line up oldest to youngest to march downhill on the coal-lined road, the autumn sun shining directly in my eyes. The October day was August hot, and my dress was tight as a snakeskin, the waist up around my ribs. How I wished I could shed it and wriggle free. The way I outgrew clothes, there'd be a day for each dress to fit regular, but today wasn't that day. We marched down Beeson Street and climbed the steps of the newly built parade stand, so soot-covered that itching your nose left a streak across your face. I heard Kostia tell his Colored friend Fergus, "You're lucky dirt don't show on you," and the boy said, "Ain't that rich?"

Ma stayed home to clean and cook for my sisters, already more important than the president of the United States. As we left for school, she was sprinkling the breakfast tea leaves on the floor so she could sweep them up and have the coal dust come away too. All the men had turned out, else Henderson said he'd dock their pay. With the mine closed for the day, they weren't getting paid either, and Pa was miffed. "We stand to lose money we don't make."

We crowded into the stands as Mrs. Collins, the postmaster's wife, plucked American flags from her bouquet to give out to grown-ups. People clapped in time to the chugging train—*huz-ZAH! huz-ZAH!*—and a ragged band of musicians featured the postmaster himself. The brakes squealed, the wheels slowed, and the crowd roared in welcome. But instead of stopping, the train picked up speed. Soon, the cowcatcher passed the parade stand, the tipple, and us. "What's the big idea?" yelled a photographer from the *Washington Observer*.

The air went out of the lot of us as the crowd moaned in disappointment. We went from puffed up and prideful to slouchy defeat. Even Mr. Collins's squeeze-box flapped, *wah-wah*! The whole of Bosses Row climbed the parade stand. With no train to meet, I thought they might throw themselves onto the tracks. But after the whistle went out of range, it came back around, growing loud and shrill. Out of the low sun, a silhouette appeared—the president of the United States coming into focus at the railing of the caboose!

"They must of let off passengers," Olga figured out before me. That meant my sisters wouldn't see me greet the president, and they'd also have to wait their turn to come back to town. Pebbled coal sprayed the hoi polloi, who flinched. Not Roosevelt, who waved and grinned, wide teeth in his wide mouth, round spectacles on his huge round head. He was fatter than in photographs, as fat as in the funnies.

"He doesn't look like a lame duck. He looks like a walrus," Kostia whispered.

Blasts of steam shot out beneath the train's wheels, heat waves shimmering from the slag. I was baking in the bowl of coal chips. Sweat plastered my dress to my back and ran between my shoulder blades, through a gap in my underwear, and down the crack of my zhopa. Miss Kelly raised her finger, and we belted out "In the Good Ole USA," like drunks in a beer hall, the photographer's flash firing—*pop! pop! pop!*

Miners in starched collars were there to ride with him to the tunnels and back, but the president waved them off, including Paddy Hanrahan's da, not even bothering with the two-bit tour. At the podium, he mopped his face with a handkerchief, and I confess I loved him for that. "Colliers, all, I greet you," his reedy voice sang out. I wondered if the miners knew they were colliers. He threw his arms wide in amazement. "This modern mine is the envy of the world—you unearth more soft coal in an hour than others do in a day."

We cheered for the men and the city they'd carved under our feet.

"But that is not all that America is, a producer without responsibilities, without heart. That is why I pride myself in knowing John and his brother David Jones, whose wife Mary Ann Feehan Jones lent her name to this thriving town."

This was news to me, that one of the owners had claimed the town for his wife and given it the name Marianna. They'd probably called the mine shafts Rachel, Agnes, and Blanche after kin as well. The Joneses must have thought they'd been granted naming rights along with mineral rights, like Adam in the Garden of Eden telling the animals who they were. Next, the president would announce that the clouds over our heads were company clouds.

"Their father was a Welsh immigrant, like so many here, who made his way to America and founded the Pittsburg-Buffalo Company. He pledged to give skilled miners a good life, with fair wages and an education for your children, who will not be forced underground before their time. I am your president, but first and foremost I am a father. And I would be proud should my sons mine the coal that runs this great nation."

The Joneses and Mr. and Mrs. Henderson clapped into the silence, as the rest of us began to realize that he was done with us. The president must have known that Mr. Jones was rich before he came to America—he bought a whole town—but the president also knew the meaning of *skilled* and *good* and *fair*. And while he knew how much the mine produced, did he know how an explosion rumbles along a seam, raining chunks of coal? Had he gotten a whiff of the afterdamp that suffocated men or felt the blistering heat of the coke ovens that stunk to high heaven?

Enraged at being jilted, I held up my hand as if I was in class, but I didn't wait to be called on. "Mr. President, over here!" I hollered. "Here we are!"

"That'll do, Yelena." Miss Kelly pushed down my arm. I was more surprised than embarrassed, because she'd never been irate with me before. Her face was raspberry red, and her freckles popped out like black seeds.

In fact, the president's arm went up, but that didn't mean he noticed me. What was at most a wave in my direction might have merely been the hot wavy air he stirred up as he said, "God bless you all and God bless America" and turned his back on Marianna. Straightaway, the train wheels took to chugging, and all we saw of President Roosevelt was his caboose.

Olga shoved my shoulder. "You thought he'd come when you called. You thought you'd have a heart-to-heart." I was drenched in sweat and shame. Even Maria said, "That was a bucket of spit," which was the God's truth. Nikki Popoff practicing his poem under the chalkboard portrait was the closest we got to the president, whose tinned speech was more hurtful than if he'd never come. To rub salt in my wounds, my friends were madder at me than at him.

I ran from the slag heap, hot as lava, hot tears in my throat. When I swept my bangs aside, I felt a slur of soot across my forehead and my fingers came away as if inked. Some man hooked elbows with Miss Kelly as Mr. Collins broke into "Drowsy Maggie." You wouldn't think she could get any redder until she did.

I spotted Max holding his flag like a spear. He was next to Mickey McBride, Miss Kelly's fella, who said, "That eejit made off with my lass—Mother of God, this day!"

Max stuck his middle finger in the air. "The bastard Jonesy come on a boat with his pockets full of gold, not packed like us, herrings in a tin. Wish I'd given him a piece of my mind."

"You'd of been canned," Mickey McBride said, "or clocked with a pipe. I pray Teddy thinks more of us than we do of him."

Max said, "Proud father, my ass! You don't see his boy leaving Harvard for this."

Bitter as I was, I coveted their flags for Ma, and I was horrified when Max snapped his stem in half. He snatched Mickey McBride's flag out of his hands and broke that in two as well. "We've been had—which noble collier's buying drinks?"

Pa's voice rang out, "You buy the first round and I'll buy the last!"

"Pa!" I was relieved to see him. I figured we'd corral Kostia and get each other up the hill, but he pushed me away. "Go help your ma."

Max squinted his narrow eyes at me, as if seeing the root of his trouble. "You're the proud American. You can have this rubbish," and he gave me his and Mickey's sad flags.

There was a steady *clop, clop,* which I took to be my heart. I tried splitting the broken flagpoles in half again for spite, but the cheap wood shredded rather than snapped. Worse, a splintered spike jabbed my palm, driven like the nail into Christ's hand. I stared in shock at the ragged puncture, which went a good inch into the meat of my palm, until the pain slammed me. Then I bayed like a wolf kicked out of the pack.

What I thought was the sound of my pounding pulse was actually horseshoes striking the road. My eyes, wild in my head, met the big horsey eye of Pezzato pulling Mr. G's wagon. Drenched with the effort of carting his load, the horse shared my righteous anger and confusion. "There, there, Pezzato." Mr. G poured water from a pitcher on the horse's mane. Sitting behind Mr. G was a young woman, her face soft with tenderness, and two younger girls wearing beautiful sky-blue coats despite the heat. I'd planned on my sisters seeing me shake the president's hand and welcome him with the songs we'd rehearsed for weeks. Instead, I stood blubbering in the street, covered in grime like gravy and clutching the bloodied slivers of a flag.

Strong, well-scrubbed men in starched white shirts ran alongside Mr. G's wagon. There were more men every few feet, yelling out to my sisters, who fluttered their heavy-lidded eyes at the crowd come to greet them. The girls looked at each other with satisfaction, and I could see that, as far as they were concerned, this is why they'd come to America.

7

MA PUT A BOWL over my head to cut my hair, and I said, "Father Dmitri won't like it."

"Father Dmitri doesn't have to comb this strigla." To Lethia, she said, "Bowl, head," exaggerating her mouth, and Lethia stuck a finger up on either side of her head.

"Bull Head," she said. And that is what my older sister called me. She was wearing a pleated blouse that Ma had ironed, and she was eating Pa's raspberry jam, which we didn't touch. In the month since my sisters had arrived, Ma and Pa had been treating them like honored guests.

Sonya called me Lenotchka, but only so I'd be her servant. I came home from school to her sitting in Pa's chair, needlework weighing down her lap like an anvil. She learned to say what she wanted me to fetch her. "Lenotchka, tea, pozhaluysta? Cherries?" At least she said please.

Ma said, "Bring her tea and your stockings with a poke in the toe for her tiny stitches."

Sonya treated everything with thread. She strung garlands of mushrooms and apple slices and hung them in our kitchen window the way Irish hung lace curtains. It reminded me of Mrs. G's kitchen, because theirs was such an Italian house, and Sonya and Lethia made our house more Russian every day. They fed Ma Suwalki stories as if she were a baby bird and not the Ma of us younger nestlings, all born in Marianna.

Lethia learned enough English to taunt me. "Your country gave you straw for hair and pancakes for bosoms." She was born first, but not here. She said, "It stinks here."

She was right about the smell. The wind coming up the hill smelled like spoiled meat. To make our soft coal worth something, the men had to burn it first. They coked mountains of it for days in the big beehive ovens, whose red-hot mouths belched out fire and brimstone.

And she was right about my thatched hair and the flapjacks on my chest. Other than my round cheeks and my big round eyes, I was flat as a griddle. Both my older sisters were wavy from the top of their heads to their bottoms, though they were only thirteen and twelve when they rode into town on the president's train. Their heavy, dark eyelids made them look sleepy, or sultry if you were a man, and men were interested as soon as they arrived.

Lethia only went outside to gather grasses for her baskets or to lure Sonya out on the porch to greet the youngest miners, walking shadows a few steps ahead of their fathers. The girls waved and hollered, "You who!" When the boys hooted back, yellow teeth flashing in their sooty faces, my sisters looked to me, and I told them whatever I pleased. "He said 'Grow up,'" or, "That means 'Get back on the train.'"

If Pa rounded the corner, he'd light out after the sparking miners, swinging his dinner pail the way Father Dmitri swung the censer in church. Pa called them wolves—"Volki! Volki!"—and said if they didn't stop their panting, the president would send them back where they came from. He acted like Roosevelt would take orders from my sisters, same as we'd been doing.

That wasn't the case for Xenia and Robert, the young couple who came along with my sisters. I never knew whether Baba gave them her and Jeda's tickets or, as Pa accused, sold them the ones he'd paid dearly for. In any case, Robert mined all day and then fixed things without being asked. And while Xenia had the beauty of a statue—smooth marble skin with her thin straight nose above heart-shaped lips—she had a warmth that drew us all close. Her stroganoff rivaled Ma's, she taught Kostia string tricks, and she practiced the alphabet with Pearl. Ma and Pa both got a kick out of her. "You are the same as when you were four," Ma said—that's how old Xenia was when they left Suwalki—and Ma seemed more comfortable with her than her own daughters. Rolling out the feather bed under the kitchen table each night, they squabbled in Russian about who would sleep where. Ma always won.

Xenia picked up English the way Nadja's son Daniil used to pick up birdsong. Ma taught her the word *newlywed*, which she loved. When I didn't know why Lethia couldn't go to church, I asked Xenia.

"She said a cousin is visiting?" she asked as we walked in the meadow.

"No." I tried to keep up with her impossibly long strides. She was Pa's height and had huge hands like him, but her face was like the princesses in my fairy-tale book.

"Lethia said she had to watch the bread rise?"

"No." I stopped in my tracks. "You said that—was it so?"

"Yes and no." She told me that women make eggs inside their bodies, like hens, and bleed them out every month. "Church says we are unclean then, that bleeding marks Eve's sin. Do you believe?"

I gathered asters and black-eyed Susans for her telling me, but as for believing, yes and no. Women making eggs like hens? The church queasy about blood? In Sunday school, Father Dmitri talked about Abel's blood crying out from the ground, God turning the Nile to blood, Holofernes gushing blood as Judith sawed off his head. Xenia said, "Men believe."

She put the flowers in an empty vodka bottle in the house, then pounded the meat and told me to make tea for Ma, who had a bellyful of Boris—Anna, if it was a girl.

Ma said, "Seven times is enough of anything." And Xenia said, "You've been carrying my whole life." They thought that was funny. Xenia was fourteen, and Ma was having her seventh baby in fourteen years.

After supper, Ma planned to cook apple butter while the stove was free. I handed Lethia the broom, but Ma said, "Not yet, Yelenie." So I swept the floor myself and carted apples to the sink. When Lethia pointed out that she'd made the apple basket, Pa said, "We are rich in baskets."

I offered my sisters each a paring knife, and they stared at my hand as if looking for the flower that should have been on the end of each knife.

"You're joking," Pa said affectionately, to them not me. "My docheri skin an apple? They'd whittle them down to peas."

Sonya yawned daintily, and Lethia agreed that it had been a trying day. They made a show of setting out cream for the domovoi before excusing themselves for bed. Of course Xenia offered to help, but Ma waved her away. "Take a walk with your muzh," she said, and Xenia's marble skin blushed pink. So I peeled and chopped the apples alongside Ma. I liked having her to myself yet resented my sisters' status, which gave them a choice when I had none. I might have enjoyed myself more had I known how things were going to change.

Robert stoked up the fire in the oven, and all night long, the cast-iron pot of apples bubbled and thickened on the stovetop. Maybe the domovoi was grateful for the warmth or the dense smell of fruit and molasses sweetening the kitchen. Who knows? Maybe it was on my side. Whatever the reason, something shifted in the night. And come morning, our apple butter was cooked, and my sisters' cream was curdled.

It was Sunday before church, and Kostia was busy cleaning Pa's boots. I was pounding potatoes with a pestle for the pancakes we'd have after services. Pa was at the table, and Xenia had steeped tea for the men and put oats on to cook. With Ma so far along, Pa and her slept upstairs again. Xenia said when Ma woke up, there'd be oatmeal topped by apple butter. Sonya was sewing roses along the collar of her church blouse, though pink buds already stretched down both sleeves, when from upstairs, we all heard a loud whimpering turn into an agonizing moan.

"Katya?" Xenia called.

But it was Lethia moaning on her way to us, practically sliding down the stairs in her socks. She came into the kitchen crying and waving her brush.

"What is it, dochenka?" Pa asked, using a sweeter form of daughter for her than for me. "There, there, now." A mouse in her bedroom? A sliver in her foot?

"Nyet!" she said. She turned sideways to show her hair matted like poison ivy on a tree, furry vines twisting down her back. She was always fussing over the ringlets that framed her face. How long since she'd combed her backside?

Pa's blue eyes flickered like the hottest part of a flame, and Kostia, who got blamed for everything, made himself scarce. Xenia and Robert went out the front door for the porch, but I was trapped on my side of the table. Pa wrapped his long fingers around Lethia's matted skein. She yelped in pain or maybe surprise, as she'd been cooed over since she arrived. "Are you gluppy?" he asked. "What girl doesn't know to brush her hair?" He grabbed Ma's kitchen shears with his free hand. "I'll fix that rat's nest!"

Sonya's needlework spilled from her lap to the floor. She was so eager to throw herself on the scissors, I was terrified that Pa would run her through. By now, Ma was in the kitchen. "Gregor, Gregor, Gregor," she chanted. "Give Sonya a chance."

Pa laughed ruefully. "You worried they would starve, worried they would feel abandoned. So now you have two more infants to feed and bathe."

"Mama and Papa loved them for us." Ma patted her huge belly with her swollen hands.

"Oy, durachki!" he waved the scissors, and as angry as he was, it was satisfying to hear him call them idiots. He roared, "Even kittens know to clean themselves!"

"That is so," Ma said.

"What man would want either of these for a wife—they couldn't boil soup!"

"Soup or soap—they can't make either. That is so."

Ma agreed with everything he said, which might be how she came to hold the scissors. She didn't stick up for them, because the truth was they did not know a thing. Her sigh turned into a sob, and then her shoulders shook with her crying. "Gregor, what's to become of them? It's as if their feet never touched the ground."

8

THE MEN WERE GETTING Thanksgiving off, paid, and Ma and Xenia wanted us to repeat all we'd learned in school about the holiday. Though Kostia's primer heaped praise on the Pilgrims, Miss Kelly said it was a wonder they survived since they ditched a leaky vessel, crowded into a single boat, and set out too late in the year, in debt to creditors they'd never be able to pay.

I said, "The Pilgrims were picked on because of how they worshipped. They thought England's church was too much like the Catholics, with all the statues and gold altars."

"Catholics," Ma said and frowned.

Xenia also frowned. "In debt as soon as they landed here. That's how it's done, then."

Ma's face brightened. "We were picked out, too."

"Picked on," I corrected. "The Pilgrims wanted their own church. That was against the law in 1620."

"Da, da," Ma said. "Almost same with us. Patriarch Nikon, then later Peter the Great. They wanted us to cross ourselves a different way, have a different calendar. That's why our holidays don't match." Russian Christmas was in January, and our Easter, as far as I could tell, was anyone's guess. It could be the same, a week off, or more than a month later.

The next day, Miss Kelly told us that the Pilgrims got planting tips from the Indians. She called them natives, and said *native* didn't mean *savage*. It meant *born*, like *nativity*.

"We're natives," I said to Kostia on our way home, and he started skipping in circles around me, patting his palm against his mouth as he chanted.

We walked in the front door to our sisters sitting at the kitchen table, gazing into each other's eyes. Ma had brushed Lethia's hair, cutting out some of the mats, and now she crimped her ringlets in a hot curling iron and pinched Sonya's cheeks for color. "No more mollycoddling," she announced. I had no idea she knew that word, and I wondered what my sisters thought it meant. Ma propped the two of them on the porch as if at the prow of a ship. Soon, miners walking by tipped their hats. "Evening, baryshnya." "Stitching for your dowry?" "Don't strain your pretty eyes."

Lethia waved a strand of birch bark like a ribbon. If there was a miner who needed bentwood canisters, she'd be a catch. When Pa came home smelling of a damp grave and whatever had rotted there, he said, "You'll be lucky to get hitched to a hunchback with a finger stump or two." She closed her heavy eyelids in disgust, which only I saw.

At supper, Lethia put her latest creations on the table, two small birch canisters on a wooden tray. With her chip knife, she'd engraved vines on them and carved the words *sakhar* and *chai*, in Russian, two words I actually recognized. Kostia, clever Kostia, had made lids. They were beautiful, though I wished she'd labeled them *sugar* and *tea*.

Robert actually spoke up. "If only they filled themselves."

Xenia said, "There's more sakhar and chai here than back home. That's why we left."

"Don't forget the blows to the head," Robert said.

Xenia ran her elegant fingers over the Russian letters. "When Suwalki changed, it was Russia, then one day Poland, then Lithuania. They beat boys talking Russian on wrong day."

Ma served Robert the last helping, usually reserved for Pa. She said, "We are punished like Pilgrims, and we came on a boat here, too. Tell them, Yelena."

I said, "Most Pilgrims froze or got sick and died the first year. Indians helped them grow corn, beans, and squash, but no potatoes. No potatoes here or in Russia for a hundred years."

"No kartofel for us or Pilgrims?" Ma was shocked. "Let's give thanks for the potato."

"Katya," Pa said, "Pilgrims were Brits who didn't know their asses from holes in the ground. You heard her, they mostly starved."

"Then let's give thanks for not starving," Ma said. "Let's have a feast of thanks." As soon as the table was cleared, she got out her penmanship booklet and lifted the oilcloth. She straightened her back and trailed letters between the ruled lines, writing better than she spoke because of all she'd copied. I read aloud, scarcely believing it. "Dear Miss Kelly, We would like to invite you and a guest to our home for a Thanksgiving supper, at four o'clock. Sincerely yours, Ekaterina and Gregor Federoff, 1212 Hill Street." She reached for her big kitchen shears, the same ones she'd had to use to cut the mats from Lethia's hair. As she snipped the page out, Kostia cheered and Robert swung Pearl around by a hand and a foot.

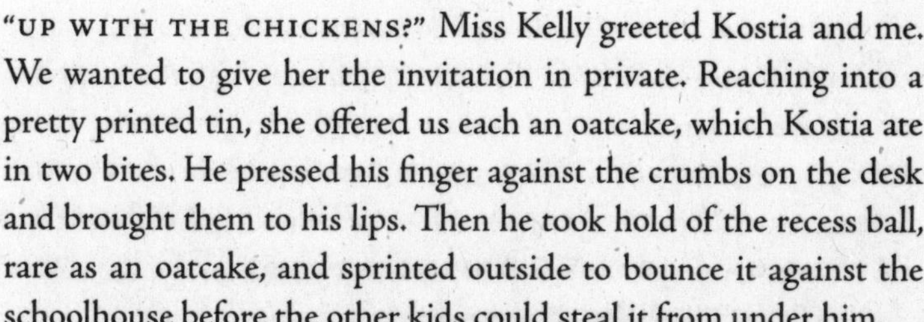

"UP WITH THE CHICKENS?" Miss Kelly greeted Kostia and me. We wanted to give her the invitation in private. Reaching into a pretty printed tin, she offered us each an oatcake, which Kostia ate in two bites. He pressed his finger against the crumbs on the desk and brought them to his lips. Then he took hold of the recess ball, rare as an oatcake, and sprinted outside to bounce it against the schoolhouse before the other kids could steal it from under him.

Miss Kelly chalked a box around the map she'd drawn so I'd know what to preserve. When she offered me the eraser, I exchanged it for our invitation, as if we were trading eggs at Easter. I was nervous she'd say no but also nervous about yes.

"I got the better of that trade," she said, and then after reading, "What an honor this is."

"Ma thinks of 1620 as yesterday." I told her how our people were banned from the Orthodox Church in 1666, because they wouldn't change a word here, a word there, so that all Russian churches would match. That's when they became Old Believers. Preserving the one true church should have protected them, but it only brought grief. "It's still a fresh wound. No one holds a grudge longer than us."

"Is that so? Have you ever met an Irishman?" Miss Kelly unscrewed the lid off a little jar of salve. She scooped out a fingerful and rubbed her hands together, and the warm smell of camphor reached my nose.

I said, "The Pilgrims didn't farm before they came here, which is like us—Pa had never picked at a seam of coal. As soon as he gets here, he owes the company for his ticket." A snootful of chalk dust made me sneeze. I couldn't see how she stood clouds of it—even more so, how the men breathed with all they took in—which got my dander up. Now that we were alone, I asked her, "How could the president say our mine is safe, that the miners have it good?"

"We have it better than some," she said, so she didn't have to call the president a liar. "Just because he's seen worse doesn't mean the company's way is right. Two things can be true at the same time."

I was working on that riddle as she slid open her desk drawer and pulled out a thick white card. Printed on the outside in fancy script was *Siobhan Mary Margaret Kelly*, enough names for her and all her sisters. She touched it to her breastbone and shrugged. "It is I." Pa said we were too poor to have middle names, and she had two of them. She wrote in straight lines, blotted the ink, and slid the card into its own envelope, writing *Mrs. Federoff* with a royal flourish beneath. After I took it from her, I curtseyed absurdly.

That night, Nadja marveled at the card, teasing Ma, "We just need two loaves and three fishes between us." And Max said, "While you're at it, pray the water turns to vodka."

For any given supper, we barely scraped together food enough for nine, and we'd invited nine more for Thanksgiving. We'd have Miss Kelly and her fella; Max, Nadja, and their daughters Martha and Rita; and three Russians who lived in the boarding house run by Maria and her ma, who were looking forward to a meal alone for a change.

Feeding this crowd would be like the stone soup story all over again. We'd have to make do with anything—everything—in the root cellar, the grain bins, all the jars Ma had put up. Also like the stone soup story, people wanted to add to our feast, but Nadja's remark about Jesus feeding the masses was closer to the truth. It was a miracle the way people pitched in when they weren't even invited, and not with a shriveled turnip or the stringy end of a roast either. Here came a sturgeon turnover to fatten up the schoolteacher, poppyseed bubliks for the single men, cherries in a jar if Lethia wanted to bake pie. Lethia collected candle stubs at church and polished the table with beeswax and beef tallow, another miracle. Robert and Pa captured two wild turkeys. Really, Kostia did. The birds were always in the meadow nipping at him, and Kostia led them into a trap. Then he fashioned a willow-branch pen and named them Teddy and Nikon.

On Wednesday, the schoolhouse got colder by the hour, and as I ran up the slope for home, an icy wind tried to push me back down. Ever since my scarlet fever, I was easily winded. My lungs burned hot and cold when I got to our yard. Pa's shirts were frozen boards on the line, and I started taking them down, planning to fold them inside. "You're a gift," Nadja said as she joined me at the clothesline. But as soon as she lifted the peg from Max's stiff sleeve, she started babbling in Russian, setting off Teddy and Nikon in their turkey pen, and then yelling at me over their blabbering. "Bits, specks all over! This is blasting too hard, too much."

She practically rubbed my nose in the sleeve to show how it was pebbled more than dusted with the usual soot. I knew Nadja was a worrywart, but I also knew that the girl who lived in my room had died after her father was crushed in the mines because he hadn't heeded Nadja.

"Here, here, this, too," Nadja said, unpegging sock and undershirt, apron and blouse.

I waited for her signal. My knees were bent, ready to sprint through the streets like the town crier. Would we tell the women up and down the hill or run all the way to Mr. Henderson?

Nadja *tsk*ed and murmured, as a chorus of whistles and wise-cracks came to us in the breeze. Dinner pails banged in time with heavy footfalls—the men had been let out early! I wanted to get to Pa, but my boots may as well have been nailed to the ground. I couldn't move because of Nadja's grip on my shoulder, an eagle's claws on a rabbit. She leaned over so we were eyeball to eyeball, and I saw the hardness in her gaze, same as when she insisted her boys wouldn't be miners.

"Chihoo," she ordered me to keep quiet. "Today's over, and no mining tomorrow. That gives the dust time to settle. Ponimayu?"

"Yes," I said. My Russian was reduced to single words like *hush* and *understand*. I thought of Nadja as gentle for the way she doted on Ma, but she'd also knock heads together if us kids talked back. "I understand," I said. I stacked our frozen laundry to thaw inside as the men rip-roared their way home. Alone at the clothesline, Nadja shook Max's shirt like she was breaking its neck.

BEFORE DARK, PA TOOK the axe to the turkeys, who ran around their pen headless and steaming for a bit. Robert wrapped their feet with twine to hang them from the porch railing. In his way, Pa soothed Kostia. "You done good, getting us those birds."

"I double-crossed them."

"You know the world isn't fairy houses with turkeys and mice for pets. Who gets to pour over books, sipping tea on a soft cushion? Priests and maybe some Jids, who loan money."

"The tsar," Kostia said.

"Yes, little man," Pa agreed. "And Mr. Henderson."

Xenia scalded the turkeys in the zinc tub that Pa and Robert used for scrubbing themselves. Kostia and I grabbed handfuls of feathers for Indian headdresses, and Pearl pretended to be the domovoi, tickling everyone. Xenia blinked behind a fan Kostia made for her—it opened and closed like a real fan—as Ma put the birds to soak in brine, like giant pickles. Then Ma punched down the dough, and we fell asleep to the smell of bread baking.

Thanksgiving morning, I got myself dressed and outside to be with Pa and Ma in the pumpkin patch. The baby inside her had scooted down to her lap, making her bowlegged, and Pa rubbed her stomach. "Here's a large, ripe one we grew."

Ma's face blanched. "Any day but today," she said.

I lugged in four pumpkins, which Ma stabbed with a fork and put in the oven to melt. Their sweet musk brought everyone to the table an hour later, and I scooped them out, Ma adding a spoonful to each bowl of kasha. "This has to last till supper," she warned.

Kostia cranked the meat grinder as I fed in carrots, celery, stale bread, pecans, apples, and fatback. Ma had said she was going to put Lethia in charge of the stuffing, but the truth was that no one could tell that girl a thing. She'd end up bossing you around and have you apologizing for disappointing her. Lethia wandered off to forage, and at least she took Pearl out of our way. After we finished the stuffing and I was working lard into flour for pie dough, Ma said, "Will you have Sonya roll the crusts?"

"When we milk chickens and cows hatch eggs," I answered.

Ma swatted me, her hand like a feather. "Umnik," wiseacre. "Teach her to make pie, peel potatoes. Her napkins will be on the table. Won't Harry Kabaloff want such a wife?"

Sonya was twelve. Also, Harry Kabaloff could eat soap for supper for what he'd done to my friend Maria, sticking his hand up under her skirt when she was cleaning his room.

Ma said, "She'll learn from you so life will be easier. Here, or in her own home."

Had Sonya even cut a slice of pie? As I slid a circle of dough into a pan, Ma's words baked in. "Here, or in her own home." Without some skills, Sonya would be our beautiful doorstop.

I called to her. "Sonya, darling sister, come learn to milk the chickens!"

"That's my Lenotchka," Ma clapped her hands together.

Bandana wrapped around my head, a flour-dusted apron from neck to knees, I was a barefoot scullery maid when Sonya waltzed in. Her deep purple skirt was stitched with autumn leaves that looked to be blowing around her shapely legs. My eyes traveled up and down her as lustily as any miner's, from her small pointy-toed boots to her hair, an onion dome on her head.

"I come to peel kartofel," she said. She swayed from side to side, then she tipped her hip and perched one hand on her tiny waist and the other below her chin like a Gibson Girl. She knew she was ridiculous. Such a relief for both of us to see her as silly.

Ma rocked herself to her feet and thanked Sonya as if she were doing us a great honor. Then Ma said, "I stuff birds at Nadja's." I figured she was taking herself next door so as not to watch.

I tied a towel around Sonya's waist. "Let's keep your ball gown out of it." Though I was supposed to teach, I couldn't recollect learning. I showed Sonya how to angle the knife in and work it around, taking off the peel in an unbroken spiral. She lifted my peel admiringly.

I said, "That's how many husbands I'll have," remembering the days when each potato yielded a half dozen husbands.

Sonya held up an unpeeled potato. "No husband." I hadn't known she could be funny. "Show again?"

"Sorry, Tsarina. Your turn." I held out the knife, which she took in her left hand.

"No," I said. "Other way." I switched the knife and potato to her correct hands, which she stared at as if they belonged to someone else. She switched them back and mimed taking a stitch with the knife. Now I understood why her sewing scissors wouldn't cut for me. "Left-handed. You're left-handed." I didn't know one thing about my sister.

"Da," she said excitedly. "Lift-handed." She took a deep breath and said, "Sorry, Tsarina," and sunk the knife in the potato. I caught her before she gouged her thumb.

"Cut away from you. Like this until you know how." As she hacked at the spud, more potato than peelings fell away. Should I stand by or save our feast? She could stitch seeds onto a strawberry, but she cut as if she was blind. That's when I saw her tears and gave her my hanky.

She said, "Your kartofel so krasivaya. I am no use."

"You'll learn," I stroked her pretty head. I thought of the shock of her new life and of growing up without Ma and Pa. Now that she'd come to us, there was already talk of who they might give her to, which turned me inside out with my usual confusion.

Sonya's skinned potato was the size of my thumb. The two of us leaned over the sink full of peelings, and Sonya said, "So many husbands."

She had managed one more spud when the grown-ups came in from Nadja's. "Look at you!" Xenia exclaimed as the men tried to make sense of what there was to look at.

Sonya held a whittled potato between her thumb and finger. "Very ugly," she said.

Pa sucked his teeth and said, "The first one is always ruined." That's what we said about the first blintz on the griddle, and I hoped he meant the potato and not Sonya.

Lethia returned bearing twigs and seedpods, and Pearl stole an onion roll before attaching herself to Pa and Robert to gather mushrooms. The rest of us sliced and grated as Ma shuttled between houses, basting the birds and fitting trays of sweet potatoes to sugar over at Nadja's. Three pumpkin pies and two apple with latticed crusts fit into our oven, the warm kitchen spicy with cinnamon and cloves and steam rising from potatoes, creamed corn, and gravy on the stovetop.

I sunk my face in every bubbling dish, but Xenia kept turning away from the smells. Ma softly asked her, "How long?" Another baby, then. More babies than potatoes in our house, except Xenia and Robert were moving on the first of December because a Russian house had opened up. I couldn't understand how Xenia could be expecting, because in our close quarters I had never seen Robert drunk, had never heard Robert and Xenia fight. That's all I knew about how each of us had come into this world.

9

MISS KELLY ARRIVED WEARING the lace collar Ma made for her before I was born. Seeing it was like seeing a piece of the true cross. Ma kissed her on both cheeks and the lips, three kisses for the Holy Trinity.

"I treasure this." Miss Kelly touched her collar. "And may I present Mickey McDarby?"

Despite his tamped-down hair and fancy tweed jacket, he was brawny as a lumberjack, his beard a woolly muff below his nose. He shrugged a leather case off his shoulder, then handed his armload of bottles to Robert, back from the woods.

Max said, "I heard of a McDarby who keeps a still."

Mickey pulled a jelly jar from his leather-trimmed pocket, sloshing with what looked to be pond water. "Here's your belly-wash. A jug of this will scutter you, I'm sure of it."

Max clapped him on the back as if his jacket was on fire.

Miss Kelly had two loaves of Irish soda bread for the feast and small presents wrapped in funny pages, one each for Kostia, me, Pearl, and my sisters, as well as Nadja's two girls.

"What a fine lady your ma is," she said to Kostia.

"She thinks she's a Pilgrim," he said. We both got pencils of our own and a drawing pad, which I squirreled up to the hidey-hole where I kept my Russian fairy tales.

The boarders from Maria's house were next, Yuri Evanoff looking dapper in a brocaded vest and corduroy pants, Lev Biletnikoff and Harry Kabaloff in crisp shirts Maria had probably ironed. Handsome Yuri gave Ma walnuts he'd gathered and shelled; Lev, who had a glowing white scar across his nose and forehead, handed Lethia a wildflower bouquet; and Harry Kabaloff, eyes like peppercorns pressed into his potato face, put two rabbit pelts in Sonya's hands.

"For you, a winter muff," Ma said to Sonya. "Harry's gift will warm you this winter." Harry gave Sonya a hungry look that made my skin crawl.

Miss Kelly and Xenia showed Ma to a chair and made sure she stayed there, when usually she wouldn't set a place for herself and would be bustling all through a meal. Lethia's centerpiece for the table was a cornucopia woven from willow branches and filled with red nandina and purple beautyberries. Yuri fondled the napkin Sonya had stitched, leaves dancing like the ones on her skirt. Although my sisters weren't useful, they were something.

"You're a marvel," Yuri said to Sonya. "Boys, isn't she a marvel?" Everyone fussed over the girls until Max brought in the roasted turkeys. Then everyone fussed over the birds.

"I hope you came hungry," Ma said to Mickey McDarby.

"I could eat the twelve apostles," he said.

There was a stunned silence. Then Max said, "You get served last for that," and roared.

Jammed together like pickles in a jar, we helped ourselves and each other to mounded, steaming dishes so heavy that my wrists shook with the weight. Stuffing, mushroom gravy, and yams glistening with maple syrup; potatoes, creamed corn, and beans; sweet and dilled cucumbers, kapusta with caraway, cranberry sauce, horseradish and Ma's hren, which was horseradish with beets; black bread, the neighbor's poppyseed bubliks, Miss Kelly's soda bread, sweet butter, and raw clover honey; sliced turkey, drumsticks, dark meat, giblets.

" . . . the middle of nine," Miss Kelly was saying.

"A small family then." That was Mickey.

Lev traced his scar. "This is from my big brother, and I still miss him, the lout."

"Makes you miss a woman's touch, seeing this spread," Harry said to Sonya.

"How about seeing these women?" Yuri asked. He had a deep dimple in his chin that reminded me of Nadja's son, Daniil. Ma and Pa seemed to have paired off Lev to Lethia and Harry to Sonya. I would have chosen Yuri over both of them.

"Beautyberry leaves keep the bugs off in summer," Lev told Lethia. He buzzed and, pretending something had landed on her arm, he swatted her.

"Bzzzzz," Lethia said, to show she understood. She followed more than she let on.

"We'll pick some in the woods," Lev said. "I'll take you to my fishing hole."

"Not so fast," Pa said. "You show me your scrip before she goes to your fishing hole."

We hadn't prayed yet, and I had to bite my cheek to keep from sinking my fork into the food. Ma tapped Miss Kelly's hand. "We pray, you pray," she said. We crossed ourselves, then Ma surprised me by squeezing her eyes shut and saying, "We give thanks for enough to eat, wise teachers, and being Pilgrims together."

"Amen," Miss Kelly and Mickey McDarby said by themselves.

"Now you pray," Ma said.

They bent their heads far over their dinner plates, and Mickey rumbled, "May those who love us, love us, and those who don't, may God turn their hearts. And if he doesn't turn their hearts, may God turn their ankles, so we'll know them by their limping. Amen."

"Amen, for heaven's sake," Miss Kelly said.

We ate like we'd been at sea for months, uncertain whether we'd make it through winter. My entire life had been thrifty and spare, and we'd never had such a spread. Caramel brown on top, the sweet potatoes were nearly pudding inside—I huffed air to let out steam, but I couldn't wait long enough not to burn the roof of my mouth.

Lev said, "This tastes like home. I never knew Thanksgiving was Russian."

Max said, "We get here and what's in our trunk? Nadja's dough bowl, horseradish long as my arm, and her pouches—dill, coriander, bay."

Nadja said, "My Max needs paska, pickles, and pelmeni." He put a hand on either side of her face and kissed her. Then it was Nasdrovyas all around for another toast, to those who come to America.

Ma said, "I swore I'd bring no more children into the world in Suwalki."

Pa's skinny smile stretched into a leer. "If I wanted to make more babies, I had to take you somewhere else. America needed miners, so I was a miner."

"Ha," Max objected. "You didn't know your pick from your pecker. Son of a cobbler, with a tongue that flaps like a shoe."

I was grateful that children were to be seen and not heard. How delicious, to eat creamed corn and spiced apples as Max told about rioting in West Virginia and taking a pellet in the shin. Stuffing studded with kielbasa to Lev's luck, picking Marianna over the Darr or Monongah mines, which had been rocked by explosions. Tart cranberries as Yuri told of his brothers sent to Siberia.

Yuri said, "You think Suwalki winter is cold, in Siberia their pee froze in the air."

"Telling stories again!" Lev scolded. "We'll see you in confession."

Yuri shrugged. "Why would my brother lie? They wrapped themselves in reindeer skins and built the church in Novosibirsk, though you won't see me in church."

I realized I hadn't seen him in church, which explained why Ma and Pa weren't favoring him. Harry put his lumpy face in Yuri's. "Why didn't they come here, your Siberians?"

"You know why," Yuri said.

"Lunatics," Harry said.

"Anarchists," Yuri corrected him.

I knew that word, *anarchist,* for the assassin who made Roosevelt president.

"Ahh," Pa said, "so that's why you can't have the powder."

"Might blast the foreman to kingdom come," Yuri said. "And Henderson knows it!"

As the Russians sucked their teeth, Mickey McDarby talked. "I long for home, though the damp did nearly drown you and the fog filled the cove like a feather bed. I'd walk the rolling green, whistling to my best dog, who kept the sheep from stepping clean off the cliffs. To think I'm underground all day, my brothers wouldn't believe it if they heard it from these lips."

"Where did they go?" Ma asked him.

"To their graves. Da was the only one of his made it through the rot. One sickness or other took my brothers, and I'm the last of the six McDarby boys here or in Ireland."

"Here," Lev said, "the last Biletnikoff."

Ma was the only one of her siblings alive as well.

Max said, "I've one sister, back in Suwalki."

"Far as you know," Harry said. That gave me a chill, but Max nodded solemnly.

It spooked me to think of these big families dwindling down or falling out of touch. Max didn't know about his only sister, and he wouldn't speak to his own sons because they married Polish Catholic girls. We had five children in our family now—me, Kostia, Pearl, Lethia, and Sonya—and a new baby coming. For the first time, I felt we were links of the same chain, hooked together as siblings. I wondered if we'd live to meet each other's children.

A bottle opened had to be finished, and you weren't to leave it on the tabletop either, not that there was any room. Empty bottles stood like ten pins on the floor, and worried that fistfights were sure to come next, I got out of my seat to serve the pies. The fast work Miss Kelly made of the dishes was proof she was raised in a big brood. I knew how to divvy up dessert from her teaching us fractions as pie wedges. Quarters cut in thirds yielded twelve pieces, which meant everyone could try both flavors without being stingy. Even after yammering that another bite might split their pants, the crowd ate four of my six pies. Then Mickey took the black case out of the corner.

"Is that an accordion?" Harry asked.

"No, it's a bathtub for an elephant," Kostia said.

"Umnik!" Pa spoke sharply, but Miss Kelly trilled a laugh.

"You and your *Foolish Questions*," she said and gave me a wink. When Mickey strapped on the box, she said, "He learned this special for today!"

Mickey played two long sad notes, pulled the box wide for the third, and squeezed for the quick fourth and fifth. It was "Ochi Chyornye," *Dark Eyes*, which set us to singing. Floor space was cleared for Pa, Max, and handsome Yuri to dance in a circle, one foot in front, one in back.

Sonya sang in her clear alto, sweet and bitter as molasses. The men wiped their tears and sweat with the napkins she'd stitched, and she twirled her finger signaling Mickey to play a third, then a fourth verse, his muscles pumping as he squeezed the box. Pa and Max fell away after the verses, leaving Yuri squatting low and kicking, Sonya swishing around him in her purple skirt and flowing blouse. They were Ma's dancer figurines come to life, and I was living in one of Ma's village stories, one with more than enough food and joy. If I hadn't eaten so much pie, I might have floated up to the ceiling with bliss.

Mickey McDarby finished in a gush of notes. As we clapped, Harry Kabaloff pulled Sonya into his lap. Rather than cuff him, Pa refilled his glass, and Yuri took his seat, alone. Mickey mopped himself and his fingerboard off, took a swig from the jelly jar, and got right to a jig. Miss Kelly stepped into the clearing—back straight, arms by her side—and puppet on a string, she kicked a pointed toe and leapt into the air, scissoring her legs. Each time she leapt, her lace collar lifted and fluttered back down as we yipped and howled. "Ay, you'll give her a big head," Mickey said at the end of it.

"Here's one for the road," he told us as Kostia scrambled to his side, gargling water and acting the ham. Mickey wheezed the accordion in, out. "Ready, my boy?"

Kostia's tinny voice matched Mrs. G's Victrola as he sang, "Beautiful dreamer, wake unto me. Starlight and dewdrops are waiting for thee." I thought of how Angelo was nice to me at his house and a pest at school, the way Miss Kelly said two things could be true at once. But listening to Kostia, I realized the song was about someone either sleeping or dead, two things that couldn't both be true.

Mickey stumbled some putting his accordion back in its shell. "Moonshine I can hold, but your brew is brutal," he said, rolling his r's. He stepped out for a smoke, and the men went, too. Smoking was a sin in our church, another thing that separated us from the Catholics. Drinking, however, was not. At weddings, the men reminded each other with every bottle that Jesus's first miracle was turning water into wine.

I worried the Russians had gone out to pee off the porch. Whatever happened out there, the men's talk had a meaner edge when they came back inside. "Mickey," Pa roared, "something I've wondered about your people, when the kartofel died. Why didn't the Irish fish? An island that starves makes no sense."

Ma said, "Potatoes came to Ireland and Russia from America!" But the men could only hear themselves.

Mickey's wide open face had closed up. He said, "Even if my people could get there, the coast is cliffs and crags. The sea swimming with treasure meant ought to us, farming sunup to sundown and Brits claiming the shoreline."

I said, "Squanto had to teach the Pilgrims how to fish in the bay."

Miss Kelly shook her big-bunned head. She said, "You're right, but I wouldn't bother."

Harry said, "Drop a line in the water is all it takes. You don't need a lesson."

Yuri defended Mickey, saying, "He's told you the Brits hogged the coast. Their own landlords were out-and-out bloodsuckers."

"Thanks, mate," Mickey said. His neck muscles twisted beneath his skin. "Whosoever had a boat sold it to buy food when the blight came. Nets, buoys, traps."

"So you're saying they did fish?" Harry Kabaloff picked up his knife and twisted it.

Mickey slammed his fist on the table. "I think you do be needing a lesson," he said.

Miss Kelly stood up and reached for his thick shoulder. "Your mouth is going to break your nose, Mr. McDarby. Saddle up your accordion. It's come time to walk me home."

"Shouldn't you be wanting to stand up for your own?" he asked.

She said, "I'm teaching my own and everyone else's. Let another have the last word."

When Mickey McDarby unclenched his jaw, the ropes in his neck went slack. "Lord love the clever lass." Then he said, "Still, I may have to give these Poles a talking-to."

That's when Harry punched him in the face. Mickey was so big, the blow just spun him so that his elbow clobbered Yuri's dimpled chin. Whether Yuri was aiming at Harry or Mickey didn't matter, for the brawl was on. Ma grabbed her Chinese pitcher and sugar bowl off the table.

As it wasn't her fight or her house, Nadja opened the front door and herded Martha and Rita onto the porch. "Max Yakimoff, I'm bolting the door with or without you." To me, she said, "I told you trouble was coming."

A sheepish Max lifted his coat off the pile on the bannister. "As always, Katya. Prostee."

There were two glasses left on the table. Miss Kelly splashed the dregs of one in Mickey's face and the other in Harry's. Harry yelled, but the spit had gone out of him. She said, "Such a shame to leave on this note." The men were lucky she didn't give their earlobes a twist.

"Prostee," Ma said.

"We say that when we go," I explained. "Forgive me for anything I've done to hurt you."

"What do people say in return?"

"Boh, Prostee. God forgives."

Miss Kelly said it, too. "Boh, Prostee. And God keep you and your children, Mrs. Federoff."

10

SNOW STARTED FALLING WHILE we put the kitchen right. Xenia sent Ma and Pa upstairs to sleep, then Lethia and Sonya pitched in, as if they didn't have to be princesses if Ma wasn't around. We chattered in whatever language we knew best, miming to bridge the gap, and Kostia and Sonya finished us off by acting out the drunks swinging at each other. "I'm Harry the svinya," Sonya said and pushed her nose into a pig snout, and we laughed all the way to bed.

I opened my eyes to a dawn pink sky, woken by bickering I couldn't place. It was Max in our kitchen ranting about Nadja, and I realized I'd heard them squabbling on the other side of the wall. "That woman!" Max said. "She sniffs my dirty socks and wants me to shut down the mine. I'm to tell Henderson himself that it's dangerous down there. Got that, fellas?"

"C'mon, old man," Pa said. "No one's been down there for days."

It was a relief that Max and Pa knew what Nadja had seen on the clothesline and weren't spooked by it. Max said, "You'd think she'd save me from getting shot in a riot or burned by a short fuse." I looked over the landing to see him shake his shriveled fist on the way out the door.

There was no school that Friday, and by the time we all got downstairs, snow covered the men's tracks and had started to drift. Ma let us eat pie for breakfast. She let Kostia whistle at the table. She stayed in her flannel nightgown, though her belly nearly busted its seams. Her hair was braided but never got bunned that day.

Lethia poured kettle water in a bowl with milk, as if making her own tea, then she added vinegar and baking soda. "Glue," she said, and held up the plate broken in the fracas. She let Kostia brush the break with a turkey feather dipped in the fixings. They had the same steady hands, and she held the matched halves together while the glue dried. Still as a stump, she moved only her lips to say to me, "Stop looking."

"Your contribution is unprecedented," I said, talking over her head to get her goat.

"Chihoo," Ma said, ending our squabble. "Go outside and blow the stink off."

Lethia gently laid the mended plate on a dish towel, then hollered upstairs, "Sonya, sneg!" I squeezed into last year's snow boots, a size too small, and bundled Pearl in someone's cast-off coat, a size too big. She was a wiggle worm eager to be throwing snowballs at Kostia, who only had to dress himself. Ma showed a little spring in her step seeing us out the door.

The drifts, not yet silted, were glittery white, and the morning sun stretched me in my tasseled cap into a dandelion sticking out of the snow. My sisters' shadows looked like full-grown women, though they ran across the snow like deer, their beautiful bright blue coats blending into the sky. Lethia leapt the way a doe runs from a wolf, or maybe for sheer pleasure. Punching through the stiff peaks didn't slow her down like it did the clunky boys, whose snowballs fell short of my loping sisters. Sonya shook a heavy pine branch and twirled under the snow she'd set free. "Sneg like home," she said, the first snowfall since she and Lethia had come.

All of us on Russian Hill squared off against the Polish and Irish kids who made their way up to the meadow. Maria stacked smooth, round snowballs into a pyramid of ammunition. Olga's brother Sergei sent me out as bait—he said I disappeared when I turned sideways.

Paddy Hanrahan picked on Kostia, saying he'd heard our pa was a drunk, and Kostia said he'd heard the same. Paddy made a fist. "Stick up for your pa!"

"I stuck up for your pa," Kostia said. "Nikki Popoff said he wasn't fit to sleep with the pigs, and I said he was." Then he ran for the forest, as familiar to him as our house.

When we stomped our boots on the porch, yelling for Ma, Xenia shushed us because Ma was back in bed. "No fair," Pearl said at the thought of someone other than her napping. She shrugged off her snow-caked layers, which stood up by themselves in the corner, and ran upstairs to snuggle. Lethia swept the porch. Before Thanksgiving, she hadn't lifted a brush to her own hair.

"Put your sewing down," I told Sonya. If Ma wouldn't teach her anything, I could. "We'll cook some turkey hash, you and me. Or maybe you want to make some pirozhki."

"I don't want," she said, sweet as butter.

"Roll up your sleeves, Tsarina. No one asks me if I want to beat the rugs. Can't you see Ma's worn through?"

I'd meant to give her a talking to, not make her cry again. "What is it?"

"Kartofel, pirozhki. You will send me away before snow melts."

"Not me," I said, sheepishly. "There's snow for months and months, you know."

"Past my birthday?"

Her birthday was at the end of March. Ma said I should teach her things so she could have her own house, but maybe if she learned things, Ma and Pa would want her to stay. "I've seen snow as late as May. Might as well learn a few things if you're going to be underfoot." That helped some, though I hadn't thought you could wear an apron wrong until she tied it high under her armpits, covering her chest like a ruffle.

Xenia joined us when I was kneading the pirozhki dough. She pinched off a ball and gently pulled it between her hands. Light shone through the stretched-out square.

"Windowpane," she said. "Okno," she said to Sonya.

"Da," Sonya agreed. "Ready for oven."

Xenia rubbed her thumb and fingers together. "I had to learn that so I didn't overwork it."

"Our baba showed me how," Sonya said. I was touched that she said *our* baba.

Ma slept the day away. Xenia said it was almost her time. When the men came home, I heard Max get a hero's welcome next door. Pa scrubbed down, ate some hash, and joined Ma upstairs. After bathing in the zinc tub, Robert put on red long johns and sat at the kitchen table in his union suit, playing Durak with us. He shuffled his cards, soft with wear, like Mickey pulling the accordion in and out. Usually, the grown-ups talked over Robert or asked him questions and then answered for him, and so it was a treat to hear his stories of taming a red fox or ice fishing for sturgeon tall as him. He won every single hand, no matter how good our cards were, until Xenia said it was bedtime.

Kostia said he didn't want the day to end, and Xenia agreed.

"Every now and then," she said, "you get an extra dumpling in your soup." She kissed each of us on the lips, the way Ma would have, and then she asked my sisters to get us ready for bed. Lethia plaited Pearl's corn silk hair. Sonya sang us to sleep, sad Russian songs with her low, sad voice. I'd never been so happy to be sad.

11

SATURDAY MORNING, I WAS listening from the landing when Pa said, "I'd stay home if it wasn't payday," and the usually quiet Robert replied with some gusto, "You and me, we have babies to feed."

"Nasdrovya!" Pa boomed. The pop of a cork meant vodka, though it was dawn.

"Gregor," Ma said, and Robert said, "Gregor, I couldn't."

"Then I'll have yours and mine both," Pa said. "Nobody tells me nothing."

It was hard not to laugh, since even I knew that Xenia was expecting. By the time I got dressed, the men were gone, and Xenia and Ma were smirking into their teacups. "What's so funny?" I asked.

Ma said, "Xenia ask me, 'Why did God make men blind?'"

Xenia was bundling herself up for a walk to Deemston. "I'll get us both some fabric," she told Ma. "Maybe a teapot," for her and Robert's house. Kostia was downstairs now, and she said, "Whoever's faster, keep your coat and boots by the door in case you have to fetch Doc Miller."

We raced around the table, bickering over who was faster. Ma yawned, and then she said she was going back to bed—unheard of. Xenia said, "Let her rest while she's able. I'm off to see the world." In her worn coat and flowered shawl for a hat, she looked like she was just off the boat, which she was.

First a snow day and now a morning without grown-ups. I poured milk in a pot, and Kostia toasted bread for milk toast, a rare treat. I brought down a stack of comics, and Pearl followed, wiping sleep from her eyes. Kostia whispered that if Ma woke up, she'd give us chores, and if our sisters did, they'd boss us around. Pearl tiptoed upstairs and returned with her shoebox of paper dolls. She brought along a gust of foul-smelling air.

"Pee-you," Kostia said, and Pearl denied it was her, like always.

Kostia had found a Little Sammy Sneeze comic about a feast, and he slowly read the first panel: "He simply couldn't stop it. He never knew when it was coming." The people at the table bowed their heads in prayer, and panel by panel, Little Sammy sneezed all the food off the table. He even sneezed the gravy out of the gravy bowl into an old man's beard. "Ah . . . chow!" we whispered, giggling.

Our doors and windows were closed, yet the smell was so strong that it burned the back of my throat and gagged me. This wasn't Pearl. At school, we got wind of the men blasting a half mile underground, and on our way home, we scavenged trash coal, which made a fire that stunk like a dirty diaper. This was worse than those smells, worse than the funk on Pa's dinner pail. I thought of a rabbit with a festering maggoty wound that Kostia had once tried to save. It smelled like that.

Milk splashed out of the top of my bowl, followed by Ma's sugar bowl clattering on the shelf. We thought that was funny, like Sammy's sneeze clearing the gravy out of the gravy bowl, but we were spooked too. My clippings started sliding from the table, and I pinned them with my elbow as the cinnamon shaker toppled over. "Yaney!" Pearl climbed into my lap. Strings of dried mushrooms and sliced apples rattled against the window, which shook in its frame, and I looked outside, where the porch swayed like a ship. Now the kitchen smelled like a forgotten Easter egg, more like a dozen forgotten eggs. I saw snow lift off roofs a few inches and land with a thud, thick sheets of it sliding down.

Ma had made it downstairs and was gripping the table edge, her face stretched with pain. "This baby's a boat in my belly," she said.

"Everything's pitching!" Kostia squealed.

As soon as he said that, a deathly calm settled, not even a crow cawing. Miss Kelly had just taught us that thunder reaches your ears many seconds after lightning flashes. Same after fireworks, she'd said. *After an explosion,* I thought, remembering Nadja's warning. My sisters stood on the landing in their nightgowns. "Bull Head, what is it?" Lethia asked. When she opened her mouth again, I heard thunder, fireworks, a cannon blast, crumpling metal, the earth splitting in two, as if Little Sammy Sneeze had sneezed the hillside clear off.

Two booms sounded, followed by sick echoes bouncing to the hill across the way and back. The sugar bowl that had made it through the Thanksgiving brawl leapt off its shelf to shatter on the floor, and broken crockery mixed with spilled sugar at our feet. When the echoes played themselves out, we listened in frightened silence.

Ma was pinned to her chair by her belly. Her whole face was white, cheeks and lips too. She tilted her head back and there was wailing, either from the mine shaft or the women running around and hollering outside. Nadja's little Rita came running through our door and threw her arms around me and Pearl. Her ma was right behind her, holding Martha by one of her half-braided pigtails. She said, "I begged them not to go, Katya, but Max would not heed me." Then she saw Ma's face and let Martha loose. "All this and the baby too?"

Ma blubbered, "Gregor, I need Gregor."

My heart sank into my socks. "I'll get Pa. Me and Kostia, we'll go."

Nadja crossed herself and announced she was coming with us. Martha pried Rita's arms from around my waist and tugged Pearl from my lap. Seven-year-old Martha would watch both little girls, and Sonya and Lethia, too, if necessary.

"Bystro!" Nadja flung us our hats, coats, and mittens, and I jumbled up my buttons in an effort to race down the hill. I ran as if bears were chasing me, toenails scraping the insides of my boots like claws. Kostia was faster still, jumping from one footprint to the next, following the path the men had made a few hours earlier. Nadja's skirt flapped farther and farther behind.

Every door of every house was flung wide, and women and children spilled down the hill like coal down the hopper. Together Kostia and I wove through the crowd to be there when they discovered our Pa was safe. Or dead, I thought, and then forced myself to unthink that thought, to go back to them declaring him safe.

The hill flattened past Little Italy, and at the schoolhouse, Kostia stopped suddenly, where there was a view all the way to the shaft. "Land sakes," he pointed, like in the comics, and I saw something shoot into the air—bodies, mule, coal car?—then scream to the ground, thuds and shouts ricocheting around us as we ran toward them. The funk was so strong I scooped up snow to suck on, so I wouldn't be sick.

Black smoke plumed from the shaft's entrance. Kostia pointed to the ravine where we'd waited for the president's train. Crumpled on the railroad tracks was the iron cage that could lift a dozen men or coal carts from the floor of the mine. The cage itself, surely a ton or more of steel, had been blown clear out of the shaft.

Mayhem swallowed us up. Vera Sokolov and Margi Popoff, the both of them in agony, clung to each other. Mrs. G's Teresa, holding her belly and rocking, wailed for "Mio prediletto." Mr. G was there, too, cursing a company man to his face. "Stronzo, bastardi! I'll slit your throat!" I remember when he'd threatened to do that to Teresa's husband.

Women were speaking every language under the shrouded sun. They clutched the sleeves of the men with clipboards, shouting their loved one's names.

John Ivill! Legs Tedroff! Horse and Pony Belsky! Red Donesty!
Fred and Nikki Popoff! Fred and Lorenzo Slovinsho! Fred Finelli!

Tears made tracks down their faces, grayed by the falling ash. Colored women swayed together, scarves tied at the backs of their heads. Their skirts were bright as Ma's, not like the drab Irish and Italians'. Kostia and I wriggled through the throngs of skirts. They'd chained off the mouth of Rachel, where we sometimes waited for Pa in the summer. Kostia clambered up a chestnut tree near the temporary tipple, which had been damaged but not destroyed, and I was right behind him.

From our perch, I saw the gruesome mess. The temporary derrick that straddled the Rachel shaft was literally blown to bits, the gangway caved in all the way to Agnes. Coal dust darkened the sky to a false twilight, and the shrill noon whistle prompted the women to scream in reply. Noon was the time their men should be taking apart the dinner pail to find the pasty, the pirozhki, the ham sandwich they'd packed. Where were their husbands or sons—or both—who'd toted pails into the mine this morning? Were they trying to claw their way out just now? Were they already dead and buried?

Because the iron chain was nothing but a sash, women had to be held back from throwing themselves down the shaft. They couldn't have if they tried: the explosion had filled the hole for a tomb. When the firedamp exploded, a single tunnel might have caved in or the whole anthill might have collapsed. If the men weren't burned or buried alive, afterdamp would have done them in.

My gut churned; despite my weak stomach, I'd never felt fear this deep. I thought of my sister's waking up to a quiet house in Suwalki, hours after Ma and Pa rode to the train station in Jeda's wagon. Had Sonya and Lethia been this afraid? Were they tied up in such knots? Sonya was so young, she might have happily sat on Baba's lap expecting they'd all be reunited at the end of the day.

"Maybe Pa was somewhere else," I said to Kostia.

Nadja had made her way down to a man with a clipboard. "Y-A-K-I-M-O-double F. His left hand is crippled. One leg has pellet shot from the Cassville riot. He's number 158—" The man made a show of checking to confirm what Nadja already knew, what she'd known from taking in the wash before Thanksgiving. "Missing," he said, at the same time she yelled "Max!" as if, at the sound of her voice, he might push the rock aside and climb out of the tomb. Her skirt ballooned as her knees buckled, toppling Nikki Popoff's ma, too.

If the men had listened to Nadja, they wouldn't be missing, and I wanted to snap off a switch and thrash the company man. Vera Sokolov did it for me, going after him with a brush she must have carried down the hill. "Zhmot!" she yelled, calling him a miser. "This is your making! You own this, but you do nothing. If my Chaz isn't dead now, he will be by tomorrow."

We shimmied down from the tree out of their sight, knowing that where Max went, Pa usually followed. As soon as someone told me Pa was gone, I'd have to go home and tell Ma. I led Kostia away from the crowd. Down Beeson Street, broken glass sparkled beneath our feet. "Bang! Kablooey!" Kostia yelled, juiced about the explosion. For once, I was grateful he lived in his own world. The windows of Mr. Henderson's office were gone, the brick buckled, and the blown-out front of the miners' tavern looked like the gaping entrance to a mine.

We saw a skinny man slouched alone at a table, sleeves blown off his coveralls and his hair standing straight up. He needed both of his thin, bloodied arms to lift a stein to his lips, and I knew him in that gesture—Pa! Even though children weren't allowed in the tavern, we walked through the missing window to throw ourselves at him. "We found you! You're here! How did you get out?"

"Chihoo!" he silenced us. "You know your pa—he has more luck than brains." We hung around his neck with relief and love. What if we had lost him?

I said, "Ma sent us to fetch you."

Pa glugged from the huge stein. "I'm celebrating. I come in walking sideways, so they put me on the tipple today. Isn't that rich? Too unsteady to go into their deathtrap."

I knew that Henderson sometimes smelled their breath as they came in, and Pa had drunk both his and Robert's shot of vodka this morning. He showed us his arm, peppered with coal from the explosion. Soon as he'd gotten out of the tipple, the whole thing had collapsed. He had a cut over his eyebrow, too, and he was drinking, had been drinking, was drunk.

A siren wound down to silence, an ambulance screeching to a stop in the street. Kostia ran out the open window to two men, who took their time getting out of the ambulance.

"Save the miners!" he ordered them.

"We will, lad, if we find a live one." The man crossed himself, Catholic style, and my runny egg of a stomach flipped over. *If we find a live one.* The breeze coming through the broken window reeked of stinkdamp but also singed hair and roasting meat.

I wanted to go home to Ma, who might be relieved to know we found Pa drunk but not dead. What about the others? I made my way past women, mothers who were wearing children like skirts, and ran to Mr. Henderson outside his ruined office. "Sir, can you tell me about Robert—?" which was as far as I got. I stood there, blinking in the hazy sun, because I didn't know his last name, only that Xenia had been "that Raskoff girl" before she married him.

"You're Gregor Federoff's girl," the foreman said. "He wasn't sent in there today. Now get along and take your pa with you."

The smoldering shaft stunk so strong that I had to breathe through my sleeve. I remembered Father Dmitri telling us brimstone was sulfur, same as in the mines. The hundreds of men who had gone to work that morning were likely trapped underground by fire and brimstone, hell on earth. Our Max, who had shown Ma and Pa how to get along, the way the Indians had shown the Pilgrims, and Xenia's Robert, who'd come to town with the president.

Two miners pushed past me, and I recognized the back of Harry Kabaloff's round head, but when I called out to him, he didn't look my way. I caught up, yelling, "Harry, it's me, Sonya's sister!" He stopped when I tugged on his coat. His eyes jiggled in his blackened face, and he yelled, "Can't hear! Firedamp took out the shaft!" He was cradling his arm against his chest like a wing, his hand balled into a fist.

I pointed to the blood all down his coat. "You're hurt." The ambulance men were sitting on their running board, and I hollered, "He's hurt, right here!" I reached for Harry's elbow. As he unfolded his arm, I saw that his hand wasn't balled into a fist. Most of his fingers were gone.

A shiver shook me, and I went clammy as the grave. The ambulance driver hooked Harry's elbow like they were square dancing. "Found a live one. Must have been a latecomer," he said. And then, "Blown clear off, the middle three." Next I knew, the sharp whiff of ammonia burned in my nose, stung my eyes. The scene in front of me was speckled gray like a newspaper photo. As it filled in, Doc's satchel was on the ground at my feet. He asked, "Does your ma need me up to your house?"

"She sent me to fetch Pa."

"Then we'd best go. Many as she's had, I'll be done and back here before they miss me." He gripped my forearm and pulled me to standing. "Too bad Gregor's tied up with the sheriff."

He said it like Pa was in a card game instead of trouble, and I hoped "tied up with the sheriff" was just a saying. We got ourselves away from the crowd, and when we passed the Catholic church, Doc said, "Saints Mary and Anne in Marianna." I couldn't believe I hadn't put that together before, and I made a loop of the church named for the town named for the woman named for the saints of the church.

We went up the hill, through Little Italy and Irish Town, where yesterday's forts and snowmen were all blackened with soot. I was afraid of what we'd find at home. When we got there, Doc sent me in ahead of him so I could tell Ma we'd found Pa. "Where is he?" Ma asked.

"What about Robert?" Xenia said. She must have known I'd have said his name if he was safe.

"Gregor broke his ankle." Doc told Ma what he hadn't told me, though he left out the sheriff. "I'm afraid Robert is missing."

Xenia clutched her sides and wailed. "I've lost them both, I'll bet." She told Doc she'd been on her way to Deemston, and when the explosions echoed in the hills, she ran home. "I ran, I ran in my condition." He asked her was she bleeding, and she sprayed him with tears shaking her head yes. "Now I have no one."

"You have us," Ma stroked her hair. "We're your family. We'll help you start over."

"Starting over is how I got here," Xenia cried.

Doc said, "It may yet come right, with some rest. Get her settled upstairs," he said to me, and then, "Where are your sisters?"

For all I knew they were bounding through the snow in the meadow, but Ma threw back her head and called, "Lethia, Sonya, priyti!"

Ma doubled over, as if Doc's arrival had started her labor. Pearl helped me cover the kitchen table with a clean sheet, and then I gave her a lump of charcoal and some butcher paper to busy herself on the floor. I was at Ma's head, wiping her brow with a cool cloth, and my sisters stationed themselves on either side of her, to squeeze a hand or hold a leg. And so Ma was surrounded by her daughters—Pa in the drunk tank and the town in mourning—when Boris Federoff showed up on our kitchen table, compact and solid as a loaf of rye bread.

SATURDAY SEEMED TO LAST a year, and my godmother Daria showed up Sunday morning with raisin rolls she'd baked and a baby blanket she'd knitted. She came upstairs to see Ma, telling her, "I only reported part of Doc's fees to the paymaster, so you'll have something." Ma thanked her. Xenia sat on a rocker in the corner, stone-faced.

"Your Jimmy?" Sonya asked Daria, and I was touched by her concern.

"He was a ways away," Daria said. "That's the whole reason he tinkers on the coal cars. Yelena helped your Harry get bandaged up," she said.

Sonya said, "He's not my Harry."

"Now, now," Ma managed. And then, "You girls have some tea."

Downstairs, I made a pot of tea and cut the raisin rolls in half. Daria slurped her tea through a sugar cube. She said, "Doc came up here yesterday because there wasn't no one to treat at the shaft. They found that old boxer's ear, and Horse's hand with his pinkie ring on." She must have volunteered to sort. "Doc knew a thigh with a Virgin Mary tattoo was Fred Finelli's 'cause he'd seen him in the altogether."

Sonya said, "Badder than dead, to be in parts." Old Believers preach that you come back how you went into the grave, so the miners torn limb from limb meant more grief for the widows. Sonya raised her heavy eyelids like curtains and asked, "What else?"

Daria put her hand on her side. "Teresa G's husband had a six-inch scar where he'd been knifed in the ribs. They dug up his whole trunk. Did you hear they pulled a man out alive?"

"I heard," I said to make her stop.

"I did not heard," Sonya said.

I fled upstairs to deliver rolls to Ma and Xenia, but not before I heard Daria say, "Even his eyeballs was shot full of coal pellets."

EXCEPT FOR THE SOUND of crying, Russian Hill was quiet the rest of that day and the next. Nadja came and went, fussing after Ma and Xenia and also railing at the company for killing her Max. She was the one who told us Mickey McDarby and Lev Biletnikoff were gone. Hearing about Lev, Lethia wept in Sonya's arms.

There would be no mining, no school, and no church for the time being. It was as if the world had stopped turning. When Mr. G and Pezzato delivered Pa to us on Monday, both men shed some tears to see Pa's new son. Mrs. G had sent a tiny embroidered shirt more fit for summer. "We call this camicino della fortuna," Mr. G explained. "You put it on the baby for good luck then pack it away—Mrs. says not to wash it or luck washes out. And she says you better not send me home with anything!"

It was good to see Ma smile. "A jar of pickled beets? Yelena, run to the cellar," she said, and sure enough, he relented.

I was wishing Mrs. G had sent something more useful, but Xenia said, "Babies need all the luck they can get." Pa hobbled over to give her a hug. His busted ankle was in a cast, and he had $3 left of his $30 pay, along with an entire newspaper they gave him in jail for some reason.

"Here, docha." Pa handed the paper over. The front page showed a casket train come to town and gawkers leaving wreaths at the toppled derrick. There was a picture of a stranger selling penny postcards, and below the fold, there were photos of Beeson Street from the tavern to the Rachel shaft, gaping windows and chimneys set crooked by the blast, and a lumpy tarp on the ground with feet and shoulders sticking out the sides. That caption read, "Body parts recovered from the Marianna Mining Disaster of 1908."

Pa said, "You're always why, why, why? Read to us."

I wanted to have it to myself before I shared it. But first, supper. I was stretching the soup, bread, and pickles to feed everyone in our house and Nadja's too. I'd rummaged through the sewing and rag baskets to make a little rabbit for Rita, just an old stuffed sock with mismatched button eyes and flannel ears.

"Give it," Sonya said and threaded her needle. She stitched a curved pink triangle for a nose so it looked to be twitching, an anchor-shaped smile beneath, and she satin-stitched pink inside the floppy ears. Then she wrapped leftover white yarn around her hand, tied it in the middle, and clipped the loops for a pom-pom tail. She worked broom straws through for whiskers behind the pink nose. It was like watching a magician pull a rabbit from the rag bag.

"My bunny," Pearl said and reached for the toy.

"No, sestrichka," little sister, Sonya said. "Our pa come home."

Upstairs in the bedroom, Lethia spooned soup into Xenia, I changed Boris's diaper, and Ma wolfed down bread with jam. Starved after nursing, Ma gnawed at a stale heel of bread.

Kostia took a tray of food and the sock rabbit next door to Nadja and her girls, whose keening came through the wall. Once Kostia returned, we sat at the table, a small crowd of six. Pearl climbed into Pa's lap and stroked his cheek, "Our pa come home." He kissed the top of her head. We crossed ourselves and glumly ate.

"Boris has a healthy appetite," I said, then wanted to take it back when I saw Pa's face. I thought he was pleased to have another son, but we didn't have crusts for the mice. I'd served myself last, so my soup was mostly broth. Whatever had fallen off the ham bone had gone to the others.

"Read to us," Pa repeated.

I smoothed Pa's copy of the *Observer*. Usually, people gave me a page or a section, and after I looked it up one side and down the other, I'd reread it to Ma as she sewed: news of the pygmy man in the Bronx Zoo or a train wreck in Pittsburgh, that mysterious city all of fifty miles north. Gathered around the table, we could hear Boris's mewling cry upstairs, followed by Ma soothing him and probably putting him to her breast. I raised my voice to read the front page.

> On Saturday, the 28th of November, 1908, shortly before 11 o'clock in the morning, an explosion commenced in the Marianna mines of the Pittsburg-Buffalo Company, and it is believed that 154 men were killed outright. The end must have come to them within minutes, if not instantly. Remarkable afterward was the absence of pathetic scenes usually enacted by the loved ones of those buried in the mines. One woman did make a commotion, saying she had a husband and two sons down there. She was a foreigner, but she had a heart and loved her family.
>
> In these Marianna mines were some of the best miners the company had, and half of them at least were Americans. Thus the company loses their services, and the world at large loses citizens who knew their duty and performed it both for their wages and also in the interests of miners of the future.

I lifted my head to see Pearl asleep in Pa's arms.

"Pa," Kostia said, "I want to be a farmer. Would you allow that?"

"Sure, sure." Pa squinted his eyes down to slits. "Run and get yourself some land, a cow, maybe chickens." He let out a creaky moan, like something buckling under. "Truth is, miners of the future means you and your brother."

"My brother." Kostia grinned.

At two days old, Boris was only "the baby." We hadn't even called him our brother yet, and here Pa was already calling him a miner. What would it take to break the spell? I thought of Daria's husband, fixing coal cars outside the shaft, or Nadja's boys working steel in Pittsburgh, fifty miles away but it may as well have been the moon.

I said, "Maybe Kostia and Boris could have themselves a turkey farm. Or Kostia could build company houses."

"Sure, sure," Kostia echoed Pa. "And maybe chickens will give milk."

Pa rubbed his whiskery cheek against the top of Pearl's head and handed her off to Lethia. "My children," he sighed. "May the future be easier than the past."

12

MARIA'S PA HAD DIED when we were four years old. He was the first dead person I'd ever seen, his flattened body dressed in church clothes and spread on their kitchen table like an oilcloth. The grown-ups told us to cross ourselves and kiss his dead forehead. After he was buried, we went to Maria's house for breakfast, but I could not touch any food on the table where he'd been laid out. Now, Maria and Olga were both without a pa, and Olga had lost her older brother Pony, who was called that because their pa was called Horse.

Casket trains came into Marianna station, and Father Dmitri chanted prayers at Olga's house for all forty-five Old Believers who'd died and were buried. We kissed the feet of an icon instead of foreheads they didn't have. After that, he performed services in houses where a shut coffin held parts they could identify. They'd found Max's dinged leg, so Nadja had a service. But Robert was a seventeen-year-old with big ears and no scars to know him by, so Xenia didn't. After the last funeral of the night, we had a church supper in a house without a coffin.

We ate our fill then ran outside to play funeral. When I was four, I wouldn't touch a pickle in a dead man's house; now, we bickered over who got the biggest pickle and who got to be worm food. That person had to stand still—it was their funeral, so no blinking or laughing—while we tucked brown leaves into their coat or pelted them with snowballs. We made a mouth of our mittened hand and pressed it to their head, smooching loudly. Olga knew the real prayers, but for playing funeral she made up prayerful jabber that split our sides. It was a horrible, wonderful time: the women wept, comforted, and fed each other, and there were no drunken fistfights.

People said, "The kingdom of heaven to him," like a chant, and Father Dmitri allowed all the miners to be buried in the sanctified part of the city cemetery, whether they'd been to confession or not. Pyotr Sokolov, whose pa and brother were dead, told me that my ma told his ma not to go to pieces, in case something worse happened tomorrow. We had a fit of hee-haw laughing, because what on earth could be worse?

At home, Pa slept downstairs, which suited his ankle, and Xenia shared the bed upstairs with Ma and Baby Boris. Ma said Xenia had been a little bit pregnant and had lost her baby—I remembered that before Boris, Ma had lost a baby.

Sonya pinched her thumb and finger together, saying, "Small thorn causes big pain." She was talking about Xenia, but at first, I'd thought she meant Harry Kabaloff and his wounded hand. Harry's new name was Penya, Russian for stump, as in "Sonya and Stump make a nice couple."

Along with the funeral suppers, Boris saved us from starving. If Pa had been hurt in the explosion instead of a brawl, he'd have been paid more, except he'd probably be dead from the explosion, a loop I followed around and around. The women Ma had been doing for all these years brought us pelmeni dumplings, borscht, or a sweet potato pie for the new baby. Pa ate angrily, waving his fork in the air. "It's the company's blood money bought this."

Ma said, "At least the widows won't be docked for supplies or booze."

"Just a coffin," Xenia said. With Robert trapped underground, she told the company she didn't need to pay for an empty box.

Miss Kelly started up school again, but the stuffing had gone out of her. The day the boys in the back row disappeared—headed into the reopened mine in the dug-out, shored-up tunnels—she handed over the chalk and spelling words to me. While I wrote on the board, she laid her head on her desk, her puffy hair like a pillow for her pale face.

Father Dmitri waited for Russian Christmas to return to the schoolhouse for services. I was ready for a little Jesus, Joseph, and Mary, but his Sunday school lesson was on Job refusing to curse God. "The Lord giveth, and the Lord taketh away; blessed be the name of the Lord," he said. "Shall we accept good at the hand of God, and shall we not receive evil?"

Why should God give us evil? I couldn't bring myself to ask that since I hadn't buried my pa and brothers—what evil had I received? My breath huffed through my nostrils, like the Bull Head my sister called me. It was one thing to take the good with the bad and another to thank the Lord for an explosion, which Father Dmitri called an act of God. Job's wife had my ear, saying God had forsaken him, and I angrily pushed the desks to the walls for service as if I was moving heaven and earth.

Like me, the women came in growling with grief and making fists of their free hands. Those who weren't carrying infants were carrying the family icons, and Father Dmitri looked more like the raw-boned, sunken-cheeked martyrs than ever. The opening *Gospodi pomiloy* set the women off again, because the men's side of the schoolhouse was nearly empty. I settled my gaze on Olga's ma—when Father Dmitri looked her way, his haunted eyes softened.

Once Sergei had snuffed out all the icons, Father Dmitri straightened his hunched shoulders and extended his arms like wings. Surprisingly, he wished everyone a good Christmas in English. "The Lord taketh away, and the Lord giveth," he said, reversing the morning verse, and thinking about that, I missed some of his announcement: " . . . make good on their promise. The company is going to build us a church."

The women talked back. "Povtorit?" "Chto eto?" Did we hear right? Say again? But there were also hurrahs, "Ura!" And "Pora!" It's about time.

Nikki Popoff's ma, who'd lost both her husband and Nikki, said, "A church with its own graveyard keeps Russians out of the city plot."

But Xenia, the youngest widow, said, "A church brings more of our people here to mine."

What would it take to get our own church? Forty-five dead men and boys is what it took, which you would have thought was a Russian ending. Except that these were American mines, in America.

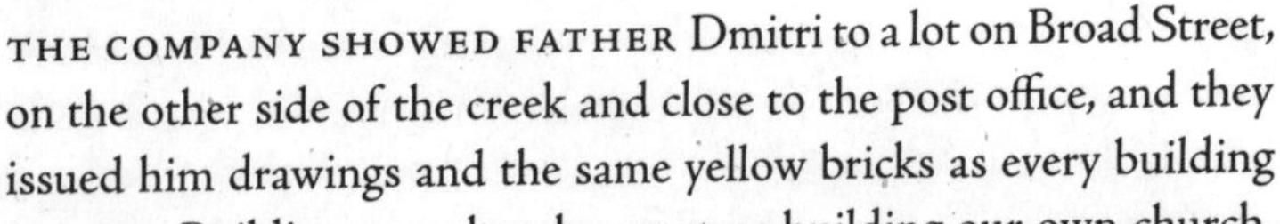

THE COMPANY SHOWED FATHER Dmitri to a lot on Broad Street, on the other side of the creek and close to the post office, and they issued him drawings and the same yellow bricks as every building in town. Building us a church meant us building our own church. Still, an Old Believer church, in America! Even Pittsburgh didn't have that.

While his ankle healed, Pa got paid to work on the church. He said the cracker-box plans must have come from a Sears & Roebuck catalog. Saints Mary and Anne was twice as tall and long as our church would be, maybe because Polish, Irish, and Italian Catholics all had to fit in there. That church also had a bell tower and arched windows, glowing with stained glass. Father Dmitri said ours came plain because they didn't know Orthodox. He finagled extra bricks to add an entry hall at the front and a cupola on top, and with the men's help, he got the shell up within weeks, a miracle Kostia and I witnessed after school on Friday, because Ma promised us a nickel apiece if we brought Pa home sober on payday.

It was a daily shock come suppertime when Pa's white face came through the door, unblackened, his veiny nose and thin sagging cheeks between great big ears. His ankle got stronger as the church went up, and he spent the winter months on ladders instead of in tunnels. At the end of the day, he peeled off layers, and Ma poured water from the kettle into the kitchen tub and then sat by the stove and rubbed his stocking feet to keep him from roaring with pain when he stepped into the hot water.

"You and your prayers," Pa teased. "My friends are warm in the mines, while I'm hanging steel gutters from a snowy roof."

"Think of the fresh air," Ma said.

He slapped her bottom. "I'll give you fresh air." Disappearing behind the folded screen, he sat down with a splash, and I chopped mushrooms as he held forth. "We'll have three crosses on top, Orthodox crosses." Ours was an eight-pointed, or four-barred, cross, an extra bar on top where they'd labeled Jesus King of the Jews and a slanted one on the bottom, where they'd nailed his feet. "No graveyard there at the church because of old mining tunnels," he said, and I remembered the map on Mr. Henderson's wall. I imagined skeletons under our church, like the catacombs Miss Kelly had shown us with her stereoscope.

"Xenia," Pa called out, "who should I meet today but Fyodor Lupowsky, just arrived? He asked after you."

"That old mule skinner," Xenia said. "He left Suwalki before we did."

"He was in Hamtramck, because Ford was paying their people five dollars a day in Detroit." Pa got a kick out of Xenia, whose gumption he admired. "Turns out he wasn't one of their people—now he's here with no wife." I was glad he wasn't offering the mule skinner to Sonya or Lethia.

"Gregor, you svat," Xenia said, which made Kostia and me laugh. We'd never heard a man called a matchmaker before. "Leave the mule skinner to the mules." Each morning, Xenia loaded Ma's giant kettle and skansi into Kostia's wagon and toted it through the crusty slush to the miners on their way into the shaft, giving away tea with every pastry bought. She also wrote letters home for Russians, Poles, Lithuanians, and Finns, new men who'd come to mine. "It's either that or jump off a bridge," Xenia said.

To our amazement, Pa was a good builder. He could nail straight boards to make a curve, so he was the one who built the bulging onion domes, the largest one twelve feet high. He attached shingles like fish scales, painted them deep blue, and burnished the surface with stars of actual gold. "They'll see my dome all the way to Cokesburg," he said. He was proud of the building crew and of Father Dmitri, who had apparently put up train stations all over New Jersey.

Father Dmitri was full of surprises. When it came time to meet the crosses in Pittsburgh, he announced that the Erie priest would join him for a blessing. "Many blessings," he said, his sunken cheeks rising up on his face. Our priests couldn't marry or remarry once they became priests, but it turned out that his calling had come only from the company. The Erie priest agreed to give him the official blessing to be our kind of priest—right after marrying him to Olga's ma! Olga was always lecturing us on right from wrong, and now the priest would be her father.

The day the onion domes were to be lifted onto their platforms, Miss Kelly walked us down from the schoolhouse and across the creek. We gawked at the hoisting tackle, ropes thicker than my arm and pulleys nearly Kostia's height. Pa waved to me from the top of the scaffold, though I wished he'd hold tight with both hands. He'd always have a limp, but he wasn't drinking much lately—he said there was no one to drink with—and so he was able to steadily guide the domes he'd built and fixed in place, their Orthodox crosses piercing the low February sky.

I imagined being inside, the floor tiled with Ma's podruchniks and flames flickering off rows of icons so tall that Sergei would need a ladder to light them all. The company taketh away, and the company giveth, is what I thought, which I didn't dare say aloud. Even so, I was puffed up with pride, sinful or not, when Paddy Hanrahan tapped me on the shoulder. He was still here to torture us because his father was working the coke ovens the day of the cave-in. "Your chapel looks furrin," he said, and pointed to the four-bar crosses. "Are those Rooskie ladders?" Miss Kelly snatched Kostia's slingshot away, but not before he got Paddy on the neck with a pebble. "Don't be ignorant," Miss Kelly said to Paddy.

The next day, we charged up the hill after school, and even though I wasn't chanting *Rooskie, Rooskie, Rooskie!* with the rest, I was afraid one of the boys would push me into the boulders of filthy snow because of Miss Kelly. Kostia ran ahead, then flopped around the kitchen like a fish out of water.

"Settle yourself," Ma said from her seat in the front room. She fed Boris from her breast and wrapped him like a blintz in blankets she said we'd softened. Little Borya, as we'd taken to calling him, wasn't much bigger at three months than when he was born.

Soon as Pa came in the door, Kostia spilled his news. "Russia was our lesson today. It was geography and history—Miss Kelly taught Russia in every class."

"To all them kids?" Pa asked.

"Let your pa in so's he can warm up." Ma and Pa stepped behind the screen, steam rising from Pa's tub of water.

Kostia busied himself with a toy Xenia had taught him to make, a string threaded through two holes of a button and tied together. He held both ends and twirled the string like a jump rope to set the button spinning, then he moved his hands like an accordion player to make it buzz and whistle. Soon, Ma folded back the screen while Pa buttoned a chamois shirt over his long underwear.

"Put that away! Everything's a game to you," Pa said.

Kostia pocketed the button and string. "Miss Kelly hung butcher paper over the board, and soon as we was in our seats, she gives it a tug—" He mimed her whisking the paper away like a bullfighter with his cape. "She drawed a huge map of Russia for us."

"Drew," I said, excited that Miss Kelly was back to her old self.

"You hush," Kostia slapped me.

So I kept going. I said, "Peter the Great changed the calendar."

When Pa turned his face to spit in the corner—*thu thu thu*—Sonya pushed me into a seat and plopped Borya in my lap. "Kostia's telling," she said, which shut me up.

Kostia took over. "Miss Kelly had a stereoscope, and she had his statue, shipyards, and palaces with gold everywhere and fountains. He built all of St. Petersburg!"

Pa grunted. In his union suit and a shirt, he should have looked silly, standing with his legs apart and hands on his hips, but his pose was defiant. "They teach that Peter was a builder?"

Kostia mirrored Pa's pose, as if they were playing a game. "He was a great engineer! His fountains ran without pumps, just the weight of the water! Peter disguised himself and learned shipbuilding in Sweden. That's how we whipped the Swedish."

"We?" Pa growled.

"Russia!" Kostia went up on his toes and clapped his hands together. Pearl echoed him, "Russia! Russia!" She'd finally learned how to say her R's.

Miss Kelly had asked us, "What if people in Pennsylvania spoke a different language than people in West Virginia?" It was a good thing she answered herself, because where we lived, every other street spoke a different language. She said, "Peter the Great won back Russian lands from Finland and Sweden. Then he unified Russia." She slipped a new piece of red chalk from a little paper sleeve and shaded Russia on the map, filling in the biggest section. "That's before Peter," she said. Then she kept shading, crossing over all the borders until the map was red from the Gulf of Finland to the Pacific Ocean. "Russia!" she announced, rolling the R and making the *sh* sound deep in her throat, like Father Dmitri. "RRRR-uhzsha!" The Russian kids cheered, and the Irish booed, because their country was tiny and they'd always be England's poor cousin. I didn't care one way or the other because I was American.

Kostia said, "Peter wanted a great Russian city on the port he won from Sweden. He wanted us to have a Venice, and so they built St. Petersburg with their bare hands!"

"They?" Pa asked.

"The peasants!" Kostia said.

"Oy, durak," Pa said, and Lethia's face lit up.

"Durak is idiot," she announced.

"Stay out of it," Pa said, and she flinched as if he'd hit her. He said, "We built his city like slaves, and then he pushed us out, murdered our priests." He pointed at Kostia. "Peasant."

"I thought peasants were barefoot and ignorant," Kostia said. He wiggled the big toe that poked through his worn boot.

I glanced away, expecting to hear a slap. But after a long cold day trying not to fall off the church's snowy roof, Pa must not have had the energy to raise his hand. He asked Ma, "Why did our son have to be such a turnip?"

I should have stopped Kostia before he made it worse. The next day, we came in from recess so Kostia could tell Miss Kelly what Pa said. While she listened carefully, it turned out she knew as much already. She'd heard Father Dmitri call Peter the Antichrist, and she'd heard the teasing when we watched the pulley raise the dome. She said, "I want you two to know your history."

Even her, I thought, saddened. I pointed to the flag. "Kostia and me are American."

"Kostia and I," she said.

She knew what I meant. I felt like she wanted to keep me back. I said, "Our parents' kin were sold with the land they worked, and Old Believers are priestless because Peter killed their priests." I thought I'd shock her, but she was the one shocked me.

Bearing down on the eraser, she wiped out the map on the board. She seemed to be speaking to the wall. "Who killed more Russians, Ivan the Terrible or Peter the Great? A regular foolish question, that one." Only halfway through the school day, she had sweat marks under her armpits and her hair had gone lopsided. She said, "American history for all, then. Maybe that's the answer."

We walked home in silence—Kostia in his head as usual and me thinking about two things being true: Miss Kelly making Kostia proud and me ashamed. As an American, I didn't care if people thought Peter was Great or the Antichrist. But after supper was over and Pa had his tea, Kostia started running his mouth like Ten Mile Creek.

"I told Miss Kelly what you said." He stood with his legs apart and hands on hips, and he imitated Pa's voice. "Peter tried to change our church—he thought he should rule instead of the priests, and that was wrong."

"You spoke to your teacher this way?" Pa asked. He was furious, which was something I hadn't considered, a third thing being true.

Kostia spoke in his own voice. "I told her what you said."

"Because you know more than the teacher?" Pa asked.

"No."

"He doesn't," I said. I hoped Kostia wouldn't tell what I'd said to Miss Kelly, and I wished I hadn't eaten so much soup because now it was sloshing around in my stomach. I didn't feel like defending the teacher or my brother. I wanted to curl up in the corner.

Without leaving his chair, Pa grabbed Kostia's arm with one hand and his plotka hanging behind the pantry door with his other. He bent Kostia over his lap, rump in the air, as the strips lifted and twirled around the handle.

"When my foreman is wrong, do I speak against him?"

"I don't know."

"You don't know?" Pa waved the plotka again, grazing a tin bowl that flew off the table to clatter to the ground. "I tell a boss he is wrong. Things work this way?"

"No," Kostia said, and you could hear the tears in his voice. "She already knew."

Now Pa raised his arm over his head and flicked his wrist, snapping the thick leather strips against Kostia's rump. Pa and Kostia hadn't squared off in the few months since my sisters had come, and Sonya covered her eyes. But Lethia looked to Ma as if she should do something.

Ma said, "Enough, Gregor. He meant well."

"Take your pants down," Pa commanded Kostia. "I'll give you something to cry about!" And he whipped him twice as hard, for all our benefit.

WIDOWS ON RUSSIAN HILL, evicted to make way for new Russian miners, gave us the foodstuffs in their pantries or root cellars. The company gave Nadja $300, lump sum plus two children, but Xenia only got $50 since Robert had mined for less than two months.

Nadja told Ma, "I'm sharing some with Xenia for helping me get our due. She understands the steps to take."

"She helps and helps," Ma said. We nodded our heads like dumplings in the soup. "And every man eats her gingerbread tells her his life story."

Nadja's cheeks parted into a wide smile, like the sun showing itself after months of gloom. "One man come from Pittsburgh," she said. "He told Xenia he played cards with a man grew up here, a man who could whistle a bird from a tree. Katya, she found my Daniil!"

They threw their arms around each other, and Ma said, "The world is cramped! Like finding you here." It turned out Nadja's boys had married cousins and had shared a house for years. The older one had two children and was moving on to Hamtramck, and Daniil was still in Pittsburgh, with a child on the way. "Here you are, already a baba," Ma said. "Such joy from such sadness."

Nadja wiped her eyes, "My Max forbid me to see them." After Easter, she and the girls were going to live with Daniil and his family. "Xenia says no one will speak against me."

Borya rooted at Ma, slobbering on her as she unbuttoned. He latched on like a snapping turtle, and she said, "Speaking of Catholics."

Nadja *tsked* at her. "I'll miss you, my Katya. Not like Vera Sokolov, with her blubbering. I earned some time in heaven taking her in."

So what did Ma do? She told Vera and her two boys they could move in with us. Years earlier, Vera had lost a little girl, who had been kicked in the head by a mule. Now she'd lost her husband and her oldest son. Ma and Nadja blabbed in Russian, pulling a curtain between me and them. I heard Pyotr's name, along with Lethia and brak. *Brak, brak, brak*—I knew that was marriage, and that Lethia would have nothing to do with Pyotr. She said Pyotr must be unlucky to lose two siblings and his pa, but I knew it was because he and Sonya sometimes sat on the porch talking and singing.

Though Nadja wasn't leaving yet, she scooted Vera over to our house right away. Vera's boys slept between quilts on our floor, two raccoons in a sack, and come morning, Pyotr headed down into the tunnel and the little one trudged to school with us. There were nights when I dreamed Pyotr's days: dark so quiet you could hear your pulse thumping in your ears as you lay on your back under the weight of the damp earth, poison air trapped in pockets of coal, and your father's ghost roaming the tunnels.

TUGGING OPEN THE THICK wooden door of our church for the first time was like opening the cover of a book. A carved sign above the door read ST. NICHOLAS RUSSIAN ORTHODOX CHURCH OF OLD BELIEVERS, and I hoped I didn't learn of a Nicholas among the Jones brothers. Widows donated their icons to the new church, and more families come to mine meant a second row of them. Taken together, the icons told our story in pictures. Sunlight and flames glinted off the enameled faces, serene despite the horrible torture that had made them saints.

Catholics built stained glass windows into their cathedrals—Miss Kelly had shown us pictures—and I realized that we'd been carrying our own windows. Old Believers had an icon for the church and every member of the family so we could come together to make a church, or make a church of home, too. Along with fresh plaster walls and sanded oak floors, I breathed in sweet beeswax, olive oil, and musty frankincense, thousand-year-old smells in a new building. Our smells. I felt Orthodox in a way I hadn't when we'd met in the schoolhouse. I couldn't believe Pa had laid the bricks, shaped the domes, gilded the blue shingles.

Father Dmitri had a special service to bless the new church and then a special supper with his new family. Olga and her ma wore matching blouses embroidered with deep green leaves and clusters of dark berries down the sleeves. I asked her where they came from, and she said, "It's my same old blouse, but Sonya sewed them. Is she after Sergei?"

"No!" I said, no offense to her brother. "She's not after anyone."

Pa had to go back into the mines now that the church was done.

"Why don't you build houses?" I asked one day as I was sweeping the floor after supper.

"Why, why, why is you," Pa said. He sucked at his teeth. "They brought me here to mine, and the town was already built. You want us to pack up for a new town?"

"Don't you dare." Ma shook her finger. "It feels like home, now we have a church."

We had to tell Xenia about the inside of the church, because she wasn't allowed in anymore. She'd gone and married a Catholic, a Lithuanian she'd met writing his letters home for him. Lothar looked nothing like a miner with his oval face and shiny skin, a thin nose like hers right down the center, and light silky curls starting high on his forehead. She turned Catholic for him, and he was learning to read for her.

I wanted to be sore at her for forgetting Robert already and for leaving us and the church, but she was still our Xenia. While we couldn't set foot in their church for the wedding, they invited our entire family to the party. "No sin in that," Pa said. Snow on the ground, everyone sat outside at one long table, a swan centerpiece carved from pond ice. Three tall fires surrounded the table, and at dusk the Lithuanians danced in circles carrying lit torches. Guests kept raising a toast to Ma and Pa for bringing Xenia here, as if they'd had a choice.

THAT YEAR, JESUS ROSE for us on the same day as he did for the rest of the town, so all of Marianna celebrated Easter at the same time. Thinking about the end of Lent started my mouth watering over paska, blintzes, and bacon. I dreamed I drank a cup of milk! But I was also nervous about this Easter in our own church because it was time for my first confession. Father Dmitri was to hear the sins of every Old Believer on the day before Easter, starting with all the girls at dawn.

Olga, Maria, and me set off for church as pink ribbons striped the sooty sky. As if keeping Lent wasn't bad enough, we had to fast before confession. St. Nicholas was down the hill, past the power plant and coke ovens, over the bridge, and a block up the hill on the other side, a mile and a half all together. In white headscarves and long black monyiks under winter coats, we huddled like starlings. Maria said to Olga, "You have to tell Father your father what you did."

"Unless I don't," Olga said, the most daring thing we'd ever heard her say.

Then we all three got quiet, and even when other girls joined us, there was no gossiping or bickering in our flock on the way to church. Father Dmitri had told us to search our hearts and "prepare to admit what God already knows." He'd question us as a group, and if you'd committed a sin he mentioned, you were to bow to the ground. He'd said thoughts were the same as deeds, so God must have known that I'd hoped Teddy Roosevelt would get mauled by a lion on his African safari. The smokestacks had stopped puffing on Holy Friday, and no slag had been dumped in the creek since then, so the smell wasn't as rank as usual.

Olga pulled the heavy front door open, and Father Dmitri swooped down on us in his big black robe, carrying a burlap bag and looking uneasy about what we might admit to.

I chose my favorite podruchnik from the quilted stack, then Father Dmitri reached inside his bag and said, "For you." I cringed, as if he were going to pull out a slap, but he handed me my own lestovka, a prayer ladder whose small leather flaps looked like tiny rungs. The ends looped together like a sash, and bumps marked special numbers: seven mysteries of the church, nine choirs of angels, twelve apostles, thirty-eight weeks Mary carried Jesus in her womb, thirty-three years Jesus lived. My lestovka was black, and he gave Olga a red one, which I envied, even knowing that envy was more trouble to my soul than it was worth. Maria also got a black one, but some other girls got a red one, too. Maria put her podruchnik on the floor at her feet and held her lestovka in her left hand, so I did too.

Ma said I'd have a fresh start with confession, which is how I felt about being born in America, but she said I'd be like a baby chick. If he wanted us to confess to anything, Father Dmitri had to speak English to us. Since I'd only heard the services in Slavonic, I never knew what he'd been reciting until I heard him ask God to "destroy the serpent nestling within me." I passed a little gas. Then he started running through sins the way we ran through our times tables. *Did you take the Lord's name in vain? Dishonor your ma or pa? Smoke at all or drink to excess? Cut your hair or wear makeup? Indulge in taunting, insults, or mockery?*

Girls bobbed up and down on either side of me, and Olga stuck her elbow in my ribs. I'd certainly taunted my siblings. But I'd never had a drink or a smoke, and I didn't cut my hair. Ma did the cutting, and she said she was allowed.

Everyone except me was confessing to everything. Our family didn't have enough food to be guilty of gluttony, and Ma wouldn't stand for us being slothful. When I didn't admit to stealing, Father Dmitri looked me in the eye. "Not even a tea cake when your ma said no?" I bowed to the floor and as soon as I stood, he asked, "Have you been proud?" I'd been proud of the very church we were standing in. "Have you sinned by having a high opinion of yourself?" I went back down and hoped to die.

Were you greedy? Angry? Cruel to animals? Did you gossip? Lie? Return evil for evil? Did you show a lack of faith, a love of praise, a hardening of the heart?

I cried to be accused so, but I was also shocked to be branded such a sinner. I was greedy every day of my life. I was greedy for Ma's attention, greedy for a second helping of stew. My heart was so hardened against my sisters that only now, six months after they arrived, was it starting to soften. And as for lying, who was Father Dmitri to judge us, having lied for years about being a priest?

Did you have thoughts of lust?

Only Maria threw herself down at that. The rest of us stood above her, mortified.

Father Dmitri chanted the usual refrain in Slavonic. I was relieved not to know what he was saying, but he pronounced our penance clearly enough. "Ten lestovka for each of you." We were to make our way ten times around the loops he'd given us, crossing and bowing for every single flap. The same punishment for every single one of us! Whether we'd had impure thoughts, lied, and smoked or not. I had a higher opinion of myself than that, but also I was angry, so maybe I deserved what we got. Ten times around meant more than a thousand bows to the floor.

We came through the doors holding on to each other and crying in great gulps. The boys, who'd been horsing around in the entry hall, were sobered by our misery as we sent them in to their confessor. Olga, back to her churchy self, suggested that we start on our lestovka in the hallway. Maria and me went along out of guilt and also wanting to get some of it over with. My knees ached with the squatting already. "We have to climb home," I said, which was uphill the whole way, and they shushed me.

I'd finally prayed my way around one whole loop—nine more to go—when the boys burst through the doors as if they'd been shot out. They couldn't believe the three of us were praying, since we could have been on our way to breakfast.

"When will you do yours?" Maria asked Kostia.

"The day before I have to," he said. "I can do two lestovkas before breakfast."

Furious, Olga swung her prayer rope at him, whipping his sleeve. "You only got two?"

The boys smoked butts they found, they stole coal and swore among themselves. They drank any vodka left in the glasses or bottles, and they gambled with not only matchsticks but pennies. Although Kostia didn't, the others threw rocks at birds and woodchucks.

"Don't get sore at us," Kostia said. "We can't help it if we're good."

And all the way home, the boys taunted us. "Sinners!" "Bad girls!" "Unclean!"

13

EASTER MORNING, MA SLICED into a round loaf of paska topped with a golden braid of dough—three strands for Father, Son, and Holy Ghost—which Father Dmitri had blessed at midnight service. I was glad I didn't have to go to midnight service with Ma and Pa like my big sisters; confession had been bad enough. I dragged a blessed slice of the sweet bread through the bacon grease Ma had drizzled on my plate.

"You'd eat that for soup," Pa said.

I didn't answer him for eating. After weeks of keeping Lent, we got to have breakfast before Easter service, and I moved on to Ma's eggy blintzes with sour cream.

Willing to do chores that were really crafts, Sonya and Lethia had boiled a pot of eggs with onion skins to turn the shells gold and orange and red. "The girls did a nice job," Pa said and picked an egg for me and him. "Hristos Voskrese."

"Voistinu Voskrese," I said. I traded my egg for his, then we kissed three times. Ma and I did the same. Then I traded eggs with Kostia, who wiped his face after my kisses. "Mush!" he complained.

Kostia cupped his golden egg in his hand, pointy side showing, and rapped it against the top of my red one, which crumpled. "You lose," he said. But when we turned our eggs over and did it, his bottom cracked.

"You lose," I copied him.

Pa raised his arm. "You'll both lose if I hear another word. Shishooks."

We ran upstairs to wake up the girls and get dressed, and our whole family joined the rest of Russian Hill to walk to service, the first Easter in St. Nicholas Russian Church of Orthodox Old Believers. "Hristos Voskrese" and "Voistinu Voskrese" greetings echoed as each family joined the crowd—we'd exchange the same greetings later with eggs. In Little Italy, Mr. G sat on his little garden chair, drinking his tiny coffee, and Mrs. G waved a dish towel from her door and shouted, "Katya, Christ is risen!" Ma happily answered, "He is risen indeed!" Some *tsk*ed, to hear their message in English.

The Catholic church bells pealed from the valley, claiming the air, but Pearl called out when she spied our blue-starred dome, which Pa had made. Just as pretty were the pussy willows, with their furry catkins, catching the sunlight. A week ago, we'd gathered them for Pussy Willow Sunday, and now Christ had been crucified, buried, and conquered death. It was a good day to be an Old Believer.

After Sergei snuffed the icons at the end of the service, we marched a wooden cross around the church three times and then followed the leader to his and Olga's house. Men who'd just come from Suwalki roasted a whole pig, though they'd cut off the feet so Olga's ma could boil them for studzien. People bickered over whether to add mustard or vinegar to the jiggly mess, a favorite of Pa's. Ma made some just for him, with pig's feet she bought at the Deemston butcher. After forty days without milk, meat, or eggs, we sucked the pork from knuckles and ribs, swallowed hard-boiled yolks whole, ate sour cream and cottage cheese on everything. Pa drank himself silly, but so did the others.

OUR FAMILY HAD THE first baby baptized and the first daughter married in the church. The week after Easter, Father Dmitri cradled Borya in his left arm, the baby's head resting in the palm of his hand and his zhopa in the crook of his elbow. Father chanted a prayer and, expertly spreading his fingers, plugged Borya's ears with his thumb and pinky. He made the sign of the cross and passed his other hand over the baby's eyes, pinching the tiny nose closed as he dunked him all the way into the copper belea, head first: once, twice, three times. Borya didn't have time to be afraid until Father Dmitri kissed the top of his head and handed him to Nadja, who Ma and Pa had picked to be his godmother, and she swaddled him and comforted his outrage.

As for the wedding, in the six months since my sisters arrived, they'd gone from precious cargo to freight. It was Xenia's marriage that sealed their lot—Pa said her going with a Catholic was proof that Russian men were scarce. Now, Harry Kabaloff came for supper after services, leering at Sonya and snickering at his own mean jokes. How could Pa shake Harry's hand for Sonya?

The Sunday that happened, I stumbled on my two sisters in a full-blown, hair-pulling spat. They were yelling in their terrible English, which shows how strict Ma was with us. Better to speak broken English than Russian.

"You have him," Sonya said. "I don't want."

Lethia yanked her sister's long golden braid. "Shame of you—Baba would wash your mouth with soap. Singing 'Ochi Chyornye' to Penya, then you sit on his lap!"

Sonya and I were the only ones who still called him Harry. Sonya stuck her finger through Lethia's precious ringlet. "He grab me, always he grab me. I tell Pa that you should have first husband, for being older. They say I'm too sweet, you too sour. Wish I was sour." She twisted the ringlet until Lethia howled.

"Serves you right. Penya won't let you get away with this."

Sonya was ugly with rage, showing her crooked teeth in a snarl. "Your Lev was so good to you."

Lethia threw her head back and yelled, "He's not my Lev! He gives me flower, says we will fish, big deal—" She pronounces it *beeg deeyul*. "Then he goes to grave."

Sonya fell into Lethia's embrace, ferocious to tender in an instant. I cowered on the other side of the stove. Now, Lethia yelled in my direction. "Bull Head! None of your beeswax," and hurled her boot at me, pointy toe first. The thought of Harry touching Sonya with his stumpy hand made my skin crawl. I wanted to brew her tea and excuse her from kitchen duties, while Ma urged her to help more.

"Forget skinning vegetables," Nadja said. "Hand her Borya for a day and a night, get her used to fussy babies making in their diaper." Borya was a handful, but he wasn't wicked—and I'd learned from my time with Pearl how screaming babies wore themselves out.

Baba sent an envelope thick with money for a store-bought wedding dress for Sonya, as well as a dress for Lethia. Pa complained, "She bought that money with my money," and Ma said, "So now your money's come back." In the months since my grandparents were supposed to have come, Jeda had died, but that was a different heartache.

On Saturday, Ma gave Kostia and me thirty cents to go to the new movie palace, and I pretended that Baba had sent that money for a treat, money for me. We were eager to get to the picture shows before Father Dmitri declared them a sin. Ma said we could each take a friend and split a bag of penny candy with them. Kostia chose Martha next door, and I took Maria.

The Arcade sign above the yellow-brick art palace was lit with rows and rows of lightbulbs, and a British boy we didn't know took our tickets. He looked impossibly fancy in his white shirt, black bowtie, and black tasseled fez. In the red velvet lobby there was a glass candy case, where we bought two sacks of licorice drops, taffy, and butterscotch. I kept petting my front-row seat, the same plush as Mrs. G's divan.

Silver pipes framed the floor-to-ceiling red curtain covering the screen, and the theater's pillars were carved with naked ladies riding fish. We were dumbstruck because we didn't know naked ladies could be art. I stared, looked away, and caught my eyes moving sideways to stare again. Maria tugged me close to whisper, "Someone carved her bosoms out of a log and sanded them smooth." The longing in her voice reminded me of her confessing to lust. Though shorter than me, she was a year older, and her breath was hot in my ear. "I wish Pyotr had to sand me."

The theater went pitch dark, except for a spotlight at the stage's edge, where the floor was sliding open. A robed figure entered, and my guilty conscience shuddered with the fear of Father Dmitri rising onstage to condemn us all. But what came up through the floor was a massive organ, four levels of keys arranged like a horseshoe below rows of pearly buttons, and it was Chins Radchenko's mother in a robe who took her seat in the spotlight. We weren't allowed music in church, or at home really, and I tingled with the sinfulness of my pleasure—naked ladies and chandeliers above us in our plush padded seats, a pipe organ vibrating my belly. And candy!

In the first picture show, Lady Florence wore a gown made of feathers, and she was wooed first by a French count and then a Prussian spy. It was thrilling the way Mrs. Radchenko waltzed a ballroom, whizzed a bullet into the spy's heart, and brought Lady Florence to her knees. She played the organ between reels, then slyly let us know that the same actress starred in every picture that day, under the duke's cape, being hypnotized, getting married. There were five pictures in all before the curtain closed. My eyes were dried up from hardly blinking.

The drama and glamour stayed with us, even as we stepped from the velvet darkness into the harsh daylight of our drab, silted town. Kostia marched, and us three girls walked on tippy-toes through Paris, the streets of Rome, the Prussian skirmish.

"Would you rather?"

"Oh yes, I shall."

"Not another morsel."

"Taste my sword, traitor!!"

We were still under the spell when we arrived home. As it turned out, we weren't the only ones who'd had an adventure. Sonya and Lethia were twirling around the kitchen in department-store dresses. They'd gone clear to Bentleyville and back, some twenty miles by bus.

I sensed we'd been had, shipped off to the Arcade to distract us from Sonya and Lethia's bigger treat. Sucking the last butterscotch,

I had the familiar taste of jealousy on my tongue as well, two things true at once. Was my day of wonder any the less for Sonya's day? I didn't know whether to hang on to the sweet or bitter when Kostia declared, "Gadzooks! Who is this before my eyes?" He took Sonya's hand in his and, bowing toward her, kissed his own thumb, making fun of us all.

Once I'd laughed, I could admire Sonya, who did look as if she'd stepped off the movie screen in her white netted skirt over a long-sleeve chemise, with her wheat-colored hair and milky skin. Lethia's sky-blue version was nearly as pretty.

Xenia was there, too, and we threw ourselves at her as if she'd moved to the moon rather than to Lothar's house.

"Now you're a Catholic," Kostia said, "tell us what their church says."

"Sorry, I can't." We thought it was a deep dark secret, but she said, "I can't tell you, because they say it in Latin!" That seemed ridiculous since Xenia understood more languages than anyone except Ma.

Kostia said, "All them Catholics, none of 'em speak Latin. Why does their church?"

"You don't speak Slavonic," she reminded him. "And whether I cross myself backwards or forwards, Lothar loves me just the same." She sighed and put her hands on her belly, which made me think she was better fed than she'd been with us.

"Boris is a good name," Xenia said. "And Kostia. The names in Lothar's family would curl your hair."

"Varfolomei," Ma said, and she cackled. "That was my uncle."

"Hedwig, Kasparas," Xenia said. Now they were both shaking with laughter, the way Ma and Mrs. G used to get on.

"Aksana," Ma snorted.

"Ruta, Grazina."

"Xenia," Ma said, the sweetest teasing. They were more like sisters than I was with mine, better friends to each other than Olga and Maria were to me.

Pyotr, the first miner home, stuck his head in the door to say he was going into the forest. He had his shovel, and he took one of Lethia's baskets. Pa came in roaring, "Who's in my kitchen?" He pretended to hug Xenia with his black-dusted arms, and he pointed to his black cheek for a kiss.

She said, "What would Lothar say if I came to him with your coal on my lips?"

"That Lugan of yours has more luck than brains!" Pa winked at Xenia and disappeared behind the screen to bathe. We hugged and kissed Xenia goodbye, and I watched her leave Russki Town for her new neighborhood, the clouds running borscht pink above her head.

After supper, Pyotr's headlamp bobbed up the walk. He'd filled the basket with spring ferns, their fiddleheads unfurling, to use in the wedding arch he was making for Sonya. She kept him company as he ate his warmed-over stew. They talked back and forth the whole while, but I only heard her side of the conversation from the dark corner of the landing. "Ma don't need to tell me. . . . There was farm next to us in Suwalki. . . . Summer, they brung bull to climb on cow. Spring, cow gets fat and has calf. So I seen."

Pyotr mumbled, and Sonya wagged a finger at him. "Bulls, men. Difference is men have vodka."

Pyotr yawned a big showy yawn, so supper was over. My heart in my chest was fast as hoofbeats, thinking of Maria whispering about her longing for Pyotr and now Sonya's words to him. Would Harry mount Sonya like the bull on the cow? We'd seen as much in farmers' fields or with dogs near the schoolyard. The more I thought about it, the more sense it made that men and women had to be drunk or fighting to behave like animals. Bulls, sheep, dogs, sparrows—I'd stupidly thought people were different. I knew drinking and fighting were involved because that's how we got here, but I also worried about sharing a bed with a man or scrubbing the coal off his belly, washing his dirty underwear. How would Sonya stand it?

In our room, Sonya's wedding trunk was open at the foot of the bed. When Ma left the girls in Russia, she had made sure each of them had an icon, and Sonya's Virgin and Child was packed for the house she'd share with Harry Kabaloff. I climbed into bed but didn't close my eyes, and when Sonya came to bed, I knelt next to her. She held out her arms, crushing me to her chest. She said, "The snow melted."

"You made it past your birthday," I whispered. At thirteen, she was a young bride, but at least she wasn't twelve. I said, "More miners will move here soon. Why won't Pa let you wait?"

"I have my fancy dress now."

I thought of Ma sending us to the movie palace while Sonya traded her future for a store-bought dress. "Why can't you marry Pyotr?"

A tear dripped from the corner of her eye to her thin pillow. "Pa says Harry thinks I'm pretty."

"You are," I told her. "You're very pretty." She must have known Pyotr thought that, too.

She rolled on her side to face me. "Lenotchka, so sweet. Pa says Harry tells miners I dance in his lap, I sing to him, I can't wait to be his. Pa says Harry is proud, with his bad hand, to have pretty girl. Pa says more men will only be more men for Harry to tell his stories."

Usually, Pa was looking for a fight. Why didn't he mash Harry's potato face? I'd thought of her as pampered and haughty, but she did as she was told.

"What does Ma say?" I asked my sister.

"Ma says to find good in the bad." She turned away from me, toward Lethia. Either to me or to her older sister, she whispered, "Dobroy nochi," and I kissed the back of her head.

WE COULDN'T TAKE OUR eyes off Sonya walking up the aisle. The sash across her chest was a garland of ivy studded with apple blossoms and wallflowers, and she and Lethia both had modest crowns and veils. Their cheeks were stained with rose petals and their lips shined with Vaseline jelly, not quite the sin of makeup. The service was the service in that we crossed ourselves and squatted and bowed, and I didn't understand very much. Harry had a gold band for Sonya's hand, but she didn't want to give him a ring because he didn't have a ring finger. People said they'd never seen Sonya look so beautiful, which was because she didn't smile at her own wedding. Her teeth leaned this way and that, and her beauty dimmed a little when she grinned.

Xenia and Lothar came to the reception, and Xenia's snug dress made it clear why she and Ma had been trying out baby names. I was as surprised as I'd been with her and Robert, and I worried that Lothar acted ugly when they were alone or that he was a drunk behind closed doors.

Lethia tied on the apron for people to stuff with money, pockets for the bride and groom, as they danced to songs played by two old men on balalaika and squeeze-box. Rita from next door stood on my feet to dance with me. I would miss her, and Kostia would miss his Martha when Nadja and the girls left for Pittsburgh. Unlike my sister Pearl, Rita followed me around and brought me dandelions in her sticky hands. The crowd drank plenty of vodka, but fewer fights than usual broke out, as there were fewer men these days.

It wasn't even a month before Sonya showed up at our door, her lower lip rising like bread dough on her face. Her eyes darted back and forth beneath her heavy lids. I said, "Ma's next door," and put the kettle on. Ma was welcoming our new neighbors on the other side of the wall, bringing them bread and salt as Nadja had done for her. Anna and Anatole were from Suwalki, which had sent yet another fresh supply of miners.

"I want Lethia," Sonya said. I saw a tiny bald spot above her ear where a patch of her flaxen hair was missing. A bruise that looked like train tracks colored her cheeks.

Lethia thundered down the steps. "Sister! What happened?"

"I'm a no good cook," she said. "Harry tasted Ma's stew, Lenotchka's pies. My food upsets him."

"I'll show Penya no good," Lethia growled.

"Please," Sonya pleaded, "I came here to be telling you don't get married."

A welt circled her wrist like the Indian burns we gave each other. The idea of Harry leaving a mark on her made me sick, and I realized the train track bruise on her face was from his two-fingered hand. In fairy tales, stepmothers and witches caused the suffering, sometimes wild animals. Men saved the women from harm, and marrying someone was the happy ending.

Sonya said, "Don't let Pa give you to Yuri or Vera's boy."

"I'm not going with Vera's boy," Lethia said, disgusted.

I said, "Pyotr's leaving. Vera has people in Morgantown, and the glassworks there are hiring." I knew no one was going with Yuri. I was staring at Sonya's wrist, so she flipped it over. Then I stared at her purpling face and her scalped patch. Had he pulled her hair out by the roots? I touched the side of my own head. I swallowed hard. "You should move back home with us."

"Nyet," Lethia said. "She has home with Penya now."

Sonya lowered her eyelids until her lashes rested on her cheeks. "Don't tell him I was here. Ma or Pa neither. Swear not to say a word. I come to tell Lethia to stay put. You too, Lenotchka." She kissed us with her puffy lip, then ran like a scalded cat before Ma came back.

I'd sworn not to tell our parents. Could I tell Father Dmitri, who was known to keep people's secrets, or Olga, who didn't? Sonya and Harry were newlyweds—how could Harry hurt her? I gazed at Lethia with the tenderness I felt for Sonya. "Good thing you're safe here."

Lethia's face puckered with envy. "I am older sister, not dumber sister." Mad as she was, Lethia seemed to think Sonya's bruises were from horseplay or, worse, lovemaking. She said, "Sister comes all this way 'cause she don't want me having what she does. I'll show her." Though she said it in English, I thought that was the most Russian thing I'd ever heard.

PART II

1910

14

I WAS SCOURING THE pots when Ma told me Sonya and Harry's plan. "You'll take Lethia with you tomorrow."

"Borya, too?" I asked.

"Does he belong to the neighbors? I'll send along pickles and beets, potatoes. I saved a tin of herring."

When she said send along, she meant send along with me. I'd be carrying my little brother and food for a crowd, and I'd be minding Sonya's baby as well. I was back to being the workhorse daughter, like in the story of the Golden Slipper.

Ma said, "You have all day for making dinner."

I had all day for doing everything. Like so many fairy tales, the Golden Slipper story had a magic fish, which showed up in the well as the girl was weeping. The fish somehow husked the barley so she could go to the ball, though should any prince come looking for me, no golden slipper would fit on my big clown feet.

Ma said, "If Pa can go back into that mine, you can give your sister a hand. Now that school is over, Sonya depends on you."

School wasn't over. It was just over for me. Sonya had a husband she didn't know what to do with. Once she had baby Alexei, I had to leave fifth grade to help her.

"And the pig gets the scraps," I said to Kostia, whose job after dinner was to dump the peelings behind the garden.

He gave it right back. "I know something you don't. Miss Kelly's moving to New York's Brooklyn. She's leaving us for them Catholic girls."

"You're sore because they give girls good teachers." I was sore, too, because I'd hoped to get back to school come fall. Without Ma or Pa's say-so, I grabbed my coat and ran out the door. A huge quarter moon was smiling at me, but I wasn't falling for it. I ran past the houses until I could see Saints Mary and Anne lit up with a mass, bells ringing in their steeple. Miss Kelly said there were bigger churches in New York, no doubt in Brooklyn. She said the faucets there gushed hot and cold Irish.

I ran past her church to the schoolhouse, where part of me still thought of her as living, and soon as I saw the square flap of her sailor collar through the window, I pounded on the pane with my fist. It gave me a mean thrill to see her body jerk and, when she spun around, her scared expression.

She opened the door to pull me inside. "Yelena, what's wrong? What is it?"

I folded my arms, a fist under each breast, so I wouldn't hug or hit her. Everything I saw upset me. She was wearing her hair in a braided bun, which, of course, Kostia hadn't mentioned. Instead of Teddy Roosevelt's portrait on the wall, Taft busted his buttons under the flag. The flag was also strange, and one sideways look told me the stars were off. Oklahoma had statehood while I was in school, but they'd waited till I left to change the flag. The worst blow was the new map. Used to, when Miss Kelly unrolled the old one, mountain ranges broke apart and countries flaked off and drifted to the planked floor. Now, they got to see the world without destroying it.

I said, "You're leaving. You're ruining everything."

"Not for another two months. There's a Catholic girls' school that needs me."

I need you. As sinful as it was to go into their church, what would happen if I ran away to one of their schools? What I said was, "I like you so much I forget you're Catholic."

"How can you, me being Irish?" She unbuttoned her high collar to reveal their kind of cross hanging from a chain. "With Mickey gone, it's best to leave. You're gone, too."

"Hey," I said. I wasn't gone the way Mickey was.

"You're gone from class. And it's not the same with Pearl." She fell into a chair the same way Ma did when Pearl was around. "That child never stops."

"Who do you think raised her?" I wanted to crawl into Miss Kelly's lap and hang my arms around her neck. I swallowed the lump in my throat. "What did you teach today?"

"Presumed innocence. How here in America, we're innocent until proven guilty."

I thought she was making up stories until she wrinkled her button nose.

"You think that's funny?" she asked.

"Yes—aren't you joshing?" In Sunday school, Father Dmitri was stuck on us being guilty from the start. "We're born guilty and have to be made innocent, starting with baptism."

"That's church. I'm talking about state, which is another thing. I'm talking about the Sixth Amendment." I got amendments and commandments mixed up. She said, "The state has to prove guilt beyond a reasonable doubt, so innocent men aren't punished."

Not in the state of Pennsylvania, where we lived and breathed. If there was spilled milk, a hole in the screen, mud on the front rug, Pa smacked the nearest one of us, and woe to anyone who blamed the domovoi. Maybe because I'd been away from school, I saw what some said against her, that she didn't know south from sideways.

"When will you finish fifth grade?" she asked.

I said, "When my sister stops having babies."

"You have a brain in your head, and your ma cares for you. That's better than some. It's better for me to be a teacher than starving in County Mayo. You can do more than marry a boy from the mines at Sonya's age."

"Or Daria's age, or Lethia's," I said, though they hadn't found anyone for Lethia yet.

Miss Kelly sighed her end-of-the-day sigh. "It's a proper epidemic, it is."

"You don't understand. I have to marry in the church."

"Aren't there churches elsewhere? All the Old Believers in America can't be in Marianna."

She was right! There were other churches, just like she was going to swim out of here and still be with her own kind. "Detroit, Erie, they have Old Believers."

"So marry a man from there. The church doesn't make you marry a miner, does it?"

I did hug Miss Kelly then, for showing me more of the world every time she opened her mouth. I helped her close the schoolhouse for the night, then she put on a blue duster and a black straw hat big enough for her bun, and we set out to her rented room among the Irish. She walked daintily in her long skirt and buttoned boots, so slow my heart didn't even speed up.

Outside her rooming house, she pointed at the moon and asked, "Crescent or gibbous?"

"Crescent."

"Waxing or waning?"

"Waxing," I said, but it sounded like nonsense. All that time I'd wasted waving my hand in the air.

"Give my best to your ma, and add on to all I taught you. You can be a student outside the classroom."

She was either speaking in riddles, or I'd gotten too dumb to understand her, and I scurried off without a word.

Pa slapped my bottom as I came through the back door. "Where've you been?"

"Miss Kelly's leaving. Kostia told me, and I went to see."

"It's Kostia's fault you're traipsing around?"

"No!" I said, flustered and weepy. Then I hugged his waist. "Good night, Pa."

"Your Ma was worried sick," he said. He gave me another pat on the behind, this one gentler than the first.

"BULL HEAD, DRAW MY bath!" Lethia woke me with her yelling. "Wash my hair."

I burrowed under the quilt and snaked around beneath the covers, avoiding her pinching fingers. One kind word would have swayed me to her cause. I heard Ma's felted slippers gliding along our rag rug. Unlike Lethia, who entered every room squawking and flapping, Ma moved like a dancer. She peeled my covers down to plant a kiss on my forehead. "Penya's friend will be on the Detroit train. Sonya says he is a good prospect."

"Who wants a bride who can't wash herself?" I said, knowing I would lose this argument. "If Lethia goes alone, Harry's friend can see her help with dinner and Alexei."

"Chihoo," Ma said. "If Penya's friend takes to Lethia, she may share his bed instead of yours." And she winked.

What kind of wife Lethia would be I couldn't imagine. She couldn't even slice the bread without squashing the loaf. As I washed her hair, I spoke lofty to annoy her, saying, "Your tendrils resemble Medusa's. I'm certain that no matrimonial prospect would rebuff you."

"Ma!" Lethia yelled. "She mocks me."

Considering Sonya's match to Harry, I might have been more help if I hacked off Lethia's hair and blackened her teeth. I said, "That means your curls make you irresistible. It's plain English."

"You are plain," my sister said. "Plain like rice, oatmeal." She said it *rise* and *utmill*, probably the only way she could talk with that sneer on her face.

I carried Borya along with a bag of potatoes, apples, and beets that weighed nearly as much as he did. Lethia had Ma's pickles in one hand and a loaf of bread in the other. Ma wanted me to make Herring in a Fur Coat, a dish usually for New Year's. I'd need to peel, cook, and slice the potatoes, apples, and beets then layer them with the herring. Maybe Lethia could beat the eggs for mayonnaise that Sonya could maybe spread over the top and sides. Maybe when I keyed open the herring, a magic fish would do it.

Walking through Sonya's door, Lethia chattered away in Russian, and Borya ran past Sonya's open arms. He didn't like to be touched. He darted beyond the table of dirty dishes and the clothes piled up since I'd been here. Every dirty diaper, towel, and garment of Alexei's was stitched with elaborate designs, from leaves to lions. Sonya knew more about embroidering his clothes than washing them.

Alexei's diaper was messy, and after I changed him, he wanted to eat. Sonya said he'd bitten her and was worse than the domovoi. I chuckled, but she growled at him. "One more tooth and you'll starve, you byess." He was no devil, just a hungry baby with an early tooth. She told us, "I give him brandy to settle him."

Lethia nodded. "Baba did that."

Ma didn't. I dipped a bread crust into Sonya's milky tea for little Alexei, who greedily mouthed the crust. Did Sonya think a baby was a cat who slept all day in a sunny spot? Borya scampered and climbed like a fat squirrel—how would she cope when Alexei was that active?

"You do too much for Alexei," Lethia scolded. She said babies at home napped outside in chicken-wire cribs. "They play in those, too."

Sonya put Alexei to her breast, and he guzzled like his father. I went after Borya, who'd wandered into the bedroom. Now, the childhood picture of the two sisters in white hung in Sonya's house, and hanging next to that was something new, a portrait of the Virgin and Child made of thread. In the embroidered version of her icon, Sonya had stitched sparkling haloes above baby Jesus and Mary, whose gaunt cheeks were more human, more tender in this soft, satin-stitched version than on the brass icon.

"This I made," Sonya said, startling me. "Do you like?"

"Yes." I stroked the threads. Mary's shining robe was out of place in our ash-dusted town, as out of place as Sonya's white gown. The photograph reminded me of how jealous I used to be, but it probably reminded her of how she used to be a princess. She didn't belong here, married to Stump and a mother at fourteen. From princess to peasant, her life was a fairy tale in reverse.

Sonya said, "I cried to give dress back. Pretty hat, too."

"Those weren't yours?"

"Oh, Lenotchka." It was her turn to pity how little I knew. She said the fancy clothes left town with the photographer, and now I saw that their sleeves dangled way past their hands. Probably their arms and legs were as bony and bug-bitten as mine. We were a people who held onto things, and so it was a surprise to let go of the envy I'd felt for years over Sonya and Lethia's finery.

A crash from the kitchen was followed by a shriek. "Borya," Lethia yelled, "your sister must be cleaning that," forgetting that she was his sister, too.

Borya had knocked over his tin cup of milk. I brought a stepstool to the sink for him to help scrub beets—really to splash in the water. I lay Alexei on a quilt with wooden spoons to clutch, then I split a cabbage in two and put Borya's hands over mine to slide the half-moon against the grater.

My sisters couldn't help because they were too busy preparing a tea tray, which they'd done as girls in Baba's house. From what I could understand, they were deciding whether to use a chipped cup and matching saucer or a mismatched cup and saucer. Sonya had few sugar cubes and neither sugar bowl nor tongs, another tight spot. But when it was time to choose napkins, she brought out a pile of linens trimmed and stitched in every direction.

Lethia's spite flared. "Too bad Penya don't eat lace and roses."

"You should sell those," I said, thinking she could eat well on her talents. "No one has towels like that."

Sonya frowned. "I do too much, they say. They want for my sewing then pay only a little."

"Too much fancy," Lethia said.

"Da," Sonya sadly agreed. "Olga's ma tell me, 'I ask for flower, you put in garden.'" I remembered the elaborate sleeves on Olga and her ma's blouses. Sonya pulled Maria's church blouse from her basket, and down the center of each sleeve was cutwork embroidery, flowers and spirals around open spaces that would show Maria's skin. Beautiful but also shocking, to think of Maria's bare arms peeking from those holes in church.

"Take it," Sonya said. "I ruin it for Maria, her ma says. Ma must sew new blouse free."

"Thank you," I gushed, then I said it in Russian for good measure. "Spasibo."

"Pozhaluysta," Sonya said. "My work ruins things."

"No. People aren't used to such nice things."

"Nice? She act like I burn it. They want to wear burlap bags and spread dirt on the flowers. A sin to make roses nice as God's, to let the skin he gave us peek out. You laugh?"

"Because it's true," I said, admiring her bold colors and lifelike flowers. "We're not in a dark hole all day. Why should we dress like miners?" I wondered if their childhood was more vivid and, when there was food, more delicious than plain rice or oatmeal.

Sonya turned her attention back to the tray. "We'll give him tea soon as they come." Harry hadn't told her his friend's name. "A head of hair. Big, strong man and no pousa"—the word for belly or watermelon.

"What color eyes?" Lethia asked.

Sonya said, "What color eyes does mine have in his head?"

Was she chiding Lethia or genuinely asking? Harry's eyes were steely gray BBs in his fat round face. He had tiny glinting eyes, a smushed button nose, and a thin upper lip. Harry had a face little Borya could draw.

The boys napped, an hour of peace to put the shuboy together. We made a circle of shingled potato slices and layered beet, apple, and herring in turns. Sonya iced it like a cake, and I found wild chives outside their back door to sprinkle on the top. When Alexei woke, he greeted Sonya's breast with a giggly smile.

She nuzzled his head with her chin. "You could even fall in love with a goat."

Sonya nursed her baby, who'd woken on dry sheets, was changed into a clean diaper, and swaddled in a sun-dried blanket because of me, even as I gathered vegetable peels and eggshells in a bowl. My beet-stained fingers looked as if I'd strangled something for supper. My apron was crusted with sour cream and cooked potato, and my oniony breath stank.

At our house, Kostia threw the scraps behind the garden plot, but neither Harry nor Sonya could be bothered to garden. I didn't suggest it for fear they'd have me dig the plot, and I swung open the front door to toss the scraps off the porch for any stray that came by. I was in motion before I realized someone was standing there. It was Mrs. Collins, the postmaster's wife, her knuckles raised to knock, as I hurled the leavings out the door.

Peels and eggshells flew through the air and clung to her in her impressive navy blue cloak. "Jesus, Mary, and Joseph!" she cried. "Aren't I come to your door just as you're tossing out slop? Fetch me a rag, dear, else the stains set."

I turned tail for the kitchen. I'd get her cleaned up and help her find who she was looking for. They were probably Catholic, to have the same names as the Holy Family.

"Just an accident," she said and dabbed at her cloak. "I'll tell myself that. You weren't expecting me, I'll tell myself."

She had a clipboard of papers and wasn't looking for Jesus, Mary, or Joseph. She'd meant to come to Sonya's house. An official at the door was never good—how much worse had I made things by covering her with trash?

Recalling Miss Kelly's lessons on manners, I said, "Won't you come in?"

"I'm afraid I can't step beyond the foyer. Aren't you Katya's girl? How you've shot up."

Sonya joined us in what I would now call the foyer, Alexei slung over her shoulder. "What is it? Is my Penya hurt?"

"I'm not sent by the company," Mrs. Collins said. The boiled wool cloak softened her shape, which was square as a grave marker. "I've nothing to do with them. My name is Mrs. Collins, sent here from the Census Bureau."

I pulled my bandana off, ready to be counted. "You're right. I'm Katya's girl."

She said softly, "I know, dear. Let me finish," and resumed her normal voice. "I am the official enumerator for Marianna. Here's me badge if you require the proof." She flipped her cloak open to tap a metal badge with an eagle perched over United States Census 1910. "Once a decade, the country is to count its residents. This is the nation's thirteenth such tallying, and my sworn duty is to visit each abode and record answers on the forms entrusted to me." She let out a sigh. "Aye, we got through that without further ado. So who is it lives here at 902 Ash Street?"

Sonya was thumping Alexei between his shoulder blades, and he let out a satisfied belch.

"That's our answer, is it?" Mrs. Collins asked and laughed at her own joke.

Sonya was shaking her head. "My Penya would not like me to talk." She must have been calling him Penya because that's how everyone knew him.

"Hmm," Mrs. Collins was unimpressed. "Is your Penya here? It's the very law—all are counted—and you can be assured that what I write is a well-guarded secret, only for the authorities."

"You see it," I pointed out.

"That I do. But I took a solemn oath to button my lip, and I believe you studied me badge. These numbers decide whether and where we get our roads, bridges—libraries."

I was swishing back and forth in excitement, sweeping the floor with my skinny self. The government could have written us off or done their head count in the mines or gone only as far as Bosses Row. Her getting all the way up the hill meant that we counted.

Mrs. Collins turned her whole body to face Sonya. She said, "Please, will you tell me your name and the name of each person whose place of abode this is? Abode as in who abides."

"I abide here," my sister said, then shrank into herself when she spoke her entire name. "Sonya Kabaloff. And Penya and Alexei."

I watched Mrs. Collins fill in the small spaces, inking *Sonya Ka-*

baloff alongside *902 Ash Street,* and *Penya* instead of Harry. Wife, female, white. "Years married?"

"One."

"Year of immigration—when did you get here?"

"1908."

Mrs. Collins recorded the date and looked to Sonya. "I remember the very day. You came into town riding President Roosevelt's train."

"We didn't know," Sonya said apologetically.

Mrs. Collins returned to her forms. "Your age—how did I miss that square?"

"Fourteen," Sonya mumbled.

"No, dear. Not the age when you came in 1908. They mean your age now. So that's sixteen then, unless you're still fifteen."

Lethia jerked her head up. "I'm fifteen."

I waited for Sonya to say her real age, but she didn't correct the census. Mrs. Collins asked Lethia, "You live here, too?"

Sonya spoke up then. "No, she don't."

Mrs. Collins said, "Very well. Then sixteen and already you have a little one. I've a mind to ask what all the rush is about, your people and mine, too. But that's not why they sent me."

I took to worrying my loose molar with my tongue, comforting myself with the rotten taste below the gum. If she suspected a lie, Mrs. Collins might have to use her badge on Sonya.

"Place of birth?"

"Russia," Sonya said, turning her mouth down to get the rich sound of it out.

"You're from Suwalki, same as all the Old Believers? That would be Russian Poland." She tipped her clipboard toward Sonya, who nodded as if reading. Mrs. Collins gave her some side-eye. "Native language, I put Russian. Say, are you able to read or write?"

"Russian and Slavonic I am able." I saw Mrs. Collins put a "Y" in the columns, so Sonya's Russian counted. "Not yet American."

"English, you mean." Mrs. Collins turned her wide face directly at me. "Americans speak English, don't they now?"

I felt my round cheeks burn red. "Yes," I agreed.

"I will speak all the way soon," Sonya said. "Lenotchka is helping me know English."

Now she was lying about me, though her saying it made me long for it to be true. When Ma had told me to help her, I could have read her the comics like I did for Kostia or sat down with what was left of Ma's penmanship tablets.

Mrs. Collins moved past Alexei, born here in Marianna, to Penya, from Russian *Poland*. I wished I could rub Harry's nose in that. Mrs. Collins said, "Alien, alien, the both of you."

Sonya chirped like a bird. "What is ale-yun, ale-yun?"

"Not citizen," Mrs. Collins said. "You may one day be American like your Alexei here, but you weren't born one and you didn't marry one." She pulled the clipboard close to her chest and lowered her voice. "Your Ma's friend, Mrs. Giordana, carried on so when I marked her Teresa such. No matter that Doc delivered Teresa at their kitchen table or that the girl's a widow now. She married herself a foreigner, and that changes the score for women." Her voice returned to normal, all business. "Didn't I feel bad, but the law's the law."

Sonya's hooded eyes were expressionless, untouched by a law she didn't understand.

Mrs. Collins got back to the task at hand. "Occupation: coal miner. Able to read?"

"Some," Sonya said. Harry could read the label on a vodka bottle.

"Out of work until the mine reopened?"

"Yes."

"Then that's six weeks of last year. Don't I hate asking, what with the heartache of that time."

Lethia piped up again. "Mine was killed that time."

"Your husband?" Mrs. Collins said. "How tragic."

Tears made their way down Lethia's face. "We were getting married. I would have baby now, but my Lev died with all them men."

Sonya handed me Alexei so she could comfort her sister. It was sad how Lethia's life was stalled by the cave-in and Sonya's was sped up. That's what I thought, but who knows? They might have been sad because they'd started fibbing and couldn't stop.

Mrs. Collins squared herself like a piece of furniture. "Here I'm yammering when I can't be spending all day with only three people living at this house. I must go on to the next abode."

I got up my pluck. "Was I counted last time, in 1900?"

"When's your birthday?"

"January 31, 1899."

"Then I imagine you were."

I counted. That's when I started blubbering, too, loud as my sisters. Mrs. Collins didn't know what was wrong or what to do with us. For her and the United States Census to look our way turned me to mush. I'd last felt this way about the president coming, and that had amounted to nothing. To be counted was something.

Little Borya padded in from his nap, saying "I's all wet," and Mrs. Collins said, "Join the club, bub." She dabbed her eyes. "For the love of Mary, how am I to do my business?"

Just then, the front door nearly flattened her as Harry and his tall friend slammed in. Harry's moon face scowled. "You're that Collins's wife, ain't you? What do you want?"

"Yes, sir. I am Mary Margaret Collins." She opened her cloak to give him an eyeful of her badge. "The United States Census Bureau has asked me to count how many residents in each Marianna abode. Now you're here, I have my count—one, two, three—and I'm away. Good day to you, then."

Mrs. Collins was out the door and down the porch steps before Harry could kick her out or slam the door on her cloak. A quick exit must have been part of her training. I figured she'd get the same reception at our house, and I had the sneaking feeling that Mrs. Collins came when she could talk to the women.

Harry started in scolding Sonya. "You have better things to do than talk to that snoop."

"We don't mind," Sonya said. "Was interesting," she drew the word out, and I was proud of her for using it.

"I don't like her in our business, badge or no badge." Harry's face had the look of fat-marbled meat that told me he and his friend had already been drinking.

"I am Drugi." The tall man stepped forward.

Sonya greeted him in her low, breathy voice. "Welcome to our home," she said, as if she'd had Miss Kelly's lesson on manners, too. Harry hadn't lied about him. Tight curls stood up from his head like a Cossack hat, and he had the muscled build of a wrestler. With one arm, he was hugging three bottles to his chest. His other hand held a newspaper cone like a dunce cap.

Harry pinched my cheek between the thumb and pinky of his spoiled hand, laughing when I squirmed. "She knew they were gone before I did," he told his friend. Although Harry's hearing had come back after the explosion, he still talked extra loud. "I could read her lips—she was yelling 'You're hurt!'—but I hear and feel nothing yet."

"What name is Drugi?" Lethia asked.

"Polish!" Harry yelled. "He's a Polack. Aren't you, my friend?"

So are you, I nearly said, having seen what Mrs. Collins wrote on her forms.

Lethia poured a wiggly column of water from the kettle, and I realized she was shaking.

"Don't give us that!" Harry picked up a bottle. "Drugi didn't come all the way from Detroit for a cup of tea. I promised him a Russian party, with Russian girls and Russian drink!"

To his credit, Drugi ignored Harry, stepping forward to present the paper cone to Sonya. "A token," he said, for having him. She peeled back the newspaper to reveal deep red roses. "Spasibo, Drugi." She kissed him tenderly on the cheek.

Harry practically bared his teeth, snarling. "I didn't bring him for you!"

Drugi picked up a teacup and said, "Lethia is a pretty name. Where I live now, in Hamtramck, there's an Old Believer church."

He knew about the eight-pointed cross, and he asked about Suwalki, not far from his family in Szcuczyn. He might as well have been romancing a potato, and I wondered why Harry had brought him. Pa would never accept a Polish son-in-law. Though he worked alongside them in the mines, Pa insulted Poles every chance he got.

Is it that way all over, that the people in the next town are worse than those across the world? Mrs. Collins had mentioned Teresa's husband, and I remembered when Mr. G threatened to slit his throat because he was Sicilian, though after the cave-in, they mourned him like a son. Poles had been our neighbors in the Old Country, and they lived on our hillside here in America. Our religion was also closest to theirs, but we were raised hearing that Catholics were our first and longest-lasting enemies.

"Where's dinner?" Harry was worse in front of his guest instead of better. "You don't give a man tea and oat cakes at day's end."

"More than oat cakes. Also shortbread, jam—"

Before Sonya could hand him the preserves I'd toted from home, he slapped the jar out of her hand. It bounced to the ground without breaking, its heavy clunk followed by the smack of Alexei's lips coming off Sonya's teat under her shawl. Alexei took the huge breath he'd need to scream bloody murder, and I swept in to save him or Sonya, or both of them, from a drubbing.

Drugi lifted the jar back to the table. He said, "You're scaring the children. I think a cup of tea might be just the thing after my train ride."

"We made shuboy," I said so they'd know dinner was coming.

Harry said, "That's a dish for Jids."

Drugi pointed to our creation. "Herring salad, right? Our people eat that." Then he took a clean handkerchief from his pocket and busied Borya with some hide-and-seek while I wasted no time getting supper on the table. I couldn't imagine why Drugi was friends with Harry. Lethia managed to slice the shuboy and grate horseradish without drawing blood.

After finishing heaping helpings, the men sucked at their teeth, Drugi loud as any Russian. He put a spoonful of jam on his brown bread, and when Harry demanded some, he handed Sonya the jar. "Here, throw this at your husband," he said, with his fetching smile.

"Did you come to stir up trouble?" Harry accused.

"I like a peaceful home," Drugi said. "Be fierce with him, Sonya. You know what they say, 'Wolf doesn't eat wolf.'"

Lethia poured Drugi a fresh cup of tea, but before she could get to Harry, Drugi poured vodka into Harry's teacup. "For your nerves."

Harry had been calming his nerves during dinner, and Sonya calmed her nerves as well, until she started singing Russian folk songs. The vodka made her haunting alto a little more merry, lending the night a sweeter spirit. I took advantage of their sing-along to have another slice of shuboy, sweet coins of beets layered beneath salty herring and wrapped in the creamy mayonnaise. The men never left the table, except when Harry got up to pee off the porch.

I had already changed Alexei and put him to bed. Now I cleared the table and washed the dishes as if I was their servant. Which I suppose I was. I made sure Borya went to the potty.

I wanted to get going before Harry struck again, because the next thing he smacked might be my little brother, and if he hit Borya, I swore I'd break a bottle over his big round head. Packing up, I saw Drugi lay his hand over Lethia's. "I could visit you again this spring, perhaps meet your father?"

"You know our church," she said hopefully. "Maybe you are being baptized?"

Harry let out a loud laugh. "Bring ten dollars and a bottle of vodka, and Gregor would let you have her."

"Penya!" Lethia protested.

"What? Sonya cost me no more than that."

Even Drugi couldn't ignore Harry now. "Your talk shames you and your bride," he said. When he stood up, his thighs were like tree trunks. He asked Lethia, "I could see you three home, if it suits you. I've been cooped up all day."

"Isn't that kind?" Sonya said, but Harry snapped, "Don't walk away from me!"

I knew we were in for it. I scrambled to gather Borya's clothes and the blouse Sonya had given me, grateful the sky was not yet pitch black.

Drugi ducked Harry's first punch. When Harry threw a second one, Drugi reached up and caught his fist, the one with only two fingers. "You already lost enough, old man," he said. "Why don't you let your Russian wife put your Russian zhopa to bed?"

Sonya kissed her older sister but not Drugi, who opened the front door and ushered the three of us out. I thought he might offer to carry Borya, who was heavier than a sack of barley, but he walked ahead, hands deep in his pockets. He was as silent as if he'd swallowed a stone.

"This is home," I said before he passed our porch.

Drugi turned around to head downhill. "He was a good friend to me once. I looked up to him when we arrived here, but he lost more than his fingers in that accident." I didn't know if he was talking to me or Lethia. "Good night, ladies," he said. "I'll sleep at the train station." He sounded eager to be rid of us.

"You'll come back? You'll visit me?" Lethia asked.

His sigh was itself a slap. "What is it your people say, 'Geese with geese, pigs with pigs'?" and turned on his heel.

For a Pole, he sure knew our sayings. Ma ran onto the porch, and I thought she might relieve me of Borya or the basket I'd been carrying. Instead, she gently led Lethia inside. "What is it, dochenka?"

My sister sobbed. "I'll never have a muzh. Here I am, fifteen and alone."

"There, there," Ma pulled out a chair and knelt at her feet. Lethia had begun to calm down until Ma said, "Every vegetable has its time."

15

"WE BURN PLANTS," KOSTIA announced at breakfast. "Coal is dug-up plants."

"Coal is rock," Ma said.

"Miss Kelly says different." He knew her word carried weight with Ma and me. "Forests got covered by oceans, which pressed them hard, and that happened for a bunch of layers. That's why there's veins of coal."

"C-O-A-L," Pearl spelled. "C can sound like K or S."

I said, "It's tricky like that." I missed the way Miss Kelly taught the same topic to kids in every grade.

Kostia said, "They call coal 'buried sunshine,' because plants grow in sunshine. The energy the plants used for growing is what gives coal energy."

"Well, sure," I said, "a million years ago, maybe."

"Miss Kelly said three *hundred* million," he happily corrected me. "But what don't make sense is she said there's soft or hard coal—all the coal I seen is hard."

"Coal is rock," Ma repeated.

I remembered Ma putting a pencil in my hand and saying, "This is coal, too. Use this to get away from the mines." I hadn't picked up a pencil in weeks. I said, "There's two kinds of coal, and ours is soft. It's bituminous. Hard coal is alluvium."

Kostia said, "Not alluvium—it's anthracite, dummy. Alluvium is fertile soil, like by riverbanks." He didn't know hard from soft, but he knew that. Then he said, "Miss Kelly let me write vocabulary on the board yesterday, seeing as how you weren't coming back."

I should have been happy for him, being on Miss Kelly's good side before she left, because everything he did at home grated on Pa. The day Kostia dragged home the *Encyclopedia of War* and had it open on the kitchen table, tracing the story of world mayhem with his pointer finger, Pa slid his hand under the tooled cover and slammed the heavy book shut on Kostia's hand. He said, "Your age, I tanned leather for my pa. Find some chores to busy yourself!" Kostia lifted the broom off its hook, but Pa yanked it out of his grip and swung the handle across his backside. "With so many sisters, why would you do women's work?"

When Kostia and Pearl took off for school, I was so glum that Ma said Sonya could clean her own baby's mess for a day. She squeezed my cheeks and said, "You are my buried sunshine," which helped some. She had me try on Maria's blouse, and though the sleeves were too short, my skin through the cutwork sleeves gave Sonya's flowers a sandy-colored garden. "Just needs long cuffs," Ma said. "You'll wear this when your bosoms fill in."

She seemed to believe that day would come, and I stepped back into my calico chore dress. I laid out a new blouse for Maria from material Ma had, and she said my way was even thriftier than hers. It was a puzzle, and I was good at those. Or I used to be.

I was still under a cloud when Kostia came home, raced through his chores, and grabbed a bucket. I asked, "Are you going frogging?"

"No." He wrinkled his crooked nose. "I'm going to the blacksmith for beef jerky."

Instead of laughing, I was mad at him mocking me, when I'm the one read to him from the comics. I'm the one taught him to read. Now I missed out on school and frogging.

Ma, Pearl, and Borya were next door, and wanting what was owed me, I took off for the woods. Right away, I picked some Juneberries that had ripened a full month early on account of the heat. Ma's rule was that we were only to pick in raggedy clothes, for you could scrub a berry stain with Fels-Naptha or borax, and it might still hang on. I should have changed my clothes and grabbed a basket, and I'd have remembered if I got to go outside more. I blamed that on Ma and my sisters for making me their serf.

If you didn't jostle them, Juneberries stayed together—not like mulberries, which seeped at the first touch. I stretched a ways to get the darkest fruit, thinking they'd all be in my debt for fresh berries at supper. Kostia would call me clever for climbing such a spindly tree—its thickest branch was the size of my wrist—and for finding Juneberries so early. For once in her life, Lethia would thank me.

Both hands full, I managed to bow a branch to reach the top berries when something stumbled through the brush. Whatever it was slashed at branches in its way, and it seemed as if, having caught a whiff, it was coming for me. Porcupines went for berries—Daria told me a porcupine needle was worse than a fishhook through the skin. Bears weren't unheard of either, and a mama foraging with her cubs would see me as a menace.

Spooked, I let loose of the branch, flinging fruit like buckshot across my dress. Berries burst on my chest and spread into a blotch no pinafore would cover. I made it worse by brushing the pieces off, mashing berry juice into the fabric. I didn't see anything trundling toward me, but now I was in a different kind of trouble. Fear pimpled my arms, which I opened wide so whatever had ruined my dress could make off with me.

I was more afraid of facing Ma than being mauled by a mother bear. If I was still in school, I could pretend I'd spilled ink, though she'd know it wasn't ink when a kerosene poultice proved useless. A squirrel skittered in to steal the berries I'd flung, making as much racket as a bear. I felt a fool, but in my own defense, I'd been feeling like a fool the whole day because of my brother. I leapt to the ground, not even startling the squirrel at his feast, and heading back, I pieced together what happened to me, or at least what might have.

By the time I got home, I'd decided it was Kostia who'd spooked me. The boys were always going at the tree like rowdy beavers, chopping and shaking the trunk. And though Pa rode him hard, Kostia also got away with plenty, like pushing me in the creek or pelting me with snowballs. As Pa said when he punished the wrong kid, this was for next time.

I came in to Ma hunched over the counter, pounding the toughness out of a piece of meat. In time to her punishing rhythm, she said, "I turn my back, so you play like a child. No chores all day and it goes right to your soft head—" she turned around and stood stock still, bloodied mallet pointing to my spotted chest. "Bohoroditsa!" which I knew was Mother of God but not because she'd ever said it to me.

I could only get my voice past a whisper. "I went for a walk, and Kostia, he scared me by the Juneberry tree."

"He threw these at you?"

"The branches, they all hit me." That was easier to say. Then Pa walked into the kitchen in his stocking feet, surprising us both. He'd kicked off his boots outside, and except for his socks and the veiny whites around his light blue eyes, he was coal black and growling like a bear.

"What's this I'm hearing? Your brother did that?"

Kostia showed up right behind Pa, setting his frogging bucket by the door. "I didn't do nothing," he said.

I was so far out on my path, I couldn't think how to turn back. If I'd shaken Ma and Pa with a bear sighting, they might be relieved I was stained and not shredded. If I'd been quicker, I might have said, Something big brushed past me. I got away with just my dress spoiled.

Pa clanked open his belt buckle, gripped it, and whipped the leather through his belt loops. With that same hand he grabbed Kostia by the earlobe, the belt dangling between them. "I've had it with your monkeyshines. You got time to play tricks, you can earn your keep!"

Kostia didn't squeal, though his ear must have smarted. "I was frogging," he said.

All eyes went to his empty bucket by the door and back to him.

"Weren't no frogs today."

Pa let loose of him, leaving a sooty thumbprint on his earlobe. Then he spun Kostia around in a terrible dance. He dropped into a chair and bent Kostia over his knee. "What'd I say about telling stories?"

"I ain't, I swear." Kostia twisted his head around to look at me. "I was at the crick. Tell him, Yelenie!"

"He-he said he'd gone frog-frogging," I panted. "Maybe it was a skunk what scared me. Or a bear, a bear with her cub thrashing." I burped up a berry in my throat, and it burned.

"One lies, the other swears to it!" Pa roared. The belt whistled through the air and hit Kostia's britches. I imagined a welt spreading like the stain on my dress. "We'll see how far your stories get you with the foreman."

Pa would whip him and then me, when I was the only one who deserved it. I wasn't thinking Kostia would be punished, though he was punished for things he did and didn't do all the time. What I was thinking was, he thinks he's so smart, still learning from Miss Kelly. This is me being smarter than him. I was thinking Ma would make him blacken the stove or spade the garden, that he'd be the one to pound potatoes instead of me always doing it.

Pa wore himself out on Kostia and didn't touch me, only sent us both to our room without supper, so Kostia was whipped and starved both because of me. I was on my bed, and he was on his. He wouldn't talk or look my way.

"You're always sneaking up and playing tricks," I blubbered. "I swear I heard a racket, a wild thing coming for me." We were raised to carry grudges, not to clear the slate, so I didn't think to say I was sorry or admit I'd made up stories. I was crying as hard as if I'd been belted.

Finally, Kostia said, "Put a cork in it, sister," his voice choked with anger. "You happy now? Or you want Pearl booted from school, too?" We were both quiet for a little while, and then he let out a wail. "You know the worst of it? You didn't bring no berries home to eat."

Lethia, Pearl, and little Borya got themselves upstairs later, followed by Ma, who sat on the boys' bed. She told Kostia, "Your Pa was looking for any excuse to get you mining. I swear you'll know more about coal than the lot of them."

"Remember Fergus?" Kostia asked Ma. "He's already down there. But just 'cause Laney can't go to school, she don't have to ruin it for me."

"That's so," Ma agreed.

"All's I did was go frogging. If there was any frogs, I'd have shown Pa what for."

"A bucket of frogs and he'd done the same. Get your rest now." She picked herself up off Kostia and Borya's bed.

"G'night," I spoke up, but Ma only fussed with Pearl. For once, Lethia didn't utter a sound.

"Say your prayers, ask for mercy," she told Pearl. "Prepare to admit what God already knows," which was Father Dmitri's line from confession. She knew I'd lied, and though I was glad to escape Pa's plotka, I wished she'd have punished me and given me a fresh start.

I watched her smooth Pearl's wild hair off her forehead and kiss her there.

"G'night," I said again, wishing she'd tuck me in and kiss me, but she left me wishing.

16

WHY DIDN'T WE PROTECT each other? Why didn't we stick together? I'd worried for years that they'd take Kostia down in the tunnels, and then I ended up being the one who sent him there ten hours a day. Instead of sitting in Miss Kelly's classroom, he sat in the cold dark, listening for the rumble of a loaded coal car. It was his job as a nipper to haul the shaft door open for the cart to come through, but if he was slow or asleep, the cart would come crashing through anyway.

I had pretended that Sonya was ready to be a wife so Harry would marry her and I could eat the food that had been on her plate. I was as bad as Lethia, who thought Sonya was lording her marriage over her when she'd come to warn her. No, I was worse than Lethia, because I not only got my brother whipped and sent into the mines but also left Sonya at the mercy of Harry after seeing the bruises on her skin. Alexei had been born nine months later, pink and stocky like Harry, except instead of gray BBs, Alexei had Pa's slanted eyes and his own shiny black hair.

Sonya showed up at our house a second time after a drunken Harry knocked hers and little Alexei's heads together. This time, Ma was home. Sonya was wearing a headscarf as if on her way to church, and she'd tied the baby to her back with a shawl. Like a hobo, she carried a bundle on a stick over her shoulder. Ma put her arms around them on the porch. She said, "It's late for a visit." What she didn't do was pull Sonya and Alexei inside.

Sonya wriggled free to get in the house, then, craning to look back where she'd come from, she shut our front door. Ma swung it open again. "We need the breeze, and your sister's out with a caller."

Sonya shook her scarf so it slid down her hair and settled around her neck, revealing a huge knot the size and color of a plum on her temple. "You can't want this for us."

"Of course not," Ma said, "but this is not always."

Early on, I'd judged Sonya as pampered, and I suppose she had been. But she'd dutifully married Harry with no love in her heart, and she'd suffered at his hands. "Mamatchka," Sonya pleaded, "I could help with sewing. I learned what you said to learn."

Ma's heavy eyes were stones in her head. "And where is there for you to sleep here?"

Sonya and I looked at each other in disbelief. With only seven living here, the house was practically empty. She set down her bundle, knotted into a sheet covered in her trademark stitching. She must have decorated every piece of fabric in her house, as if to make her mark. She said, "You took in Vera and her boys" and pointed to where the rolled-up mattress used to rest against the wall.

Ma said, "Vera lost her husband in the cave-in. You have a husband."

Lethia was at the picture show with Sergei, and I told them what she'd told me. "Lethia says she'll be married and gone by her birthday."

"Maybe she will, maybe she won't," Ma said severely. "Lethia can't tell the future."

Sonya lifted Alexei's glossy hair to show us the goose egg on the side of his head. Ma ran a rag under the cold spigot and pressed it against his temple, *tsk-tsk*ing. I expected her to ask, "Who knocks a mother's head against her own baby's?" I waited for her to soothe Sonya, maybe say, "Sit, talk. With that milk tooth of his, Alexei can chew some butter cake." Surely she'd let Sonya know she wasn't to blame, tell her, "It's not your fault that Harry's a hothead."

But what Ma said to my sister was, "Lethia sees you've come back, she may stay with us as well." I wouldn't have believed it except that I heard it with my own ears. She said, "Penya's your husband, and your home is with him."

Ma folded her own shawl into thirds, spread it on the floor, and lay Alexei down on the makeshift quilt. "Let him sleep that off while we have tea."

If I could have gone against Ma, I would have taken Alexei upstairs and slid him between the covers of my bed. I put my arms around my weeping sister, fourteen and caught in an ogre's trap. Ma lit the burner under the kettle, not budging an inch about Sonya's place being with Harry. When Sonya complained about his drinking, Ma said, "Do this. He says it's bad luck not to finish off the bottle, you ask for a glass. Maybe you pour it in your mouth, maybe in the dirt." She waved at the shriveled ivy by the window. "Don't make the mistake his mutka did, drinking like a fish when she carried him." Sonya showed her where he'd burned her, and Ma said, "You need to stay away from the stove with that one."

A ball of snakes writhed in my gut. Ma made it seem like rescuing one daughter would set a bad example for the other. The way I saw it, saving Sonya from Harry had nothing to do with Lethia's prospects. Lethia as Lethia was enough to scuttle her prospects. And maybe we didn't need to be pushing Lethia out of the nest.

Eventually, Sonya scooted her cup to the middle of the table and lifted Alexei from the floor. She said to Ma, "Send me home with jam, so he'll think that's why I come."

"I'll be there in the morning," I promised.

Ma wrapped some gooseberry preserves in a dishrag she'd just crocheted. The last thing she said to Sonya was, "There's Father Dmitri, too, to talk with."

She could talk to Father Dmitri or she could talk to a wall. Anymore, instead of Father, Son, and Holy Spirit, I saw the trinity as the church, the mine, and vodka.

I watched my sister take herself and her baby out of our house, Ma already putting the kitchen right. "Maybe you never saw your sisters squabble," she said to me. "Sonya gives good as she gets, and that could be same with Penya."

I remembered the spat I'd happened on when she and Harry were matched, but the most I dared to say was, "Sonya wouldn't hit him."

"Marriage is for better or worse. We give her tea, let her run her mouth. You'll see for yourself tomorrow."

What I saw for myself was that Sonya and Alexei still had goose eggs the next day, but she didn't complain. I saw for myself that each day there were more empty vodka bottles for me to clean up. And then I saw for myself a drunken sampler of her rage.

I thought maybe Borya had upended her sewing basket because tangled skeins of thread were out of their tidy pouches and embroidery hoops were willy-nilly rather than one tucked inside another. One hoop was clamped on a tea towel planted with radishes, but another hoop held a muslin mess of fury, a sampler of jarring colors, jagged lines, and jumbled knots. The clumped threads on the backside reminded me of Lethia's uncombed hair, and there were bloodstains, too. Having seen her portrait of the Virgin radiant with motherly love, I was shocked by this angry vision. She'd stitched ugly angels and horned demons, two-headed serpents, and a lion feeding on a naked woman. I saw for myself that Sonya was sewing her heart out, chain-stitching and French knotting, jabbing the needle in the muslin—or herself—when she might have stuck it in Harry's eye.

LETHIA WAS SET ON marrying before she turned sixteen, and she was lucky to find someone as sweet as Sergei, who was practically royalty in Ma's eyes. When he showed up at our door with wildflowers, I thought of Lev Biletnikoff that memorable Thanksgiving before last.

Lev taught us the names of what all he'd gathered—henbit, dog fennel, black-eyed Susan—and two days later, the firedamp got him. How strange that I remembered those as good times, but Kostia and I were in school back then and I was one of Miss Kelly's best; Pa mostly drank too much only at parties; and, though they brought us Lethia and Sonya, Xenia and Robert were a joy to have in the house.

"Bull Head," Lethia asked me, "do I let them choose him?"

Sergei was surprisingly not her only suitor, but what I said was, "It's your funeral," knowing she always did the opposite of my advice.

Ma told Lethia, "If you are given something, take it," which took me back to Sonya, because the other half of that saying is, "If you are beaten, run."

With Sergei and Olga's ma married to Father Dmitri, the church biddies treated the wedding like a coronation, and Lethia was well-suited to her new role. She asked for a sash of roses and for roses on the tables, and she got them. She wore the store-bought dress Sonya had been married in after Ma let out the seams. For the bridesmaid dress to fit Sonya, who was still nursing, Ma let out the bust but took in the rest. She said, "Penya's kotleti, Sonya's lapshoy": Harry's becoming a meatball, Sonya a noodle.

The night Lethia moved into Sergei's bed, Pearl and I switched from sleeping three across to the two of us stretched lengthwise. As much as I used to yearn for Lethia to be out of our house, the bed felt too big without her. Instead of torturing me, Lethia would be kneeing Sergei and hogging the quilt off his backside while I only had to fight Pearl for the covers. So why couldn't I sleep?

All four of us were restless, wound up from the wedding revelry or the house emptying out. "You're not leaving, are you, Yelenie? Don't go," Borya said, working himself into a state.

"She will go," Pearl said, to be honest or mean, I couldn't tell, and Kostia told them, "They're not lining up to take Yelenie from us anytime soon." To me, he said, "Read us your book, like the old days."

I smiled in the dark. To Ma and Pa, the old days meant when they were in Suwalki, but I knew that Kostia meant before our sisters came. I opened my book of Russian fairy tales and read about Prince Ivan capturing the firebird's golden feather and then, in pursuit of the bird, his beloved horse falling dead beneath him, and the gray wolf showing up to help. I got as far as the wolf telling Ivan to hop on his back and promising to take him to the firebird before I was sure the younger two were asleep, and I closed the book and turned out the light.

Kostia's reedy voice spoke into the dark. "Why'd you stop?"

"They're asleep," I whispered. But really, I was fed up. "First, Ivan steals the firebird's cage and then he steals the golden horse reins, and the wolf keeps on helping him. Why is that?"

"It's make-believe," he said dismissively. "Shh, quiet." A fly was whining in the space between our beds until Kostia slapped it dead in midair. Borya didn't stir at the sound. Kostia said, "Ivan fesses up to the wolf that he's greedy and couldn't help himself. He's not as bad as his brothers, who lie to their father."

"Who lied?" Pearl piped up.

"Nobody," I said, and Kostia said, "Not you."

"Be that way," Pearl pushed closer to me, taking pleasure in pressing her cold feet against my calves.

A minute later, I heard her regular breathing but not Kostia's whistling nose, and I whispered, "The wolf should have eaten him."

My brother answered with the old refrain, "Wolf doesn't eat wolf."

"Ivan's not a wolf." But though I'd read the story a hundred times or more, he'd put a new thought in my head. "You think maybe the wolf was a prince?"

There was a long pause, then Kostia said, "Or a princess."

I pictured the gray wolf getting Ivan out of trouble, making rules that he kept breaking. You can have the firebird but not the cage, the horse but not the reins. Each time the wolf helps, Ivan is more greedy than grateful, until he meets Beautiful Helen, who is already promised to the tsar. I could see the words on the page, and I whispered, "'So the wolf turned itself into a young woman like Helen.'"

And Kostia said, "Either the tsar married the wolf or Ivan did."

It was the same story I'd read and read, only now it was about a wolf who put Ivan through his paces to make him a worthy husband. "How'd you think of that?" I asked.

"What do you think I do all day in the dark, trying to stay awake so's I don't get crushed? I look behind their stories to find better ones."

17

BEFORE SONYA HAD HER second baby and Lethia had her first, I had a mind to finish fifth grade. I'd been gone for almost exactly a year, and I thought I could pick up where I left off, stepping into the same spot like in jump rope. Except I'd been gone for almost exactly a year, and the teacher was Mrs. Henderson, the skunk-haired sourpuss from the company store. Kostia said he'd rather be in the mines than her classroom. Pearl said she'd rather be in the mines, too.

I'd always been taller than Olga and Maria, the two of them almost done with sixth grade now, but I'd shot up so much that I was tall as Mrs. Henderson, who had a skunk's glassy eyes. She didn't turn me away but didn't meet me with bread and salt either. What she said was, "You'll have to keep up."

I was sure everyone could see the bulky rag of my monthly in my underwear as I squeezed into the fifth-grade row. Worse than being uncomfortable, with my clodhopper feet sticking out into the aisle, was being stumped. Either I was the highest stalk of corn or Mrs. Henderson aimed to humiliate me. A gerund, Yelena? A dangling participle—Yelena, can you tell us? I knew eight parts of speech, and she didn't ask me one of them.

At recess, I popped from my desk like a cork from a bottle. The sixth-grade girls were nice enough, letting me join their hopscotch game, but hopping on one foot from square to square hurt my bosoms. I mashed my arms across my chest for some relief, and Maria, who saw me hunched up and tender, said, "Don't you mind. We'll help you catch up."

I felt old and young at the same time, going from running my sister's house to wearing not only a diaper but also a dunce cap. Mrs. Henderson started in on something called percent, drawing a symbol on the board that looked like the fraction zero over zero, which wasn't allowed. She said there were three ways to look at percent. Five is what percent of twenty? Six percent of eighty is what? Ten is thirty percent of what? The whats were a moving target. As soon as one came into focus for me, she'd point to another. Used to be, math was easy and I was good at it. My chilled skin was pimply as a plucked chicken, and my sleeves bunched up under my armpits, as if I'd put on Pearl's blouse instead of my own.

"Five is twenty-five percent of twenty," Olga said, which made me feel worse. I didn't want her to be slow, just slower than me.

"You have a question, Yelena?" Mrs. Henderson asked when I raised my hand.

No, I'm pointing to the moon. But I said, "May I go to the outhouse?"

Her skunky stripe had gotten thicker in the last few years, as had she, and she clomped in front of my desk. I squirmed under her gaze, wondering if she remembered Ma standing up to both her and her husband years ago, but she laid a hand on my arm and the deep creases around her eyes softened to lines. "You're clammy as a fish. You may be excused."

I followed the stink and the buzzing flies to the outhouse, latched the door, and hiked up my skirt. When I pulled down my panties, they were soaked with syrupy blood. I looked through my legs to the back of my skirt, stained through as well. The times I'd bled so far, one rag had lasted all day, so I figured this for something else. I hadn't heard of any other kids bleeding to death after lunch, but some children died young, like the girl in our house. Ma said scarlet fever could have killed me, too. Also, after Lethia and Sonya, Ma and Pa had a baby boy in Suwalki who'd died, though I never knew from what.

Dying would save me from confession, which was coming up at

Easter. *Have you remembered offenses done and returned evil for evil? Did you bear false witness?* I cramped up with the guilt of sending Kostia to the mines, among other things. I was grateful to have gotten to Scenery Hill and to Deemston in my lifetime, though I'd always hoped to see Pittsburgh.

Knuckles rapped on the outhouse door. "Yelenie!" Olga scolded. "You're in trouble for taking so long."

"Bring me Agrippina's shawl," I said, asking for one of Mrs. Henderson's history props.

"What for—you practicing a play in there?"

"I messed myself. I'm sick." Cold sweat pasted my bangs to my forehead.

"She'll give us both a paddling if I don't bring you back." Olga yell-whispered, "Is it your monthly? Lethia gets green around the gills then."

Olga, who used to couldn't conjugate a verb or do long division, knew all about what was happening to me—from my sister, who was now her sister, living at her house. What kind of loop was that?

She said, "Lethia has Ma steep chamomile buds for her, and I make up a hot water bottle to put across her belly." That was Lethia, all right. "Not always, only when it's the baddest."

"The worst," I corrected her, to show I knew something. Now that I was dying, school didn't seem so important, and even if this was my monthly, now that I could have a baby of my own, maybe I didn't belong. Mrs. Henderson could chalk me up as a girl done in by percents and dangling participles, if she wanted, or just grown out of my chance. I'd be giving her what she expected of me, which got me bawling down the front of my blouse. My second and third buttons popped open to my ragged undershirt.

Olga gave up waiting for me, and I took off my blouse to tie it around my waist, grateful that it was warm enough for just an undershirt. A few months ago, no one would have noticed, but that day my chest bobbed up and down with each step I took away from school. Inside my undershirt my soski stuck out like two thumbs.

SONYA'S NEW BABY, A daughter named Eva, was born in June. She was olive-skinned and delicate, dark eyebrows arching above chestnut-colored eyes. I trimmed her nails with my teeth and rubbed oil into her scalp to ease her cradle cap. Her puckered rosebud lips and her arched eyebrows high on her forehead always made her look surprised. Even when her eyes were closed, she looked that way, as if she had big dreams.

All that summer, her slightest cold turned into custardy congestion. She used her strength to suck in enough breath, and her limbs stayed limp. To firm her up, I sat her in my lap facing me, made her hands to grip my thumbs, and gently pulled her forward up to sitting then laid her back down. This thrilled her to no end.

My little brother Borya played with Anna's children next door, so I had only Sonya's two. Alexei nodded along as I counted the baby's toes, and we sang a song where the only word was her name. Eeee-vah, Eva, Eva, Eva, Eeee-vah. I taught Alexei his colors with green peas and orange carrots. Rolling two peas to one side and three to the other, I taught him addition. He knew more than he could speak.

Sonya complained to Ma that I was pushing him, and Ma said, "Let her teach. If she wasn't helping you, my Yelena might have been a teacher."

I cut the crust from Alexei's fried cheese sandwich. I took him outside even in the rain, letting him squish mud between his toes or dig for worms. Sonya's milk gave out early with Eva, so I fed her a bottle as soon as she was hungry. I rocked her to sleep rather than listen to her cry. At three months old, she was a baby who told you what she needed, but Sonya snapped at me for coddling the children. Maybe because Sonya had been raised to get what she wanted, she thought Eva shouldn't be waited on.

Sonya was so unhappy with Harry and unsettled by Alexei that one day I said, "It's a pity you had another so soon." And my sister shrugged. "This is what happens when you drink. You have another and another."

Sometimes I came home from Sonya's house mad at Ma. I'd listened to her pine for her girls for as long as I could remember, and after working so hard to get them, she gave them away—Sonya to a crippled drunk.

Lethia's marriage panned out for her. Father Dmitri's dead daughter would have been her age, and he and Olga's ma thought she was a peach, this Russian girl who'd been raised by the man who inked the church prayer books. Lethia brought them the wisdom of Ma's ways without the actual hard work, like the company foreman. Olga's ma praised her bossiness. "She knows just what I should do for her baby," and she took care of Lethia's Vadim, born just after Eva.

But if Lethia's marriage was a bridge, Sonya's was a cage. The night Ma sent her home to her husband, Sonya took most of Ma's advice: she returned to Harry and poured herself vodka, except what she poured went to her and not the plants. "The warm spreads down to your toes," she told me. And when the bottle was running low, she told me she finished it off and asked Harry to open another, as long as he did it in their bedroom and not near the stove.

Eva had Sonya's wavy hair but darker. Her deep, dark stare unnerved some people. It unnerved Sonya. "She mocks me," Sonya would say. I set her straight. Eva had her eyes on her mother, and she wriggled free from me to reach for her when Sonya paid her any attention.

By the first snow, Eva scooted along on her hands and knees. I bundled her, Alexei, and sometimes Borya up so we could go outside, though I kept her in my arms. She liked to touch the snow with her bare hand and scream at the shock of it. When I put her down for her nap, I wedged a pillow under her back to help her breathe a little easier. She woke up, sticky and smeared, and I wiped her cheeks with a soft facecloth dipped in warm water. Her dark eyes with those pretty bowed brows peeked at me above the cloth. By winter, two-year-old Alexei could say anything he had a mind to. As I cleaned the clotted goo from Eva's tiny nostrils, her big brother chanted, "Eva, Eva, full of cottage cheesa."

18

January 31, 1912

ON THE LAST DAY of January, I got up as usual to pack the dinner pails, and Pa wished me "Mnogaya Leta."

"Yeah, many years," Kostia said, taking his pail from me.

It was my thirteenth birthday, which was exciting, though Pa had sprung Harry on Sonya just after she turned thirteen. I said, "You didn't forget."

"Of course not," Pa said. "What kind of father forgets his docha's birthday?"

Ma said, "Get moving, you two," no mention of my birthday. She said the men had best be going and that we needed to get Pearl to school and Borya next door to Anna, who'd had two babies since she and Anatole moved next door. Ma said she was taking me all the way to Bentleyville. Only me.

I took it for a treat until she went on about the twisty bumpy bus ride—we were none of us good travelers—and gleefully listed all I'd have to carry. Twenty pounds of flour, ten of sugar. "Good thing you slung those babies around, so's you can do the toting."

My birthday was turning to stale bread. Sonya and Lethia had their babies, but I did more diapering and laundry than they did. Now, Ma wanted to take me along as the family mule. I looked at my scuffed shoes to keep from talking back, and Ma lifted my chin to give me a wink.

Once the men and Pearl went on their way, we got Borya settled with Anna's brood, then the two of us walked to Maple Street hand in hand. The bus driver cheered up when he saw Ma. "Morning, Miss." There weren't enough smiles aimed our way in Marianna.

Ma smiled and spoke English to him like a boss's wife, if a boss's wife rode the bus. "Good morning, Mr. Walichevski. We thank you for the ride." She dropped a nickel in the fare box. We didn't tell him I was thirteen, so I was still free.

With every step, Ma's skirt swayed as if her pockets were weighed down with coal, and when we took our seats, she showed me why. She'd tied two cornmeal sacks around her waist, one on each side, but instead of cornmeal, they were full of coins! "Yours and mine," she said.

Everyone knew that Sonya's needle could plant a rosebush on a handkerchief or spill a cornucopia of vegetables down a tablecloth, but my talent was sewing tiny even stitches that rivaled Ma's machine. I hefted one of the sacks, bumpy with coins, and Ma laughed at her caper. I'd given over whatever nickels and dimes I earned, unaware she'd saved the lot. We sped away from Marianna, clutching the moneybags like bank robbers on the lam.

The bus motored along at a fast clip. Usually, we walked through fields and pastures to town, knapsacks on our back and children to carry or corral. What a treat to ride in a heated bus, feeling the warm winter sun all along one side. The square fields flew by as if farmers had dealt playing cards in suits of snow, cows, winter wheat, and plowed dirt.

I'd heard about Bentleyville from my godmother, Daria, who took her nursing training there. In the three years Daria had been married, she had two children and still managed to make her weekly class and help Doc. Sometimes Ma watched one of her babies for the day. From the time Daria escorted Ma to Miss Kelly's desk, the two of them had been pulling for each other.

Sitting in the back of the bus, I didn't feel the least bit queasy on the winding roads. The curves smushed me against Ma at the window or made me lean out toward the aisle, and it was fun. Stopping at Scenery Hill, Cokeburg, and Ellsworth, we still reached Bentleyville within an hour. One hour to go farther than I'd ever been.

For everything Marianna had, Bentleyville had three. Plus a public library, a trolley from Donora, and entire shops devoted to a single item: dress shop, millinery, men's haberdashery, dry goods, and candy. An entire candy shop! Ma said I could go in all of them if I wanted but that we'd find what we were looking for in Perkins Department Store. I had never heard of a department store, and she guided me to a tall building where people pushed through a door like a wheel. Inside, we walked past displays of carved furniture like in Mrs. G's parlor, china dishes, lamps with painted glass shades, and parasols. Every direction was a revelation.

I followed Ma to the second floor and then the third, where we rounded the landing to an open, high-ceilinged room that reminded me of the Arcade, our movie palace. Instead of naked ladies or dolphins, the beams were carved and painted like a garden. Wisteria vines dripped with carved blossoms, as if Sonya had embroidered the timbers.

Swiveling my head on my neck, I took in the array of fabric. Bolts of material lined up in formations, giant dominoes standing on end in rows and clusters. There was more fabric in this one room than I'd ever seen, more colors than I'd ever seen. Common browns and grays to heathery blues and greens, tweeds and herringbones, tartans and paisleys. Wafting from thin slick silks to rough buckram, the smell of dye, sizing, and freshly cut cloth was the smell of new.

Ma was the daughter of a seamstress and a tailor, and so while her English could be choppy, she was fluent in fabric. We touched everything. No one stopped me from rubbing swaths between my fingers as Ma practically sang: hodden, broadcloth, cheviot; frieze, gabardine, and serge. In the cotton display, she had me touch stiff calico, soft challis, textured jacquard, dainty dimity.

A girl came toward us wearing a measuring tape around her neck, open shears dangling from a rope at her waist. "May I help you?" I dropped the dimity I'd been stroking.

Ma said, "We shop for fabric. It is my daughter's birthday."

"Happy birthday," the salesgirl said. I wanted to scream with pleasure the way baby Eva did when she touched her fingers to snow. She took the tape from around her neck to figure my size, thirty-four because of my chest.

Ma talked fabric with her: "If she wants a peplum, three yards for the blouse?" "I'd like some soutache to trim collar." "Do you think cheviot or jacquard?"

"A real seamstress," the girl said. "Take your time." Her kindness was a gift.

Ma escorted me beyond the bolts to the notions room. Tall dressers with small drawers featured buttons of oyster, bone, wood, jet, glass, and brass. I counted twenty-four dressers across and twelve drawers in each so I wouldn't exaggerate when I told Daria: 24 times 12 meant 288 kinds of buttons. Revolving stands held more buttons sewn on cards. I thought my head might start spinning, too. Notions also meant hooks, frogs, and snaps. So far, we hadn't spent a penny, and it was already the best day of my life. Ma led the way to trims: soutache, brocade, grosgrain. I never saw so many choices.

The back of the notions room had a tilted counter and a large sign that said Tissues of Dreams in cursive. I thought of the sign Pa passed every day by the coke ovens, Danger Zone, in six languages with a skull and crossbones.

Women sat on high stools beneath the sign, leafing through pattern books. Ma hoisted her wide bottom onto a stool, patting the one next to her. I stared at the endless fashions as she turned the illustrated pages, so out of my reach I didn't even think to desire them. It was like the movies that way.

Ma said, "I make same dresses, maybe puff a sleeve, round a neck. Pattern is in here." She tapped her head with her finger. "But today is for something new."

We paged through the book, and she asked me what kind of dress I wanted. None of my dresses had ever been the first made from a piece of cloth or a skein of yarn. I unraveled sweaters we'd grown out of for Ma to knit our next sweaters. What kind of dress did I want? Faced with the Butterick catalog, I wanted them all. Ma was tempting me with "smart suits," "attractive gowns," or "new coat lines," none of which I'd have reason to wear in Marianna. I chose a blouse-waist with a well-shaped collar over a gored skirt.

The salesgirl must have heard our coins clanking, because she pointed to the remnant table, "Seeing as how patterns are now a quarter." Then she pretend-whispered, "These are the last few yards from the bolts at nearly half the price." For the skirt, four yards of red jacquard at eighteen cents a yard; for the blouse, three yards of brushed poplin, in a color called "seed pearl," at twelve cents a yard. Running the tab in my head was like being in school again. Two yards of off-white soutache, nine cents a yard, and a dozen red shell buttons, two for a penny. Plus the twenty-five-cent pattern. Ma spilled open a cornmeal sack to pay our $1.57 bill.

I steeled myself for scorn, but the salesgirl said, "Money is money," and helped count pennies. Afterwards, she wrapped our goods in tissue and slid the parcel into a Perkins Department Store bag with its own rope handle, which I planned to keep forever.

Ma had packed us a lunch, which we ate in the heated lobby of the post office building. No one seemed to mind our liverwurst and onion sandwiches smelling up the place. I thanked her for everything, and she said, "Some present, fabric and paper. Thank me when you wear it."

We got a four-cent chocolate bar apiece and gawked at the shop windows on Washington Street. I saw hats stuck with feathers of every kind, the latest sewing machines, and velvet pillows topped with jewelry, which Ma pretended was hers. "So that's where I left my ruby ring," she said, and "Pa's solid gold watch has diamond fob now." Her joking was rare as jewels. She tried to hold my hand, but I was clutching the Perkins bag for fear I'd leave it behind.

She led us into a bank building that looked like a Roman temple we'd seen in Miss Kelly's stereoscopes. We waited in line for a spot at the teller's window, where the woman counted pennies and nickels into the tray. She slid five silver dollars to Ma. "Two for you, three for me," Ma said to me. She put them in her change purse rather than the cornmeal bag. "I hold yours," which was fine by me. I'd only worry about losing so much money, or Pa finding it first.

We boarded the bus for the trip back to Marianna, where the beehive coke ovens hadn't taken the day off. The harsh dark smoke blew in the bus windows, and the town's seven smokestacks striped the afternoon sky with ash. By the time we headed up the hill, violet and yellow streaks crosshatched the smoke columns as the early winter sun began to set on my birthday.

Children played on their stoops, and looking through kitchen windows we could see women cooking. The men were still in the mine, and me and Ma walked the empty road in the last light. Pushing against an icy headwind stung my cheeks, and I was a little out of breath when we got to the porch. The day's sun had melted the snow from Kostia's old collection of creek pebbles, still in a pile by the bottom step. I felt I'd been away for years or gone to another country. Inside, I laid my precious bag upstairs on my bed and went next door to collect Borya from Anna.

After the quiet of our empty house, theirs was like a hornet's nest. Borya launched himself into my arms, which was unlike him, and Anna was frantic with news. Ma followed the commotion, so she was next to me when Anna told us how Doc Miller had come to our door, knocking and shouting for Katya. Where had we gone, when would we be back? She'd begged Doc to tell her what we should do, and he had said: go to Sonya's.

I said I'd go, then Ma said I should stay with Borya and she'd go. We ended up taking him with us. He could run up the short steep hill to Sonya's faster than we could. I was sick with fear that while I'd been thinking this was the best day of my life, Sonya had seen fit to send for Doc Miller, and he'd come looking for us.

I remember seeing my breath in front of me, puffs of steam like a train as we chugged there, our feet crunching snow and gravel. And then we were at her steps, up her steps, and on her front porch, where Doc's black satchel was sitting unopened. It didn't make any sense, that Doc had been at our house looking for us and said to go to Sonya's, but his bag sat on the front porch like he'd had no use for it.

I remembered Daria visiting the day after Boris was born and her telling me he hadn't needed his bag at the cave-in because there was no one to save that day. Ma was looking at me looking at his bag. My teeth started clacking in my head.

I heard a siren coming from the house—I must have thought it was a siren because it was like that day of the explosion, when the ambulance was whining but there were no people to put in it. It was Ma who flung the door open to Sonya crying like a siren, a keening wail of despair that was her stretching out her baby girl's name: *Eeee-vah.*

Sonya was rocking her baby, whose face was a dull blue. The heathery blue of the wools I'd been stroking a few hours ago, when Eva was alive, the blue of a healing bruise, like the ones Sonya had endured in this house. Sonya had her bunched in a blanket rather than wrapping her like a blintz, and one of Eva's arms hung out, her fingernails trim as I'd pared them yesterday with my teeth. When I reached for her, Sonya clutched her close and gave a guttural growl.

"I'm sorry," Doc said. Ma sank to the floor and wrapped her arms around the legs of her daughter, who was rocking her own dead baby daughter. She babbled away in Russian.

Me, I wanted Doc Miller to say what he'd seen. "Was she breathing when you got here? Did you check her for bruises?" His eyes were bloodshot, and then I could see them bugging out because I was shaking him by his shoulders. "She gives the babies brandy if they're fussy!"

Next I knew, Doc Miller had me by my shoulders, though I don't remember him turning the tables. Where I had been shouting, he spoke calmly, like a hypnotist. "Pneumonia is what I'm thinking. You saw her yesterday."

"She wasn't sick then."

"She was probably warm. Sonya says she was congested—is that right? Might she have had a cough?"

"Of course she was warm. I kept her warm. And she was always congested. She was our Eva, Eva, full of cottage cheesa!" I spun around looking for Alexei.

"She wouldn't stop crying," Sonya howled. "What to do when baby won't stop?"

Alexei was wedged between the stove and the door, shaking like a leaf. I squatted down, and he ran to me. Had he seen all that had happened?

I answered Sonya. "You soothe a crying baby. Change her, bathe her, rock her."

Doc Miller said, "Believe me, Yelena. If Sonya gave her a little brandy, it wouldn't have made any difference. Eva died of pneumonia. See? That's what I'm writing on her certificate."

I didn't believe him. He didn't even believe him. He was saying that so Sonya wouldn't throw herself off a bridge. For all I knew, she'd shaken the baby harder than I'd shaken him. Or maybe she'd set Eva crying on the bed and had a swig of brandy her own self. Or picked up yet another pillowcase to stitch with a flower, and her crying baby had rolled off the bed and hit her head. I could imagine a dozen ways my poor Eva died, and none of them was pneumonia.

Doc Miller and Ma put Sonya to bed, and we took the children home with us. I carried Eva in my arms, wishing I'd taken her with me yesterday, or the day before, or every day that she'd been alive. I could barely see for sobbing. I almost threw up I was so sick about what had happened while we were in Bentleyville. I told Ma, "Don't sew me that dress—I could never wear it." That did me in all over again, that my best day was now my worst, and that I was selfish enough to think about my birthday.

Ma said, "You couldn't know," which made me feel worse. Because I knew and she knew plenty.

I held Eva's body to my chest until Ma filled the little washtub, pouring in water from a kettle on the stove and testing it with her elbow, as if it mattered. Ma and me washed every inch of her with warm soapy water, her crusty nose and rashy bottom. We dressed her in what had been Pearl and Kostia and Borya's white baptismal gown, maybe mine too, which was heavily trimmed in lace because that was Ma's talent. It was a spring gown, but Eva didn't need a blanket or a quilt now except to cover up her unbearably blue skin.

For the next two nights, Baby Eva lay in our front room—not Sonya's—while Olga and her ma took turns chanting prayers at her side. People came through to pray and kiss the baby's forehead. With her arching eyebrows and rosebud lips, she looked surprised to be dead.

19

BECAUSE EVA HADN'T BEEN baptized, Father Dmitri would not bury her in the sanctified hillside of the cemetery. Sonya had been waiting for spring to baptize her, so that Eva wouldn't come out of the copper belea into the unheated church. Now it was too late.

Lethia begged Father Dmitri, her own father-in-law, who'd buried all the miners up top whether or not they'd been to confession. But he wouldn't budge, because those miners had been baptized. Sergei defended his stepfather, and Sonya swore she'd never enter a room with Sergei in it other than church.

I'd been listening to Father Dmitri say all my life that we come into this world with the stain of Adam's sin, yet I did not believe that he could open his mouth and say that Eva was born a sinner, that Eva was not going to heaven to be with Jesus. Eva could only be buried in the swamp, alongside sinners who hadn't gone to confession and Zlata Slivinsky, who'd swallowed lye on purpose.

On the first day after Eva died, Pa made her coffin and asked me to sand it. I gave that coffin what for, working off my rage at Sonya and her drunken bully of a husband, at a God who would let Eva die and a merciless church that would condemn her, and at this horrible, horrible town, where the men go down to hell every day and then drown their sorrows every night.

On the second day, Pa came home late, and he hadn't been drinking. He'd asked Mr. G for a ride out to the cemetery after work, and he'd dug her muddy grave with his own pick and shovel. "How could you?" I sobbed, not caring if he smacked me across the face, but he put a hand on my shoulder and said, "My poor dochenka, we'll bury her under the willow tree."

On the third day, Pa and Harry carried the tiny coffin all the way to the cemetery, which was quite a ways, and we followed behind. Mud sucked at our shoes in the swamp, and I thought of Eva's gummy, crusty nose as they lowered her into the hole. We left her there not only dead but also condemned and alone. I cried until my throat nearly closed shut.

I felt nothing for Penya, except for wanting him to be dead. If he went into the mine shaft tomorrow and a pile of rocks buried him, I wouldn't lift a finger to help. But my rage at Sonya sat like a hot coal in my stomach, though Ma said Sonya was suffering enough.

I remembered Father Dmitri telling us that Jesus said, "Suffer the little children to come to me," and that "suffer" meant "permit," which wasn't how Russians used the word. Part of me wanted to have nothing to do with Sonya, who couldn't be bothered to mother her own children. Another part of me wanted to take Alexei from her to keep him safe and to teach him what she wouldn't. I was facedown on my bed when Ma came in to hold me.

"Some babies die," she said. "They might be twisted up inside or eat something they're not ready for—or not eat."

"Eva was perfect," I blubbered.

"You told me about her sticky breathing, how you propped her up for sleep."

I couldn't bear that I'd treated her snot-filled nose as normal.

Ma said, "Back there, I lost a little one, my first baby boy."

I'd heard the same stories so many times that I sometimes missed it when Ma was ready to tell me the whole story.

She said, "He was my Eva, Ivan was, and he had your eyes."

I hated my big round eyes. Everyone was always asking if I'd seen a ghost. Now Ma was saying that someone had my eyes before me, that I'd had an older brother with the same pond-colored eyes, a brother she loved the way I loved Eva and who had died. I felt a jealousy that made little sense. Had she been thinking of him all these years, even the years me and her were alone? That picture of my sisters still bedeviled me, but I'd never seen Baby Ivan. "Why don't you talk about him?"

"I had to leave him behind me. So much suffering," she sighed.

There it was again, but her suffering I was interested in. "My eyes wouldn't be strange if he were here now."

"New country, new lives—that's what Pa said. He doesn't like talk about Ivan, our only boy until Kostia. You were my first American, but he was my first boy," she said playfully, though tears flooded her face. "One morning, I told Baba he'd slept like a stone, and she shrieked that he'd go to the devil if he wasn't baptized. She wasn't either," she said, reminding me that Baba was a Jew. "I wanted to finish the lace on his gown, but she dragged in the priest to baptize him before Pa came in from haying. Pa was spitting mad."

That was easy to imagine, furious that Baba had his son baptized without him around.

She said, "When you have children, you think you're in charge. But what happened was that Baby Ivan slept longer that night and could barely lift his head come morning. The next night, I put him to bed and he never woke up."

"The kingdom of heaven to him," I said.

"Oh, Lenotchka," Mom choked. "The kingdom of heaven to him."

"Is Eva's gown my gown, the same as Ivan's?"

"Yes, for baptism I made it, and you wore it, each one of you."

I'd always wanted a white flowing dress, lace frilling the top and bottom, not knowing I already had one. "You buried her in that dress, like she'd been baptized." As if we could trick God into bending the rules. The last time I saw Miss Kelly, she told me that in America, people are presumed innocent. Why wasn't that true for babies? Then I was beside myself all over again, flailing in Ma's arms. I said, "Why couldn't you be New Believers in your new country?" Father Dmitri was always saying we were the church. If that was so, then we should be able to change the rules that made no sense.

"No, no, shh." She rubbed my back. "If you must have anger, have anger at me. I left Sonya at two—what kind of mother does that? And Baba kept them like dolls. Sonya finally comes to us, her family, and we send her to play house with Penya."

"She was my age," I said.

"We couldn't marry her off fast enough. I thought Penya could feed her, and then I could better feed the rest of you."

I'd blamed my sisters for stealing food from my plate, and I'd blamed them for horning in on Ma, when she'd been with me all my life. I said, "Sonya never held a baby until she had one."

Now we were both blubbering, but we were clutching each other, too, because Ma came to America to make a life for me. I'm the one she asked to help her and the daughter she taught everything to. I wanted to be in school, but at least I knew how to pickle and stew and darn socks to last another winter. I knew how to comfort a crying baby and that even if you feed, burp, change, and rock some babies, they still might cry, because they're babies and that's what babies do. And I knew that if that wears you down, you don't spoon brandy into a baby or shake some sense into her or give her something to cry about.

MA SOLD MY BIRTHDAY material for more than she paid, to a Scottish woman I'd never met and good thing, or I would have seen that material for years, all the way to podruchniks on the floor at church. I would have bowed to the floor weeping for my Eva. We took more trips to Bentleyville to bring back remnants to sell or sew, mostly housecoats or Russian shirts, though Mrs. G's friends liked church dresses in wool crepe and a few Irish asked for tweed skirts or jackets. My talent was straight seams, rows and rows on any fabric. I could thread a needle in the dark. Tucks, pleats, smocking fell to me.

The tiny pinafore I had been cross-stitching with chickens and eggs stayed in the sewing basket, and the alphabet book Borya and

I had been making for Eva would be forever stuck on G. Eva gave me her first smile, she learned to crawl so she could crawl to me, and they buried her without a blessing.

"Mooning all day, moaning all night is you," Pearl said when I was thrashing around in bed. If I squirmed to adjust my nightgown, she hissed, "Sleep on the floor in your fart sack, or I'll tell Pa you're keeping me up."

Ma splashed cold water on herself each morning and faced the day. Was this having a backbone or being a fool? You could stand on your head and family wouldn't make sense.

Pa's bum ankle was from drinking and not mining—he had all ten fingers and breath in his lungs—so I was luckier than most. Or so Ma said. And then there was the church. When Ma talked about the misery our people had endured, I used to see us as slowly rising, the way Father Dmitri swung his censer so spirals of smoke ascended to heaven. But Eva's death made me feel caught in an endless cycle. Instead of rising up, we were just going round and round.

Sure enough, Doc Miller was back at our doorstep within a month. Three-year-old Borya had lit a tin of black powder that Paddy Hanrahan gave him along with matches. Though Paddy had a history with Kostia, no one expected him to take it out on a three-year-old. Paddy told him that he'd get a surprise when he lit the tin, and good thing Borya threw his arm over his eyes a second before the surprise hit. The explosion burned his arm, knuckles to elbow, and singed off his eyebrows. His new skin grew in wobbly and melted, but his eyes weren't harmed.

Ma said, "Might have ended up with his own apple cart." Blind Mike, who sold apples in the street, had done the same thing as a kid.

Doc nodded. "Lesson learned, though I'm sorry it doesn't come free." It was Daria's job to report Doc's fees to the paymaster, who took them from a worker's wages.

Pa flicked Borya on the head and said, "You don't have the brains God gave you."

What God gave Borya was a trusting nature and a tender heart, like Kostia at his age. I volunteered to change his bandages, so I spent my days with him and Alexei at either Sonya's or our house. Borya was my comfort that winter. His arm still wrapped in gauze, he tugged Alexei and me outside to build snowmen and families of snow babies. The three of us sledded on our hill and ice-skated on Ten Mile Creek.

BY EASTER, SONYA WAS pregnant again. Of course she was. And when baby Leon was baptized the next February, a year since Eva died, I noticed that Sonya didn't drink any of the toasts. She'd clink and clink her full glass, never bringing it to her lips.

That winter, Ma and I put up enough yams and maple syrup to share some with Mrs. G, and starting in the spring, we pickled everything imaginable. So much pickling. "Such is life," Ma would say, "as sweet as it is bitter."

The fight she brought to each battle sent me reeling. She wrestled a dozen demons out the door every day, only to have as many or more rush in. Kostia working in the mines meant twice the soot-stained overalls to be boiled clean but not so much more money. I cranked the sopping clothes through the mangler.

Pearl pestered Pa to take her mushroom hunting. If Kostia had gone on like that, Pa would have lifted the plotka off its nail.

"Leave an old man to his rest. I've taught you all you need."

"You're better at it." Only seven, she already knew to flatter him. She swung the mushroom basket, saying, "Stay away from the white gills, right? The brown gills are never poisonous, yes? To test, I'll just take a nibble."

To this day, I don't know which mushrooms to avoid, because sometimes she said it right and sometimes she said it wrong. "I'll pick the pretty ones. If we string them up for decoration, they'll keep robbers away."

Pa laughed. "We keep robbers away by having nothing to steal."

Pearl plopped into his lap. "When I'm married, you'll wish you'd gone with me. What if I poison my husband and end up in jail?"

Pa set her on her feet and fetched his scarf. Though she'd gotten the better of him, he cheerfully buttoned his coat and unfolded his cap. "I pity your husband, my silly docha."

I couldn't imagine anyone marrying Pearl. I had never understood how Ma married Pa, Sonya married Harry, Sergei married Lethia. Pearl wanted me married and out, the same way I'd been eager for my older sisters to leave. Maybe this was how we were made, one eaglet pushing another out of the nest, but it hurt, as did Pearl being Pa's favorite. Both us girls were better off than the boys—Kostia could do no right, and Pa considered Borya a fool.

Borya could get sparrows to eat out of his mangled hand, and he took in finches who woke us in the morning. I remembered the way Daniil's bird whistles used to wake me when I was Borya's age and Daniil was headed downhill for school. After our neighbor gave Borya a canary and two eggs, he gathered wood scraps and talked Kostia into building a crib-like cage in our room. Borya combed the creek for wild millet the birds loved, and under his care, three canaries soon became ten. When he started selling canaries to the miners, Pa said he might amount to something. He got some of his girl canaries to sing, which was rare.

It all ended on a freezing February night. Pa said Chins Radchenko and Humpy Kuznetsov would be by later if they could brave the ice. Humpy hauled things for people. A barrel, a three-legged table that might have a use—he'd hump it up to Russian Hill for a price. Olga tried to get people to call him by his given name, Manfred, because she fancied him.

Pa said, "Today was a two-canary day. Good business for you, Borya."

Borya's sparse eyebrows fretted over Pa's words. He pulled me into our room, where the canaries flocked to the front of the cage, singing with joy at the sight of him. Miners who came brought flat wire boxes that looked like a contraption for toasting bread, and

Borya showed each one how to call to his canary, how to get the bird to perch on a finger, and where to scratch so the bird arched with pleasure. Humpy and Chins had bought birds from him before.

"Yelenie, do they pit my boys against each other? Do they fight them like roosters?"

Though he put the men through their paces about caring for the canaries, I thought my little brother knew the bird's fate. "No . . ."

He gasped. "Do they eat them?"

"No."

"Are they cruel? Tell me!"

I didn't want to. By now he was all of four years old, and I don't know why I assumed that he'd put two and two together. I said the men had a stick that looped through the top of the cage, and they waved it in the tunnel ahead of them. The canaries helped the men because the birds had trouble with firedamp and the like.

"Trouble," he repeated. "You mean it's too much for them, like for Gleb."

We'd told him the story of Nadja's boys, which had happened before he was born, and how the canary named Gleb had given his life to save Daniil. Borya's mouth started twitching like his eyebrows. Seems he'd thought the canary in the coal mine was a companion, a portable pet the men were allowed, life underground being so dull and dreary.

I didn't put my arms around him at first, because he didn't like to be touched. I said, "Your canaries save their lives."

"I raised them all from eggs, from babies." He was hiccupping with misery.

"Your birds are so sweet. Humpy's probably sad about it." I would never say the same about Chins Radchenko.

"Humpy Kuznetsov can jump in the creek!" He ran past me to open our window, then he struggled with his bad hand to unlatch the cage. I heard Pa limping to our room, and he was at our door when Borya got the hasp open. Frightened canaries fled from their cage and flapped around our room like a yellow twister. Several tried to perch on Borya's finger, but he kept his arms flapping. A few hit the top half of the window but recovered quickly, and eventually all of them made their way into the icy dark.

"Oy, durak!" Pa was shouting, calling him an idiot and worse. "They'll freeze out there."

I thought Borya might crack in two realizing he'd given his birds a death sentence rather than their freedom, but he shooed them out the open window and said, "At least they'll die flying."

PART III

1913

20

VIKTOR EMERGED FROM A cloud of soot the day after he and his brothers landed in America for the second time. Having docked at the Port of Baltimore, they made their way to the train station, where the company supplied them with tickets to Waynesburg, for some reason. They slept in a field and, in the morning, walked twenty steep miles into Marianna, carrying their possessions all the way up to 1212 Hill Street.

I didn't know all that when I was giving our rugs a good what for. I pretended Pa was the red and black one, and I beat his rivals right out of him, running my mouth all the while. Away, you stupid foreman who passed over Pa every day last week. Is it any wonder he went on a bender? I swung at the gray rug, who was Kostia. Take that, company clerk, docking Kostia's stolen pick from his pay. I aimed to send that gritty soot packing. Was it my fault that I had to give every member of the family a drubbing?

Ma had carried the rug beater here from Russia, bent loops of birch my jeda had lashed to a stick. So many things left behind, why had she found room for this? Had she brought it so her father wouldn't use it on Sonya and Lethia? Ma had taken it to Borya's backside twice, once for tripping Blind Mike and once for returning Mrs. Hanrahan's lost purse without her money.

I hoisted our braided rag rug up and over the clothesline like a movie curtain and walloped away, mimicking the Mohawk Medicine Show announcer we'd seen at the Arcade: *Buster Keaton's pa socks him in the jaw, busts him with a frypan, knocks him into the base-*

ment, but he can't, bust, Buster! Each swing loosed the dirt from what colors were left. I fixed my sights on a stripe that had gone from feed sack to skirt to apron to rug. Then someone sneezed.

I stood stock still inside the dust cloud I'd raised. A second sneeze, closer than the first, and a call of "Nasdrovya," which is for after a sneeze or before vodka. A crowd of legs had gathered beneath my rug, and I drew the curtain back from the clothesline to four strangers. The short one closest to me wiped his nose with a handkerchief rather than his sleeve. His noggin teetered atop his scrawny build. In a row behind him, like stepping stones from left to right, were three statues carved with muscles and broad shoulders.

The one out front had the same big head, stone face, and deep-set eyes as Buster Keaton, who I'd just been yammering about. He would have been handsome if someone had fed him. His three followers pushed him forward, chanting: "Viktor!" "Viktor!" "Viktor!"

He lifted one eyebrow and laid his hand on his chest, as if accepting and mocking a coveted invitation. Then he smiled right at me with his teeth blazing, and while I was mortified at their witnessing my rug-beating act, I couldn't look away. Almost no one in the mines had a full set of teeth.

Taking his own sweet time, Viktor set his huge scruffy suitcase and his oversized knapsack on the ground, then he reached inside his coat pocket with the grace of Buster Keaton as well. He might have drawn out a string of silk kerchiefs knotted together. While he had all his fingers, his slender hands were crisscrossed with the scars of a breaker boy, and he drew from his coat an envelope addressed in Ma's careful penmanship. Our own address was in the corner. He looked me up and down, which was a first, and then the biggest surprise of all, he spoke in lightly accented English.

"You might be Yelena."

Bull Head, Lethia called me, which Pearl repeated because it needled me. I was *Docha* to Ma and Pa, *Lenotchka* to Sonya when she wanted something. To the Italians and Irish, I was *Rushie girl.* To hear a stranger call me by my given name made my ears ring.

"I beg your pardon," he spoke to me as if I was royalty. "You *must* be Yelena."

Now, a warm tingle spread from my crotch to my bosom. I dropped the rug beater and ran for Ma, who swung the front door open with an accusatory slam. The three others gave a hearty laugh at the bottom of the porch steps. At the sight of Ma, Viktor's smile blazed anew. He said, "Ekaterina Federoff, I promised your own mutka we would find you."

Ma's face relaxed into the pure joy of the Madonna looking at Baby Jesus. "Viktor, Viktor, Viktor," she said, just as they had chanted. She put her arms out to the tall one behind Viktor, who looked to be the youngest. "Here is spitting image of Josef Gomelekoff come to my door."

"This one is Pavel, born in West Virginia," Viktor said. "We lost both Josefs, Pa and our brother. Here is Anton, and here is Stash, Mutka's baby after we said goodbye to you and Gregor."

"You speak like an American," Ma said.

"We spent eight years in West Virginia, and then Mutka took us back to Suwalki. Sadly, she just passed."

"Dear Olga," Ma said. "The kingdom of heaven to you boys." She kissed each of them on one cheek, the other cheek, the lips. She squeezed the one slightly taller and broader than Viktor. "Anton, you were a baby. I cannot trust my eyes!" Her tenderness made her look younger, walking on tiptoes as she dipped toward each of them.

Viktor had written the company, which had jobs and a house for them if they were willing to live among the Poles. "Suwalki is Russian Poland," Ma said, another shock, and as they caught up in Russian, Polish, and English, I pieced things together. Josef and Olga Gomelekoff left Suwalki two years after Ma and Pa, but they went to West Virginia, where Pavel was born. Forty miles between us may as well have been an ocean.

Borya slipped in from the meadow with sprouts and sprigs for his lone canary, and he and I gave the men a tour of the upstairs. When we got to the big cage in our bedroom, he wrapped an arm around

Viktor's thigh. "I raised them from eggs and set them all free, but Fyodor came back," my brother said. Viktor scratched Borya's fluffy head as if he were a baby bird, and Borya let him.

"So many windows in your hut," Pavel marveled. West Virginia patch houses were little more than shanties, and Suwalki may have been worse. Anton said, "We lived in two rooms, with heat from the stove." Each sentence they spoke was less halting than the one before.

"We had a life there," Stash said defensively, but then he tipped his head into the water closet and said, "Your life is better." His brothers piled in and gathered round the commode, then Borya yanked the chain with his wobbly hand and they marveled at the gushing water. They all took a turn sending the water on its way. "West Virginia, too, we had to go outside," Stash said.

Anton said, "You'd hardly notice winter this way."

Pearl stormed up the hill after school, and when Pa and Kostia walked through the door, she was the one who announced our guests. "Look who's here!" Kostia was puzzled, but Pa's blue eyes lit up his coal-smeared face. As he and Kostia went behind the kitchen screen to scrub themselves, I got potatoes on to boil, enjoying the Suwalki stories for once without longing. They spoke of Nadja and Max, Xenia and Robert, as well as families I barely remembered and ones I'd never heard of.

Viktor said, "We might have heard something about Lethia marrying the priest's son."

"Yes, but only nine or ten times," Anton said, and they all had a hearty laugh. Then he sighed. "Sonya and I were the same year in school. The kingdom of heaven to her baby."

Ma said, "We try to get my ma to come here—"

"'Maybe later,'" two of them interrupted, and again they laughed at Baba's familiar refrain. I'd never heard of these men, but they knew all about us. Though I'd just met them, I already wished Sonya had been matched to one of them instead of Harry. I took Pa's and

Kostia's buckets outside for a lick and a promise, hurrying back to see Pavel unwrapping a porcelain tea set of their mutka's that they wanted Ma to have. "She always said you were such a help."

Ma wiped away more tears. "I left school to watch Josef and Viktor—you were terrors."

"Josef was," Viktor corrected her with the straight face of a comic.

I didn't know she'd gone to school. Viktor brought out photographs of one family after another huddled in dirt-floored huts, pocked grins and dirty faces that Ma and Pa recognized. How he'd kept all his teeth seemed more and more remarkable. Every dog in the raggedy town had ribs like fence slats. Viktor had a picture of Baba, taken after Jeda died, and Baba's face looked like Ma's face pulled down like putty.

Ma and I hustled to put together supper enough for all. Black bread sliced, pickled beets and beans, a string of her homemade sausage links sizzling in the pan with onions and Pearl's mushrooms. After draining the potatoes, I put a scoop of sour cream, butter, and garden parsley in the pot, shaking it with the lid on to make a creamy sauce.

Viktor and his brothers faced the kitchen corner where our icon hung on a nail that the family before us had driven into the wall. They gathered around the Virgin Mary the same way they'd circled the toilet, and we all crossed ourselves before sitting at the table. When I brought the steaming bowl of Russian potatoes to Viktor, he said, "Gregor," insisting Pa be served first.

"Viktor," Pa spoke with real concern, "you been down there and still you came back."

"I did," was all he had to say, eyes on the platter of sausage coming toward him. He speared a kielbasa and lifted it high. Anton did the same, his forkful a prize, and I saw that his big wrists were bony. On closer inspection, their clothes bulged because they'd outgrown them. I admit that sausage was a treat and that supper was sometimes only cabbage with brown bread and lard, but they were newly astonished by every chunk they jabbed. Pavel was practically face-down in his plate eating like a stray cur. I didn't have to be fluent in the babble and snort of brothers to understand their amazement.

"Is this kielbasa on my fork?" Kostia asked, and little Borya piped up, "No, it is a yak hoof from Mongolia."

Pa bounced his spoon on the top of Borya's head, but Viktor laughed. He said, "Are we all brothers? No, we are circus clowns who ate our own makeup!"

"You know *Foolish Questions?*" I asked.

Viktor turned his big head my way and cupped his right palm against my cheek. "I remember from when we lived in West Virginia, America." Even after he took his hand back, my cheeks flushed. I was not used to being touched so tenderly except by Ma.

"A-mary-cuh?" Anton asked, and "A-mary-cuh!" Pavel answered.

Stash said, "Circus clowns, the lot of you," and Pavel said, "Don't be such a hothead."

"Four men with no mutka, no wives," Ma said. "You'll eat supper here as long as you want. Until your news runs out," she joked.

Viktor was twenty-one, three years older than Lethia, and Pavel was just a year older than Kostia. They all looked older because their skin stretched taut across their faces, like the saints in our icons. We were poor, but these men were starving. In my upside-down understanding, the people here had left treasures behind in Russia. Women pined for their parents and precious children, samovars and reindeer boots, birch-log beds piled high with down-stuffed quilts. The fairy tales, too, were of princes and tsars, castles and golden apple trees. Proud as I was of being American, I'd been jealous of their tales of feasts and abundance. I remember Kostia simply saying it was make-believe. How could I have believed it for so long?

"I am back where I started," Pavel said and began clinking his glass to everyone else's.

"Why do you speak so good?" Pearl blurted out.

Pavel put his glass next to his plate and recited,

Dinner time. The yard resounded,
Horses stamped and men dismounted.
Thick-mustached and ruddy-skinned,
Seven lusty Knights walked in.

"Pushkin," Ma said to my surprise, because I'd never heard it. "The Princess and the Seven Knights." She looked around the table counting off the boys, and she frowned. "Little Carl, between Viktor and Anton."

"The cholera outbreak," Viktor said, and Ma crossed herself. He said, "Before that, with Pa and Josef, we were Ma's seven knights. She read us the poem in English so we wouldn't forget."

Now Stash recited, too, with almost no accent:

Tell me, pretty looking-glass,
Nothing but the truth, I ask:
Who in all the world is fairest,
And has beauty of the rarest?

Viktor shrugged his shoulders, and his collarbones stuck out as if he'd swallowed a stick sideways. Even his wavy hair was thin. I wondered if he'd deprived himself to feed his younger brothers. He was handsome with kindness, and I could not take my eyes off of him. Neither blowhard nor bellyacher, Viktor told us about their years in Suwalki, along with the years in between, when he'd been underground in the dark West Virginia mine. He spoke almost entirely in English, throwing a word to a brother here and there.

"Soon as we arrived, I worked. That's probably why Pa picked West Virginia—with the hard coal, I could be a breaker boy at eight, next to my brother Josef."

"There are laws now," Pa said. Every law a loophole, the Italians said, and they'd shown Pa how to get an age blank for Kostia. Pa had paid Mr. Collins a quarter to plant his seal on a new birth certificate, and Kostia grew two years older in a day.

Viktor said, "They had us in the tipple on benches over a conveyor belt, a river of coal running beneath our feet." He hunched his back to show how they plucked slate and rocks from the coal as it rushed past on its way to the washers. "Boys would lose a finger trying for every rock, or they'd mangle their hand in the belt. A foot in the gears was a foot crushed. Me and Josef weren't after every chunk. Some said we were choosy and some said glupyy."

Or graceful, I thought, remembering how he'd pulled out Ma's letter like a magician sliding a card from a deck.

Anton said, "My godfather, Chechi Kryzinksy, was killed in the gears."

"Chechi Kryzinsky," Pa said. "His pa lit the icons in church with my cousin."

Viktor stretched out his hands, spiderwebbed with scars. "You see what the slate did." Then he laid his palms against his chest. "You can't see what the soot did, kicked up in the commotion. Josef was two years older than me, bigger boned too, so he become a miner. When I turned twelve and hadn't lost a finger or got the breaker boy humpback, they made me a nipper."

Kostia spoke up. "I was a nipper at the start."

"Then you know," Viktor said. "Was yours a swinging door or pushed along a track?"

"Swinging," Kostia answered. "They pump the fresh air in for the miners, and my door kept it from going up the shaft."

Viktor said, "That is so. Though we nippers sat on the other side from the fresh air."

I'd often imagined Kostia alone in the pitch-black tunnel, ankle-deep in cold water and breathing who knows what for ten hours a day. He had to spring to his feet when he heard the thunder of a coal car coming down the tracks.

Kostia said, "Sometimes I'd sit with my ear to the door. Other times, as far away as I had room for, twisted in a pretzel so I wouldn't get comfortable. 'Napping nippers never wake.'"

Viktor's laugh turned into a cough. When he got his breath back, he said, "The cart don't care if the door is open or closed when it's barreling through. The coal on its back is worth more than slow or sleeping nippers."

Kostia said, "One of ours got crushed. Not my buddy Fergus but a boy our age. Pa told the foreman I knew how to blast so I could pick alongside him."

"Good man, Gregor," Viktor said. "Toward the end, if a spragger was down or out, they'd give me a bundle of sticks to slow a car going full tilt. You've got to be quick to wedge a sprag in the wheel of a loaded coal car." He brandished his fork like the pirates in the picture shows. Then another coughing spell caught him, and Pavel stood up to clap him between his shoulder blades.

Anton said, "Word of Marianna reached us in West Virginia 'cause Pa's cousin was in there, Freddy Popoff."

Ma said, "Kingdom of heaven to him and his boy."

Trying not to cough bugged out Viktor's eyes, and I refilled his tin cup from the pitcher on the table. "Much obliged," he said after he sipped the water. "It wasn't but two months later that Pa and Josef got smoked into a blind tunnel." Now, the four boys crossed themselves. "I rode the elevator up with their dead bodies, the one time any of us was allowed a ride."

"Kingdom of heaven to them," we all said.

Mother Gomelekoff took them back to Suwalki, and after she'd died, Viktor got Ma and Pa's whereabouts from our baba. "The army was coming for me," he said, "so we come here."

They were sized in reverse order from their age, and I imagined each of them pushing extra food to the next one down the line instead of every man for himself. Stash was the skeptic of the family; he said someone had to be. Most of their stories were about being hungry and cold. "To be fair," Stash objected, and I expected him to say it wasn't that bad but instead he said, "it wasn't just at home. We spent a lot of time hungry and cold in church."

"You kept your brothers together," Ma said to Viktor. "Of five siblings, me and Sofia only made it past ten years old, then Sofia died with her first child."

Their talk took me back to that first Thanksgiving, when most of the guests were the last ones left in their families. No one had spoken to me, and I don't know what came over me to speak up. "Peter the Great had fourteen children and only three survived."

I dreaded Pa spitting on the stove, *thu thu thu*, or knocking his spoon on my head. But it was Pavel who answered me, as if we were having a conversation. "Really only two lived on, since Peter killed his son Alexei before Alexei was to be executed."

Then Anton scratched his chin, and in a deep, accented voice said, "Maybe. Maybe he choked on a chicken bone." Stash took on the same accent. "Pity Ivan the Terrible, full of woe, for accidentally killing his favorite son while beating him."

"You knew Pa," Viktor said. "How he'd say two things at once."

Pa squeezed Stash's muscled arm. "I can hear Josef himself say—how did it go?—'I would rather be respected than loved, said the man who struck his wife.'"

The four Gomelekoff boys let out a whoop at sharing their pa with ours.

"Why did you come to America?" Viktor asked.

"America came for me," Pa said, as he always did. "And now we are content to flush the commode all day and look out our many windows, aren't we, children?" He reached behind the icebox for a bottle. "Katya says we must spend our money on necessities, but then we have nothing left for vodka. I say buy the vodka and we will not miss the necessities. Nasdrovya!" He poured all the brothers a glass, even Pavel.

Viktor raised his glass with the others and returned it full to the table. Pavel pointed to our family icon in the corner, and when Viktor looked, he passed Viktor's glass to Anton, who drank it down and returned it. Each time Pa filled the cups, a different brother distracted Viktor before drinking Viktor's vodka. The next time his glass was within reach, I snatched it up. "There!" I handed it over, realizing the instant I did that this was a joke between brothers.

"Ohhhhh," all four bayed, leaning away from the table.

Viktor rested his hand heavily on my arm so that the scars criss-crossing his palm were like threads against my skin. "Sweet Yelena, come to my aid," he said. "And yet I got us all to your table, didn't I?"

21

BOYS CIRCLED OUR HOUSE like dogs soon as I turned fifteen—I scooted inside when I saw them coming. Humpy Kuznetsov's cousin came right up on our front porch, faking an interest in Borya. "Slingshot, huh? Used to, I could hit a sparrow in the eye."

Borya said, "No, you couldn't, and who'd want to anyway?" My little brother pulled back the sling and aimed all the way to Lethia's porch, where he neatly toppled Sergei's boot. Humpy's cousin slunk away, and Borya and I had a good laugh. I could see Harry's big boots on Lethia's front porch as well. Sonya had recently made her peace with Sergei, and the families often shared supper.

Worker that I was, Ma and Pa weren't so antsy to marry me off, though any calamity could change my lot. When a girl two years behind me had to have her appendix out, going all the way to Washington City for the operation, her widowed mother went and matched her to Humpy's cousin. Now she was his problem.

Viktor and his brothers usually came for supper on Sunday, my new favorite day of the week. They thanked Ma for feeding them, and Viktor recruited Pavel to clear the table with him. We were slack-jawed when Ma accepted their help and sat down to enjoy a cup of tea. "Don't mind if I do," she said.

Sonya and Harry sometimes joined us. I remember standing outside church the first time Anton and Sonya were reunited. He lifted my sister into the air, and she flashed her uneven smile. When Harry looked at him sideways, to my amazement, Anton lifted Harry up as well—they'd known each other in West Virginia—and Harry actually took it in stride. Nights we had a crowd, Viktor rigged up a churn to make ice cream from snow. Another time we had a taffy pull to celebrate the birthday of Sonya's youngest. Sometimes Stash stayed home from the rowdy suppers, for some peace and quiet his brothers said, and no one missed his grumpiness.

With me done growing and Ma such a seamstress, my clothes actually fit these days, and they weren't made from flour sacks or black wool either. On my monyik, palmettes repeated like wallpaper on the deep purple background. Olga called it too daring for church, but Ma had orders for two more after I wore it. Ma said, "Church is not a funeral," which I repeated to Olga, who said, "Maybe not, but it ain't Photoplay neither, and you're no Lillian Gish."

I didn't disappear anymore when I turned sideways. Ma said I'd grown two plums in the front and a peach of a bottom. My skin stayed smoother than some girls', and my cheekbones under my rosy-red cheeks stood out beneath my wide-open eyes. Boys made themselves silly over my eyes, calling them mossy green or dill weed. I wanted to plug up my ears, and I wanted them to say it louder. Even my hair had thickened some, and a potato-peel rinse from a recipe in the newspaper lent it some sheen. What had been a dull bowl cut was now a shiny bob.

"Afternoon, Miss," the mailman said one day, and he handed me a letter.

I said, "Thank you kindly," which I'd read in a book. Then I ran inside, waving the envelope with Xenia's back-slanted penmanship. "Letter from Xenia!" Ma dictated news of marriages and babies for me to write Xenia, and she sent us stories from Pittsburgh, that nearby faraway city. We saved the letter until after supper, and when I opened the envelope, a clipping fluttered to the ground, an article with a woman's photograph and the headline, "Suffrage Leaders Meet in the National Capital." Along the margin of the picture, Xenia had written, "Look familiar?"

Ma snatched it out of my hands. "Does she want a dress like

that? A plain jumper, and no collar makes that girl's big nose bigger." Then she stuck the clipping under Pa's big nose. "Bohoroditsa. Gregor, look!"

Pa sucked his teeth the way he did when was putting two and two together. "If I have eyes in my head, that's Agata Wenclawska's girl."

"Rose Winslow," Ma read, and sounded out "suffrage—what is that, she is suffering? Yelena, read!"

"'Rose Winslow, who has risen in the ranks of the National Women's Party, recited wrongs done to American working women. Miss Winslow, born Ruza Wenclawska, is an immigrant from Suwalki, Poland—'"

"Russia!" they objected in unison.

"'Her father has been a steel worker, and she was put to the loom at the age of eleven but developed symptoms of tuberculosis. As Miss Winslow is of the working class, she was chosen to voice the Working Woman Deputation to President Wilson. Primary among their demands, of course, is that women receive the vote.'" I said, "That's suffrage, Ma, you knew that."

"Ruza," Ma scowled the way she did when the biddies gossiped. "Troublemakers, the whole lot. Everyone in that family, troublemaker." I remembered when the biddies called Ma that.

Kostia put a finger under his chin and talked in a Kewpie Doll voice. "Give us women the vote so we can vote for John Barrymore—his nose, so straight; his hair, so curly."

Pearl and Borya laughed. I didn't think Xenia meant the clipping to be funny, the way I sent her funnies I thought she'd like. "You knew her?" I asked Ma and Pa.

"Listen to your ma," Pa said. "That family come here and their girl bosses the president around, big surprise."

I kept the clipping for myself and read them Xenia's letter, how her youngest picked all the green tomatoes in the garden on a lark, how Xenia was selling drozdzowki and kolacz to the Poles. "What they don't know is that they're really eating your skansi and paska,

Katya!" She'd had to learn how to make potato bread and bacon-and-onion rolls for the Lithuanians.

In my room, I reread the clipping, which didn't make enough of Rose Winslow's courage or pluck. Pa was always telling me I ask too many questions, that I think and talk too much. Here were things I'd never thought or talked about with anyone. She was chosen by six hundred delegates who pledged to storm the White House. This group of women started meeting after the Civil War—this was their forty-fifth convention asking for the vote! I tucked Rose's picture into my book of fairy tales, where she would have good company. What I wanted to know was how did a Polish girl get up the nerve to join other girls and demand anything?

TRAINS INTO MARIANNA BROUGHT more Russians, but they also filled up with folks going back. In West Virginia, the Eccles cave-in at the southern tip took 180 men to the grave. Then the Layland mine explosion up near the Pennsylvania border killed 115. The fact that 50 were rescued was considered a miracle, though a storekeeper a block from the drift mouth was thrown against a post and killed. Between the mine accidents and the war, traffic went both ways.

Pa said, "Afterdamp or mustard gas, pick your poison. Some would rather be shooting Fritz than swinging a pick."

He got into shouting matches after church about what the tsar should be doing, and Ma said that figured, that Russians loved to fight unless it was for something. I thought of Viktor leaving the country to avoid the draft.

"Pray this country has the sense to mind its own business," Ma said.

I told her that her kind was called an isolationist and that President Wilson was with her.

"Wilson doesn't know squat," Kostia said. "Being a mile underground is what I call being an isolationist. I'd join up if I could. Better to be buried dead than alive."

That chilled me through. Not long after the Layland explosion, Olga got matched to Humpy Kuznetsov, which she seemed thrilled about. She gave up trying to get people to use his real name, Manfred, and within a few months, she was already pregnant.

I might have predicted that Maria, who'd bowed down to lust in our first confession, would be the first one married, but cooking and cleaning at her ma's boarding house changed her tune. "Men live like pigs," she said and shuddered. She kept a wooden spoon in her apron pocket, and she'd bloodied the nose of one boarder who squeezed her bosom and another who'd pressed himself against her.

Making sure I stayed busy worked until I turned sixteen, when suitors wore a path through the snow and tried to soften up Pearl to get to me. They'd start off, "My pretty Pearl," or some such palaver. No matter how sweet they talked, Pearl stayed sour and crisp as a dill. "Yelena saw you coming and slammed the door! She doesn't like strong men, so don't waste your time."

She knew I'd set my sights on Viktor, and for whatever reason, she approved. I liked strong men just fine, and I imagined that if I were cooking for Viktor, his pants would no longer bunch like a paper bag and he'd be as muscular as any of the miners sniffing around our house. Viktor was more American than many born here, speaking good English and riding a bicycle up our steep hill through the snow. He'd ended up with a castoff, the way Ma got herself a sewing machine. He asked Kostia to help him take the bike apart and clean it, and then he let Kostia borrow it for Sunday rides. Wasn't that clever of him to befriend my brother?

When Maria and me went to the Arcade for a new Buster Keaton picture, I thrilled to see Viktor's double on a giant screen. They called Keaton the "Great Stone Face," because he sidestepped every sort of mishap, gamely carrying on. His quaking house collapsed as he sat at an open window, the housefront folding forward to leave him unharmed, window frame and rubble at his feet. Dumb luck but he could also be nimble.

Viktor played it straight as well. He could seem a bit feather-brained until you remembered what he'd been through. I pointed that out to Maria when she said he was soft. Also, what did we know but hard? We were surrounded by loud, barrel-chested men whose only compliment was a belch after supper or a slap on their wife's behind.

One spring evening in the fading light, I heard him whistling "By the Beautiful Sea" as his rickety bicycle grew closer to our house. You wouldn't think he'd have the wind for riding and whistling both. I changed into the blouse I'd been saving, Maria's very blouse that Sonya had ruined with the open work down the sleeves, and scooted into the porch glider as Viktor coasted into our front yard, swinging a leg over to walk his machine the last few feet. He leaned the handlebars against our porch and, raising his eyebrows at the sight of me, said, "Mind if I join you, Miss Skinclad?"

I blushed at the name from the funny pages—Miss Skinclad was the comic's shapely cavewoman. "I suppose that would be all right," I said. In the time that it took for us to glide forward and back, here came Borya and Pearl.

Pearl was downright saucy. "If it isn't Mr. Bonescraper," she teased. He was the caveman who wooed Miss Skinclad.

Borya wanted to share a Rube Goldberg panel I'd given him, which he flapped in Viktor's face. He said, "All these fancy cars, but the motorcycle cop stretches like rubber to snag the guy in a jalopy. The chump says, 'Some night they'll drag me out of bed and tell me I'm sleeping too fast.'"

Viktor pointed to the cop's reach, "That's the long arm of the law for you."

"Good one!" Borya said, shaking with his silent belly laugh. His blasting powder accident had cost him half his hearing, and he laughed deep in his gut, no sound coming out.

I said, "Shoo, you two! It may be light, but it's still your bedtime."

Pearl was forward with Viktor, knowing he'd be straight with her. "Where do you make in the mines? And if it's so deadly dark, why don't they poke holes up for daylight?"

"You should run a mine, and I'll work for you," he said. "But as it is, since we've no toilet, I'm grateful for the dark." Having answered Pearl to her satisfaction, she and Borya went inside, and he turned to me. It was better than sweet talk to have his big head looking my way. "Time for long sleeves again, though yours are right breezy."

This is how I fell for Viktor, and I well remembered whatever he noticed. "It would take me all day to button those boots." Or, "You're wearing shorter hair today. Did you save a lock for anyone special?" I wanted to be seen, to count to someone. One day not long after this, I asked him if he thought I wanted too much. "Long as you want me," he said.

My sleeves fluttered as we glided along, and he recited from the Pushkin his mutka had taught them, "Wind, o Wind! Lord of the sky, Herding flocks of clouds on high."

I liked thinking about that loop, her reading them the Russian poem in English in Russia. He pointed to the grass moon rising through the white oak, sprouted in new leaves. "Moon, O Moon, my friend! Gold of horn and round of head." This was how we talked in pretty poetry without fear of an eavesdropping Pearl or Pa. After we'd glided for a bit, he said, "There's a card game waiting for me at home, but I thank you for this chat and wish you and yours dobroy nochi."

I answered for all of us. "Dobroy nochi."

He righted his bicycle from where he'd leaned it against the porch and gave me a sweet salute, then he rattled down to his house in Pole Town.

"Viktor took off?" Ma asked when I came inside. "I meant to ask him if Pavel could join our supper on Sunday."

"Pavel usually comes," I said.

"Pavel alone for a change. Give us time to hear his stories, his plans." She leaned toward me, leering. "Pavel's big and healthy, isn't he? And he is the one born here, not the others. That's like you."

"Like me? Ma, Pavel is younger than me."

"Sixteen, fifteen. What's in your head, what's on your head?" she said, which meant don't be an idiot but also what's the difference.

What was in my head was saying good night to Viktor, so I hadn't made sense of what was on my head. Both my sisters had been married off by my age, Lethia willingly—she would have married a goat—and Sonya out of duty. Once my parents had said Sonya and Harry's names together, she was doomed. Even in America, it worked this way.

Ma was still talking. "You're not getting younger. He makes you look young, that's good."

She may as well have slapped me across the face. Had Ma and Pa already talked to Viktor about Pavel and me? Was Viktor helping find Pavel a wife? When he asked if I'd saved a lock of hair, did he mean for Pavel? For a girl who thinks too much, I hadn't thought of this, and now I had to think of a way out. My only hope was to get Ma and Pa to say my name with Viktor's.

I said, "Of all the brothers, Pavel is not for me."

"Who said you choose, little miss? You think I chose Pa?"

I clamped my mouth shut, chin quivering. I wondered if Sonya knew they had chained her to Harry the first time she met him. Pavel would make someone a good match, maybe even Pearl, but he didn't hold a candle to Viktor, who'd been wiping Pavel's nose until a couple years ago. I fled upstairs, Ma calling after me, "You get too picky, there will be nothing to pick."

Pa spoke of every lug as a son-in-law, bragging about what Humpy could shovel or who his cousin had laid low, but they'd never said my name with anyone. Ma saw and didn't see that I listened for Viktor and stayed outside. Pearl and Borya listened for him, too, though talking to children was thought a waste of time.

I knew Viktor cared for me, and I also knew that if Pavel came to dinner alone, I would be Pavel's wife. I couldn't disobey Ma and

Pa, but I couldn't obey them either. I thought of Rose Winslow in the newspaper story, the troublemaker who stuck up for herself. She did more than that; she took women's concerns all the way to the president.

IN THE MORNING, I worked the bread dough over, punching its puffed-up hopes flat. That helped, the same way I used to beat the rugs as if they were my family and I had to knock the ash out of them. But remembering my rug ritual led to remembering the dust clearing, Viktor having made his way to us. I pulled the dough like taffy, imagining the white silky ropes were his muscles and the loaf his weary back that I was kneading at the day's end, before we would sleep in each other's arms.

"We want bread not leather," Ma said, and she flicked me on the head. "What are you thinking?"

I looked at the lump, so overworked it might not rise again. I said quietly, "I was thinking about Viktor." It made me giddy to speak his name aloud. I was probably smiling like a half-wit. "You know how his brothers look up to him, especially Pavel. I can see why."

"Viktor?" Ma considered. "He's good to them, like he's good to Borya. A grown man listening to a child reading—it's something." She pushed her hair off her face with her wrist, a signal she was done with this topic. But then she said gently, "He's tetchy, Lenotchka. His own mother, Olga, the kingdom of heaven to her, told me when he was a baby. Like you with your scarlet fever, we almost lost you."

"I barely remember that." Sometimes I thought I'd dreamt those fevered nights and Ma's sweet concern. Or that I'd put myself in the place of the girl who'd died in our house before us, whose book I had. Time was when I'd wished for a cough to worsen, to get Ma's attention.

Ma took my dough out from under me, then sat down at the table and motioned for me to sit. There were strands of gray in her dark brown hair. Although she always had more stamina than most, she'd recently turned thirty-five. She said, "Viktor brought his brothers here so they'd have a life, maybe care for him."

"I could care for him," I said.

"Oy!" Ma said, put out with me. "Can you knit him a new pair of lungs? I hope you're more of a help at Sonya's than here. Go on with you."

I wasn't used to Ma scolding me, and I scooted out of the house with my tail between my legs. Sonya's children kept me running, which might have taken my mind off my troubles except that Sonya had named her newest baby Pyotr, and she cooed and fussed over him as she hadn't over the others. I couldn't help but remember Pyotr living with us and them talking quietly in the dark. She knew then that she was matched to Harry.

Ma served us soup and pickles for supper. She handed Pearl a knife and the loaf of bread I'd baked that morning.

"No yeast today?" Pearl held up the loaf, which looked like a cow patty. She passed around the misshapen slices. Eating them was like chewing on a belt. I'd worked all the flavor out of the dough, so that even butter and salt wouldn't save it.

"See what happens?" Ma said.

My younger siblings didn't know what was up, though Pa must have told Kostia because he offered to take Pearl and Borya to the woods to look for the owl Borya had been hearing after dark.

Ma led me back to the table, where Pa had steeped his cup of tea, spooned jam into it, and stirred in milk. His knuckles were knobby, his little finger bent at a funny angle because he broke it and never saw Doc for a splint. I wondered how he shoveled with a bum ankle and a broken finger, and then I wondered how much he suffered every day just to feed us. His fingertips were black, as if inked.

"Listen to me," he said. He stirred his tea for some time and sighed. "You have a good head on your shoulders. Ma taught you well, though you have me to thank for your brains." He laughed—*hah hah!* Even taking credit for my brains, this was praise I'd never heard.

"You tell anyone who will listen that you are American. American born, American made. I respect that."

"You do?" I asked, thrown by his understanding.

"Yes, that is why we chose you an American. We have matched you to Pavel." He leaned forward and tipped my chin up. "He's a good man."

I sniffled but I couldn't stop the tears from splashing off my cheek. "He is," I said, looking into my father's blue eyes, which had drawn Ma to him. Pavel was a good man. He wasn't the man for me. Because Pa had praised me, because I wasn't disagreeing with him about Pavel, because it was my life, I said, "I want to be matched with Viktor."

Pa let go of my chin to wave his crooked hand in the air. "Who says you choose? Pavel, too, leads me to Viktor, as if he was Viktor's pa. But Pavel will come around."

I didn't want Pavel. I wanted the one who had led them out of Suwalki.

Ma said, "Pavel is most like Viktor but also least like him. Look with your two eyes, Lenotchka. Every bone on Viktor's body shows, and you need someone to care for you. The fever you had may well have weakened your heart."

I stared at the two of them, my face heating up. Not once in my life had Ma suggested I take it easy. When I dragged the featherbeds outside for airing, lugged heavy wet overalls to the line, or pounded potatoes to pulp, no one had ever said, "Careful, Yelena, think of your heart." They only mentioned it now that they were prepared to break it.

Pa said, "Viktor's not strong enough. He can't draw a breath without spitting sopli."

Ma added, "You'll be a widow before you're a mother with that one."

I said, "He's been working since he was eight. He brought himself and three brothers back—that takes brains and grit." Viktor did look worn out for being twenty-three. Meanwhile, what Pa called strong was being a hothead. I couldn't say that, but I did say, "Because he doesn't start fights, you say he's soft."

"I didn't call him soft," Pa said. "I said he was sickly."

"Maybe he wouldn't be sickly out of the mines."

"He's a miner! And he's Russian." He tapped the top of my head as if testing a melon. "You could take him to the moon and he'd be Russian. Pavel was born here, like you."

Pa stood up to pour his tea in the sink and fill his cup with vodka.

"Gregor," Ma growled, and Pa growled back.

"It's like talking to a turnip! She throws her life away and for what?" He drained the cup and slammed it on the table. As he stormed out, he said, "Use the brains I gave you."

Just as they saw and didn't see my love for Viktor, I heard and didn't hear what they were trying to tell me.

Ma said, "More than for your sisters, your pa made a choice with you in mind."

If Pavel wouldn't agree, Pa's choice meant nothing. Instead of pointing that out, I said, "Viktor's not tetchy. He has irritabilities. Like when Kostia was stung by those wasps."

"He's been stung?" she asked, genuinely curious.

"No, but there are foods that give him hives or swell him up. Like you with goldenrod, how your eyes itch and water. The soot and slag in our air chokes him."

"He can't breathe the air without being sick," Ma said. "You'll wear worry like a headscarf with that one."

I said, "That time he went with Doc Miller? The Pittsburgh doctor explained. There are foods he can't digest, like milk and beer. Potatoes."

Ma said, "You're talking about a weakness, the kind of ailment in people's heads. Lazy people invent such complaints." At least she didn't say he'd been cursed or was sick because he hadn't kept Lent.

I said, "Father Dmitri says weakness is caving in to someone despite your beliefs."

I could see the misgiving in her face. She said, "This is about your beliefs then?" She leaned forward and kissed me on the forehead, like when we were young, and maybe because they'd brought up my fever, I remembered her doing that and saying, "You'll live."

Ma said, "Milk, beer, Lenotchka. These are drinks that fortify. I mended clothes for you children to have milk and cottage cheese."

"They make him sick, Ma."

"He doesn't like them, is what you're saying. Mother's milk is how a baby lives. No one gets sickened by beer. That's why people drink the both of them."

Used to, I would have kept my mouth shut. Before I'd lost Eva or met Viktor, Ma's opinions outweighed mine. Her gray hairs reminded me that she was from another time, that her opinions would fade and would leave me to make my own. I thought of what Kostia had told me about spending his dark days looking behind their stories to find his own. And I stood up for my Viktor. "The Pittsburgh doctor calls them allergies; he says Viktor is allergic to such things. His throat closes so it's hard to swallow. His stomach cramps."

"He's telling tales, that one. His mother could talk the pork off a chop."

"I believe what he says."

She was blotchy in the face, angrier than when Borya or Pearl disobeyed her, more frustrated than when Pa called her a shrew. "You believe him over me, your mamulya?"

I swallowed hard. Though neither of us ever said it, we were the most alike. I was her comfort and her sounding board. I was her first American, as she said, and we'd learned English together. I helped her raise Kostia, Pearl, and Borya, and I helped her introduce Sonya and Lethia to this country, though I could have been nicer about that.

I said, "Yogurt is different; even buttermilk and sour cream, it seems. But he drinks a glass of milk and doubles over in pain. He passes gas. He gets the runs."

"Beer, too? That has to be a lie."

"He has yet to lie to me," I said. "He tells me about living in Suwalki, the way you do, and about working in the mine. It's almost like I'm there."

Ma made a face. "Pa doesn't want to be in the mines—why would I want him to drag me in there?"

I said, "What this means, Ma, is that he doesn't drink. Remember the game his brothers play, drinking his glass down for him?"

Slowly, Ma's expression changed. She rubbed her jaw, where Pa had hit her just a few days ago for hiding his bottle. "At all? He doesn't ever drink?"

"Not beer, not vodka, and not milk either. He drinks tea and water. He says he's had ginger ale and apple cider, fruit juices, too."

"Look at me," she said, and I stared into my mother's dark eyes. "He cannot drink vodka?"

"No," I said. "And he's not lazy either. You've seen him work. When he's well, there's no one the men trust more."

Anger drained from her face, and I saw in her smile the contentment she showed after pressing a seam. She opened her arms for me to come close. "Then marry him, Lenotchka, before he gets away. I'll talk with Pa. And may your children have such allergies."

Ma hugged and rocked me, and we were both crying. This is what I wanted, to marry Viktor and to have her blessing. He was part of the life I was choosing for myself. But marrying him also meant giving up other plans, and that's why I kept crying when she was already dabbing her eyes. "Ma," I said, "you won't be upset if there aren't grandchildren?"

"He is allergic to children? I have seen him play with Borya as if he were his own brother." And then she gasped. "He is allergic to being with a woman?"

I'd only just taught her about allergies, and I already regretted it. "He is not allergic to being with a woman." What I was worried about was a different matter. "If he doesn't drink, how will there be children?"

"Drink or don't drink, the babies keep coming. Don't your sisters tell you anything?"

Daria had told me about how much it hurt and how much blood she lost, but that was Daria. I sputtered, "Sonya said . . . And you, too. I came along after Pa drank Max's vodka and took a swing at him." Maybe it was more about fighting, though I didn't want Viktor to hit me either. "You said Borya was because Pa had been on a spree."

Now it was Ma's turn to slam the table, though she wasn't mad. "Drink makes them like animals, that is so." She cackled like a hen. "Oh, my Lenotchka, always asking your foolish questions, never getting the answers that matter. What have you learned that really counts?"

I hid my face in my hands as Ma explained how bull and cow is different from man and wife. When she was done, I felt even sadder about baby Eva. I'd mourned for her, ignorant of how she'd come to grow in Sonya's belly, unaware that it was hugging and kissing—and more—that had brought about my sweet Eva.

Ma said, "The men show us so little kindness. There is more wooing of vodka than women. It's no wonder you put the bottle in bed with them."

I'd given up school and time with my friends for the women in my family. Why hadn't they bothered to prepare me for my life? No one shielded me from pregnancy or babies, because they needed my help. At nine, I'd set Kostia straight when he said Ma had pooped Borya out—I'd stood at Ma's head when Borya was born. I'd felt babies swim and kick in Ma and my sisters' bellies, and I'd seen enough breastfeeding, dirty diapers, and baby spit-up to last a lifetime. But I'd seen little enough of tenderness or romance.

Having witnessed the outright pain, mess, and heartache of babies, I'd made my peace with foregoing children. Except I thought that meant living with a sober husband and covering my glass when someone was eager to refill it.

22

MA SET VIKTOR'S AND my wedding date for February, just after my seventeenth birthday. "A winter wedding warms the village," she said. "If Kostia catches us a rabbit, I'll make you a muff."

"He'd trap a dozen rabbits to be rid of me."

"How I fussed about my sisters," Ma admitted, "four in a bed every night. 'Sofia kicked me! Botcha stole my blankets!' And how I miss them. It will be like that for you two. Ye bo ho." I promise.

Borya would miss me, but Pearl might only miss the chores I did. Lately, I was so distracted, I measured salt for sugar, and I threw the soup broth out with the dishwater.

Viktor and I were allowed to be alone for an hour on Sundays. Walking in the woods with him, I confessed my ignorance—that I'd thought men had to be drunk and swinging for a woman to get pregnant—and he said I was only half-wrong. For a sickly man, he had swagger.

He said, "Looks like I found myself a true innocent."

With that remark, I couldn't stop myself confessing, as if he had to know the worst about me. I told him it was my fault that Kostia got sent to the mines and maybe that Eva had died. She might well be alive if I'd taken care of her that day.

Viktor gave my hand a squeeze. "Now, now, save something for after the wedding. And don't expect to see my dirty laundry until it's in the washtub."

Ma sold three lace collars and a dozen trimmed handkerchiefs to buy five yards of cream silk with a flaw down the center. She swore the blemish would cause no trouble, and sure enough, she easily pieced my gown from either side of the scumbled stripe. "Be grateful their loom jammed so we could get this material."

I hoped no girl had been docked for scrambling the threads. After each session, I wrapped the pieces in a sheet and stowed them under her and Pa's bed to keep my dress safe from ash that blew in through the cracks. Pa and Kostia in the mines, Pearl and Borya at school, we made excuses for fittings when I wasn't helping Sonya. "We don't want the bodice to pucker," she'd say. "It would be a shame if the neckline's too low."

Below the empire waist, the swish of the long skirt lent volume to my hips, and Ma made a long-sleeved overdress of white netting like Sonya's dress. It crisscrossed my chest and belted with a thick satin sash under my bosom. Down the center of the overdress, the netting parted, trimmed with a satin border that Ma planned to embroider with pale pink roses and barely green leaves. Ma fit a half moon of muslin under my armpit. "For sweating," she said. "You and your nerves."

"I'm only nervous that I won't get the chance," I said, and Ma said she'd spent so much time on my gown that if the worst happened, she'd bury me in the dress.

I meant the worst happening to Viktor, who'd been sounding as if he were breathing underwater. But Ma's remark gave me a strange thrill, thinking of myself like Pushkin's princess, "In a coffin made of crystal, they laid out the body fair," a church full of mourners looking down on my beautiful corpse.

IN THE DRY WINTER air, my fine hair lifted up and away from my head, crackling with every stroke of my hairbrush. "You'll catch fire," Ma said. She wet a comb to paste down the flyaways and smiled approvingly into the mirror. I felt regal in the plaid skirt and fitted Norfolk jacket she had made me. I took Pa's tea upstairs to him so he'd get a move on.

"Docha," he greeted me sleepily, "you're dressed up for the Mick?"

I merely curtsied, not wanting to egg him on or argue with him. I was looking forward to seeing Mr. Collins, who used to give me sections from his newspaper and listen to me go on about being American, "eyelash to toenail," as Ma once said about the wolf who eats the bride.

Pa stomped downstairs in his heavy boots, saying, "So this is what a day of lost wages feels like." He'd fretted that his mark would probably be used against him, and to be fair to the devil, everything he'd ever signed had been used that way. To Ma, he said, "You were fourteen when you took me, and Sonya was even younger. We didn't need a license." And to me, "You've no birth certificate, so tell him you're eighteen."

Though it was Mr. Collins who got Kostia a birth certificate to make him two years older, I said, "You can't tell him whatever suits you. This isn't Russia."

My father eyed me with a satisfied smirk. "You'll be Russian again soon."

Again? I said, but only to myself. I had never been Russian, and I didn't intend to start now. Ma laid fried mushrooms on his plate and unscrewed a fresh jar of raspberry jam with a *pop!*

"Tea in bed and the guest's jam. This is how the other half lives, eh?" He pinched Ma's bottom. "Our docha gets married, maybe we need a few more to take her place."

"Gregor!" She pushed him away.

"Katya," he pleaded, "I'm sober as a skunk."

"And twice as smelly," she said, but they kissed deeply right in front of me.

Their tomfoolery gave me a warm rush of pleasure. I had never seen Ma and Pa flirt and rarely seen them kiss. What else would I be privy to now that I was old enough to marry? The only words he and Ma had that morning were over a pour he added to his cup.

"You promised," Ma said.

"Not to get drunk is what I promised. Ye bo ho," he said, giving his word. To me he said, "What good is a day off if you can't have a drink?"

I didn't know how to answer without stirring him up, so I fetched his coat and gloves and waved away the slice of bread Ma offered to put in my pocket, as if I were off to play in the woods. Pa looked nice, with a collar buttoned to his shirt and a short, old-fashioned tie around his neck.

Miners' wives called out to us, their arms plunged into their washtubs. On a bright windless morning like this, clothes would dry or freeze before getting ashed. Widow Joedsky was in her yard, surrounded by her hens. She said, "Where are you going with my man's tie around your neck? Both of youse, so dapper."

Pa snapped, "I can't walk in the sunshine with my docha without you ko-ko-ko-ing like a hen?" He hooked my arm and brought his face down to mine. "Our business is our business." The vodka on his breath was so strong I blinked. He must have had more than the splash I witnessed. I wished I'd accepted Ma's slice of bread so I could have given it to Pa to soak up his drink. I watched the edge of the road, but no wild mint poked from the snow on our way to Mr. Collins.

"Yelena, my dear," the postmaster greeted me as we came through his door, then he tipped his head to the side. "And Mr. Federoff, I've the pleasure of your company today."

Pa was addled by his sociability, suspicious that he was being mocked. Fortunately, Viktor arrived just then. He'd grown a mustache since Russian Christmas—to warm him until our wedding, he'd teased. It made him more dashing and less like Buster Keaton. He said, "I'd like a mail-order bride, please." Pearl would have said I blushed from the hole in my stocking to the hole in my head.

Mr. Collins laughed. "You skip work to come here, I know it's serious now."

I had to lick my teeth, they were so dried out with smiling. How I wished Ma could see the fuss being made over me.

Pa reached his muscular arms around Viktor, and though Pa was a towering bear, he nestled into Viktor's embrace. Then Viktor kissed me on the cheek and shook hands with Mr. Collins. "They say you're the man to see about a wedding."

Mr. Collins said, "If you have this gentleman's permission, I might be."

Neither Pa nor I understood who was a gentleman until Viktor nudged Pa. "Gregor? May I have your daughter's hand?"

"Yes, yes, already," Pa said.

To hear him give his approval made my heart rise and fall, a jump rope in my chest. I hadn't had to disobey my father to be with Viktor, and once I got married, I would not have to answer to him. God, the church, my family—before Viktor, there had always been a reason I couldn't do what I wanted.

Mr. Collins recorded my name and Viktor's with his fountain pen. "Allow me," he said and read solemnly from the form: "'Is applicant an imbecile, epileptic, of unsound mind, or under guardianship as a person of unsound mind? Is applicant under the influence of intoxicating liquor or narcotic drug?' That would be a 'No.' For the two of you, anyway." And he sniffed the air.

I hoped Pa had missed Mr. Collins's sleight. His questions were like the litany at confession, and my skipping heart was more anxious than gleeful. What if Mr. Collins got to a question of unsound body? Viktor cleared his throat and spit into his hanky. While such hemming and hawing was common among miners, Viktor had it worse than most.

Mr. Collins slid the marriage license over the counter and pointed to a line where I was to "herewith affix" my name. Type tinier than newsprint covered the legal document, the first I'd seen since Pa's mining contract.

"You're not related by blood, I presume," he said, "and I don't suppose you've had the time to be married once or twice before."

His teasing wrung me out. I was accustomed to being ignored—it was Viktor noticing me that had made me fall for him. Now, no matter where I looked, either the postmaster, Pa, or my future husband was staring at me. Tea slopped around my stomach like in a wash bin, and I lurched forward to catch my balance, stepping hard on Viktor's foot at the same moment he caught my arm. "Steady, there," Viktor said.

A burp in my throat went out into the air, and I put a hand on my gurgling belly just below my ribs. When I looked up at Mr. Collins, his face had closed as surely as if he'd pulled down the curtain at his postal window. I said, "I'm not having cold feet."

"I wasn't thinking you were, my dear." He was no longer chipper. "And whatever you might be having, 'tis none of my business, is it?" To Pa, he said, "So she needs to marry soon, despite being underage." He asked me, "You understand you're marrying a foreign national?"

He tapped the form, but I might as well have been reading soup, the paragraphs bobbing up and down like dumplings. I thought he was casting a vote against Viktor. "He's going to become an American."

"Be that as it may," he said.

Viktor took hold of Mr. Collins's pen to sign in two places, then Mr. Collins showed me where I had to sign in three. Unnerved by the men's attention and the change that had come over Mr. Collins, I signed without reading. And Pa put his X where it mattered.

COAL WARMS YOU TWICE, they say, digging it out and burning it. But within a week, Viktor worked past warming himself, his feet in icy puddles as he picked along a vein, and Stash ran to our house to say that his brother had come home with his teeth rattling. I boiled up horseradish soup and poured it into Kostia's dinner pail, which I'd just scrubbed out. The heavy pail swung me off balance, and like a drunk, I walked weaving and staggering to their house.

Viktor's eyes were craters in his stone face as he sloppily sipped soup. I read to him from his *Farmer's Almanac,* how best to stake tomatoes and a story about a loyal dog. Having made off with Kostia's pail, I had to go home, but Ma let me return in the morning, after

Viktor's brothers left for the mine. She said, "Where's the harm? In his condition, there'll be no monkey business."

He was worse than how I'd left him, delirious with fever. I'd brought a cool cloth to his face when I heard pounding at the front door and my godmother Daria calling, "Yelenie, I'm here from Doc."

I ran downstairs in a panic, pulling her inside from the cold. "Who's sick?"

"No, it's not that." She stomped snow from her boots. "We're only sick of winter is all."

"You scared me." When she took off her coat and scarf, the smell of Doc's office was on her clothes, so she'd already been down the hill and come all the way back up. I filled the kettle and rattled around in the boys' cupboard for their tea tin. "Bread? Jam?" Everything they had that was sweet was something I'd brought.

"Tea is all," she said and sniffed at the potions I'd laid out. "Katya's mint oil." I had hot pepper salve to rub on Viktor's chest and willow sticks to chew on for aches. When I put a cup in front of her, there was a new vial on the table with a skull and crossbones etched in the brown glass.

"You selling door-to-door?" I asked. I didn't want to put money out for half-baked cures.

"No," she said sternly. "Have you heard of miner's lung? They showed us in nursing class how coal dust turns a pink sponge into a black rag."

The bottle's black stopper had a rubber dropper like a nipple, and I ran my thumb across the etched glass. Chicken bumps covered my arms. "You brought me poison?"

"This is morphine. Store it somewhere safe, where no one can take a swig by mistake. Viktor gets to coughing, he could break a rib or worse. And if he can't sleep for hacking, or he coughs up blood, put a drop in hot water for him to drink."

"This will cure what ails him."

"No," she said again, as if I was thick. "Doc says mining will make him worse. He give me this bottle free of charge and shoos me up the hill. He knows you're a good egg, like your ma, and that I'm your godmother. If anyone can get Viktor out of here, it's you."

"Me?"

"My Jimmy says Viktor's handy, and I seen machine shops in Bentleyville, sign-makers, too. Think he could do that? Because this work will surely kill him."

Daria was never one to gloss over things. I'd wanted away from the mines since I could smell the coke ovens, and now she was saying it was up to me to get Viktor away. I was terrified and grateful for her honesty, angry and obliged that she knew my business. She took both my hands in hers. "You don't have to marry him, Lenotchka," she said. "But if you do marry him, you have to help him."

"I have to marry him," I told her.

"Then that's that," Daria said.

IT WASN'T AN HOUR after Daria left that Viktor coughed so hard he spat up blood. I was grateful that he hadn't grown a beard. I squeezed a drop from the skull-and-dagger bottle into his broth, and he drank the potion down.

"Why did you choose me?" Viktor managed to ask, and shame on me, I couldn't help myself. "Who said I chose?" I asked.

"You have to confess your lies come Easter," he said weakly.

I told him that I was lucky Father Dmitri hadn't kicked me out of the church, the way I'd pelted the priest with questions, no matter how many times he said that God didn't have to answer to me. "Why couldn't we have a ham bone to thicken the soup during Lent?"

"What will you tell our children when they ask?"

I told him my old suspicion, that the church made rules to turn poverty into piety. I said, "Since no one could afford meat, why not forbid it?"

He twitched his mustache and said, "Our children will be lucky heretics."

I kissed his wide forehead, stoked with fire, and my kiss put him to sleep, or the morphine did. I left him resting and returned in the morning as his brothers were leaving.

"Not a peep all night," Anton said. "You're a fine nurse."

When he finally opened his eyes, Viktor said, "I dreamed you felt sorry for me."

I mopped his face with a cloth I'd brought from home. "Are you trying to get out of your promise? Because sorry is not what I feel for you. The first time I saw you coming through a cloud of dust to me, you might as well have been on a white horse."

"I'm allergic to horses," he said and halfway smiled his rare, beautiful smile. "You were beating a rug to death. You were yelling at the dirt."

With anyone else, I would have been embarrassed. "I was sending that blasted coal dust back to the mines."

Trying to laugh, Viktor coughed and had a hard time stopping. I pulled him up to sitting. I worked Ma's pepper salve under his shoulder blades until his muscles let him get a breath, then brought him tea the way he liked it, with two spoons of honey in the bottom but not stirred up, which he said was too sweet.

He sipped and nodded, a little color coming back into his face. He patted the quilt. "Sit here."

Some said if you sat on a bed you wouldn't marry for seven years. "I don't want to cause any mischief."

Beneath his mustache, his thick lips were a straight line. "You said yourself, that poor in everything else, we are rich in rules." He spoke without effort, as if from the heart rather than his ragged lungs. "Between the church and the foreman, we don't get many choices. But I want you to know that I chose you without any other voice in my head." He reached out for my hand, and still standing by the bed, I gave it to him. He said, "I don't have a mutka or a butka. And no priest makes my decisions for me, either."

"What are you saying, that I'm not the boss of you?"

"No, Lenotchka, the other side of the coin. I'm saying let's you and me make our own decisions."

I plopped down on the corner of the bed careful not to slosh him with hot tea. "I did that with Ma and Pa. I chose you," I admitted.

"Pavel told me as much. Last night, with all those dreams, I had myself a time of it. I traveled the world talking to the dead and seeing visions."

In the pocket of my jumper, I fingered the brown bottle. "From fever, you reckon?"

"Guilt pangs, I imagine, as there's something I have to confess. Doc thinks my mining days are numbered, that my chest doesn't take to that dust."

After the mines had stunted his growth, scarred his lungs, and buried his father and brother, he'd had the wherewithal to return, climbing down the same hole as before.

"I never wanted to marry a miner," I said. "But if we're confessing . . ." I took out the tiny poison vial of morphine and told him about Daria.

"You drugged me then?" he said.

"Doc's orders," I said. "And I stuck up for you when Ma said you were sickly, so we best get you another line of work."

"Couldn't see your ma or pa pushing you in my direction. I'm a dark horse."

"You're allergic to dark horses," I said.

"You're not usually this sassy, Miss Skinclad." He turned to lay on his side, and I kneaded the thin dough of his back. "I hope this isn't a dream, too," he said, drifting off.

He fell back asleep not even knowing how he'd changed me. *Let's make our own decisions*—choosing him was one of the few decisions I'd ever made.

23

MA WELCOMED MY HELP candying fruit from jars we had put up. And she was happy to have me pick nutmeat from the hickory stash that Borya and I had harvested. Through the summer, I'd washed, peeled, and pitted that fruit; fall, I'd husked hickories, sorted out floaters, and cured the nuts, never once imagining I'd be stirring them into my wedding cake. All this time, I'd been unknowingly preparing the ingredients to grant my own wish, weaving my own red carpet.

And my dress—oh, my dress! Sonya embroidered my sash, and Lethia actually sewed seed pearls on my veil. "Your easy days are over," Lethia said. "Once you marry, you're not the little girl at home." Either she never noticed how much I did or she'd forgotten.

Sonya agreed. "Is always time to cook or wash. You can't believe how much, cleaning pail and filling pail, wash out day's coal every single day just to dirty." Her tiny chain stitches along my sash would wear another woman out, but she grew livelier with each vivid bloom, fussing about the biddies who said her needlework made their towels too beautiful to wipe up a spill. "They say I act like I'm too good for them," she said, showing us her work. "I am." She wrapped me in roses that went from budding to blowsy.

Ma asked my opinion about stroganoff or paprika chicken for the wedding supper, and she had me pick my shoes from the Sears & Roebuck catalog, since no other brides had feet large as me. But when I piped up with particulars that Viktor and I had decided on, she let me know that's not how things were done. "What's got into you?" she asked, hands on her hips.

Let's make our own decisions. We wanted children to be welcome at the supper, we wanted lemonade to drink along with the vodka, we wanted wedding toasts in English. I invited Doc Miller and Mr. and Mrs. G to the reception, and we asked to borrow their Victrola. We were making a dozen decisions a day, together.

Maria was my maid of honor, and Pavel was Viktor's best man. There was every reason to suspect that the two of them could be next. The church had swelled in number with so many new miners, and everyone was invited.

During the ceremony, I was deeply grateful to be Orthodox, despite not understanding most of what Father Dmitri said. The church had brought me Viktor, who was a miner but not a drunk. And he wouldn't be a miner for long. To think that my jeda had inked the prayer books that the priest was reading from, and that nearly everyone there had ties to the same village as Viktor and me—I was doubly and triply bound and watched over.

I struggled inside my extravagant dress to bow to the ground, get up, and bow again. When we promised to make our own decisions, I almost decided that this rigmarole was for the birds. Habit took me through the motions, and I wondered if we'd make our children do this, a thought that rapped me on the head like Pa's spoon—*our children.*

When Father Dmitri swung the elaborate silver censer, Viktor pushed his finger across his mustache, an effort not to sneeze. Allergic to incense as well as vodka. He might be the first Staroobryadtsy not to drink at his own wedding!

Although vanity was one of the deadly sins, I loved my dress and the way I looked in it. Pride, of course, was another sin—the worst—but this kind of pride couldn't possibly be sinful, could it? I stood up in front of my community, with a man I loved, the people I loved at my back. I wished I knew the meaning of every prayer that Father Dmitri said over us and every word we repeated together. Winter's murky light came through the high windows to slant across the icons.

In this harsh church of brittle rules, whose heroes were martyred rather than make a single change, I'd been taught blind devotion, sin, and shame. But singled out for blessings at my wedding, I was lifted up and carried along rather than penned in by the church. Viktor already knew these prayers that our people had been chanting for hundreds of years. Ma and Pa recited theirs together each night before bed. We could do that too.

I was every inch the blushing bride with the pleasure of becoming Yelena Gomelekoff. The thrill of making our own decisions thrummed through my whole body, no jitters in my stomach or tears in my eyes. Good thing, because crying would make black paste run down my face. Although wearing makeup was a sin, people looked the other way at your wedding, and Lethia had lengthened my eyelashes with a paste of ash and Vaseline. As for cutting my hair, Ma had skirted that for years. Now that I was a woman, I'd have to grow it out. Unless we made our own decisions.

Viktor and me left the church hand in hand, husband and wife. I almost wished we could walk right past the crowd and go to his house, where his brothers had turned over a bedroom to us and moved in with friends for a few nights. From my disgust at learning how babies were made, I'd come around to the idea of Viktor's hands on me and more.

"After we celebrate with everyone," Viktor said, "we'll celebrate alone tonight." He whispered the last lines of Pushkin's tale in my ear, "Never since the World's creation, was there such a celebration. I was there, drank mead and yet, barely got my whiskers wet."

Mr. G and Pezzato were waiting for us, his cart adorned with paper roses, to lead the procession to Ma and Pa's house. A great feast was set in our house and the one next door: bread and salt followed by cheese with apples, nuts, and pickles, then barley, mushrooms, and paprika chicken from coops up and down the hillside, including Widow Joedsky's and Mr. and Mrs. G's.

Sonya had made me a wedding apron with two lace-trimmed pockets that she'd labeled *His* and *Hers*. Maria and Pavel went table to table, greeting the guests and either collecting money or encouraging them to fill my pockets. The two of them sang to the guests: "Let's drink to Olga, she's such a fine cook. No one in the world bakes bread as fine as Olga's." People clinked and cheered as Olga's husband Humpy stuffed money into the *His* pocket. "Let's drink to Humpy, he's still got his looks. Nowhere in the world will you see such a head of hair." Viktor kissed me with each toast, our guests beckoning us to turn the bitter wine sweet, though our own glasses were full of cider. And then the dancing began: women, couples, single men and women, just men. I danced with my new husband and wanted to hold onto him all night. Anyone else who danced with me paid for the privilege, and the men joked about which pocket got their money while the women made a show of transferring money from the *His* to the *Hers* pocket.

Pavel toasted us with another of his father's sayings: "Out of respect for God, who breathed life into us, we don't smoke. And out of respect for God, who gave us alcohol as a gift to make life more joyous, we drink!"

Pa began the Cossack foolishness, and he urged Viktor to follow him as he squatted and kicked out one heel then the other. Pa wouldn't be walking tomorrow, and the day after would be worse, as the dance worked its way through his muscles.

Our wedding was a joy until it was too much for Viktor. First, his brother linked arms with him to circle around his father-in-law. Then Pa wanted his attention. "Dance with me!" he commanded. "I give you my Yelena, don't I?"

They let go of each other to cross their arms in front of their chests like a ledge. I was impressed at Viktor's bounce and kick. It was as if he were made of rubber, the way he stretched up and then down, flinging out one leg and then another.

"Go! Go! Go!" the men chanted, so loudly they did not hear him bubbling up. I saw it before I heard it, clouds of hot air puffing out in front of him. Viktor separated his hands to cover his mouth. Dipping under the circling men, he began a full-blown spell.

"Some air, pozhaluysta." Pavel asked for space in the crowd.

I stayed behind Pavel's outstretched arm until Lethia tugged on my apron. I'm ashamed to say I twisted out of her grip—old habits die hard. My sister's hooded eyes welled with concern. "Go to your husband, Yelena. He needs his wife."

All the names Lethia had called me had never been my own, and I stood there, disoriented. "Yelena," she'd said my name with such urgency, and she told me to go to my *husband* who needed his *wife*. Viktor and me had become each other's responsibility. Although we had repeated as much in front of everyone in the church, it was Lethia's plea that shocked me into married life.

Pavel's arm readily yielded to my push. He hadn't meant to keep me out. I was the one Viktor needed to rub between his shoulder blades and get him to sip water. While I hated seeing him hack up coal dust on our wedding day, I felt privileged to be in the clearing his brothers had made. With every minute, I was growing toward Viktor and away from this place.

I'd dreaded being married off to one of the miners to repeat the life my mother had already lived. But me and Viktor had a voice now, and helped by the money in my apron pockets —his *and* hers—we would get him out of the mines and us out of Marianna. We'd made our vows in front of God and everyone. As Viktor spit gray gobs on the ground at my feet, he was cementing a vow I was making on the spot, that we would be gone come spring and he would no longer descend every morning into the sooty underworld he carried deep within his lungs.

24

IF OUR WEDDING NIGHT wasn't everything I'd dreamed, the next day was. Viktor got home to our bed with only enough energy for hugging and some sweet talk. I slept in the crook of my husband's arm and listened to his wet snores. He simmered like a pot of porridge, bubbling up a time or two. But come morning, when I threw back the quilt, he caught the hem of my nightdress to show how a good night's sleep had rejuvenated him.

The company allowed men a day off after their wedding, without pay. And in broad daylight, under the wedding-ring quilt Ma had stitched, my new husband embarrassed and thrilled me and caused me some amount of pain with that kielbasa of his. I didn't know what I'd tolerate as a married woman until Viktor got long and stiff again, and he guided me on top of him. We were tender with each other but also, as the days went on, randy as rabbits.

Anton, Stash, and Pavel returned to their house, our house, at week's end. They said they were better off piled in one bedroom if the princess was willing to boil their laundry and their beets. Not much of a princess, I wasn't even a decent wife, seeing as how Viktor was getting skinnier, his paper bag pants bunching worse than ever. "I was raised on nothing," Viktor said. "That must be all I need." We were the same height and weight, but where I stored some fat in my hips and my bushy tail—like a squirrel, he liked to say—he had none to store.

Stash pounded new holes in his belt, too. He said, "Wish I had some of your ma's potatoes. She made us the best kartofel."

"That was me," I told him. "I know a hundred ways to make potatoes."

The next day, they came uphill tossing what must have been a forty-pound sack back and forth like a playground ball. Stash also had two bottles of vodka, one in each of his coverall pockets. I scrubbed the spuds while the men scrubbed up, then Stash nudged me aside. "Don't bother peeling," he said, quartering and plopping them, skins on, into a pot of water.

I hadn't thought to serve up what Viktor couldn't eat. Once the potatoes were tender, I added butter, garlic, and parsley, coating them in their own creamy starch. For Viktor, I roasted parsnips, tossing peels to their canaries. Gleb and Boris came from Borya, who'd gone back to raising birds solely for Old Believers.

Stash said, "What kind of Russian can't eat potatoes?" and he lifted his fork like a blessing. He said, "What kind of Russian can't drink vodka?" and drained his glass. He thought that was funny, but it was Anton's teasing that got us all going.

Anton pretended the pot was too heavy to lift, then he set his face blank except to raise one eyebrow and somehow shrink himself down from a brick wall to a column to resemble Viktor. He scooped mounds onto his plate, making fart noises as he spooned. I was horrified at first, until Viktor twitched his mustache my way, and then we all howled with laughter, setting off the canaries in their corner cage. Pavel said, "Our princess is a good sport," which was nicer than saying our princess had stuffing between her ears.

I packed dinner pails for Viktor and his brothers, cooked their suppers, scrubbed their laundry, and mended their clothes. I put up tomatoes, beans, and pickles galore from Anton's garden. I cooked their soup and their soap, knitted their sweaters and their socks. If one of them was sick, I watched over him. Though if anyone was sick, it was likely Viktor.

At night, Viktor and me lay on our sides in bed, my bushy tail in his lap. He said we'd need a car to get to Pittsburgh, let alone Erie or

Detroit. Really, a *car?* Might as well ask for a towel that could turn into a river, a comb that could turn into a forest. I thought he was finding ways to keep us back, like his take on the Coloreds. He said their kind had been as eager to come to Marianna as I was to get out, but that people had it in for them.

When Viktor talked, he tickled my ear with his mustache, which gave me a good shiver. He said, "Black Toby had an uncle strung up in West Virginia for building a house on his own land. Our people got on the boat of our free will and showed up for a paying job, but Coloreds come here before us and not because they wanted to. Seems like they try to make it on their own, everyone's against them."

I didn't come to this country; I was born here, and I said, "I'm not against them." Aside from Kostia's friend Fergus, the only Colored person I knew to talk to was Doc Miller's housekeeper, Myrna, who handed over his mending to me or to Daria to give to me. I thought her name was beautiful. One time, I put my plain burlap hand by Myrna's velvet brown one. Then I lifted up a hank of my hair, straight as hers was springy. "Aren't we knit from two sacks of wool?" I said.

"Black sheep, white sheep," Myrna answered back, and we'd shared a laugh.

A car was enough of a hurdle to our leaving, but I asked Viktor, "What's their troubles got to do with us?"

"Folks get worked up about us knowing our place, too. At home, they'd say, 'A goose is not a pig's friend.'"

I'd heard as much years ago from Harry's Detroit friend, after Lethia asked if he'd visit her again. "You want to stay here with the pigs?"

"I'm used to pigs," he said. He brushed his horse lips against my neck as if I had a sugar cube tucked there. Then he let out a long, ragged sigh. "You know what I been through, going from pillar to post twice now. We're among kin here. Maybe we make our own decisions and stick around."

If he suffocated from coal dust or was crushed in a cave-in, I'd be a widow in this pigpen. His chest was pressed against my back, so I felt the gurgle in each breath he took with his percolating lungs. Stay or go? It was the same choice Ma and Pa had to make.

I turned over so we were nose to nose. I wanted me and him to have a future together, and I reached under his nightshirt. "What we could do is make our own family." The whites of his eyes shone in the dark. I could feel that he liked that idea, too.

"If you say so, Miss Skinclad."

"That's Mrs. Bonescraper to you," I said.

He pushed my nightshirt up to my waist and soon enough I had my Bonescraper between my legs. I'm sure we made quite a ruckus. With the bed squeaking under us like a rickety wagon, we practically scooted out the door.

"ERIE'S SNOW STARTS AT Thanksgiving and is chest high come Russian Christmas." Olga swayed her little Manny side to side. "Meanwhile, Detroit lost their priest, so there's no one to do baptizing, and where the Russians live, in Hamtramck, there's Poles and Coloreds."

Maria said, "We all went to school together—Poles, Coloreds, Irish—so what?"

"We were kids then," Olga said, picking up steam. "Detroit's twice as far as Erie, and Viktor's a miner. He can't drive, what does he know about making cars in Detroit?"

He could drive, I would have said, if I could have gotten a word in edgewise. Jimmy, Daria's husband, let him drive their car, and they worked on it together. I said, "Nobody makes a whole car. One man attaches a bumper. Another screws on the headlight." I didn't tell them Viktor wanted us to somehow buy our own car.

Olga opened her housedress, pushing her soska into her baby's mouth as he thrashed in her arms. "So hungry he can't eat, the little fool."

I'd spent so much time raising other people's babies that I knew to stroke little Manny's cheek, from ear to chin, which stopped him flailing. I said, "Those are their sucking muscles—you have to remind them sometimes."

She said, "You ain't seen fussy until you seen Lethia's Ivan. With that one on her hands, Ma hardly has time for mine." So Lethia was keeping her from her own ma.

Though Olga had a bushel of reasons we should stay, Maria gave the only one not to go. She said, "You can't take Viktor from his brothers." That was my worry, that after all they'd gone through together, I'd be the wedge that split their family tree. The longer we stayed, the easier it was to stay. Some mean corner of my heart had always blamed the mining families for wallowing in their own misery, but I wasn't doing any better, even hearing Viktor's cough and knowing that each day in the mines could be his last. Then, as the leaves fell, I was the one who started feeling poorly.

Hadn't I said we should make our own family? Viktor and me were thrilled, except for my being sick as a dog and trapped, my growing belly a boulder I'd rolled directly in my own way. I was supposed to be getting us out of here; instead, I'd made it harder to leave.

"You're getting big so fast, might be twins," Daria said. "I ripped like a sheet with my youngest, and that was just one. Doc had to stitch me back together. Two layers of stitching," she said with some pride. "Doc said miners who'd busted their head open didn't bleed as much as me." She touched my ballooning stomach and scared me silly.

But Daria also walked with me down to Doc, who to my relief felt only one head and one bum in my womb. He saw me having a rough time of it and gave me menthol drops to suck on, which he said I could share with Viktor if he had a coughing fit. "Daria?" he said, and she scooted out the door so we'd be alone.

"A few more weeks of this is all," he said, "though for some it lasts longer," then he was done talking about the baby. Pacing the length of the exam room, he opined over what damage is borne by a lifetime of mining. "Some can endure but not all," he said. When he said he'd expected us to have left by now, I said I'd die trying. That's when Doc Miller planted himself in front of me and took me by the shoulders, like the time we faced off over Eva. He said, "He'll die first. You have to get him away from here."

STILL, WE DIDN'T LEAVE, we didn't leave, and we didn't leave. Moving cost money, Viktor had no job prospects, and I could barely keep food down. On a good day, I retched two or three times. Bad days, I stayed in the toilet. My sickness wasn't letting up, and every week there was a reason to wish we'd left two weeks earlier. On our first anniversary, I cooked a hearty breakfast of buckwheat groats, dried cherries, and brown bread with honey. As the boys burrowed into their porridge, Viktor surprised me with a calico pouch I suspected Ma might have made. Inside was a Russian cross on a chain.

"Yelena," he said. "Thank you for marrying me. It's steel, though you deserve silver."

"Steel," Pavel scoffed.

"Don't," I stopped him. We'd been counting every penny, and I didn't want to hear that Viktor had splurged on silver but told me otherwise. I would have bawled even if I wasn't pregnant. I gave him the socks I'd knitted in red, his favorite color.

"Here's for putting up with us this year," Anton said. He handed me a baton of newspaper, tied with twine, a gift of paper on the first anniversary. He knew I used to horde whatever scrap I could get my hands on, and here was today's unread edition: February 6, 1917.

Pavel said, "Like a squirrel with a nest you were when we met you."

I kissed each of them on the cheek. The newspaper was no longer a luxury, though having anything first still was. They'd usually pawed through the pages by the time I got my turn. With a tug, I unfurled the day's news, and the huge black headlines made me drop the paper like a hot potato. Had a mine collapsed nearby? Had America joined the war? The boys huddled around the table as I read: "No More Orientals—Immigration Act Official." Beneath the banner was a scowling President Wilson. He'd rejected the law three times in as many years. This time his veto hadn't stuck.

I stared at a map with the "Asiatic Barred Zone" striped like a prisoner's suit. Instead of the Immigration Act, it should have been called the Anti-Immigration Act.

Anton said, "We're here—they can't make a law against us."

I fingered the cross around my neck to show Viktor I already cherished it, and I bit my quivering lip. They had to get going down the hill, no matter what the new law said. My knights gathered their dinner buckets, and Viktor flashed his ankle to show me he'd slipped on his new socks. He put his scarred hands around mine. "Lenotchka, we'll figure this out together."

On the porch, I heard a scuffle. "You numbskull," Stash said to Pavel.

"Durak," Pavel called himself an idiot. "That went over like a fart in church."

I wished we were already settled in our next town. I wished Ma and Pa had taken my advice and applied for their papers to be Americans. I wished Viktor had been here long enough for that. I stayed in my kitchen chair, too puny to do much of anything. Why clear the table or scrub the porridge pot? I couldn't see that anything made any difference, and here I was bringing a baby into this mess. Though Russia went all the way to Asia, Suwalki was in Europe—did that matter? I read the paper top to bottom. Were foreigners allowed to leave the mines if the company had paid their way here? Were there rules about hiring foreigners for work? What would happen to families who got separated? There were still men who mined here in the winter and returned to Suwalki for farming in spring—what about them?

None of the answers I wanted were in the paper, and then Olga and Maria dropped by.

"Humpy agrees we need to keep out the Chinese. And them that can't read or write their own language."

"That would have ruled out Humpy's family," Maria said.

"My pa, too," I said.

Olga tensed with her baby's eager sucking and pressed her free arm against the other breast. "Keeps me from gushing." It didn't keep her from talking. She said, "Daria tells me Doc patched up the Piserelli cousins from a knife fight, and now the company is sending them back. Foreigners need to keep out of trouble."

Maria said, "A few of the men at our house registered for their citizenship test. Mr. Collins has a booklet that Viktor and you could study."

I said, "I don't need to study up. Or take any test."

Manny let loose a milk burp, souring the air, and I took little sips of breath to keep from gagging.

"What if men leave the mines," Maria asked. "That's what the boarders want to know. Can they stay in America?"

"You won't know till it's too late," Olga said, but then she bent my head against her shoulder and let my tears fall on the head of her squirming baby, probably a future miner. The Coloreds, the Chinese, us—when they needed us to break our backs, they handed out tickets. After that, we were not for village, not for town, as the old Russians say.

I'D LOST MY GET up and go, except to be sick in the toilet. Then I sat on the floor itself looking through the grimy window I hadn't managed to clean. Fat white flakes swirled down with no thought to where they'd roost. It was the coldest March anyone could remember, and I sat there envying the snowflakes coming at me. How did Ma endure this again and again, most of her life? She'd had seven babies. Viktor's mutka had had six. Sonya had already had five. Also, they'd each lost a baby—Viktor's ma had lost a grown son, too—which would have laid me lower if I wasn't already on the floor.

The sheets on the line needed to be brought in, and I should have been stoking the stove and starting up a meal. All the snow had to do was fall from the sky, mounting into drifts that simply followed nature's bidding, gathering black dust and crusting over until they finally melted, running willy-nilly down the hillside.

That was low, envying the snow. Lower still was turning into a ninny. When the boys came through the door that night without Viktor, I panicked. "Where is he?" I dashed to the porch, imagining grisly accidents and devious ways Russia might force him into battle. Or maybe America was the problem, and they'd weeded him out as weak.

Anton assured me he was fine, but I didn't believe him until "Buffalo Gals, Won't You Come Out Tonight," wafted uphill. For a man with such breathing trouble, Viktor sure could whistle. I bawled at my husband returning unharmed but really at what might have been.

Viktor folded me into his long arms. He told me that on the walk home, he'd asked Mrs. G if she had something for my stomach—he pulled a netted bag of herbs from his pocket. "There, there," he kissed my head. "Tell Junior I'm doing my best."

Stash said, "You may be doing your best in Germany."

A look of anger passed from Viktor to his brother, something I'd never seen.

"What?" Stash shrugged. "Someone had better tell our princess."

What Viktor hadn't said—why he'd sought out Mrs. G—was that the tsar himself had stepped down. He handed me the evening paper, rolled tight as a stick of dynamite. I was starting to hate the paper, which I unscrolled to read, "Tsar Nicholas Dethroned on Way to Petrograd."

I still thought of Petrograd as St. Petersburg, renamed because *-burg* was German. The tsar's train had been stopped in Pskov, and right there sitting on the train he was forced to sign away his throne. "Who's in charge if not him?" I asked.

"Nobody knows," Anton said. He pointed farther down the page, and I read, "'Russia today is neither a republic nor a monarchy. The form of government is in suspense.'"

Tsar Nicholas gave Old Believers nearly as much trouble as he gave the Jews, so this might be one less worry for those in Suwalki. And the tsarina wasn't even Russian; she was a German princess—granddaughter of Queen Victoria—who'd had to learn Russian when she married.

I scrambled to get food on the table as the boys, apart from Viktor, toasted the tsar's demise. "Is Russia over?" I asked.

Viktor's face was flat as my iron. "If it is, then my father, my mother, my dead brothers, and my country are over."

Poor Viktor. My father, brother, and mother were all here in Marianna, the only home I'd known, and here I was counting the hours until we could leave.

In the next few days, we learned that Russia wasn't over, but no one knew who was in charge, either. Just as upsetting was America joining the war, though our men and theirs would be on the same side. Miners twenty-one to thirty-five had to report to Mr. Collins, who registered them for the Selective Service, citizen and noncitizen alike.

Another boulder rolled in our path. If we moved and Viktor was drafted, I'd be pregnant and alone in a new city. That night, I practically rocked the bed with my fretting, scared when the baby kicked and even more scared when it settled down.

"Shh, it will all come right," Viktor soothed me. "As for the service, the talk is that you have to pass a physical. Who'd want me wheezing and sneezing in their foxhole?"

We scooted as close as we could with me six months along, nose to nose and toes to toes, Viktor called it. I said, "I'll make you a big bowl of mashed potatoes just before the exam."

"You'd do that for me?" He kissed my swollen breasts. If they stamped him as unfit for service, they might deport him. I told myself I should enjoy him while he was mine.

ANTON AND STASH HAD an announcement to make at dinner. They counted, "Odin, dva, tri! We're enlisting!"

"You're too young," I said to Stash.

"For Selective Service, I'm too young. Men over twenty-one have to register, but you can enlist at eighteen."

"We're thinking we'll be better paid and better fed in the service," Anton said. "No offense, Yelena."

I hadn't taken offense until he said that. Lately, I was just as likely to burn as bake the bread, and with meat costing an arm and a leg, I hoped Uncle Sam could better afford to feed them. Mr. Collins told them there was a volunteer bonus, which Anton wanted to share with us. They also figured that enlisting lessened the chances that Viktor would be needed. Pavel would be eighteen soon enough and could join them. That was three men before America would have to call on Viktor, was their reasoning.

We spent some of our savings for their train tickets to the recruitment center in Pittsburgh. At the sendoff, Ma did most of the cooking, because I'd lost my touch. She fussed that I'd been neglecting the domovoi, but she was cross with me as well. "You gave them your moving money?"

I put my arm around my husband. "Our money," I said, though spending money to sign up for a war did sound glupyy.

"Butt out," Pa said to Ma. "We made our mistakes, let them make theirs."

She slipped a hanky into my pocket, laying her hand flat on my hip so I knew to wait until we got home to find two silver dollars in there. I was sure they were the ones she'd been saving for me since my birthday in Bentleyville, the day Eva died.

But it takes a lot of coke to make ships and a lot of coal to power them. And while Anton and Stash were getting themselves to Pittsburgh on our dime, President Wilson was declaring the mines essential to the war effort. The two hadn't even finished filling out their recruitment forms when miners were deemed exempt from serving—the recruitment center took up their registrations to rip them in half.

After all that fuss, the two of them were back at our supper table by week's end. Anton said, "Saved me from failing their test. Get a load of this."

He'd made off with his Devens Literacy Test, a page of yes or no questions where the order was "No" and then "Yes," maybe as the first test of literacy. It started sensible enough—*Do dogs bark? Is coal white? Does a baby cry?*—before it began reading like *Foolish Questions: Do ships sail on railroads? Do stones float in the air?*

"Dogs bark and coal ain't white," Stash said, "but four or five in and I was skipping around the page, underlining five-dollar words. You know all these?"

Should criminals <u>forfeit</u> liberty?	No	Yes
Is a <u>dilapidated</u> garment <u>nevertheless</u> clothing?	No	Yes
Is <u>irony</u> connected with blast furnaces?	No	Yes
Are milksops likely to <u>perpetrate</u> violent offenses?	No	Yes

"I want to," I said, and Pavel laughed.

Viktor said, "That's why I married her, boys, aside from her love of milksops."

Anton said, "I'd chewed my pencil to a stub when the big brass came in. Don't the president sound like Pa? 'Miners are too valuable to serve in the army and must return underground.'"

The boys had gone gallivanting around Pittsburgh and missed two days' wages besides. I felt relieved. I felt robbed. Though their train fares gnawed at me, I'm proud to say I didn't begrudge them riding the Monongahela Incline and feeding bears at the Highland Park Zoo.

Cooking Sunday supper, I scorched the rice and sliced off the very tip of my finger dicing onions. It was ridiculous, considering I'd been slicing and dicing since I could stand on a stool by the sink.

Pavel wrapped my finger tight for the bleeding to stop. He said, "This baby can't come soon enough. You'll whittle yourself down to a stump, and then what kind of mother will you be?"

My finger throbbed in time to my head. Good or bad, I'd be a mother stuck in Marianna. While Anton and Stash had tried to help, there was no escaping their sooty tomb even for a battlefield. *Is irony connected to blast furnaces? Does a baby cry?*

25

MA SAID A MORNING would come when I'd shake the spiderwebs from my head and have double my dash, two hearts beating blood through me. I was nearly seven months along when that day finally arrived, and wasn't Viktor delighted to see me through windows wiped clean of thick coal dust, turnips peeled for the pot, and neatly folded and mended clothes? I put some trout lilies and salt-and-pepper sprigs in a bottle, as if we lived in a meadow and not above a slag heap.

Anton had left me his literacy test—*Is coal white? Is misuse of money an evil?*—and I intended to give the rest a go. I missed tackling Miss Kelly's tests and showing what I'd learned, but instead of school, what came back to me was sitting at the kitchen table with Ma. "We patch our patches. We make broth from a bone." She'd made our drudgery sound like music, and then she'd told me to use the coal-filled pencil to get away from our coal-filled life.

I flipped Anton's test over, and on the blank side, I started writing a letter to Nadja's Rita, as if we'd been pen pals for years. Ma stayed in touch with Nadja, so I knew that Rita and her husband had moved to Erie and brought Nadja to live with them. Though Rita had left as a child, I wrote to her as if we were bosom buddies who could ask anything of each other. I told her we hoped to move as soon as my baby came, but I had such qualms. Could she help me and Viktor the way Max and Nadja had helped Ma and Pa? I wouldn't have thought I could do that until I waved my magic wand over the page. I signed it "Always, Yelena."

Then I wrote Xenia, too, signing it the same way, and it was her answer that came first. She said we could stay with them and their four children in Pittsburgh as long as we could stand it! I hadn't seen Xenia since Sonya's wedding, but Viktor hadn't seen her since they were eight years old in Suwalki. When I heard from Rita, she wasn't appalled that I'd asked for so much. She said to come as soon as we could, and she told me about her husband, Leo, and their baby, Irene, who'd just been baptized.

Viktor and me read the letters back and forth. I presented him with Ma's wadded-up hanky, which he unwrapped. Lifting out one of the silver dollars, he said, "Well, what do you know?" He perched it on his thumb, ready to flip. "How about heads, Erie, tails, Pittsburgh?"

He didn't mention Detroit. From reading the papers, I knew about the black sky in Pittsburgh. Also, there was no church there. "Erie," I said.

Rather than flipping the coin, he held it up so that Miss Liberty's head faced me. "Erie it is then," my husband agreed.

I told him the dollars were for the car fund—"Only ninety-eight dollars to go"—and he laughed, showing his beautiful mouthful of teeth.

"I hear the first two dollars are the hardest," he said.

Although I wanted to hold on until Fourth of July, America's birthday, Hazel Angelina Gomelekoff arrived on July 1, 1917, a whopping nine pounds. I came up with the name Hazel as soon as I looked into her big round eyes, green flecked with brown and gold. My eyes.

For her saint's name, we chose Angelina, which I rested in the middle because Father Dmitri said naming a baby for the closest saint's birthday was more a tradition than a rule. That was a first, for him to suggest rather than decree. It made me feel rich giving her a middle name. Pavel and Maria agreed to be our baby's godparents. At her baptism, Father Dmitri said that Angelina was the rare saint who hadn't been burned or flayed or stretched on a wheel, what he called a lucky life. She had died of old age after burying her husband, Saint Stephen, and her sons, Saints John and George. A lucky life, indeed.

Two months later, Viktor and I were climbing the hill from church, Hazel tied to my back, when he led me into the Irish Quarter. As we walked past a coupe parked in the street, a rare sight, he offered me his arm and asked me, "Wouldn't you rather ride than walk, Mrs. Bonescraper?"

"Why, yes, Mr. Bonescraper," I replied, and wasn't I surprised when he strolled us up to Paddy Hanrahan's very house? The door swung open to Paddy's red-nosed pa, who clapped Viktor on the back and put out his hand. I freed my arm and took a step back, I was so shocked. Digging deep in his pocket, Viktor brought out Ma's hanky, spreading open the lacey edges to reveal a stack of bills with the coins on top. "One, two," he stacked our silver dollars in Hanrahan's palm, then counted out dozens of dollar bills, fives, and even two tens up to a hundred dollars. He folded the edges of the hanky over the top like an envelope.

"Missus," Hanrahan called out and presented the tidy package to his wife, who fingered Ma's lacework around the edges. Viktor followed him to the street, where he opened the wide door of the dark green coupe, keys dangling from the steering wheel. "It's peace you've brought to my household," Paddy's pa said meekly, but he showed his Irish when Viktor wouldn't drink from his flask.

"I'll send all our brothers to share a drink," Viktor said, "seeing as how this was mostly their doing." He turned to me. "You think Borya can hold his liquor?"

"My Borya?" I asked. Borya was all of eight. I figured Anton, Stash, and Pavel had kicked in, but my brothers, too, even Kostia?

Viktor twitched his mustache. "I promised to keep it under my hat, but you two beat it out of me." He told me, "Now that you know, you can make them each a pie."

"That's some deal, a pie for a car," Hanrahan said.

"You've never had her pies," Viktor told him.

I untied Hazel so I could twirl her around. "Uncle Kostia, Uncle

Boris," I said. "Uncle Anton, Uncle Stash, Uncle Pavel." I was giddy with their generosity, unearned as grace.

ON OUR LAST DAY in Marianna, we drove the coupe down the hill. Viktor wanted to get gas and a once-over at the filling station, and I wanted to say goodbye to Father Dmitri, who was preparing a service for St. Andrew the Fool for Christ. The priest laid one hand on my head and the other on Hazel's, blessing us right there in the middle of the church. Back up Russian Hill, the rutted roads bounced us like a buckboard past Beeson Street, Maple, Oklahoma, Ash, Hill. Tomorrow morning, we would coast down this coal-pocked, godforsaken road, and I would finally see Pittsburgh. Maybe someday I'd get all the way to Oklahoma. Anything seemed possible, the two of us with our tiny Hazelnut, who would grow bored of hearing me tell her that she was lovely and smart and precious.

I baked all afternoon, and once the boys were home and had scrubbed the workday off themselves, we piled into the coupe instead of walking. I'd left cherry pies cooling in the kitchen for Viktor's brothers, and on the floor at my feet, I had two for my own. I thought of the time Kostia chucked a nickel Ma gave him into the reservoir so Pa wouldn't find it, and I hoped he hadn't given his last nickel to us. And Borya, who imagined every canary he raised saved a miner's life, may very well have saved ours.

Soon as we pulled up to Ma and Pa's, children ran at us full tilt. Only Sonya's youngest and mine were girls. Lethia claimed Hazel, Borya claimed the pies, and Pa grabbed hold of Pavel's vodka. Inside the rowdy house, I was issued an apron and a paring knife.

"Did you take a joyride when you knew we were waiting?" Ma said, accepting flowers from Stash.

As Pavel struggled to open the tinned herring, Pa said, "Be grateful you didn't marry this weakling."

Lethia told Pearl, "If I'd known you were making your poppy seed cakes, I'd have brought one of Sergei's cousins."

And Borya said, "Pearly, you baked bread instead of your bricks?"

A stranger might not have been able to tell that folks wished us well. *I heard Hanrahan say that his car was a waste of gas. You'll have to do your own mending in Erie. Thank me after you clean the pan. Did you pull a muscle figuring that out?* I tried to remember if I'd ever heard someone on Russian Hill say, *I'm glad for you and I wish you well.*

These people had such a hard life, and then they turned around and made themselves hard to love. We would eat in shifts, whatever bottle was opened would have to be finished, and by the end of the night, there could well be words. I wouldn't be surprised if Stash took a swing at Harry, who brought out the worst in people. I was leaving in good health, of my own free will, and with their help. Not many got to do that, not enough.

I'd already packed the baby clothes Sonya had stitched for Hazel, some from our little Eva. I'd wrapped them around the blue-and-white pitcher Ma prized because it wasn't Russian, the one she'd threatened our lives if we broke. "Where's the Chinese pitcher?" someone would no doubt ask at tonight's meal, and the answer from now on would be, "At Yelena's house." In Ma and Pa's trunk, which we were also taking, I'd put in some of Ma's worked lace, a prayer service her father had copied, my book of Russian fairy tales, and a pocket-sized icon of St. Nicholas that Pa got from his pa and gave to Viktor and me. Ma's tin had stayed in the trunk, and I scooped ashes from our stove, so that domovoi or not, I'd have the devil I knew with me.

WITH EACH MILE WE drove away from Marianna, the world opened wider. I thought of how Pearl and me used to gather daffodils still in bud, because they bloomed already dusted in ash. And how, while fresh air was easier to come by on Russian Hill than in the stripes below us, it still reeked of rotten eggs. Out on the open road, fall was going great guns, such that the trees seem to catch fire.

I raised my nose into the wind to smell cows, grass, skunk, hay, apples. The sky was the color of laundry bluing.

A few miles before Washington City, Viktor said, "I have something to show my girls." He took us to a covered bridge I knew from postcards. Other than the cave-in of 1908, when I saw windows blown out by the explosion and caskets lined up near the train tracks, I hadn't witnessed something in person that had been on a postcard.

Viktor drove onto the red-planked bridge, a barn floating over a creek, pulling on the headlights to see in the cavernous dark. Our thudding wheels echoed in our ears, and when we came out the other side, there was a sloping field waiting for us. Viktor parked facing the bridge.

I spread our worn quilt between the coupe and the stream, whose current paraded a show of leaves, then I filled Hazel up until milk bubbled out of her mouth. Viktor coaxed a burp from her as I unwrapped drumsticks, sliced turnips, pickles, and apple cake. Nursing made me so ravenous I could barely chew for swallowing.

Another family pulled in looking like Sunday drivers in a magazine advertisement. Their children tumbled out of the car to throw pebbles in the water and giggle at the wind whirling leaves into little twisters. The father snoozed by a tree. We looked much the same as them, Viktor in his herringbone flat cap and me in my felted wool coat, our chubby-cheeked baby warming in a spot of sun by our shiny car. I felt that I was finally starting to live my life.

A few miles beyond our picnic was Washington City, where a domed courthouse topped by a statue of George Washington filled an entire block of Main Street. Viktor had heard that it cost a million dollars to build. "How many zeroes in a million?" he asked, and I counted up.

"Six," I said. I'd never imagined anything costing that much, and I welcomed having to think bigger. We stopped at a traffic light behind a line of cars—two more novelties—and then a third: a woman on the sidewalk held my gaze as she took a long drag off a cigarette. Viktor rounded the corner to drive through a gate in front of a majestic red-brick building with two towers.

"Are we allowed here?" I asked.

"It don't say 'No Trespassing.'" A tombstone sign was carved WASHINGTON AND JEFFERSON COLLEGE, AN INSTITUTION FOR PRESBYTERIAN MEN. I'd never met anyone who went to college, unless Teddy Roosevelt counted. Young men in suits were doing what Ma would call lollygagging, paging through books or talking in clusters around the green groomed grounds. Near a rose garden, couples sat on benches. I figured I had as much right as they did to be here. I can't explain why I felt proud, but I was beaming. When the circle around campus returned us to the gate, Viktor asked, in a lofty voice, "Shall we be on our way?"

"Yes, let us commence," I answered.

If Washington City was all that, I expected Pittsburgh to be even more so, having longed to see Steel City since I started reading newspaper scraps to Ma. The closer we got, the less I could see. A strip of grime lined the rivers like a bathtub ring, and I lost count of the smokestacks striping the sky, on a Sunday no less. When I said that Anton and Stash never mentioned the gloom, Viktor said they didn't want to complain about the lark we'd treated them to.

Viktor drove onto a bridge whose open gratings hung by a steel thread, and the river reek rose through the gratings, stinkier than a messy diaper. Spewing barges chugged beneath us, with more barges docked along the banks. We rolled the windows up, we rolled the windows down. Pittsburgh smelled like an outhouse—sewage and the ammonia of burning coke—with an oily stench far worse than Marianna. My stomach flipped like a runny egg.

Manchester Bridge was topped by the carving of a coal miner bent to his work, a carved cone of light coming from his cap. In my head, I toyed with the loop of crossing the Allegheny beneath this miner who was carved from the rock that bore the coal he mined.

Viktor hadn't been bothered by the hayfields or orchards of the countryside, but the dustpan air of Pittsburgh had him sneezing in threes. I worried he'd wrench the wheel and send us careening off the bridge, its shadowy edge marked by streetlights at three in the afternoon. Murky hills rose in the distance, and every which way was another river. "The Monongahela, the Allegheny, and the Ohio," I said aloud.

Viktor said, "Your ma's a scholar, Hazel."

And I said, "Thank you, Miss Kelly, wherever you are."

Viktor had been here once with Doc Miller, who'd taken an interest in his ailments. "The wind was blowing like mad, and Doc said it was the first time he'd seen the skyline."

Though he wanted to show me the sights before we headed to Xenia's neighborhood, we couldn't make out a blessed thing. On Stanwix, Viktor pointed toward Jenkins Arcade, outlined in lights. "There's fancy shopping in there." Plumed-hatted ladies came through a revolving door, same as on my trips to Bentleyville. At the start of Fifth Avenue, the Buhl Building stood out because it was covered with blue-and-white tiles reflecting whatever light there was.

"That will be gray soon enough," Viktor said grimly, and I thought of his lungs. Cars had their headlights on, and gas lamps lining the street were already lit. Viktor announced one large building after another. "That there's the Carnegie Building. That's the Frick," he said. I knew the names from the newspapers and that Carnegie was busy these days giving his money away. So far, I preferred reading and dreaming about Pittsburgh to visiting.

"What's the use?" Viktor asked, once he'd told me where the Oliver building and Kaufmann's would be if I could see them. "Doc called the place 'hell with the lid off.'"

Everyone did, but I'd thought that had to do with Catholics, crowds, and chorus girls. I said, "If Carnegie has so much money, why doesn't he clean up his mess?"

"Can't carve your name in air," Viktor said.

We stayed on Liberty Street all the way to Xenia's neighborhood, Polish Hill. Still separated and labeled, even in a big city, though

Lothar was Lithuanian. The steep road rose up above the railroad tracks and riverside factories to Immaculate Heart Church. Shabby houses came almost to the street's edge, with graveled front yards and few trees. Halfway down Pulawski, four tow-headed children waving and jumping were as good as a house number. Xenia stood in front of a tidy yellow clapboard sandwiched between two houses the color of moldy bread, shutters hanging by a corner. She had melted into a wider, shorter woman, though she might once have seemed tall because I was so young. Her smooth marble face was now tanned and lined. Three boys and a girl ran to the car to greet us, and I put my sweet baby in Xenia's outstretched arms. "My dear Yelena." She kissed me three times, and then, "Viktor Gomelekoff, as I live and breathe!"

Hazel's eyes grew wider than mine as the children joined hands around us, chanting, "They're here, they're here, they're here." Gretel tugged at my sleeve, eager to show us to our room, which turned out to be Xenia and Lothar's. I tried to refuse, but Xenia said, "Hazel's crib is already here. Your parents stretched nothing to feed two more people. They slept on a bedroll on the floor for me."

"You brought their precious Sonya and Lethia over."

"Don't remind me," Xenia said, and we laughed together, the way she used to laugh with Ma. I heard the glee in my voice when I talked about her living with us, probably the hardest time of her life. Fifteen, newly married, and bunking with strangers—widowed within two months. But the squabbling and singing! Our first Thanksgiving! Carting Vera's samovar on Kostia's wagon!

Xenia said, "Gregor took Robert under his wing. And then after, he tried to be my matchmaker." Her memories made me miss the man Pa once was.

Lothar came home wearing a suit and tie. His forehead claimed most of his head, his golden curls now on the heads of his children, and his skin wasn't shiny anymore. I wondered if that was because he didn't need to scrub himself clean of coal dust every night. He worked for a hotel so big, he said, it was like a small city, and he managed cleaning and cooking staff, porters, and big events. He showed us a special menu he'd printed on a letterpress.

Xenia had prepared a feast starting with borscht and pickled herring, followed by a pork roast. The children were as excited as I was. When Viktor passed the mound of Russian potatoes on, Xenia sliced him more black bread. "They were always trying to fatten you up," she said.

I wanted to hear Xenia and Viktor talk about Suwalki. Baba and Jeda and my young parents walked through their stories, as did Sonya and Lethia and Viktor's family.

Xenia sighed. "I had my heart set on your brother Josef. The kingdom of heaven to him."

"He was a prince," Viktor said.

"You remember Ruza," she asked, "same age as him? My ma taught us to knit, because Ruza wanted to make hats for the poor children."

"As if there was anyone poorer," Viktor said.

"Ruza Winslow?" I asked. "That woman from the clipping?"

"The very same," Xenia said. She put her hand on her husband's but addressed Viktor. "When your family left the same day as Ruza's, I lost my boyfriend and my best friend. Of course, they didn't either of them know that."

To think that before Viktor was mine, he and his family had been Xenia's, and that her heart had fluttered for his brother. The world is cramped. Looking from Viktor to Lothar, I sensed a kinship in their kindness and their slightly blank expressions, neither dismissive nor stern. For the short time Xenia had been in our lives, she had made a lasting impression on me. I wondered if I would have known to choose Viktor if she hadn't first picked Lothar, or Robert.

Our wonderful supper ended with a chocolate log Xenia took from an icebox.

"Tinginys," Lothar said, "the lazy one."

I must have given him the stink eye, because their oldest, Hedwig, pointed at me and laughed. "Papa means the icebox cake. That's what is the Lazy One."

"Eat, eat," Lothar passed us plates with generous slices. When he forked a bite of cake into his own mouth, he hummed in approval.

The best was before bedtime, alone in the kitchen with Xenia. She had let her hair down for the night and wore a striped seersucker robe over a simple white nightgown, eyelet trim top and bottom. That we could share a cup of tea, her in her nightclothes, was as big a gift as letting us stay with them. She held Hazel so they were face-to-face and she could take stock of her, which thrilled me. This wasn't just another baby, even if my family treated her that way.

She said, "I know these green and gold eyes well. Oh, *Hazel*, that's right."

Hazel's round cheeks were probably like mine had been too, though there were no pictures of me as an infant to prove it. Because I could speak my heart without being put down for bragging or bringing on bad luck, I said, "I've taken care of so many babies, and Hazel is the best baby I've ever known."

Xenia said, "That's how your ma feels about you." She shifted my girl to her hip and slid open the roll top on her Hoosier cabinet. Reaching behind the flour hopper, she retrieved a booklet for naturalization and a wide roll of satin ribbon.

"You're going to be American!" I said.

"I put in my petition after Lothar's hearing. He said they asked him ten obvious questions, but I'm taking citizenship classes and studying. He has more confidence than I do."

"I wonder how many Americans could pass." I had always been proud of Xenia, now more than ever. The first step stopped most people in Marianna, as the nearest courthouse was twenty miles away in Washington City, and the petition cost money. Xenia tugged on the ribbon I'd assumed was from celebrating Lothar's citizenship, and a sash unfurled proclaiming *Votes for Women*.

"Look at you!" was all I could manage. I petted the sash, the same buttery yellow as their house. The letters had been satin-stitched in purple by a machine. "Were you there when she talked?"

"Ruza, Rose, yes. Rose goes right up front to speak for the working woman. She's brave like your ma."

"Ma called her a troublemaker."

"So Katya remembers!" Xenia said, excited. She lowered her voice. "She just got herself arrested and started a hunger strike in jail. Did you read about that?"

I shook my head, vowing to myself to keep up. "You think Ma is brave? She'd have no part of this." Xenia had left before Sonya needed Ma's protection, before Eva died.

"Brave for Marianna," Xenia said. "Didn't she learn English and invite the teacher to Thanksgiving? She got Gregor paid in cash. And didn't she pick out Sergei for Lethia?"

The last was news to me, that Ma had made that match. I said, "I went with her when she got money for Pa's work. Pa was mad she stirred the pot."

"Brave," Xenia said again. "And you, you showed plenty of courage getting out."

I told her about Viktor's lungs and my promise, along with my guilt about being so lucky. The mine disaster didn't kill Pa, like it did her Robert. Pa snapped at me and swatted me plenty, not like how he beat my brothers. Sonya's baby died, and my Hazel was healthy.

"Don't feel guilty," she said. "That might be who can get out, those who aren't beaten down, singled out. I can imagine what our friend Olga said about your leaving."

"She didn't call me brave," I said, and we both laughed.

She kissed Hazel once on each chubby cheek. "You'll stir the pot, too, won't you?"

WE DROVE AWAY IN the morning, Xenia's children waving two arms apiece. Viktor said, "She landed on her feet. A good man in her life and a litter of four. If they aren't careful, they'll have nothing to complain about."

I hadn't asked Xenia whether Lothar knew about her sash, if he approved, or if she cared whether he approved. I hadn't asked if she actually wore the sash. I remembered how the papers called Rose not only Miss Winslow but also Ruza Wenclawska, their way of pointing out that she was both a spinster and a foreigner.

It was 130 or so miles to Erie, nearly three times what we'd driven the day before, but the coupe was comfortable and Hazel napped in my arms. Viktor and me took turns naming what came in on the breeze; in our assembly-line car, I enjoyed being just another American on the road. When Viktor gave a light honk and a wave to those we passed, most of them waved right back. *Hello, there. Why, hello to you, too.*

We bought cider and apples at a roadside stand and kept going until Meadville, pulling off by an abandoned lockhouse. The temperature had dropped a few more degrees, and we huddled over our picnic. On a Monday afternoon, we were the only ones. Hawks circled above us, and tree branches were embroidered against the blue sky.

"This air," Viktor said, taking the crisp air in without a cough.

Beneath the food Xenia had packed for us was an envelope with my name written in her backward-leaning writing. I opened it, expecting her good wishes, and read the short note aloud. "Lothar didn't get to dance with you at your wedding." Folded inside the envelope were five ten-dollar bills. I lifted them up, my mouth wide open. Fifty dollars was half a car!

"You should send that back to her," Viktor said. I could tell he was a little insulted.

"It's not addressed to you," I said. I thought of the girl saved from the witch with her towel that could turn into a river, comb that could turn into a forest. In America, that magic was in money. I tucked all five bills into my nursing corset, daring Viktor to come after them. With her gift but also her nerve, Xenia had already made me bolder.

26

TAR FUMES FILLED THE car at the same time I spotted the marker, ERIE—1 MILE, so you could smell our new town a mile away. Rita had written that there were Russians at the paper mills and breweries, at the locomotive, stove, and cast-iron plants. There were Russians making pipe organs! A forest of smokestacks belched into the air that Viktor would have to breathe, but I tried to see them as hundreds of factories needing workers. For the first time, working underground had some appeal.

We turned onto Parade Street as the streetlights were coming on, and their flickering made the view out our windshield look like a movie. Tall oval windows decorated the red-brick Schultz Warehouse, marquis lights circled the signs outside the White Eagle, New Wilkay, Isis, and Plaza—four movie palaces in as many blocks. Packed trolleys clanged on both sides of the street. The Parade Street Market stretched the entire block of 10th Street, and people flowed in and out loaded with hatboxes, string-tied packages, grease-spotted bags, and cones of fresh flowers. A few blocks after Kraus's Department Store on 8th was Rita's turreted house on the corner of 5th and Parade.

When Nadja opened the etched-glass front door, I nearly swooned into her arms. Out of sorts from something I'd eaten, Hazel had gone through my diaper supply with her watery messes. Nadja took our soiled bag from Viktor, and she kissed him on both cheeks. Turns out, she'd known him in both Suwalki and West Virginia.

Rita, who used to cling to me in Marianna, now cradled my bawling baby, sour as the night air. Leo's first words to me and Viktor were, "We've seen worse."

Following Rita through the apartment, which took up the entire downstairs floor, I marveled that Little Rita had finished eighth grade, grown taller than me, and was pregnant with her second baby. She led me to a fluffy stack of clean diapers in the nursery, the sock rabbit Sonya and I had made her years ago up on a shelf.

"It lasted this long because I mostly looked at it," she said. "That was a terrible shock, to lose Pa and then leave you." She'd always been able to speak her mind, without rancor or dark humor, and I was grateful she hadn't grown out of that. I admired her baby, Irene, asleep in the crib as she cleaned, powdered, and changed my Hazel. From our first night back together, we got on like pickles and dill.

The rest of them were talking a mile a minute when we joined them, and I lay Hazel in the cradle I recognized from when Rita was little. Leo's pa had been a timberman in the very West Virginia mine where Max had been shot in the leg and Viktor's father and brother had died. How was it that everyone already knew Viktor? Nadja warmed salty beef broth to ease his wheezing. Viktor coughed and spit into his handkerchief.

"That's from the mines?" Rita asked. "We'll take you to our clinic for a TB test."

Viktor said, "I came here to work. Might the results scotch that?"

Leo agreed. "There's not much for it, anyways. They sent Carp Plevich, he was in the Ellsworth mine, to a sanatorium. No paycheck and no visitors."

I worried that we'd made things worse. "We ran from the wolf to the bear."

Nadja said, "Those who don't run are no better off."

"Let's just wait and see," Rita said. "What was left for you where you were?"

IN MARIANNA, THE OLD Believers worked in the mine with all the other men in town. In Erie, they worked throughout the city, one church member getting another hired at the next drill press at Jarecki's, building train engines at General Electric, enameling stoves at Griswold's, pulping rags at Hammermill, filling cream assortments at Pulakos Chocolates. They also fished Lake Erie and Presque Isle Bay together, from the shore, a boat, or through the ice. Friday nights, everyone showed up for the fish fry at the CYS Club, the "Community of Young Staroobryadtsy." There were bowling alleys, card games, and drinking there; everyone called it the "Russian Club" except me.

Our first night at the club, I said to Rita, "I hoped I could be American in Erie."

"Can you do that after the Russians get Viktor work and you have a place to live?" she teased.

Leo convinced the dock foreman to hire Viktor to hump cargo. All those years of me worrying about the seeping afterdamp, Viktor came home freezing and reeking of fish, exhausted from heavy lifting. He said it was a comfort to look up and see the church domes glinting far above the dock.

That was our church he saw on high. A city landmark, Church of the Nativity overlooked the drop-off to the railroad tracks and the docks. Inside, three rows of icons, some as tall as four feet, lined the walls. Every service, boys climbed ladders on wheels to light them and then snuff them out. Father Timofei held services on Saturday and Sunday as well as feast days, funerals, and every day during Christmas and Easter Lent. How much church did you need? We went on Saturday along with Rita's whole family. Without Ma, I followed Nadja's lead.

The Old Believers neighborhood was five blocks on a side, from Front Street to 6th, between Peach and Parade Streets. We lived a block beyond Front and Parade, where the pavement gave out and the drop-off to the tracks served as the town dump. We shared the carved-up house on Sobieski Street with three Old Believer families from the Old Country. These families led the chanting in church and knew when to cross themselves and bow without prompting. The husbands didn't shave, and their beards looked as scraggly as the hobos who made it up from the train tracks. None of them set foot in the CYS Club, certainly not for fish fries or pinochle.

While I wore a print housecoat and a bibbed apron, my hair in a bob, the women in the other apartments kept their hair covered and wore sleeves to their wrists and skirts to their ankles. I made Russian tea cakes and blintzes, which the two families above us appreciated, but the Vasiliev family on our floor refused my offerings. Built like an icebox and twice as cold, Mikhail Vasiliev actually spit on the ground when I walked past. His wife, Tatiana, was missing several teeth and had a fearful scowl, and their two boys had dirty or maybe bruised faces. Their dog was tied outside to a stake in the ground, his ribs like a birdcage. I'd sneak a raw chicken neck now and again to Pyos, whose name meant *dog*; probably, I should have given the chicken neck to the boys.

Viktor said the Vasilievs were pure Suwalki stock. Mikhail came outside to hit Pyos with a switch now and again, and once a mug flew out their window, in anger or at the dog, I didn't know. "Arkady and Evgeny should be in school," I ranted to Viktor. "That's the law." There was a young girl, too, but we only ever saw her in church.

"They may not have what it takes for school."

"What do you mean—shoes, pencils? They've lived here a year."

My husband pulled me into his bony lap. "Do you want to get them help or arrested?"

Ma would have said I carried fire in one hand and water in the other. I wanted them to learn English and better themselves so people wouldn't judge me by their ways.

Viktor said, "At least the boys aren't in a factory or picking rags. Father Timofei says they're good eggs. The parents speak Russian and Polish, can't write at all."

So he'd mentioned them to Father. "What else did Father say?"

"The war's brought out the worst in Suwalki. They ran all the Jews out."

I thought of my baba, Ma's ma, who had died a few months earlier. She was the only Jew I knew in Suwalki, not that I knew her.

Viktor said, "Our people had no love for the tsar, but the ones who took his place believe in nothing—no church, no priest, no God."

"Nothing," I repeated. Whatever my struggles with the church, I couldn't imagine stepping outside of it.

I slid off Viktor's lap to pick up the broom. "Rita says that I tried and they weren't interested. Let them stew in their own juices." Hazel and I had been with her and her new baby this afternoon. Just two weeks old, Max was already ten pounds.

Viktor held the dustpan for me, a simple kindness. "My parents and yours left with somewhere to go to. These people just fled. They're wary."

Weren't we all? "We need to file your citizenship petition. Xenia told me you have to get it in years before you apply for citizenship."

"I'll need a witness willing to swear I'm not a plut."

"English, please," I said, "or they'll send you back on the next boat, crook or not."

It was one of my fears, though Erie Russians scoffed at the idea of anyone being sent back. Who would make the town's streetcars, engines, or boilers; their boots and buttons; their paint, paper, or pickles? Who would slaughter the meat or tan the leather if Russians were sent back?

The makeshift dump down the hillside served as Arkady and Evgeny's stomping grounds. The boys ran wild during the day, and it was only a matter of time before one of them stepped on a rusty nail or worse. A few blocks beyond was the city sewage plant, where they skated on the frozen runoff.

When I was up in the night with Hazel, stewing in my own juices, I was already planning our next move. I'd hear people's cars putter and stop where the pavement ended, then they'd chuck their trash down the embankment. Seagulls picked at the hillocks and rats tunneled through the mounds, steaming with spoiled food and rancid oil. I went round and round my loops of worry as if I was praying the lestovka. I'd dragged Viktor here, taken him away from his brothers for his health, yet his longshoreman work paid less and was just as dangerous. Out in all weather unloading cargo ships, he could catch a stray cargo hook in the thigh or shoulder, not to mention loads sliding off ramps or wagons to crush him.

Before any of those things could happen on the icy, fish-slicked pier, Viktor's wet cough turned to bronchitis, and the dock let him go. The money Xenia had put in our picnic basket kept us in carrots and soup bones through December. Ma begged us to visit for Russian Christmas, but I put her off. I couldn't bear going to Marianna, no job and no gifts. After services on Christmas Eve, we joined Leo, Rita, and Nadja for a huge batch of Nadja's pelmeni dumplings. The dish she fed my parents on their first night in America she now fed to me, my husband, and our baby. They pushed presents on us for Hazel, saying they knew we'd do that for their Irene and Max. When Rita said there'd be something soon for Viktor, I wanted to believe her.

Strolling home in snow like sifting flour, I wondered how much punching down we could take before we couldn't rise anymore, before the flavor was worked out of us. Now Father Timofei and the church were helping all the families in our Sobieski house with food, including us—who was I to be ashamed of the others?

We woke on Russian Christmas to six inches of snow, and for once I was relieved that Viktor didn't have a job. I'd saved bacon for Viktor's Christmas breakfast, along with turnip hash and a sliced apple for his tea. "You're too good to this slob," he said, then he took his dirty dishes to the sink. He and his brothers were the only men I knew who cleaned up after themselves. I'd knitted him a pair of mittens, lined with leftover flannel pajamas. He gave me a brand-new book, *My Ántonia*, only the second book I'd been given in my life.

"It's about a Bohunk girl come to America," he told me.

The cover said she was "all impulsive youth and careless courage," and I kissed Viktor impulsively all over his face. Loaves of snow covered our stoop and walk, and children's boots had already broken through the drifts. I woke up Hazel and wrapped her like a present so the three of us could walk to Front Street, where the drop-off was blanketed in a white quilt. Snow masked the abandoned tires and rotting pumpkins into gentle white lumps. The gold church domes shone beneath pointy hats of snow, and the church bell would be pealing soon.

I was looking out to the lake beyond the bay, whitecaps churning with chunks of ice, when Arkady and Evgeny's war whoops sounded on either side of us. Out of the corner of my eye, I saw Arkady leap onto a wooden panel to sled over the snow-covered mounds of rubbish. Now I could make out paths their runs had flattened, even crossing the train tracks at the bottom of the ravine. Twenty feet away, Evgeny launched himself headlong off the overlook and thumped down the iced iron steps on a giant sheet of cardboard.

It was bad enough when they skated on the frozen sewage called Shit Creek, where the worst that could happen was falling through uneven ice to the stinky muck. Evgeny's stomach met the last icy step, which he hit with a smack. He and his makeshift sled kept trundling toward the tracks, and I heard the engine fixing to round the corner. The trains didn't stop for Russian Christmas.

"Evgeny!" I yelled out his name in terror.

"Bohoroditsa," Viktor said. Mother of God.

The boy was sledding face down, the flaps of his hat over his ears. Could he sense the rumbling train? He must have heard the shrieking whistle, which shook snow from branches above us. "Evgeny! Evgeny!" I shouted, and Viktor yelled "Stop!"—the same word in Russian and English. I held Hazel in one arm and waved my scarf with the other.

There's no steering a cardboard box, and Evgeny had to lift his chin to see what he was in for. He showed quick thinking, abandoning his craft and rolling down the steep embankment like a log, but the same danger awaited him there. Train brakes squealed, I screamed, and Hazel bawled for good measure. Viktor ran for the cast-iron steps and instantly fell on his zhopa. Evgeny's head took a bounce, but he had enough of his wits about him to claw at the snow just as Arkady suddenly reached him, grabbing him by his sleeve. Miraculously, the two stopped a foot from the tracks. Hissing in relief, the train brakes let up—they would have put the boy's death off a second at most—and the cars barreled through. The whistle carried a long ways in the crisp air. My shaking was wobbling Hazel's head on her neck until Viktor somehow returned to us and took her from me. My rib cage pounded with the chugging of the wheels, which would have cut Evgeny in half had we not been standing there.

Grinning like a maniac, Evgeny brushed himself off at the bottom of the ravine, and he showed his brother there was no harm done. That's when Arkady hauled off and punched his brother's arm, a gesture I understood. Since he'd nearly gotten himself killed, I wanted to pummel him too. Evgeny swiveled his head, and maybe he caught sight of my rage rather than my fear and concern, because his grin turned to a grimace. His gaze rose above my head at the same time I heard Mikhail's boots clunking heavily behind me.

"Malchiki!" Boys! he barked. Icy as the slope was, both boys quickly scrambled up the embankment. When their father pounded the ground with his boot, they came to his side like nails to a magnet.

I would have hugged Mikhail around his big boxy shoulders, but he was so stern, no doubt angered by their carelessness. I expected him to talk to me finally, a simple "spasibo" for worrying and for calling out a warning. Instead, he made the same grimace Evgeny had, then he spit on the snow at my feet—*thu!* "Jid," he said and spat three more times—*thu, thu, thu!*

"Ona byla polezna." She was helpful, my husband said.

Mikhail nodded at Viktor, seeing him in a way he never did me. "Ekaterina Federoff's docha, da?"

"Da," Viktor said.

"Gadkiy Jid." Mikhail grabbed each of his boys by an ear, the way Pa held onto Kostia before a beating. They winced, but neither cried out as he marched them through the snow—across the street, past the first house, and into theirs, which was also ours.

I'm not sure how I understood his slur. I remembered *gadkiy* was vile, filthy, and I must have heard the phrase at least once in the past because I knew. *Gadkiy Jid* was filthy Jew.

"What makes him say that? For heaven's sake, we were all of us at services last night."

"He must have known your baba in Suwalki."

Viktor's remark cut me to the quick. Ever since I could remember, I had yearned to have Baba fuss over me as she had over my sisters. I hated that Mikhail might have been a neighbor of the grandmother I'd never gotten to meet before she died. "So what?"

He handed Hazel to me and said, "Jews believe it comes through the mother."

"Ma's not Jewish, and neither am I!" As the words came out of my mouth, I realized what Viktor was telling me, what Mikhail was saying about Baba, Ma, and me. The chugging train wheels thrummed in my head—I am my mother's daughter. When I'd wanted Ma to defend herself from the church biddies long ago, she didn't deny their claim. Now, Mikhail had picked at the very scab that hadn't healed, might never heal, maybe shouldn't heal. I squeezed Hazel tight, though I probably should have unwrapped her and pinched her to boot. You had to have skin thick as an elephant to endure these people.

I am my mother's daughter—there was no denying that—but Baba and Ma had done a lot so I could make my own history. How long before people gave me credit for belonging? Dirty Russki, filthy Jew, Bull Head, Rushie girl—how long until someone recognized me for who I was?

27

VIKTOR SOLVED THE CHURCH'S boiler trouble, don't ask me how, and after that Father Timofei paid him to enclose the foyer and install a second set of doors, so winter wouldn't blow in with every person. That work led to a few house repairs for church members. I nagged him to agree to prices up front. If he didn't, the Russians assumed he'd be happy with a bottle of vodka.

Staying out of debt took everything we had. How had Ma and Pa raised so many on so little? I took in sewing and baked for Stephanski's, selling the soft cabbages and onions Mr. Stephanski gave me back to him in pirozhki filling. If we put five dollars together, one of the coupe's tires went flat. I was anxious to file Viktor's citizenship declaration, but we could never scrape together the court fee. We did, however, manage to play the numbers every week. A nickel got you a three-digit number, and a quarter boxed them in, which meant three numbers in any order won. Wednesdays, I'd bring my pirozhkis to Stephanski's, grocer and number runner, and give him back a quarter to play our house number boxed. Viktor and I raced to check the front page of the paper the next morning—if the last three digits of the US Treasury balance matched our address, we won. When we won big on our second anniversary, Viktor took me out to the Russian Club for a nice dinner. "It's found money," he reasoned.

At the end of March, Griswold Cookware hired Viktor as a grinder, shaving the burrs off cast-iron skillets and waffle irons. Salary and insurance, sure, but I saw the end of that job coming almost as soon as it started, reading Viktor's hanky the way Nadja used to read the clothesline. Night after night, we stared at his filings-filled snot, trying to judge if things were getting worse. Viktor asked, "What can it hurt to breathe another few months of this?"

"I guess we'll find out," I said. We didn't really have a choice. Fortunately, people took to Viktor, and he'd been canny enough to join the Ironworkers Union on day one. They promised to help him if he lasted six months. I took his hanky to the sink for a soak.

On the other side of the kitchen wall, I heard a smack that could have been Tatiana pounding a piece of tough meat. It was suppertime, after all, but then there was Mikhail's angry voice, which set my teeth on edge. A higher voice followed by another slap might have been Tatiana getting on with her stew, or not. I scouted around for a few pears that should be eaten tonight or some hard candy for the children—any excuse to show up at their door.

Viktor was watching me. "You'll only make trouble."

I wished I had the courage to make trouble, when the truth was that I'd already lost my nerve. I thought of *My Ántonia* and her "careless courage," of Ruza Wenclawska fighting for all women when I couldn't even defend my neighbor.

Coming back from Stephanski's the next day, I saw Tatiana and Arkady, who was wearing one of his mother's headscarves tied in a sling, his arm cradled inside.

I didn't have much Russian, but I called out, "Dobroye utro sestra," choosing *sister* between familiar and formal. She surprised me by saying in English, "Not today." She didn't stop to explain if it wasn't a good day today or if she couldn't talk out in the open today.

That night, I baked Viktor squash the way he liked, a mash peppered with a few pieces of meat I'd beaten tender. "Mama, Papa"—Hazel babbled more than usual, and I showed Viktor her latest trick. When I pointed, our talented baby said, "Look, look."

"The little princess speaks Russian!" Viktor said. He teased the two of us by pointing at his tied shoes, "luk," Russian for bow, and the vegetable bin, "luk," onion. After I'd poured honey in his tea and warmed a biscuit for him, I mentioned Arkady's arm and the way

Tatiana had skittered away like a crab. I said, "I think we should call the truant officer."

"Then it's lucky we can't afford a telephone," my husband said. He touched the calico of my skirt. "You're wearing a clever apron."

"Ma sent it." She'd invented a one-piece wonder that slipped over the head and didn't need tying; the straps crisscrossed in the back.

It was true that Viktor had done more than speak my name to win me over. He'd romanced me by simply noticing me. But I would not be derailed. "What if Mikhail decides to break his other arm?"

"I hope he does not," Viktor said wearily. "You can't live their lives for them."

"That is so." I couldn't stand Tatiana's helplessness or mine. I said, "Women better get the vote soon. That's the only way anything's going to change."

"Hmph," my husband grunted, the strongest disapproval he ever voiced. "I thought we were talking about the boys next door. You're sounding like Ruza from home, Xenia's friend."

Maybe he didn't like her because she was Polish. Xenia's Robert had once told me that when he couldn't ice-skate across the lake to school, the Polish kids beat him up on the way there and on the way home. I wondered if that was true for Viktor. I said, "Ruza stands up for factory workers, and for families."

"She doesn't have a job or a family, Lenotchka! You want to go in the factory? You want to go to war? Women like her wish they were men."

Russia had just left the war, but we were still in it. Viktor started gathering the supper dishes into the middle of the table, and he sucked at his teeth, the way Russian men did to have the last word. When we'd agreed to make our own decisions, I didn't mean for him to make them and for me to follow like a sheep. I wiped my clammy hands down the front of my apron. "I don't want to be a man."

"Of course you don't."

"But I want to have a say, and men don't like that. Father Dmitri was always telling me things were as they were because God wanted it that way. But when woman wanted to know what was what, he didn't like that."

"Father said that?"

"No, I did." I'd been chewing on this apple for years. "Eve asked, 'Why are we naked?' and God could have answered her. Probably he had a reason, but he said, 'Who told you that?' and he deported them."

Viktor sucked at another tooth, raising his lip in a sneer. "Women should be grateful that we're in charge, that we take care of you. And you have it better than most. So many husbands can't walk by a bottle without draining it."

I stared at my poorly husband, who couldn't drink a toast at our own wedding. On a good night, he blew out iron filings in his snot. Bad nights, he coughed blood into a pot on the side of our bed. "I'm supposed to thank you for not getting drunk, for not beating me?"

"I don't beat anyone," he said.

"And here I thought I was special." I saw his hand clench around the honey spoon, but I didn't stop. "You're not going to war. With your health, we'll be lucky if you can hold a job. May the union find work that doesn't kill you. You look down your nose at Ruza, who wants better treatment for both of us."

"She wants attention, is what she wants. Those rich women put her in front because they've never worked a day in their lives. They use her, Lenotchka."

"Maybe she uses them!" I snapped back. "She was in the mills, and now her lungs are like yours, only we don't know what you have because a doctor's report could get you fired. You say men are in charge. If you were in charge, you'd be a coal miner in Marianna."

"And I'd be having supper with my brothers."

I gasped like a fish on a hook. "Is that what you want?"

"Right now it is!"

"Bub, bub, bub." Hazel shuddered with fright at Viktor and me yelling, then she let loose with such a piercing howl that Pyos chained outside joined in. The Vasilievs pounded on our shared wall, which made everything worse, them objecting to our fighting.

Viktor tugged his jacket and hat roughly off the hook. "I'm going to the club."

He didn't kiss his little princess or me. Out the door, he had a fit of coughing that sounded all the way down the front steps. I lifted Hazel from her chair to hold her tight, quieting her ragged sobs.

As for me, I calmed myself down and worked myself back up a half dozen times. I thought, good for him for going to the CYS Club, until it made me madder. I could never storm out of the house alone at night and drive to the club to meet a group of women. Women weren't allowed in unaccompanied, and none of the other women could get away from their babies and out for the night. How dare he ask for thanks because he didn't hit me. I didn't do anything that deserved a beating. But neither did any of the women who got hit.

Proud as I was of being American, I didn't choose to be born here, just like he didn't choose to be born a foreigner. Pa chose to be a coal miner, though he was really choosing to leave Suwalki. I might have married Pavel—or someone as sturdy—but I chose Viktor and defended my choice against Ma's wishes. I chose Viktor from the lot at church. God knows, I didn't choose the church. I didn't choose my parents or my siblings. But I chose my husband. And I chose Erie.

After Hazel wore herself out with crying, I slid the dresser drawer all the way out onto the floor, because she'd grown so heavy, and I laid her in like a doll. Then I finished off the dishes and tackled the bottom of the pots with baking soda to work off some anger. That just got me more worked up. Viktor was out on a lark with the boys, and I was scrubbing the kitchen.

The way it usually went at the club was that Viktor won the most because he wasn't drinking, and then he turned around and bought drinks with the money he won. But as I dried the last pan, the coupe's fan belt whinnied in the street. He hadn't been gone long enough for his usual cycle, though I was relieved to know he was back.

Soon as he was in the door, resentment rose up in me like water in the kettle. Except it was Viktor, and whatever hot water I was in, we were in together. I was torn by having a choice, which was that I could choose to hold a grudge or I could choose not to. Another man would have stayed away for hours. I swallowed the bitter taste in my mouth. "No one at the club?"

"It was packed." He hung up his hat and coat.

"Too crowded?"

"No," he said. He didn't have the stench of vodka that grown men had before I met him. He smelled like birch beer. "Drank myself a mug of sarsaparilla, cleaned the Morosky boys out, and came home to my wife." He held up his hand, fanning out one- and five-dollar bills.

"Spasibo." I thanked him. Plucking the bills one by one, I thanked him in all the miners' tongues I remembered. "Grazie, danke," my meanness melting into gratitude with each bill. "Dziakuj, ačiū." He pulled me against him and growled into my neck. "No, thank *you*, you, you, you," until we couldn't stop thanking each other.

WHEN VIKTOR LEFT FOR the factory in the morning, I made my own decision to bake a batch of skansi, not for Mr. Stephanski. The yeast was already bubbling in the warm water when Mikhail slammed the door to leave for the paper mill. I mixed the filling and gave some to Hazel, who smeared the sweetened cottage cheese around her tray and sometimes in her mouth.

As I rushed to get the pastries in the oven, a free-for-all broke out next door. "Byess!" Tatiana yelled, and I remembered Sonya saying Alexei was a devil, too. An hour later, when the skansi were baked and cool enough to touch, I gathered Hazel in one arm and gripped the plate in the other. At the last minute, I tucked my collection of Russian fairy tales under my arm.

Pyos strained at his chain outside, whining and wagging his entire body. Tatiana saw how happy he was to see me, and her shoulders relaxed from up around her ears. There was a gash over her eyebrow I hadn't seen yesterday.

I pressed the pastries toward her. Arkady came to the door to glare at me, and I handed him the book before I could regret its loss. He didn't deserve the book, and I didn't want to part with it. That's what made it a gift. "Like God's grace," Ma would have said. I was doing this because of what Ma had fought for, but also because of what she hadn't, with my brothers, Sonya, Baby Eva.

Tatiana tugged me into their front room and closed the door. Arkady had sunk to the floor and with his good hand was tracing the firebird's feathers on the cover, just as I'd done in Mrs. G's parlor.

"Spasibo," the boy said.

"You're most welcome," I said.

Their little girl came running into the room on her tiptoes, grabbing at a chair to keep her balance. She was maybe two, but such a wobbly two, and she didn't look anything like her brothers. "Nazovi mne!" she squealed. "Nazovi! Nazovi!" Gimme!

"Klara!" Tatiana tried to shush her.

The girl's militant selfishness reminded me of Sonya's Harry, and then everything about her did. Klara had a flat face, no ridge between her nose and thin upper lip. A face like a child's stick drawing, like Sonya's Harry. Her tiny, dark eyes were deeply sunken, as if in dough. Tatiana put the pastries high up and reached for her girl, who swung at her mother the way Harry smacked Sonya or Alexei. Ma had told Sonya that if she poured the vodka out rather than drink it, she wouldn't have a son like Harry. I'd thought she was talking about a superstition.

Arkady tried to block Klara, who hit him on his sling. He yelped, then he swatted her using the book I'd armed him with. I had a mind to take back my beloved fairy tales, if only to hit him over the head with it.

Hazel let out the same howl as the night before, and I carried her to the opposite corner to comfort her until she settled. Who knows what I'd been hearing through the wall or how Arkady had broken his arm? I felt bad for them all, holding back from judging Tatiana. Now that I'd made the match between Klara and Harry, I thought of kids from school who'd looked like Harry, kids we'd teased for being slow. Chins Radchenko was in that boat, and everyone knew his ma was a drinker.

Evgeny arrived—to fight or break up the fight, I wasn't sure—and his eyes bugged out at the plate of skansi, warm and shining. Tatiana snuck up behind Klara and crossed her arms tightly over the girl's chest, like the apron Ma had sent me if I'd decided to wear it backwards. Tatiana asked Evgeny to put the kettle on, and Klara sobbed. "Prostee, Mama, prostee," begging forgiveness.

Tatiana laid her cheek on top of Klara's head and gave me a thin-lipped smile. "Durak," she said about her own daughter. That was my father's word for Borya and other numbskulls, but she was telling me that Klara was in far worse shape than that.

"Prostee." I repeated Klara's request.

"Boh, prostee," Tatiana said. God forgives.

I thought I'd best say why I'd come. "Arkady, Evgeny go to shkolu." I marched my fingers along Hazel's back, miming the two of them walking.

"Oh, I think not," she said, shaking her head emphatically no. She'd let go of Klara, who wandered off as if nothing was wrong. Tatiana rubbed her fingers together. "Many dollars, da?"

I waved my hand level to the floor, then remembered the word for nothing. "Nichevo. And I could go with you. Or watch Klara."

"Da," she said decisively. She stood and reached for her coat on the hook by the door.

Viktor and I might have to move off Sobieski Street sooner than planned, I thought, when Mikhail found out about this. But I was also heartened that she was eager to help her sons. "After tea?" I asked.

"Da, da," she said. "After skansi."

SOBIESKI STREET LOOKED DINGIER than ever that spring, and I scrounged what I could to spruce things up. With a single sheet of sandpaper, I sanded the kitchen cabinets and the swinging door, then rag-painted them with paint I mixed from milk and colored chalk. I spread the *Erie Daily Times* on the linoleum, and I dripped paint on the world's sorrows: the Spanish influenza, infantile paralysis plague, the Kaiser's Battle on the Western Front, and a powder plant explosion in Montreal. "War Gives the Virus Wings" read one headline about the flu.

We bought remnants from the wallpaper store on Holland Street and spent a few Sundays wallpapering the kitchen and tiny bathroom, using flour and water paste that Viktor made. He also planted a garden, helping two other families put in plots. For fun that summer, we went to the peninsula with Leo and Rita nearly every Sunday, joining CYS families there after church. Playing with Hazel in the lake's gentle waves made me glad we'd come to Erie.

Someone in the CYS crowd tipped me off about Mrs. McNulty, whose rooming house was near St. Hedwig's, the Polish Catholic church around the corner from our apartment. Nine men bunked three to a room at her place, heading out to the paper mills together every morning and home to their little towns on Friday nights. I paid Rita a little something to watch Hazel with her Irene and Max two days a week so I could strip beds and scrub toilets side by side with Mrs. McNulty, who took a shine to me. She liked to say, "One day, kid, this will all be yours."

A few months in, I had the idea to sell the boarders bagged lunches. I'd make the bags and the lunches and deliver them each morning for cheaper than they ate at the mills. Mrs. McNulty said, "Go crazy, kid." Then she led me to the cellar and, next to her wringer-washer, lifted a dusty tarp off a pedal-powered sewing machine the same vintage as Ma's. "Your people are always celebrating something late. Happy Orthodox Flag Day." I hugged her around her doughy middle and tried not to get teary, else she'd say, "Spare me the waterworks."

The day Viktor and Leo carted the machine home, it took them an hour to go the last block. Russians kept running out to announce that the tsar and his family had been murdered. With the cast-iron stand finally wedged into our bedroom, the two headed to the club, whether to toast the tsar or his demise, I wasn't sure.

I stayed home, threaded the needle, wound a bobbin, and pumped that pedal to beat the band. Sewing with a machine was like riding in the coupe after walking all week. *Zzt-zzt-zzt*—I put together a dozen drawstring sacks from scraps. The men would never know they were carrying a housecoat or a toddler's sunsuit. I had all sorts of futures in my head, including earning a school certificate and moving to Parade Street. I imagined us doing what Mrs. McNulty did, Viktor turning a wreck of a rooming house shipshape.

"Henry Ford would be proud," Viktor said, as we do-si-doed around each other to make lunches. He laid waxed-paper squares on the oilcloth; I dealt two slices of bread on each. He slapped the mustard down; I spread the mayonnaise. He put two pieces of cheese on the mustard; I put two pieces of bologna on the mayonnaise. He dealt out the top bread slices; I stacked and wrapped the sandwiches. Everyone got two sandwiches, a scoop of peanuts or oyster crackers in a waxed-paper envelope, and cookies or fruit.

We made a nice lunch for thirty-two cents—$1.60 each week—and they usually rounded it up to $1.75. Friday night, when I came home with their payments, we shook the coins in a can, *cha cha cha*.

Viktor danced me around the kitchen as Hazel clapped. "And you said we could make anything except money," I chided him. We cleared at least seven dollars on the lunches, and if a man lost or ruined his drawstring sack, I charged a quarter for a new bag, when all it cost me was thread. Viktor delivered the lunches to Mrs. McNulty's on his way to GE, where the Union had gotten him a welding shift. He'd been sweating all summer, wielding an acetylene torch inside the belly of a giant engine.

Just shy of thirteen months old, Hazel learned to walk so she could greet Viktor at the front door. She knew the sound of her pa shuffling home to us, his light footfall climbing the stoop with the wobbly railing.

"My little princess," Viktor would say and lift her up in the air.

I felt a twinge from when I was the princess in the house with him and his brothers. It was almost a swoon, but Mrs. McNulty and I had spent the July afternoon scrubbing floors.

The next day, Evgeny and Arkady were out playing stickball with boys they'd met at school. They'd learned enough English to get themselves a paper route, and I paid Arkady a nickel to come over twice a week to read from his Russian fairy-tale book—or if not read, tell Hazel stories from the pictures. So I had a Russian kid in America reading to my daughter in English from a Russian fairy-tale book that I had gotten from a Russian girl who'd lived and died in the American house where I was born.

"Mrs. G, Mrs. G," they waved. That gave me a twinge back to the Giordanas, who'd made such an impression on me as a kid. Before I knew it, I was crying. I went inside I was bawling so hard, with no real cause. Hazel was rashy from the heat but plenty lively. As I changed her, my stomach curdled and I ran to the toilet. I blamed myself for keeping milk too long, then realized why I couldn't face walking all the way to the store. I counted backwards and forwards and, soon as Viktor showed up from work, flung myself into his ropey arms.

"Why, hello to you too," he said. He dropped his welder's mask on the porch, coaxing out my news. "Yelena, Yelena, Yelena," he chanted my name in church cadence, and I tried to stop crying before he said it forty times. Then he laid his hand on my belly and asked, "Is it bad as all that, bringing another Gomelekoff into the world?"

28

I WAS HAPPY ABOUT having another baby, but I'd been happy just having Hazel. Besides, being pregnant wasn't my strong suit. Each week, the less I could keep down, the more the garden offered up. I cooked, canned, and gave away so much squash that even the hobos who came up from the train tracks didn't want it. Then I ground to a halt. The air that August was too heavy to blow the stockyard fumes and the tarred air out to the lake. Poor Viktor: often as not, supper was boiled eggs and pickled beets. He decided to take me and Hazel home for the Dormition of the Mother of God Feast, which must have been the first time in history that anyone went to Marianna for better air.

We surprised everyone, especially Ma, who teased me after she heard our news. "You sure he doesn't take a swig or two?"

Viktor laughed. "That's not how you get a baby, Katya—didn't you know?"

"You told him!" She was amazed I'd share my ignorance with my husband. Her hair was shot through with gray—by the time our new baby came, she'd have eight grandchildren.

Anton introduced us to Svetlana, and my old friend Maria was there, officially Pavel's girl. They begged us to come back for Thanksgiving, and we reminisced about Ma writing Miss Kelly an invitation, ten years past. That Thanksgiving, we'd had Miss Kelly's Mickey McDarby, along with Nadja's Max, Xenia's Robert, and Lev at our table. Two days later, they were buried in the mine. Was it any safer down there these days?

"Nope," Anton said. "We're hoping to follow you to Erie."

"Don't you go to Boston," Borya announced. "The Spanish flew in there and killed a bunch of people."

"The Spanish influenza," I said gently, as family started shouting him down. What had swept through Boston in the spring was starting up a second time.

Borya leaned against me like a dog. "Father Dmitri won't let us spit 'cause of Spanish influence."

"Influenza," I repeated. "What about Mrs. Henderson?"

"She never let us spit," he said.

Sergei said that it was hardest on people twenty to thirty. "Those with symptoms in the morning are gone by nightfall."

Lethia chimed in to add details. "They get high fevers, but what kills them is they can't get a breath in edgewise. What I heard, they drown in their bodies."

"Where are you hearing?" Sonya asked, and when Lethia pointed back to Sergei, Sonya harrumphed.

Sergei said, "The healthiest are faring the worst."

"Then I'm safe," Viktor said matter-of-factly.

Pa knocked Borya on the head with his spoon. "Look what you started."

"We're celebrating," Ma reminded everyone. She went around the table offering squares of studzien. For the Dormition Feast, she'd added veal to the jiggly mix.

Viktor took two squares. "You spoil me."

"Not you. No one tells me you was coming!" She mocked giving him the back of her hand, but he caught it and kissed it.

Pa scoffed. "We have to live with her when you drive back."

Platters went in both directions, as did arguments about vinegar or horseradish on studzien, sour cream or cottage cheese on blintzes, and who got more than his share. We'd stolen the stage, showing up and telling our news. Or maybe we started the ball rolling, because Anton and Svetlana announced their wedding plans and

Pavel said that he and Maria had agreed to join them. A year older than me, Maria was considered almost a lost cause, and I'd always hoped they'd marry.

Stash said, "I'll be the only bachelor in town," and I felt bad for him.

When Maria asked me to be her maid of honor, Pearl protested. "No fair, Yelenie's a matron." She put a hand behind her head and cocked her hip. "Pick a fair young maid."

Pavel brushed dirt from her skirt. "You'd have to promise to take a bath."

"Comb that rat's nest," Maria added.

"And leave off insulting the men for a day, if you can," Stash said.

I stood up for her. "Say what you will, there's no one to fill your apron like Pearl."

My baby sister rubbed her grubby hands together. "Lenotchka's right—I'd have you dancing with Father Dmitri himself."

When I took Hazel upstairs, Maria came along. She unrolled a towel on top of Ma and Pa's quilt, and I lay Hazel down to change her. My squirmy girl reached for the cross that dangled from my neck. "Remember when I was jealous of yours?" I asked.

"You got your own and then some," Maria said.

I knew why she'd come upstairs when she asked, "Is there work in Erie?"

"There is and there isn't," I said, unsure how much to tell about our struggle. "It's not like the mines, where you show up and they hire you. You have to look for a job, put in applications. But the church people watch out for each other."

"Pavel's so talented, don't you think? I tell him he could do other things, less dangerous things. He could only leave his brothers behind for family."

I thought of our tiny apartment, the squabbles of other families echoing down the hallways, the smell of their dinners blowing into our kitchen. Still, I said, "If you come to Erie, you can start out with us."

"I told Pavel you'd help!" Maria clapped Hazel's hands together, and Hazel crossed her eyes watching her own palms tap and open in front of her. We came downstairs to hear Viktor making the same offer to all three of his brothers.

Anton said, "What about my garden? Finally got the dirt to how I want it."

"There's plenty of dirt in our yard. Right, Lenotchka?"

"We have dirt," I agreed because I wanted to be agreeable. Viktor had brought his brothers here. I'd taken him and left town.

His generosity shamed me so much I extended the invitation to Kostia, who shrugged me off. "Most days it's not so bad," my brother said, then his voice sped up as he explained a bellows he'd invented to bring fresh air into the shaft and spread through flexible ducts. "The foot pedal works like on a sewing machine. Mr. Henderson, he gave me a bonus for that."

"Pa must have loved that!"

"He would if he knew," Kostia said.

"If I knew what?" Pa bellowed, and Kostia answered, "Nothing, old man." So some things had changed. He said, "I'm likely to leave for Pittsburgh. Nadja's Martha is still there, living with her brother's family."

"You're in touch?" I asked, though I already knew from Rita that they were pen pals.

Borya snuck in between us. "Look what Kostia made!" He handed me a flat glass box the size of the canary cages men took into the mines. On top, a cigar-sized tank was connected to a rubber hose that led to a corner of the box.

Kostia unlatched the glass front and closed a metal grill across the opening, like an elevator car for a canary. He said, "Borya loves his birds. My Basil—"

"I raised Basil from a egg," Borya said.

"Basil goes right in here on this perch and breathes what we do. But if the blackdamp gets him before me, I swing the glass shut and turn the valve for air from this tank. Then we both come out alive." He put his arm around his little brother, who let him. More changes.

"That's swell," I said admiringly. "It reminds me of the contraptions in the comics." Many a day we'd traced Rube Goldberg's crazy steps for buttering toast or petting the cat.

Kostia said, "Anyone who wants one I give it to him. They say I'm glupyy, I don't care."

He never had. "Remember when we played as kids?" I said. "You had more in your head than any of us."

"I did," Kostia agreed, and he looked pleased with both of us.

Hazel flitted among her relatives. Sonya's Alexei, now a tall eight-year-old, took Hazel's tiny shoes off her and danced her around the kitchen. "Don't get citified," he teased. "Don't go soft." She got a sliver in her big toe, but Ma sang and tickled her while working the sliver out with a needle.

Late that night, Ma and I sat up talking, and when it was time to leave on Sunday, she clung to me. "I don't see why you had to go so far," she said.

I settled into the back seat with Hazel, hoping we could sleep through the drive, but the coupe shook me up like a seltzer bottle. The other side of Pittsburgh, Viktor pulled off so I could throw up in a ditch. He wet his shirttail with water from the jug and pressed it to my forehead. "All that talk of the grippe has you spooked." He fetched a blanket and the shovel from the back, and after he scooped dirt over my vomit, he covered Hazel and me with the blanket. "Let's get you home." Home meant Erie now.

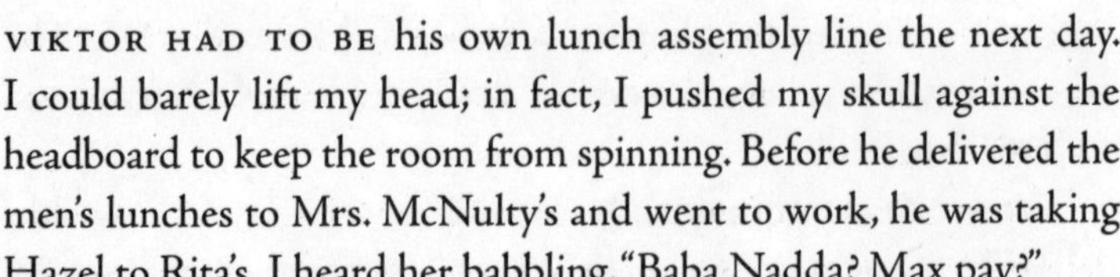

VIKTOR HAD TO BE his own lunch assembly line the next day. I could barely lift my head; in fact, I pushed my skull against the headboard to keep the room from spinning. Before he delivered the men's lunches to Mrs. McNulty's and went to work, he was taking Hazel to Rita's. I heard her babbling, "Baba Nadda? Max pay?"

"Yes, Baba Nadja's," Viktor answered her. "You show Irene and Max a thing or two."

We couldn't afford for me to stay in bed on a day when I was supposed to be at Mrs. McNulty's. I wondered if there were any new medicines for morning sickness, but we couldn't afford a doctor, either. We were still paying for Viktor's last bronchitis episode. I closed my eyes and didn't wake up until Viktor plopped on the edge of the bed with all his weight. "Are you off to work?" I asked.

He raised one eyebrow nearly to his hairline. "Did you sleep the whole day away?"

"Mama!" Hazel ran into the bedroom, smacking her lips. At the sound of her voice, my engorged breasts leaked milk. "Quick, quick," I pulled her to me and unbuttoned my wet nightgown. I wanted to think my body knew what to do, but my stomach reeled from the cabbage smell in her hair. I craned my head above hers, sipping air through my mouth.

"I can't be as sick as last time, can I?"

"You're asking a man with only brothers," Viktor said.

He took her for the final burp, and I tried to buck up. "Maybe she'll have a brother."

And he bounced Hazel on his thigh, singing, "A new baby for Hazel! Baby, baby, baby."

"Baby Aza." She pointed to herself. "Max." She pointed outside.

I looked past Viktor out the window. It was pouring on Sobieski Street, which meant a shower for the top of the trash heap and water for the dump flowers, hollyhocks and tiger lilies that bloomed among the hillocks. Last go-round, I'd sat on the kitchen floor watching the snow come down, eager to leave Marianna. I hadn't intended to live by the dump on a dirt road with drawers full of babies, but I should have thought of that when me and Viktor went about our business.

When I finally got myself back to Mrs. McNulty's, she wouldn't let me scrub on my knees, though she said that was only for my second. "After that, you're on your own." I had the get up and go of a rug. To take my mind off my queasiness, we sang, "Oh, How I Hate to Get Up in the Morning," and I told her she was onto something. She said, "I went through plenty of Irish girls before you came along. We're worse than your people, with the babies."

In the afternoon, I picked up Hazel from Rita, and Arkady came over to read. Hazel squealed for him the way Eva used to squeal for snow. The best thing that could happen to Arkady was for someone to be glad to see him. That and staying out of his father's way, which he'd gotten good at. I certainly stayed out of Mikhail's way, but I didn't live with the man.

Arkady put the nickel I gave him in a change purse and showed me his stash of coins. "I'm marching in parade. This I save to buy Ma and Klara balloons so I see them when I pass." I told him I was proud of him, and his mouth fell open.

That night I felt steady enough to send Viktor to the CYS Club to enjoy the last game of the World Series, early this year because of the war. They were rooting for the Cubs since their Pirates hadn't made it into the series. I'd gone to an earlier game and found it funny to hear them cheering like they were in the stands, when they were just listening to Brick Myeroff read out the telegraph reports of each play to the crowded bar.

For weeks, Arkady practiced carrying a flag for the Liberty Loan parade, which the *Daily Times* touted as Erie's biggest and best. The paper printed the rectangular route the troops would march, followed by schools, bands, and bigwigs. From Perry Square, they'd go down State Street, over 3rd, up Parade, and then back on 6th to the square, where Mayor Kitts and his ilk were to speak. The mayor's claim to fame was that he'd personally sent off every train carrying troops that left from Erie. As much as I wanted to see Arkady, I couldn't stand the thought of being hemmed in by a crowd. With Hazel on his shoulders, Viktor headed to Parade Street to watch for Arkady in the procession, and the bands and chants wafted into our bedroom window while I rested.

By the time Rita took me to see her doctor, I was coming out of my fog, and he declared me a healthy eleven weeks along as if he deserved the credit. I wondered what an unhealthy pregnancy felt like. "Watch out for the influenza," he warned. He didn't say what to do if it came my way. Viktor had read about more cases—Boston, New York, Philly, and Chicago—on every side of us.

"Let's get out to the peninsula before the weather changes," Rita said as we pushed our three little ones in two strollers. "A picnic and a beach bonfire, think you'd be up for that?"

"I can always sleep on a blanket."

"Downwind of the food," Rita said. Then she leaned in to tell two-year-old Irene, "We'll play on the beach—build a castle?"

"Irene splash. Swim swim with Daddy," she waved her arms around.

I was just as excited, looking forward to seeing the sun set over the dunes. When Friday's paper reported that the flu had hit Pittsburgh with twenty cases, I tossed the front section because I didn't want to worry Viktor about his brothers.

We caravanned to Presque Isle on Sunday, Leo's rickety rowboat on their car's roof. The warm September day was nicer than we often had for the Fourth of July. Blankets covered the sand patchwork-style, and close to the lake, Hazel filled and emptied her bucket with purpose. I urged Viktor to roll up his sleeves and pants legs to get some sun, which was moving along on its path without me feeling the earth spin. Such sweet relief to feel pregnant instead of sick.

I ate and ate, and so did everyone else. Kielbasa and burgers on the open coals, along with a pike that Viktor caught from the rowboat. He brought the fish to shore still flopping about. "If I throw him back, will he grant me wishes?"

"I wish I weren't hungry," Leo said and clubbed the fish on the head. As Leo cleaned it, Viktor sharpened a stick, and they skewered the pike over the coals. I heard Viktor telling Leo that his brothers were joining us soon. "Anton's your age—you remember him from West Virginia?" Viktor asked.

"Smarter and more likeable than you, yeah, I remember," Leo

said, and Viktor doubled over laughing. I wouldn't hear him laugh again for months.

As the light faded, we pulled our chairs around the fire and shook out blankets to swaddle the little ones. Leo piled on driftwood that shot out beautiful sparks. Awed by the fire and the rising moon, Hazel stayed awake for a mouthful of roasted marshmallow, then glued her sticky face to my shoulder. We sang "Hinky Dinky Parlez-vous" and "It's a Long Way to Tipperary," before someone broke into "Ochi Chyornye," *Dark Eyes*. That brought twelve-year-old Sonya to mind, just off the boat from Suwalki, singing to us in her dark alto. Instead of sadness, I felt an early thrilling flutter in my belly.

Holding Hazel on the way home was like hugging a smoked sausage, and the car breeze was thick with the smell of burning leaves, as if we'd driven out of summer into fall. As soon as Viktor took the picnic basket through our front door, he disappeared. I stuck Hazel in her high chair so I could walk back and forth unloading the car, then bathed her in the sink, finding where her buckets of sand had ended up. I put her in her little bed, a crib mattress in the corner of our room. Gathering our sandy things and wondering where Viktor had run off to, I was taken aback when he scuffled out of the bathroom in his pajamas and a robe. This type of weather, he usually slept in boxers, but here he was, buttoned up to his skinny neck.

"Mind if I turn in?" he said, teeth chattering.

"You're sick," I said. It was him asking my permission that alarmed me.

"Too much sun in that boat. I may have caught a little chill." His mustache twitched when he shuddered.

I touched his forehead. "You're a furnace."

"Then why do I feel like ice?"

I pulled out a kitchen chair and wrapped a quilt around him. When I returned with the thermometer, we sat knee to knee staring into each other's eyes. His were shiny and red-rimmed. His teeth were still knocking together, and his pulse was racing. The thermometer read 104 degrees. "Are you achy?" I asked.

He tilted his head back and forth, as if it were too heavy to hold up. "Now that you mention it, I've had a crick in my neck all day. And my knees are swollen—where you going?"

I hadn't realized I was backing away from him. "You're sick," I whimpered.

"This is a hard turn. It's the grippe, isn't it? It come to Pittsburgh in the last few days."

"You read about it?" I asked.

"Leo did. It's taking the healthy down fast, but you know me. I've never been healthy a day in my life. I told him I didn't leave the mines to catch a bug and die. Anton and them, if it's close quarters what spreads it, they're goners." Either fear or fever was making him jabber, which scared me more than if he'd given me his deadpan smile. "Stuck underground, breathing each other's stink, and except for a broken bone or two, they've been healthy as oxen. Leo says to me the healthy go quickest . . ."

I got him to bed, where he shook the whole frame as much with his shivering as with his quaking breath. I remembered when we were three in a bed and Ma's fairy tales made Kostia tremble, but Viktor shook even as he slept. I picked up my sleeping Hazel and dragged her mattress to a corner of the kitchen, where I laid down next to her, my long legs and big feet hanging off the end.

THE SPANISH FLU CAME through Erie like a gully washer. It was the Liberty Loan parade, the returning troops walking through the heart of town and cheering crowds on either side, that apparently spread it all over. Viktor was one of the earliest cases, but by the next night, the Petrovskys above us and their three children were sick. Never clear, Viktor's lungs filled up. He gurgled as he moaned. His nose bled and he hacked up blood.

Desperate to get his fever down, I gave him one sponge bath after another. Poor Hazel was in her playpen most of the day. "Don't cry," Viktor kept saying, delirious, when he was the one with tears crusting his eyes. "Please don't cry. You should go back to Marianna to be with your family. Tell your pa he was right—he's bound to outlive me now."

I didn't want to take Viktor to the hospital, where the sick people would do him in. He couldn't look any more like a skeleton, his long taut face and his slender rack of ribs rattling with each cough. Delicate as a canary, he'd survived so much. How much could a man stand in one lifetime? The GE plant closed and was turned into an infirmary. They shut down the schools, churches, and movie theaters. Barely a week after cheering the greatness of Erie, Mayor Kitts was telling people to leave town. For where?

Leo dropped by to tell me he'd taken his mother-in-law to the hospital, and Rita didn't think I should bring Hazel to their house. So far, Irene and Max were all right. They had a phone, and Mrs. McNulty had called them to say she wanted me to stay away, too. I hated to think of her cooking and cleaning for nine men. Turns out I didn't have to, because with the paper mills shut down, they'd all fled home. The hope was that little towns would be safer because they were less crowded. Wasn't there a chance they'd spread the flu hither and yon?

I swabbed Viktor down or piled quilts atop him. I fed him broth and crackers, tea and toast, mashed bananas and rice cereal—same diet as Hazel. And before I picked Hazel up or fed her, I scrubbed my hands and layered a clean housecoat over my regular one. Two mornings later, Viktor still asleep, I walked Hazel to the corner grocer. A sign propped in the window read, "Remember the three C's: Clean mouth, Clean heart, and Clean clothes." What did "clean heart" even mean? I bought a newspaper and a loaf of bread, and I didn't waste a nickel on the numbers. The cashier wore a white mask over her face, tied behind her ears, which made me nervous. Was she unclean, or did she think I was?

"Read me the paper," Viktor asked when I got home. "How are my Cubbies doing?"

He'd been to the CYS Club for the last game. "It's over, remember? The Red Sox won."

"Poor Cubbies," he said weakly. "What's happened since I've been away?"

"They say the Allies are making progress." I wasn't about to show him the paper. Each day in Erie was more dire, and my only solace was that Viktor wasn't one of the casualties they chronicled. I stared at the headline "Partners Die the Same Night." Four women playing bridge in Lawrence Park were all struck with the flu Friday night; by Saturday, three were dead.

"Nadja's home," I said, which was true but no relief. The doctor told Rita to keep her comfortable, and Nadja could barely catch her breath for coughing. It sounded bad as it could be. Father Timofei had come to take her confession, and yesterday, Leo had come down with the flu.

With the church closed, Father Timofei was up and down the blocks granting confessions and final rites. His black cassock flapped by our window. When I was on Parade Street and saw a SPIT SPREADS DEATH sign on a passing streetcar, I knew the miners were in big trouble. They spent their lives worrying about the walls caving in, the deadly air, a coal cart running awry—turns out one man spits in the shaft and they're all dead of Spanish flu.

I cleaned the kitchen from the doorknobs to the dish drainer, adding a capful of bleach to each bucket of wash water. It roughed up the diapers so that I just about chapped Hazel's skin off her little zhopa. I wished I could ask a doctor about flu and my pregnancy, but I wasn't sick so I couldn't take up his time.

That changed soon enough, when Viktor cooled down and I heated up. My eyes in the mirror were crisscrossed with red. We'd switched places, and now Viktor was taking my temperature, sounding a whistle at me hitting 104 degrees. "If we had a telephone, I'd call your ma."

"Where's my Hazel? Does she have a fever? Call Ma."

"Hush, now. Hazel's fine—Maeve McNulty fetched her for a day. Maeve wants you resting, and that's what Hazel and me want, too."

Sweat ran down the tips of my bobbed hair, puddling behind my neck. I'd just gotten my wheezing sneezing husband out of danger. I said, "Father Timofei has a telephone"—his house was on the church grounds, two blocks away—"and Doc Miller has one there. Or go to Leo and Rita's. Bundle up good when you go," I told Viktor.

That shows how bad off I was, ordering him to bring Ma to me. Viktor phoned, sent a telegram, and wired her a train ticket, all three. I didn't ask him how he paid for it. Mr. G got her to the Marianna station the next day, and from the Erie station, Rita picked her up in Leo's car. I hadn't known Rita could drive. Ma showed up in a flowered skirt, a matching mask like a podruchnik over her face.

"You sewed that?" I managed to ask.

She untied the mask and held it out. "I made it for riding the train," she said.

Her smooth, milky skin pooled beneath her cheeks as she bent over me in bed. She looked as if all the air had gone out of her, strangely both fatter and more gaunt at the same time. We'd celebrate her fortieth birthday next month, if I lived that long.

"Baba, Baba, Baba," Hazel sung from the doorway, and that didn't make Ma smile, so things at home were bad. I twitched uncontrollably with shivers. "What happened? Is it Pa?"

"No, Pa's too old, tough as beef jerky. And Kostia's fresh air machine—who knows? Maybe that's kept him." She lifted the quilt off me, raised it up in the air and let it fall back down, making a welcome breeze. "My docha," Ma said, and then to Viktor, "My syn." She sat on the edge of our bed.

Viktor's stone face looked to be carved with misery. He held Hazel in his arms.

Ma said, "We lost Anton and Stash so quick—if they suffered, it wasn't for long. Maria cared for them how you did, Yelena. And Viktor, how you did for years."

Viktor squeezed Hazel to his chest. I heard her high muffled voice, "My papa."

Ma said, "Stash, he climbs from the tunnel to lay down on the dirt. Says he can't walk the hill, and them two brothers carry him all the way to his bed, like Nadja's boy years ago. By supper, Anton's wobbly, too. They can't neither of them keep a thing down. When Pavel get me in the morning, I see their cheeks already with the spots. Not even a full day—we lost them by sundown."

I struggled to make sense of her story about two lost boys. Such bad fortune, so swift and merciless, like the tale of a forest witch, except Ma was talking about Anton and Stash, who lived where she lived when she wasn't at the edge of my bed. "They're not lost, they're gone," I said. "And me expecting again."

"Life for life," she said.

"Pavel?" Viktor asked.

"Pavel is healthy, only his heart is broken because he lost his Maria yesterday. She swabbed them other two, gave them broth. He was holding her hand at the last. Her lips were blue as a robin's egg."

Ma's voice was a distant echo. She kept saying lost when she meant dead. Viktor's brothers and dear Maria, dead. Those generous men, who pretended I helped them when they did so much for me, and my sweet friend. Pavel alone.

"Shoosh," Ma soothed us like babies. "You need your strength. They were good boys, and we took care of them. God didn't want for them any more suffering. Shoosh."

I was too spent to grieve. I woke to Viktor hacking away, breaking apart, and then Ma and him talking. He said, "I saved myself and left my brothers behind—is that how we live? I should have been there."

"They had each other," Ma said. "Three brothers stood up for each other is something."

Viktor pounded his own chest. "I turned my back on them." Then quietly, "I promised Mutka on her deathbed they could count on me."

"And they did. You brought them here for better."

"How is it better? At least Mutka and Butka found each other to marry. They got to have children in Suwalki, and they had the church, which Mutka loved. I brought my brothers back here and for what?" I'd never heard him so angry.

Stay or go? It was harder than I'd imagined for Viktor. He'd have died if we stayed. What if he died from going? I roused myself to say, "You'll give yourself pneumonia," and he came over to squeeze my hand, his palm hatched with the breaker boy scars of his childhood.

All Viktor's coughing may have drained something because the next morning I heard him whistling a dreary folk song. He was still sad—maybe he would always be sad. Ma gave him a steam treatment, leaning him over water boiled with willow sticks she must have brought, a dish towel tented over his head. She gave him a toddy of honey-lemon water with a little rum, which she'd either brought or bought. "You said he couldn't drink," she reminded me.

"Are you here to prove me a liar? Is that why you've come?" I tried to smile.

"I'm here to see the sights," she said, smiling back. "And my Lenotchka, with a little one on the way. Don't leave us."

She washed clothes, scrubbed floors, cooked soup, stuffed cabbage, and baked black and brown bread. It all tasted like ash in my mouth. She walked to the church and brought Father Timofei in to wave the censer around the house, which didn't even stink. They chanted over me.

She made her way to the sewing machine in the corner, and I could hear its *zzt-zzt-zzt*. She let Hazel come as far as our bedroom door to show me the doll her Baba had made for her, complete with an apron and yarn hair. When I woke up each morning and wasn't dead, I felt a little less kinked and ravaged. I'd chipped a tooth from clacking my teeth together as I shivered.

Finally strong enough to stand in our stingy shower, I let water run down my swelling breasts to my belly, a melon in the bowl of my bony hips. "The baby gets what it needs," Rita's doctor had said, which I hoped was true.

I dressed and went to the kitchen. On the table were three days of newspapers, headlines announcing the score like sports: 238 reported cases, 275, 320, alongside deaths: 35, 67, 55. I poured myself a glass of city juice, as Viktor called tap water, and drank it down. Hazel and Ma were buzzing like flies in the front room, Hazel telling her the story of Stupid Emilion, though I'm not sure Ma recognized her version. "He marry princess for magic pike he no eat. And that's that," Hazel said, and her baba laughed. "That's that," Ma repeated.

I looked in to see Hazel's legs dangling from a chair, both hands looped through a skein of blue yarn, helping Ma wind it from a hank into a ball. Ma said, "Next batch, I might give you the second blinchiki, warm and sweet." The second blintz, because they say the first one is always ruined. Remembering that let me know I was coming back.

"Mama here!" Hazel wriggled and dropped from her chair to the floor, trailing yarn.

Ma's shoulders relaxed from her working hunch. "You're out of that bed," she said.

I sat on the sofa as if falling, Ma in my side view already changing the bedsheets. Hazel scrambled into my lap, somehow keeping the yarn on her arms. I had to shade my eyes from the sunshine blazing in through the front-room window. Coming from my dark cave, I saw the two of them as bright angels, halos around their faces. Hazel's hair looked to be spun of gold. Her baby teeth were tiny as white corn, and she chittered away with her mouse voice. "Mama, I help Baba! I big help!"

It was unusually quiet outside, and I realized Pyos wasn't tied up barking himself hoarse. Had they gotten rid of the poor animal, or had he died? Had they died?

"Where's Viktor gone?" I asked.

Ma was back at my side, and she dabbed at her nose with a hanky, lips trembling. "He drove to Leo and Rita's." That's how weak we were, that he drove the six blocks. Then Ma crossed herself, and I knew that Nadja had died. Her first friend in this country, a welcome face when Ma had traveled across the ocean. I put my arms around my mother. "The kingdom of heaven to her," I said.

"She's with her Max now," Ma said. The way she choked back her tears sounded like chuckling, and I thought of all those games of funeral we'd played as kids, after Max and so many others died.

Hazel laughed back at her Baba. "Baby Max?" she asked.

"No, vnuchka."

My little one was dressed in a royal purple skirt and a yellow blouse with puffy sleeves; the sash at her waist was stitched with yellow roses. Ma had sewn her an entire outfit while I was sick and had made her a matching doll to boot. Two drawings were tacked to the front window, white butcher paper smeared with finger paint. Orange and yellow leaves littered the yard outside, and a blue jay dive-bombed a red-wing blackbird. In the shuttered sickroom, my world had been like newsprint, in black and white. Now I saw colors and knew I wouldn't cry forever. I smelled a hambone simmering.

I took the heathered blue yarn from Hazel's arms and laid her hand on my belly, because the baby had the hiccups. "Jumping bean," I said, and she giggled.

Viktor pulled our deep green coupe to the curb. He was never healthy, and certainly never pregnant, so he didn't have as far to go to be back to normal. Still, the flu had taken its toll. His coat hung on him like Father Timofei's cassock, and his face looked more like a skull with a hat than like Buster Keaton.

Freed from her yarn, Hazel ran to the window, purple skirt ballooning out. Nadja was gone, his beloved Anton and Stash and my Maria were lost to us, yet somehow he closed the wide coupe's door with confidence and gave us, his two favorite girls, a wave, and we waved back. Stooped and too frail for a man of twenty-six, he walked eagerly toward us, a yellow canary feather in the band of his fedora.

29

January 7, 1920

WE OPENED OUR HOUSE for Russian Christmas, doing the holiday up right for the first time since we got married. Last year, influenza had nearly done us in, and the year before, the mines nearly had. You don't want to ruin your good luck, but you had better make some memories of good times, too. After forty days of Lent without milk, meat, or eggs, I cooked up blintzes and meat pirozhki, added chopped tongue to the Russian salad and baked cabbage and egg pies. I had a long string of kielbasa links at the ready, to go with the sauerkraut Viktor brewed in the basement barrel, and I put a roast in the oven, its pretty rump resting on a bed of carrots, onions, and potatoes.

Thank goodness Christmas comes every year.

We'd moved to Parade Street in the spring, a few months after Viktor got hired back at Griswold's as an enamel setter, putting the baked finish on stoves. We lived downstairs from none other than Rita and Pavel. Those two knew loss. Rita lost everyone to the flu except Max: her girl, Irene; her husband, Leo; and her mother, Nadja, all died days apart in the epidemic. She still had her sister Martha in Pittsburgh—she and my brother Kostia lived on a little farm outside the city.

In Marianna, Pavel buried two of his and Viktor's brothers and his intended, Maria. He came to Erie with Svetlana, Anton's match, only to watch Brick Myeroff steal her away at the first wedding after the flu ban. Rita and her little Max were eager to make Pavel feel better, which they did. After Pavel and Rita married, they moved upstairs, and we took over the downstairs.

For all the times I'd brought it up, Pavel was the one who got Viktor to file his Declaration of Intention papers. We still had two years to wait before he could petition for citizenship, which Pavel said should give Viktor enough time to find two people willing to stand up for his character. Pavel could not have been more different from Rita's Leo, who I missed, but I saw how a different fit could also be a good one. He'd made my best friend my sister-in-law, and the reunited Gomelekoff boys loved that Rita and me were in cahoots.

Lethia also ended up in Erie. Her Sergei was a sheet metal cutter at GE and went to night school to study drafting. It was Sergei who'd gotten me a training manual to be a switchboard operator.

Here was Lethia's brood and two other families at our door: Brick and Svetlana, along with Leo's Uncle Marco and Aunt Olya, toting all their children. Hazel was excited to have so many people in our apartment. The crowd had worked their way up Parade Street after services, singing the tropar and kondak to families along the way and drinking steaming cups of sbiten, spiked for the adults, who were liquored up by the time they got to us. Their church garb hidden beneath fur-trimmed coats, the women had stuffed their headscarves into their coat pockets and swiped lipstick over their devout lips. Olya said, "That's what confession is for."

Viktor ushered them in from the porch. "Sing to us in our front room. Leave the cold out there." I missed Ma when they belted out the kondak, remembering how Nadja and her sang the St. Nicholas hymn. "You preserved them from danger and death as they labored beneath the earth." I hadn't known the meaning until my old neighbor Tatiana translated for me.

The Vasilievs—Tatiana, her husband, Mikhail, and their children—went back to Russia when their poor addled Klara stopped speaking altogether. Tatiana said she'd get more help in Suwalki, and I hoped she was right. I wondered if my parents ever wished they'd returned to Suwalki and let Pa be the village cobbler.

The commotion in our front room drew Rita's gang downstairs. "Trying to leave us out?" Pavel asked. Viktor kissed his baby brother on each cheek, and he did the same to Rita, whose belly stretched the seams of my old maternity dress.

Viktor said, "Don't worry, none of these people were invited either." He squatted down to Rita's little Max, who practically leapt into Viktor's arms, and Viktor carried him over to Hazel.

Svetlana handed her rabbit-fur muff to Brick, who pulled a full bottle of vodka from the muff's center. Brick and his ilk at the paper mill had been working overtime so they could buy up as much liquor as possible in the countdown to Prohibition.

Rita said, "Who knew Russians were so ambitious?" We went through the swinging door to the kitchen, where I had every pot out and cabinet open, and she helped me load food onto trays. "Merry Christmas, TomTom," she said to my boy, and we both watched him for a reaction. I would have thought he'd recognize her birdlike voice. Tommy stared at her, bored.

We heard another cheer from the living room. As far as I was concerned, the men were not so much honoring Christmas as racing the clock.

Rita said, "If women had the vote, Prohibition would have come earlier."

"And you wonder why we don't have the vote," I said, but there'd been news she might have missed in the holiday flurry. "Did you hear?" I unlatched the broom closet door, where I kept track of Hazel's height along the inside edge, and at the top, hash marks tallying the states. "It passed Kentucky and Rhode Island this week. Only twelve more." Another reason to love Rita was that she cared as much as me about the amendment passing.

"Save your breath to cool your soup," she said, and I laughed because her mother, Nadja, used to say that. I'd already thought of Nadja as I got ready for this crowd, the way she and Ma could make soup from nothing. Rita finished stacking the pirozhkis, and she put a towel in Tommy's hand, trying to get him to grip. She asked, "Would you starve yourself for the vote, like those women in prison?"

I said, "Most of them didn't grow up hungry, I don't think. Except for our Rose, they're all of them college girls."

"Our Rose?" Rita laughed. "Nobody claims her but you. Notice the paper has to put her in her place, saying 'Rose Winslow, born Ruza Wenclawska, a mill worker.'"

"She doesn't care what the paper says about her," I said. As if she were actually my Rose and we'd had a good long talk about it.

Rita said, "Think it's easier to go on a hunger strike when you've grown up hungry? Or harder?" She rolled up a blintz, dabbed it in the melted butter I had by the griddle, and ate it plain. "Mmmm, eggs and butter. They force-fed them eggs, you know. Could be that's why they've been on my mind."

"You made it through," I said.

We'd bickered about her keeping Lent. Pregnant women were let off, but she was determined to honor her ma. "The baby gets what it needs." She'd quoted her doctor. More and more, I worried that Tommy hadn't gotten what he needed when I had the flu.

Lethia swept in just then. "Viktor tells us you've been cooking, so show us a morsel, why don't you?"

I handed her the stuffed peppers I'd arranged on our new tray, a baking sheet painted with holly leaves and red berries. My sister held it at arm's length. "Ma painted us a tray. Is this from her?" When I nodded, she said, "Yours is nicer. She probably practiced on mine first."

Like us, I thought meanly. It was a reflex with Lethia, wanting to poke her back, and I held my tongue. My sisters arrived in America and I imagined I was the girl in the Golden Slipper story, whose mother loved her other daughters more. Years later, when Arkady read the story to Hazel, I realized it ended with the neglected daughter rising to the top like cream. For Christmas, Ma had sent me the tray and a stack of quilted hot pads, as well as her lacquer box painted with Emilion and his magic pike.

Lethia was still inspecting the tray of peppers. "The stuffing's coming out of these," she said and carried them off.

Rita said, "New year, same old Lethia." She straightened Tommy in his high chair, stuffing hot pads into the gaps so he couldn't flop sideways. The batch Ma had sent were smaller versions of the church podruchniks she quilted for when we bowed our heads to the floor. Viktor had jokingly tossed one on the linoleum and pretended to pray for dinner, all in fun, because he hadn't missed a day of work for four months and I was still at Mrs. McNulty's, which is how we could feed everyone and also buy a tree.

Rita picked up a platter of pirozhki in one hand, a tray of kielbasa in the other. "I promise to pass these around. Honest, I won't eat them all myself. Really," she teased.

Alone with Tommy, I wrapped tissue around my two Willow Ware teacups and saucers, Viktor's Christmas gift to me, and put them back in the striped Boston Store box. I wished he'd taken me with him to buy them. I only went there to look, and it would have been a joy to be waited on, to pay, to be thanked, to be asked to come back. *Erie's Boston Store, Where You Choose from More.* I yearned to choose from more, and I was staring down the box when Viktor came in. I said, "Christ is born."

"He is born indeed." He kissed me on the forehead. "There's a party in our house, you don't want to use your new cups?"

I hugged the box to my chest. "Not yet. After Lethia has tea, she'll fill it with vodka." I took one of our thick white coffee mugs from the dish drainer. "For Lethia," I said.

"Suit yourself," Viktor shrugged. It wasn't so much that I was being selfish—I *was* being selfish—it was that he would never have thought to hold back. Maybe with his health, not to mention his losses, he didn't see as far into the future as I did, when we'd have an entire set of cups and saucers.

I didn't begrudge the crowd eating us out of house and home. We'd had a high time at Brick and Svetlana's last night for Christmas Eve. I was happy to host tonight and proud that I'd prepared so many favorites. Viktor took Tommy from his high chair and followed me in. The crowd had been in church for hours, standing and bowing, and here were the foods they hadn't touched for forty days. They cheered my arrival, or the rump roast's.

"Blintzes and pirozhki?" Pavel asked, his eyes big as eggs.

"And a roast," I practically danced the platter from the counter to the card table strewn with food.

"I hope you didn't pay good money for a dead tree." Leo's Uncle Marco emptied a handful of dried pine needles on our floor—by Russian Christmas, the tree was nearly bald except for ornaments—but he changed his tune when he lifted one of my heavy pirozhkis.

His little girl pointed to my platter. "Is that meat?"

We laughed, so happy with our good fortune. As Lethia plucked a carrot with her fingers, I mimed knocking her hand with a spoon, the way Pa used to. I said, "Remember Ma tearing apart a stringy brisket to flavor a stew?"

Lethia said, "She might have put old shoes in there, cut to bits."

Pavel licked his fingers. "We thought youse were rich. That day we arrived at Gregor and Katya's, Stash stuck a fork in his bowl and found kielbasa. Then we all did. Such a memory, the four of us waving our forks in the air."

"Four of us," Viktor repeated, and the two brothers clasped arms in a moment of grief.

"Yelenie," Brick said, sounding desperate, "we need to scrounge up glasses. Should we help ourselves?"

Svetlana muttered, "Here, you help yourself. At home, I have to wait on you."

I said, "They aim to drink all the liquor in town before it's illegal."

She agreed. "After that, it will cost them more." Their children ran wild, but so did Lethia's, racing around the apartment. Her youngest ran smack into Sergei.

"Settle down," Sergei said. He turned to Lethia. "So? What did she think?"

"She doesn't think yet," Lethia answered. She unbuckled her

pocketbook and handed me a flat parcel wrapped in paper and tied with a bow. "Happy Christmas, Yelena." I looked at the parcel, then at my sister, and then back to the parcel.

"Don't be so shocked."

But I was shocked. Her giving me a present and calling me by my name were two Christmas miracles. Ma had begged me to welcome Lethia and her brood to Erie, and I made an effort, despite Lethia saying Tommy should be crawling, or her asking how many more years of work I thought Viktor had in him. I slipped off the ribbon and tissue paper to see a delicately painted icon, the image as familiar to me as the photograph of my two sisters. The Virgin Mother held Baby Jesus, whose round eyes and thin column of nose stood out in a beautiful, loving face. It was a miniature version of the icon Ma had given Sonya when they left the girls in Suwalki. The square had gold-leafed edges like a frame and an eyehook at the top looped with red string.

Lethia said, "I know, I know, you are American, but also you are Orthodox."

The wooden square, twice the size of a postage stamp, was so intricately painted it showed the folds in both Mary's sky-blue robe and the infant's chubby thighs. I hadn't seen anything this special at the church bazaar or the stores where I'd shopped. I said, "It's exactly like Sonya's." I'd stroked her stitched icon, Mary's satin robe and a golden halo of thread.

"Da," Lethia said. "I copied hers."

This image had gone from Ma to Sonya to Lethia and now to me. "It's beautiful," I said. "I didn't know you could do this."

She said, "Our jeda taught me to paint before I knew you."

She still didn't know me, or she would have known I'd hidden my new cups rather than let her use them. Lethia's delicate, expressive strokes caught the Virgin's thin face tilted in adoration and also modesty. Lethia had grown up across the globe from me, and she'd painted this ornament herself, for me.

"Spasibo," I said. The Virgin stared down at her newborn with her long-suffering gaze, a woman pushed out of her home, and I hung her on a high branch of the Christmas tree in my line of sight. I was deeply moved by Lethia's verdict, that I was American but also Orthodox.

"You can say 'thank you' how they say it here. Sergei and me are Americans now."

"You're citizens?" I asked. It was just like Sergei to file papers, help her study, get witnesses.

She said, "Fresh off the boat," which she must have thought meant brand new.

Rita had just said, "New year, same old Lethia." But that wasn't true.

Sergei rushed over, and he was studying my face. "What? What do you think?"

"It's wonderful," I said, for both the ornament and their news. They must have started the citizenship process when they were still in Marianna. I gave Sergei a warm hug and then opened my arms for my sister. I said, "Welcome to my country!"

WITH THAT, CHRISTMAS BURST forth for me. Our guests had hours of celebrating left in them, and even Leo's Uncle Marco didn't get in my way. First, he wanted answers: "How can this be a great country without vodka?" Pavel waved him off, and Brick told him to go back to Russia if he thought vodka made the country. Then Marco wanted all the children to join in—"I knew the taste after my mother's breast." The children made faces—"What? You drank from a teat too!"—and they pelted him with sugar cubes until I made them stop. Once again, not my children.

When our house grew overheated, Brick and Marco stripped off their Russian shirts and good shoes to sit around on our furniture in undershirts and long pants, the same as they'd wear on the peninsula's sandy shores. Except we were in Erie in January, which meant the dunes piling up outside were snowdrifts.

"Sing, princess," Viktor lifted Hazel onto the sofa. She was red-cheeked as I'd been, but the bows in her thick curls stayed put. Sturdier than me or any of my siblings, she had pudgy knees and dimpled thighs. Viktor moved behind me, and I leaned into him, happy to feel him at my back. He said, "Her hands are like two little skansi." They were doughy delights.

That's how Viktor had won me over, showing me that he noticed.

Hazel took hold of her skirt on either side of her hips, swaying on the sofa cushion. In her squeaky voice, she sang a tune Ma had taught her in Russian, one we had sung: "I was already dancing, I was already blushing. Come on over, be my fellow, come on and I'll kiss you."

Someone yelled, "Can't speak Russian but already sings it!"

Lethia had settled next to me, and I said, "I never saw you paint."

"Where was a brush? An egg yolk to use for paint when we fought over strings of meat?"

"Like asking for the moon."

"I was useless," she said. "I'd never combed my own hair, and you could make pies and pelmeni. You pounded rice into baby food for Borya! No one needed what I could do."

Until Sergei, I thought, realizing that she'd chosen a family tied to the church like the grandfather who'd raised her. All those questions I pestered Ma with, I'd never asked Lethia or Sonya about life in Suwalki. They hadn't gone hungry, like Viktor and his brothers—or like us, for that matter—and Baba and Jeda had pampered them. Still, if Mikhail spit on the ground and called me a filthy Jew, they must have faced that and worse. I hoped that was behind her now that she was a citizen.

Hazel scrambled down, collecting kisses and coins. People passed Tommy from lap to lap. "So content." "What a quiet one." He sometimes forgot how to nurse overnight, and we had to start over nearly as strangers in the morning.

By the time we got everyone out of our house, it was three in the morning, and I'd had a few vodkas myself. Our guests had gone through the entire roast and all the kielbasa, even the extra links I had in the icebox. The sour cream and cottage cheese bowls were as clean as if someone had licked them, which they may have, and there was one lone blintz. No matter how many you cooked, a single blintz was always left.

Folks had spirited deviled ham from the pantry, saltines, brined apples, and jarred plums. I found pickles abandoned by children, their tiny teeth marks like Christmas mice let loose. Other than that, there was no food left to put away or clean up, not a sprig of dill. Only dishes and glasses everywhere, so I went to bed, pressing my cold feet against Viktor, who was snoring louder than the coupe when its muffler broke free.

30

I DIDN'T HEAR VIKTOR leave for the factory in the morning, and I made it to the rooming house late with Hazel and Tommy in tow, which I'd only done once before.

Mrs. McNulty said, "When you go to the phone company, they won't allow children."

"They might be grown by then. Turns out there's a lot to running a switchboard." I closed my eyes most nights with the operator script in my hands. In my sleep, I wore a drop-waist dress with a knife-pleated skirt, and I used proper grammar to help Erie's citizens reach their intended party. To *whom* am I speaking, please? I assured Mrs. McNulty I'd still work for her, then we talked about the rowdy crowd I'd fed last night and all that they'd plowed through. While my little ones napped in the buggy, I managed to strip and change the beds, get the sheets in the wash, and run a carpet sweeper through the rooms.

TomTom started fussing when I crinkled up newspaper to wipe the windows down. Mrs. McNulty waved me off. "Go home and take your small fry with you." I promised to come back before the boarders returned on Sunday. She said, "You Russians have three holidays for every one of ours," but she didn't say it meanly.

Parade was a little farther than Sobieski had been, and by the time we walked the extra blocks, Tommy was asleep in the carriage. Hazel trailed me around the apartment picking up doilies and trash. I let her drop napkins down the trash chute, then I stacked dishes in the sink. I put a clean pot on the floor with a tin cup and some soapy water for her.

"Washin' up from big potty," she sang, scooping and pouring. We both did our jobs, though she was more cheerful about it.

Viktor dragged himself home from the plant and draped his arm around my neck.

"I'm afraid there's nothing for you but crusts and gristle," I apologized. I made the children rice cereal and him some scrambled eggs and toast, which he ate without complaint.

He sipped his tea and commenced to suck at his teeth. He said, "Thank you for the dinosaur chops, Mrs. Bonescraper." And I said, "You're most welcome, Mr. Bonescraper." You had to prize a husband who saw us as sweeties from the comics. Hazel, who had laid her cheek on the table, fell asleep clutching her spoon.

"See, Tommy," Viktor said and pointed. "Your big sister's saying her prayers." We shared a laugh at our exhausted girl and at Father Timofei, too, facedown in his dinner plate at the last church supper and calling it praying.

I ran a washcloth under the tap and handed it to Viktor, who swabbed Hazel's face, neck, and behind her ears. Then he tipped her toward me for a peck on the cheek. I cleaned the crumbs from the table, and he was back empty-handed. "You said her prayers over her?" I asked.

He crossed himself in answer, a smirk below his mustache. I looked at the clock, rubbed my eyes, looked again. What felt like midnight was only seven. "Why so peppy?"

"The Morosky boys will be at the Russian Club tonight. Pavel and me thought we might teach them a lesson."

"Go, go, go." I egged him on before he could talk himself out of it. "They might forget how to lose if you wait another month."

I almost asked him to come home between beating them and treating them to drinks, but I didn't want to spoil his fun. What with his health, the babies, and the bills, I worried that he felt me breathing down his neck day and night. He flapped the end of his Christmas scarf and said, "Red to match my eyes," the same thing he'd said when he'd unwrapped it the day before.

"Don't leave it behind—the way I knit, you won't get another until next Christmas. Are you driving?"

"If the car starts, I'm driving everyone."

I heard Pavel galumphing downstairs from his and Rita's apartment before the coupe started up, stalled, and started again. Viktor beeped twice as they sped away from Parade Street.

I took my time putting dishes away. I checked on Hazel, who'd kicked off her blanket, and returned to fill the sink for Tommy's bath. Gently holding his wrist, I poked the suds with his fingers. "Pop." I burst a shiny soap bubble. "Pop," I repeated. I might as well have been playing with Hazel's doll. I hoped to get him settled and go to sleep myself, but as Mrs. McNulty would say, Jesus had other plans.

Just as I'd lathered the baby's hair, our buzzer sounded. "I'm bathing TomTom," I hollered, expecting Rita to let herself in for straight pins or a cake of yeast. Instead, a voice chirped, friendly and fancy, "Shall I return a bit later?"

That told me it wasn't one of us. My own ma would have said, "You're too busy for me." Reciting from my switchboard-operator script, I asked, "To whom am I speaking, please?"

"Frances G. Byrne. I'm the census enumerator for this neighborhood. Shall I start upstairs?"

Again with the shall. "Yes, please," I said.

I'd read in the newspaper that census takers would come round, though it hadn't said when. Heels clacked up the stairs, and Rita's buzzer snored through the exhaust vent. I heard Rita's puzzled greeting; far along as she was, she was probably bushed, too.

I got a second wind at Frances G. Byrne, complete with middle initial, sent to take our measure. Ten years ago, when the postmaster's wife made her way from Bosses Row up to Russian Hill, we'd all burst into tears at being counted. That and Sonya lying about her age. Lethia had been there, too, to meet Harry's friend from Detroit.

It wouldn't do to have the enumerator see me with a baby in the sink and clothes heaped on the floor, the stink of dirty diapers rising from the pail. "Let's sit up and be counted, TomTom."

His darting eyes worried over the black-and-white cow and pink pig mounted on the high chair. By his age, Hazel was greeting the animals as old friends, reaching to spin them. I slid the diaper pail beneath the sink and swept under the tree, surprised that the dried needles had any pine scent left. I scurried around, putting away things we used and getting out things we didn't, like my new Willow Ware cups and saucers.

Tucked between the percolator and the icebox was a wedge of pound cake that last night's crowd had missed. I cut the piece in two and dusted the slices with powdered sugar to freshen them, then filled the kettle. Heels tapped down the stairs, and I smoothed the wrinkles from my housedress after the buzzer moaned.

My heart lurched in my chest when I opened the door to Frances G. Byrne. She looked to be my age, hair bobbed like mine, but everything else was ritzier: T-strap shoes and a green wool coat, collared in fur. Beneath her coat flashed a bright white blouse with a striped tie like a man's. A column skirt hugged her narrow but shapely hips.

"I regret I was occupied earlier," I said, another line from the switchboard script.

Her cheeks colored, though that might have been blush. "I'm sorry for the interruption." With her slim figure and tapered fingers, she looked like the women in the pattern books Ma and I used to page through. I was skinny but knobby-kneed and round-faced, bustier than usual from nursing TomTom.

"You are the second of two families living at this address," she said.

"That is correct." I sounded like a stiff. "Please," I warmed my welcome, inviting her in with a sweep of my arm. I had us sipping from my blue-and-white cups as we talked about hem lengths, but she would only come in far enough for me to close the door against the cold. "You're dandy to offer"—dandy—but she simply could not. She waved the clipboard in one hand, mother-of-pearl pen in the other. I smelled Sen-Sen on her breath and wondered what she was covering up.

She said, "Don't think I'm not tempted, but I have the rest of the block to get through." I admired the pin tucks of her white blouse, her short, striped tie. She wrote some numbers in the vertical column with her gold-nibbed pen. We were the 589th family she'd visited, maybe since she'd been issued her sheaf of forms.

I stepped away to turn the burner off; the kettle's sighing whistle echoed my disappointment. She consulted her rectangular wristwatch and nodded, so that when she asked my name, I thought she had the time to make my acquaintance. "I'm Yelena," I said. What I wouldn't have given for the two of us to drink tea from my new cups.

But, of course, Frances G. Byrne was asking for her form. "I know how to spell that," she said, "E-L-A-I-N-E." With one stroke of her pen, I became Elaine, and I couldn't bring myself to set her straight. I had a lump in my throat, remembering Mrs. Collins adding years to Sonya's age and Sonya letting it go. It wasn't entirely a lie, Elaine being the American version of my name. If I got hit by a streetcar before I had a chance to go to confession, they'd bury me in the swamp.

"And who is the head of the household at this abode?"

Last I'd heard the word *abode* was from Mrs. Collins. "My husband, Viktor Gomelekoff. I'll spell that for you."

She pointed to the line above ours. "Same as upstairs?"

"Oh, yes. Pavel's his baby brother. My husband is Viktor. With a K," I stressed.

Hearing his spelling, she said, "That's distinctive," then sounded *Gomelekoff* out slowly, *Go-mail-a-cough*, an expert on the second try. "And where was he born?"

"Russian Poland," I said, remembering how Mrs. Collins had corrected us about where our people were from. "Suwalki."

She pointed at Rita and Pavel's line again. "I have his brother born in West Virginia."

"That's right," I said, and it was my turn to blush, as if she knew I'd been matched to Pavel first.

"Do you rent or own?" she asked, and it occurred to me I could tell her anything. To Frances G. Byrne, I could be Elaine who owned this house and worked at the phone company. "Rent," I said.

She took a dainty step toward Tommy, who didn't blink. "Who's this pretty baby?"

"He's a boy," I said out of pride, but it came out like a correction.

"Handsome, then. A handsome fella."

I said, "Thomas. He's nine months old."

I watched her record his name and draw a circle on the form. She said, "That's zero, for 'age at last birthday.' Any others?"

"Our daughter Hazel's nearly three and in bed for the night. Such a dear."

The tidy cursive written between the lines sent me further back, as far back as I could remember, to when Ma practiced endless rows of cursive loops. Miss Kelly had taught Ma penmanship, and Ma's written invitation had brought Miss Kelly to our table—*Siobhan Mary Margaret Kelly*. I was thinking of all that at exactly the same time, as if the ink in her pen had once been in Ma's inkwell, the past and the future looping together.

"Here, I'm skipping all over, when I meant to go across for each. What's Viktor's age?"

I told her he was twenty-seven.

"Very good," she said. "His year of immigration?"

"Well, the family went back and forth. Viktor came over again in 1913."

She brought the small print of the form closer for a moment, writing the numbers as she talked. "Nineteen, thirteen. Has he been naturalized?"

"Not yet," I said, "but he's filed for it."

She made a loop in another column like the zero she'd made for Tommy's age. Then it was more names and dates and me grinning like a sap, the two of us chuckling at father's mother tongue and mother's mother tongue. She sped up to ask, "Can he read? Can he write? Can he speak English?" Her litany was something like Father Dmitri at our first confession.

"Can he read?" I tried not to take offense. "Viktor recites Pushkin."

"But can he read?"

"He got himself and his brothers here from Suwalki. Of course he can read, and write, and speak English."

She smiled slightly, obviously relieved. "Occupation?"

"Enamel setter, over at Griswold's. He coats the cast-iron stoves."

Frances G. Byrne raced along, tallying us as white, married people who rented our apartment and worked as a laborer and domestic. I wanted her to write that we drove a Ford, that I made Fannie Farmer's meatloaf for Sunday supper, that I saved Green Stamps.

"Now, it's your turn," she said. "Age, if you don't mind?"

"I'll be twenty-one in two weeks," I said.

"Oh." Her painted lips puckered for an instant. "I thought you were older, married and with little ones. Twenty, then, like me."

I said, "Rita upstairs is younger and expecting her third. Her Pavel's nineteen."

"Right, I have that. Can you read? Can you write?"

I nodded my head. That she even had to ask. With a lighter touch, she said, "And you obviously speak English."

"It's my mother tongue," I said.

"Place of birth?"

"Marianna, Pennsylvania. Viktor and me moved to Erie soon as we could." I wanted her to look at me and not the form. "Are you from Erie?"

Again, she puckered, then answered my question. "I'm from Titusville. I came here to go to Allegheny."

"You're in college? A college girl?"

"Not right now, it's winter break." She pointed her fountain pen at Tommy. "The baby," she said. He was spitting up.

He did this sometimes after his bath, and we'd have to start all over if it got into his curly hair. It usually happened when I was worn out, and I figured on those nights maybe he was tired, too, and that affected his digestion. He wasn't the least troubled about his mess, which already soured the air. I wished she had seen Hazel.

I got a dishcloth from the sink, stumbling over my own feet. I was the last to blame a baby for losing his supper or to judge a person whose baby made a mess. Babies didn't know. They didn't care, either, and here I was caring too much. In Frances G. Byrne's tally, I'd married too young, had children too fast. My husband wasn't naturalized, my baby couldn't keep his supper down.

"Is he sick?" she asked.

"No," I said, a little sickened by the smell of his curdled spit-up and her licorice-scented breath—if I weren't having my monthly, I'd have worried I was expecting. I lifted my baby from his chair and gently swabbed his chin and neck.

Tommy didn't narrow his eyes with pleasure at his mother's face. He didn't see me, but with her as my witness, I saw him. "I had the Spanish flu last fall, not long after I started carrying him. At nine months, his sister stood on her own and pointed for what she wanted. If he wants something, it's a mystery to us all."

She shifted her weight from foot to foot. "That must be a worry," she finally said.

I wondered if she'd learned that in college, or maybe from her census-taking script. I unbuttoned his sleepsuit and peeled it off, then swaddled him in a blanket. I could at least show that I knew how to tend to him. I said, "I'll be twenty-one at the end of the month. Will you be twenty-one by November? This neighborhood is up in arms about Prohibition, but Rita and me, we're watching to see if we get the vote."

"Oh, my," she said, and this time there was pity in her voice. "Oh, Elaine."

She was talking to me. I was Elaine to her.

I was watching every mark she made with her gold-nibbed pen, so I was watching when she filled in the box that separated the sheep from the goats. Where it asked "Naturalized or Alien," she made the same loops for me that she'd made for Viktor, where I'd thought she'd written in a zero. I couldn't understand what I was looking at. "Naturalized or Alien" were choices for foreigners.

On Rita and Pavel's line, those boxes were blank, as mine should have been, the three of us all born here. I could see higher up where she'd visited Lethia and Sergei on Parade, and their boxes were marked with a capital N. N for naturalized, which had just happened.

That was the clue that slipped the knot, unraveling a thread that had been just out of my reach. What she'd written in my box made as little sense as Ma's penciled corkscrews, which weren't words or even letters. Frances G. Byrne, in her practiced penmanship, had inked in cursive *Al* for alien.

"Alien!" I pointed at the form. "No, you got that wrong. I was born here." In my head, I heard Sonya repeating, "ale-yun, ale-yun," asking why she and Harry were being called that.

She said, "It isn't right. Women who marry foreign nationals are no longer citizens. For now. They're working to change that."

"You're saying Viktor is a foreign national."

"Well, I'm not saying it, but yes, he is. And it doesn't apply to men—isn't that unfair? When we learned about this in class, I never thought I'd be in the middle of it."

She wasn't in the middle of anything. I asked, "So am I Russian? Russian *Polish*?" Next she'd tell me up was down and south was sideways. "I'm American."

"You should be," she said. "It's a silly law, a stinker from Teddy Roosevelt," and she tittered the way we had over "father's mother tongue."

Nothing about this was silly. I remembered the president's law about boys in the mine and how families got around it. Every law a loophole, the Italians had taught them. Italians, I thought, Mrs. G's daughter dangling in my memory. Born on the Giordana's kitchen table down the hill from us in Marianna, Teresa was made a foreigner by marrying a Sicilian. Now that I'd tugged at the thread, I saw all that was strung along it, from Pa matching me with Pavel to Maria pushing her citizenship book my way.

Frances G. Byrne said, "My civics teacher said people were worried about the Chinese marrying our women."

You are *our women,* I thought, born the same year in the same state as me. She might as well have stuck her pen in my gut. She might as well be Father Dmitri, her swanky coat his cavernous black robe. "Yelena, Yelena, Yelena," he'd say my name, my real name, whenever I questioned the church's silly laws. "God cast Adam and Eve from the garden for asking why this, why that."

Alien was such an ugly word. I thought I was seeing loops like Ma's elegant penmanship when she was branding me an alien. I'd imagined I had more choices than Ma and Pa, but I couldn't choose to be Elaine, an American girl working for the phone company and voting for president. My country, church, and family—my personal trinity—had always been thorn as well as balm, as capable of showing malice as mercy.

"What a bother I've caused," she said, no comfort in her Sen-Sen breath. "I need to be on my way, and I do thank you for answering all our questions."

At that, Frances G. Byrne capped her pen and scooted herself into the foyer, just the way Mrs. Collins had when Sonya's Harry showed up. She tapped down the hallway in her T-straps on her merry way to the next house, where she could wave her pen around like a gavel. The kick pleat of her skirt fluttered like a flag beneath her smart coat.

You're meant to count everyone, not judge them, I wanted to yell after her. I heard her heels clacking down the wrought iron stairs to the street as I fell into my chair at the kitchen table, hugging Tommy. Saying I wasn't American was like saying my children weren't my children. What would she have me do? Get on a boat to Russia, where I'd never set foot? Might as well swim there. Might as well drown.

I felt useless as an egg that's been cracked and emptied. And worse for the shame of doing the same thing, telling Russians to go back where they came from. Because I'm American, or was. Americans with their libraries and meatloaf, their department stores and county fairs. I fell for it all.

My parents had matched me and Pavel because he was born here, and I'd made a choice. *Who says you choose?* both my parents had asked, though they didn't want an answer. People had tried to warn me that marrying Viktor might turn me into a Russian girl, and I'd called them silly. Question after foolish question popped into my head, when the truth was, this was something I'd known about my country but had not allowed myself to believe. So eager to be the bride, I'd forgotten about the wolf.

RITA MUST HAVE HEARD me bawling from her apartment and thundered downstairs. "What did that woman do to you?" She took Tommy into her arms, flapping open the blanket as she toed his soiled sleepsuit on the floor. "TomTom, didn't you like your dinner? Let's give your ma a moment's peace."

When she returned from putting Tommy down, I blubbered to my friend, "I married Viktor, and now I'm not a citizen. Even if we get the vote, I can't vote."

"She told you all that?" Rita gave a snort. "Well, she doesn't know everything." She lit the burner under the kettle I'd filled for Frances G. Byrne.

I was grateful for Rita's distrust of her. Maybe checking a box doesn't necessarily make it so. I fanned out my hands and turned them one way then the other, as if I'd changed my spots. "I'm American. They can't take that away from me, can they?"

"Oh, Yelena," she reminded me of my name. "You're asking me? The mines took away my father. The flu took away my mother, my husband, my baby. Really, they can do anything they want."

I meant the law, but she meant death. Rita and Pavel had lost so many, yet they carried on. They were both Americans, and whether or not they were expecting the worst, the worst happened to them, until they found each other.

For a fleeting second, I wondered if I'd been put in my place or set free in some way, a citizen of the world. Except for the vote, which still wasn't settled, what had I lost? Tommy's soiled pajamas on the floor set me off again. "And Tommy," I said. "A mother knows."

"Maybe," Rita said. "Pavel tells me Stash didn't speak till he was three."

"That's so." I'd forgotten that.

"Tommy's lucky he's yours. We're all bone tired, and then that nosey girl comes by to play Twenty Questions." She pointed to the plate near the sink. "I see two pieces of cake there. You want company, or would you rather be in bed?"

"Take them upstairs for you and Pavel," I told Rita, when the truth was that I wanted to be alone. "You're good to me."

"We're in the same lifeboat." She kissed me good night and picked up the cake plate. On her way out the door, she said, "I won't vote until you can."

The kettle screamed like a freight train, and I wished it would just run me down. Frances G. Byrne had knocked on my door and told me this country passed a law to reject me. Tommy and Hazel were now the Americans in our family, like I had been in my family. Unless new laws changed that. When I poured water into my Willow Ware cup, the swirling and sinking tea leaves brought to mind the schoolboys who drowned the rat in the rain barrel, angered by his gumption. I'm not a rat, swimming for my life, I thought. We finally have two dimes to rub together, I'm not pregnant, Viktor isn't coughing up blood.

When Ma talked like this after Eva died, I questioned whether she was brave or foolhardy. Were we bettering or just repeating ourselves? After all, I ended up with a miner, an Old Believer like my parents, born in their hometown of Suwalki. Ma said there's always a way, but no matter its effort or outlook, the rat in the rain barrel drowned.

I remembered reading "Prince Ivan and the Firebird" to my siblings for the hundredth time and getting stuck in my usual spot. Kostia came up with a new ending he'd discovered without changing a word, a trick he'd taught himself while trying to stay awake in the dark underground.

The coupe, which used to whinny, sputtered, because it's always something, and I heard it turn the corner and come to rest in the driveway. After the engine coughed, Viktor did, too, stepping from the heated car into the wintry air. His lungs may well give out or the flu come back and finish us off, but tonight my husband went out for some fun with his beloved brother and came home to his family. He won't be drunk, and he won't strike me. If our baby turns out to be slow, he'll be disappointed, but he won't take it out on me or Tommy.

Say I turned the tables on Frances G. Byrne and waved my own pencil around to make my mark the way she did, the way Ma told me to. Would that make any difference? If Ma showed up in my kitchen tonight, I'd throw my arms around her and cry into her soft bosom.

"What can you do?" she'd ask, the same as saying you can't do anything. "Lose one tooth, you don't stop eating."

In the morning, I told myself, I'll get myself over to Mrs. McNulty's to do the job she pays me for, and I'll keep studying to be a switchboard operator. Sergei said if I can read it without sounding like a foreigner, I'll have a shot. That was funny at the time, because I wasn't a foreigner. Funnier still tonight, after seeing on the census roll that I am an alien and that he and Lethia are not. Those two Russians got themselves a different American ending.

How may I help you? Are you having an emergency? I will connect you to the fire department. Here was a chance to ask useful questions and answer them, too. *How may I direct your call? Allow me to connect you to your destination.*

Pavel's belly laugh—*ho, ho, ho*—was like the American St. Nick, jollier than the Russian version. "We won big tonight," he bragged like the American he is.

Viktor said, "We? You have more luck than brains."

"I have you," Pavel said.

I had him, too, though he was the reason I am an alien. The way I heard it, Viktor wasn't the one who changed my story, President Roosevelt was. Like in a fairy tale, my wish came with tangled strings attached. The stroke of a pen gave me my man and took away my country. Wrecked as I was, I didn't wish I'd married anyone else.

On the steps outside, Viktor said, "See that, mine left the home fires burning."

"Our window's dark," Pavel said. "No light on for me until after Rita's due."

"You had your luck tonight. It's my turn now. Maybe we'll have a little one to keep yours company."

What he meant was babies, maybe we'd have more babies. *We?* A spark flickered, not ire or regret so much as spunk. I might not lead a hunger strike or speak to the president, but I could say to Viktor, Let's not have more babies than we can feed. Let's find a doctor to help us with the baby we have. I could say, I'm not who I thought I was, and it's because we made our own decisions.

I sipped tea from my delicate cup, a gift from the man I chose. Russian ending or American ending? I reject them both. I'm only twenty, so with any luck, my own ending is a long way away, and I won't let America write me off the page. I will look behind the story this country keeps telling to find a better ending, one that includes both of us.

Lose one tooth, I won't stop eating apples or crusted fruit pies. And like a kettle at full boil, I'll whistle. Like the priest, I'll send smoke in all directions. That's the only way to make us count in ten years, in a hundred. Old beliefs may be set, but there are those who crumble stone with a pickax or a pencil. I know that as well as I know that a grudge does not keep you warm. That is the story I will tell my tender American children.

Appendix of Immigration Laws Related to This Novel

Alien Contract Labor Law of 1885, also known as the Foran Act, made it unlawful for companies to pay for the transportation or importation of alien laborers—except for skilled workmen who "cannot be otherwise obtained."

Expatriation Act of 1907 deemed that "any American woman who marries a foreigner shall take the nationality of her husband."

Immigration Act of 1917, also known as **The Literacy Act** or **The Asiatic Barred Zone Act**, excluded from admission into the United States: "All idiots, imbeciles, feeble-minded persons, epileptics, insane persons . . . ; persons with chronic alcoholism; paupers; professional beggars; vagrants; persons afflicted with tuberculosis in any form or with a loathsome or dangerous contagious disease," along with felons, polygamists, anarchists, and "natives of any country, province, or dependency situated on the Continent of Asia."

Literacy requirements prohibited the entry of anyone over sixteen "who can not read the English language, or some other language or dialect, including Hebrew or Yiddish." An admissible alien or citizen "may bring in or send for his father or grandfather over fifty-five years of age, his wife, his mother, his grandmother, or his unmarried or widowed daughter, if otherwise admissible, whether such relative can read or not; and such relative shall be permitted to enter." The literacy test was proscribed "for the purpose of ascertaining whether aliens can read, the immigrant inspectors shall be furnished with slips of uniform size, prepared under the direction of the Secretary of Labor, each containing not less than thirty nor more than forty words in ordinary use, printed in plainly legible type in some one of the various languages or dialects of immigrants."

Cable Act of 1922 was "an Act Relative to the naturalization and citizenship of married women," and included the following pertinent sections.

Section 2: "That any woman who marries a citizen of the United States after the passage of this Act or any woman whose husband is naturalized after the passage of this Act, shall not become a citizen of the United States by reason of such marriage or naturalization; but, if eligible to citizenship, she may be naturalized upon full and complete compliance with all requirements of the naturalization laws."

Section 3: "That a woman citizen of the United States shall not cease to be a citizen of the United States by reason of her marriage after the passage of this Act, unless she makes a formal renunciation of her citizenship before a court having jurisdiction over naturalization of aliens: Provided, That any woman citizen who marries an alien ineligible to citizenship shall cease to be a citizen of the United States."

Section 4: "That a woman who, before the passage of this Act, has lost her United States citizenship by reason of her marriage to an alien eligible for citizenship may be naturalized as provided by Section 2 of this Act."

Acknowledgments

Thanks be to my husband, Gary Zizka, for his loving encouragement and genealogical research, and to Eliza Zizka, Theo Zizka, and Amelia Raines for egging me on. The DC Commission on the Arts and Humanities and the Virginia Center for the Creative Arts offered vital support.

I am grateful to my mother, Millie Zuravleff, who often reminded me that I was named for my two grandmothers, Mary and Kay. She told me stories of life in the mines, Erie, and the church and was an invaluable reader. I also loved listening to aunts and uncles now gone, including Victor Federoff, Pearl Plevich, and Anna Golubov.

So many friends and writers helped me keep the faith, including the collective DC Women Writers, HIVE, and WOM, and the singular Bridget Bean, Michelle Brafman, Susan Campbell, Lisa Gornick, Linda Hopkins, Miriam Karp, Mardi Jo Link, Alice McDermott, John Mauk, Jenny Moore, Lori Nuffer, Karen Outen, Sarah Ridley, Karen Sagstetter, Laura Scalzo, Susan Shreve, Maureen Taft-Morales, and Margaret Talbot.

Robin Miura, Lynn York, and Kathleen Anderson championed this novel and brought it to the page, thank goodness. Laura Williams designed the stunning cover, April Leidig the beautiful interior, and Arielle Hebert and Kaye Publicity ushered it into the world.

This is a work of fiction with touchstones in family lore and history, including Teddy Roosevelt's visit to the Marianna mine and the 1908 mine disaster. Religiously, the Old Believer faith runs through both sides of my family. While I included the gold dome and richly painted interior of Erie's Russian Orthodox Old Rite Church of the Nativity, those features came much later, under the loving leadership of Archpriest Pimen Simon. I relied on my childhood memories of the church before him. All mistakes are my own.